A Sydnee Marcola Adventure

AGU:® BORDER PATROL

CLIDEPP
DEJA VU

Book 3

BY

THOMAS DEPRIMA

Vinnia Publishing - U.S.A.

AGU:®

Clidepp Deja Vu

AGU:® Border Patrol – Book 3

ISBN-13 (print):   **978-1-61931-031-5**

ISBN-10 (print):   **1-61931-031-7**

Cover by: Thomas DePrima

Appendices containing political and technical data highly pertinent to this series are included at the back of this book.

To contact the author, or see additional information about this and his other novels, visit:

http://www.deprima.com

Acknowledgements

Myra Shelley, my editor at Independent Author Services, and her proofreaders, came through for me once again, allowing me to release this book in record time.

My good friend and military protocol advisor, Michael Norcott, also found the time somehow to review it and offer suggestions in time to include them before publication.

༶ **Thomas DePrima** ༶

Novels and series by the author:

The AGU:® series:
A Galaxy Unknown ®
Valor at Vauzlee
The Clones of Mawcett
Trader Vyx
Milor!
Castle Vroman
Against All Odds
Return to Dakistee
Retreat And Adapt
Azula Carver
Changing of the Guard
The Invasion Begins

AGU:® Border Patrol series:
Citizen X
Clidepp Requital
Clidepp Déjà Vu

The AGU:® SCI series:
The Star Brotherhood

Colton James novels:
A World Without Secrets
Vengeance Is Personal

When The Spirit... series:
When The Spirit Moves You
When The Spirit Calls

Table of Contents

CHAPTER ONE
~ November 11th, 2286 ~

As the twin doors slid noiselessly apart and temporarily disappeared into the bulkhead on either side of the doorway, the young Space Command officer entered the captain's private office adjoining the ship's bridge. Walking to within a meter of the large desk, she braced to attention and announced in a calm and clear voice, "Lieutenant(jg) Sydnee Marcola reporting to the captain as ordered." As always, or at least as was usual when she was to be briefed by the captain, Commander Bryant was seated in a side chair to the right of the desk facing away from Sydnee. Without expression, the ship's XO turned slightly and glanced momentarily over his left shoulder at Marcola.

"At ease, Sydnee," Lidden said. Glancing up from the report he was reading on a viewpad, he added, "Have a seat."

Commander Bryant swiveled his oh-gee chair to face Sydnee as she sat down in a chair facing the captain's desk.

"I need an answer to the offer I made three days ago," Lidden said as he put the viewpad down. "Do you accept command of the new mission to Yolongus with Marine Captain Blade?"

"Yes, sir, I do. I've given it a lot of thought and realized you're right. We do owe the Clidepp minister something for all we've unfairly put him through. As much as I don't look forward to another clandestine mission inside Clidepp space, I'll take him home."

"Good. Blade reported aboard yesterday with his Special Ops team and the package you'll be delivering."

1

"And how are we to treat the package on this trip, sir? As a prisoner or a guest?"

"As a— detainee, but with consideration that he's guilty of nothing except being used as an unwitting pawn by the Clidepp Rebel Command. Special accommodations have been created for him in the Marine habitat container. While basically a brig, the size is several times normal cell size and outfitted to appear as normal living quarters. Obviously, we cannot give him the run of the ship, and he's to have no contact with anyone except his guards. Also, no one is to converse with him. We don't want him to learn anything about the ship, the crew, or the mission. He's been led to believe his trip from Yolongus to Simmons SCB took place aboard one of our newest and largest battleships and that he's being returned the same way. He knows we've cleared him of any culpability in the bombing of the Trade Show and that we're taking him home. The Clidepp government only knows he's been missing. They aren't aware Space Command was responsible, and the GA Senate Council insists we maintain deniability. Not even the full Senate knows about the kidnapping— or at least *shouldn't* know. It's always so difficult to get politicians to maintain security. The package will naturally report the true facts as he knows them as soon as he's home, but by then you'll be on your way back, and there must not be any *proof* that Space Command was responsible or that we were even there. Once he relates the details of his ordeal, the Clidepp High Command will probably accept we took him and that our speed capability is no mere myth, but our double-envelope travel has become almost common knowledge anyway— at least with the intelligence service of every nation with whom we have regular contact. As far as Space Command is *officially* concerned, his alleged kidnapping was a ruse devised by him so he could enjoy a year-long vacation with one of his numerous mistresses. And SHQ wants no muck-ups on this trip."

Sydnee opened her mouth to state she was not responsible for the shipboard problems that had occurred inside the Clidepp Empire but then shut it just as quickly without uttering a word. Lidden was familiar with the facts and knew she wasn't to blame for the events that had plagued their last mission. She realized Lidden wasn't making an accusation but was merely giving voice to the frustration they had all felt during the mission.

"Marine Captain Blade and Major Burrows will meet you in the conference room on Deck 12, Frame Section 78, at 1400 hours to discuss the mission," Lidden said. "Any questions?"

"One, sir. Will the *Justice* have a full crew on this mission?"

"A full crew?"

"Yes, sir. On the last mission I had just seven crewmembers. Because we were so shorthanded, I had to leave the ship to perform as the backup MAT pilot once we were on the planet. Our crew size was perfectly adequate for a brief mission or simple training exercise, but I quickly learned that an extended voyage needs at least twice that number. And for a covert mission in hostile space, like the one we just completed, I believe that a full complement of twenty-four crewmembers is required to adequately respond to the demands of such an undertaking, as well as provide replacements for key personnel who might be injured or lost during the mission."

Lidden took a deep breath and released it slowly before saying, "Commander Bryant and I have already decided that eighteen, not counting the captain, should crew the ship this time. We agree that eight was woefully inadequate on the last trip, but twenty-four might be too many. There's not much to do in a vessel the size of a CPS-14, and too much downtime can create its own problems. This is just a quick foray into Clidepp space to drop off the package and an equally quick exit back to GA space."

"Yes, sir. And if everything goes smoothly, eighteen will be perfectly adequate. But if we should encounter even half the obstacles we faced last time, the extra hands would help considerably. We were all pretty ragged when we returned from the last voyage."

"We're aware of how taxing that mission was and reported it as such to headquarters. Commander Bryant and I will discuss your request and reassess the situation. Is there anything else?"

"Have you heard anything about the investigation into the speed anomaly we experienced on our last mission?"

"No, nothing. But that's not unusual. Research into such matters usually remains Most Secret until reports are verified and the science can either be reproduced or declared impossible to replicate. And at our level we probably won't hear anything unless— and until— it's deemed safe for general shipboard use. Even then the information can remain highly restricted and privileged, with only the senior officers and senior noncoms privy to much of the information until it becomes part of the normal routine. In the service we always like to have an edge our enemies don't know about, and we tend to hold our cards close to our vests, to use an old term, until we're called and it's time to lay our hand on the table. Look at the situation with the speed advance that took us to Light-9790. We had it available and were using it for two years before the information became generally known even to the security forces of other nations. When the Milori and then the Tsgardi and Uthlaro nations attacked us, their militaries had no idea we could fly circles around them. Their maximum speed at the time was only about Light-460."

"Yes, sir. I understand."

"Anything else?"

"No, sir."

"Then you're dismissed."

Sydnee stood, braced to attention, then turned on her left heel and left the office.

◆

As the doors closed completely behind Marcola, Lidden swiveled his chair towards Bryant. "What do you think of her request for a crew of twenty-four?"

"She has a point. When we discussed the matter, we were looking to determine the optimal crew size for an extended mission in GA space. We merely wanted to maintain a full presence on the bridge at all times. Eighteen crewmembers, plus the commanding officer, would accomplish that. But perhaps for a covert mission inside enemy territory we should increase that to the twenty-four she requested. Space Command did design the crew's sleeping compartment aboard the CPS-14 to accommodate twenty-four, so SHQ must have come to the same conclusion at some point."

"Yes, that's true. But my main consideration in this instance is putting a junior officer in command of what approaches a small warship with a full crew of twenty-four. The commanding officer on a mission of this type and with a crew of that size should at the *very least* hold the rank of Lieutenant, and I'd actually prefer to see a lieutenant commander in command. Sydnee is the logical one to send only because she commanded the first mission, has proven herself capable, and has Blade's unwavering support. I again recommended that Sydnee receive an early promotion of one grade in recognition of her accomplishments, but I've heard nothing back."

"You're not worried about losing her if they do agree to early promotion?"

"Not really. With things settling down slightly in Regions Two and Three, our patrol area is just as important as any other in GA space— perhaps even more important than most. The old *Perry* has finally gone to the scrapyard, may he rest in peace, and hopefully the stigma of being posted aboard that ship went with it. We're the *Denver* now, and we've proven our worth. And we still don't have the full crew complement approved for this destroyer class, so we do have an open O-3 bridge officer position. Most ships in the fleet are presently understaffed, but I'm fairly confident that SHQ won't reduce our crew size further by removing one of our most able junior officers."

◆　◆　◆

Everyone who had participated in the recent mission aboard the CPS-14 *Justice* had been granted two weeks downtime following their return to the *Denver* three days earlier, but after ten months of almost constant worry and activity, it was difficult for the *Justice* crew to come to a complete stop unless they were sleeping. Sydnee hadn't been assigned any shipboard duties aboard the *Denver* yet and apparently wouldn't be until she returned from the new two-month mission, so after completion of her meeting with Captain Lidden she changed into her sweats and headed to the exercise hold where a running track was available when the hold wasn't filled with supplies and materials. Since it had been designated as an exercise area, that particular hold would only be used for other purposes when there was nowhere else available for storage.

As Sydnee entered the hold, she saw there were six other runners already using the track. She hung her towel on a hook provided for that purpose and fell into line behind a runner. Over the next thirty minutes, a dozen other crewmembers came to the hold to run while earlier runners dropped out and left. When Sydnee tired, she left the track, wiped the sweat from her head and brow, and walked back to her quarters. A hot shower briefly reinvigorated her, but the tiredness returned as she dried off, so she lay down to take a quick nap. She arranged for a wakeup call from the computer before closing her eyes and drifting off to sleep.

◆　◆

As the computer announced it was 1130 hours, Sydnee's eyes fluttered open. She jumped out of bed, dressed, and was on her way to the officers' mess before noon. The nap had refreshed her, and now she intended to sate an appetite heightened by her recent activity.

After selecting her food at the serving counter, she took a seat at a table where several bridge officers, including Lt. Milton, were discussing shipboard matters. Since her return, she had caught up on current events and was able to join in such conversations.

During a lull, Lt. Milton looked at Sydnee and said, "Scuttlebutt says you'll be leaving us soon, Syd."

"Leaving?"

"Another away mission, we hear. Any truth to that?"

"I'd tell you if I could, Milty."

"That's not a yes or a no."

"No, it isn't. Sorry, but it's the best I can offer right now."

"I understand. Well, best of luck."

"Thanks. And I know *Lifeguard* will be there again if we need him."

"Let's hope he's not needed."

"Amen, Milty."

◆　◆　◆

Following lunch, Sydnee wandered the corridors in silence as she thought about the previous mission. It had taxed her to the limit, and she certainly didn't relish another secret mission to Yolongus, but someone had to go. And on this mission there would be no hiding in lakes while waiting for the Special Ops team to capture their quarry. All they had to do was drop the minister off in a safe but slightly remote area where he'd be able to get help without much difficulty while the *Justice* used that time to ensure their safe departure before an alarm could be sounded. The *Justice* had had its space trial, and all the kinks had been worked out.

When it was almost time to report to the conference room, Sydnee took a lift to Deck 12, then a transport car to Frame Section 78. As she stepped into the area outside the room where the sensor would verify her identity using her CT, the door opened immediately.

"Come in, Sydnee," Major Burrows said as he looked up from the viewpad he was scanning from his chair at the conference table. Marine Captain Blade was seated next to him, and Marine First Lieutenant Kelly MacDonald sat across the table from both. Sydnee took a seat next to Kelly, facing the two more senior officers. Although Major Burrows held the same official O-3 Marine rank as Marine Captain Blade, he was in command of all Marine forces posted to the *Denver*, and was addressed as Major. There can only be one captain

7

aboard ship, so captains in the Marine Corps had to be addressed as *Marine* Captain. However, a shorter title of Major was commonly used for the senior Marine Captain aboard ship.

"Captain Lidden tells me you've volunteered for the new mission into Clidepp space," Burrows said. "Is that correct?"

"Yes, sir."

"You understand that this new mission is another unannounced incursion into the space of a neighboring nation and, therefore, doesn't have the official sanction of the Galactic Alliance Senate?"

"Yes, sir. But it's necessary that we do it."

"You don't exactly sound like you're ready and anxious to get underway," Blade said with a grin.

"Ready, yes," Sydnee said. "Anxious, no. But that won't prevent me from performing to the best of my ability."

"The purpose of this meeting is to lay out the objectives of the mission," Burrows said. "If you still wish to participate when it's over, it'll be up to you to recruit your crew and be ready to depart within seventy-two hours. All hands must be volunteers. The *Justice* has been prepped and ready for two days. In addition to the three simulated cargo containers the *Justice* carried on the last mission, five more have been added. You'll be maxed out on this mission."

"Five more? That'll give us a cargo section ninety-four meters long by twenty meters wide and twenty meters high. Once it's attached to our keel, the overall length of the *Justice* will be a hundred sixteen meters. Why the extra containers, sir?"

"Four of the additional containers house the new DS-sheathed Marine FA-SF4 fighter aircraft, plus pilots, maintenance parts, and all support personnel. Since each container carries two aircraft, you're receiving two full squadrons. You'll have your own Wing for this mission."

"Uh, isn't the commanding officer of a Marine Wing usually a colonel?"

"Usually— aboard a cruiser or a battleship. In this situation, Lt. Colonel Dennier will command the *Justice's* smaller Air Wing."

Sydnee groaned silently as she recalled the difficulties she'd had with Blade during the last mission. It was entirely understandable that Marine officers didn't like reporting to Space Command officers of lower rank or less seniority, but that didn't make the confrontations any less unpleasant. A lieutenant(jg) had the military pay grade of O-2, while Burrows and Blade, as marine captains, were O-3. As a lieutenant colonel, Dennier had to be an O-5. "That might be a bit awkward, Major."

"Because of the disparity in rank between Dennier and yourself?"

"Yes, sir."

"Essentially, the *Justice* is simply providing a ride for the Wing. Lieutenant Colonel Dennier requires little contact with you until it's time for her and her Wing to take part in the mission. She's been informed that *you*, alone, are the mission commander. She understands that while the Wing is aboard the *Justice*, command is compartmentalized but that *you* have the final word in *all* matters aboard the ship. The pilots naturally report to their own command structure, but even they know their commander is subordinate to you while they are aboard ship, just as Marine Captain Blade has been." Glancing briefly at Blade, Burrows returned his gaze to Sydnee and said, "Captain Lidden felt it important that there be no second-guessing on this mission. Once you actually launch aircraft or transport the Special Ops or fire teams to a dirt-side location, their senior officer is in command of carrying out their mission. But until then, and following their return to the *Justice, you* are in command."

"The aircraft are a welcome addition if we need support for ground operations. I wish we'd had them last trip. But who defines the mission parameters of the pilots *before* they launch?"

"That's your responsibility since you'll have overall command of the mission, and Dennier has accepted that she only has the latitude to change the mission parameters if the unexpected occurs. She also knows she must be prepared to formally explain her deviation afterwards and justify her actions."

Sydnee shifted her gaze immediately to Blade. He nodded and said, "Me too. You're the boss aboard the ship, Syd. I promise not to second-guess you this trip, which is not to say I will automatically agree with everything you order, but on our last mission I learned to trust your instincts, judgment, and command abilities. Those, combined with your intense concern for the safety of the people under your command, inspired great loyalty in not only your people but mine as well."

"I've known Blade for a long time," Burrows said with a grin, "and that's about the highest compliment I've ever heard him give any Space Command officer."

"Thank you, Marine Captain," Sydnee said to Blade, then turned to Burrows. "May I ask why Lt. Colonel Dennier isn't at this briefing?"

"SCI insisted that only individuals whose participation was dependent upon their having knowledge of the main mission be briefed at this time."

"Main mission? I thought there was only *one* mission— to return the package to an area near his home."

"That's the way it began. The mission parameters have since been greatly expanded."

"I don't understand. Is there another capture required on this trip?"

"No, not a capture. It's more of a release."

"I don't understand. Release who?"

CHAPTER TWO
~ November 11th, 2286 ~

"Not who. What. Upon arrival at Yolongus, you're to place eight micro-satellites into orbit around the planet. After departing Yolongus, you'll visit all other inhabited and inhabitable planets and moons in the Clidepp Empire and seed satellites around each. Since we no longer have diplomatic missions in Clidepp space, we're unable to monitor activity on the surfaces of those worlds. We need the intel the satellites can deliver. The satellites are sheathed with Dakinium, so they're invisible to all Clidepp electronic detection technology. Their coloration and small size makes them virtually impossible to spot visually, and the energy the Dakinium absorbs from suns and other energy sources as a natural by-product of its composition will fuel them indefinitely. If they're bumped by a ship in space, they'll simply reposition themselves afterwards to their original placement location."

"So you're saying we're to travel around the Clidepp Empire planting spy satellites *everywhere*?"

"Yes. Colonel Dennier has already been briefed on the satellite placement operation. She will receive her full briefing after you depart."

"And I'm expected to deliver that briefing?"

"Yes. Don't worry; she'll do what's required of her when the time comes. This is an important operation. We've been unable to get any cooperation from the Clidepp Empire whatsoever, so we're being forced to deal with the Rebels ourselves. We'll monitor all outgoing conversations on all frequencies on every planet until we identify the Rebel leaders. Then, we'll act to take down the leadership responsible for the attack on our space station."

"So we're going in to help save the Empire's backside from the Rebels? Why doesn't Admiral Carver simply come in and kick their collective buttocks into the next century, then take over that part of space? The inhabited worlds in the Clidepp Empire will definitely be the better for it. The Empire has been run by one group of grisly murderers after another, and the Rebels have already shown they won't be any better than the current Triumvirate. They might even be worse."

"The legal government of the Clidepp Empire hasn't attacked us, so we can't legally attack *them*. We're only doing what we must to protect our nation and its citizens from further attack by the Rebels and bring the Rebels responsible for the attack on Freight-One to justice. Besides, the GA has already absorbed more territory than we can adequately safeguard with our available manpower and resources. We're stretched to the breaking point. The Clidepp Empire is substantially larger than Region One of the GA. Given our present staffing levels, we have no way of taking on the added responsibility for a new area of space that large."

Sydnee grimaced mildly. "So how many inhabited planets are there in Clidepp space?"

"I only know of about— thirty-six, but an SCI officer will brief you on that part of your mission."

"Thirty-six? In an area substantially larger than our Region One? It'll take us more than a year to reach all those planets and then place a satellite in orbit."

"Actually, SCI wants from three to as many as eight satellites placed around every inhabited planet to ensure full coverage. The size of a planet and its population density will determine how many satellites we place."

"How are we supposed to transport all those satellites?"

"They're quite small, and the entire inventory fits into just one of the twenty-meter-long containers that attach to a CPS-14. That's what's in the eighth container you'll be getting."

"When I was offered this assignment, Captain Lidden told me it was a quick in/drop/exit operation."

"To the best of his knowledge it was— until two hours ago."

"What happened two hours ago?"

"That's when an SCI officer arrived with new orders from SHQ, along with the Air Wing and a cargo container full of the newest spy satellites. He briefed Lidden and then Lidden briefed me. The captain said that since the mission has changed so radically you may withdraw if you wish without it reflecting badly on your record. But, speaking for myself, I wouldn't if I were you."

"Why not?"

"First, the importance of this mission. And second, the captain told me that when informed you had volunteered to command this new mission, the SCI officer who had briefed the captain seemed quite pleased. Your past missions have definitely been noticed by people in positions to add a considerable boost to your career in Space Command. This is an opportunity to again show them what you can do."

"I didn't volunteer for this mission because I'm hoping it will earn me a half-stripe promotion."

"That doesn't mean you shouldn't take full advantage of side benefits a mission such as this offers. You don't want to remain a Junior Grade forever, do you?"

"No, sir. But I've always believed the rank will come in time."

"But there's also no harm in speeding it along a little, is there?"

"I suppose not."

"Then what's your answer? Do you agree to command the mission, or not?"

Sydnee took a deep breath and exhaled it slowly as she glanced at Burrows, Blade, and then MacDonald. While she'd hoped never to visit Clidepp space again, the mission was an important one. "I'll do it, sir."

"Good. I'll inform the captain of your decision. By the way, owing to the greatly expanded mission parameters, the captain approved your request for twenty-four crewmembers for this mission, so you should get busy recruiting your crew. This conference room is yours for the rest of the day. Present your crew list to the watch commander before midnight. Once that's set, contact me and I'll make the arrangements for your briefing from the SCI officer. Good luck, Sydnee."

"Thank you, Major."

♦ ♦ ♦

"*Another* mission you can't talk about unless we first agree to go?" Lieutenant(jg) Peter Caruthers said when Sydnee welcomed the crew of the previous mission to the conference room and told them she was assembling a CPS-14 crew for a covert mission.

"That's about the size of it, Pete. Interested?"

"Is this as important as the last mission?"

"Some would say more— much more."

"I'm in," Lt.(jg) Weems said.

"Okay, Jerry. You're number one. How about it, Pete? Are you going to be number two?"

"I know I'll feel that way if I don't sign on," he said with a small snicker. "Oh, you mean will I be the second to join up? Okay, *Captain* Marcola, I'm in."

For this first meeting of the day, Sydnee had only invited Lieutenants(jg) Weems, Caruthers, Olivetti, and Templeton, and Chief Petty Officer Wilson Lemela. Lemela had served as com chief on the first mission. Engineering CPO Luscome was still recovering from his back injury and wouldn't be available to go for that reason, but Olivetti, Templeton and Lemela likewise signed on for the new mission without knowing any of the particulars. Sydnee believed their seeming lack of hesitation was a vote of confidence in her abilities, and that brightened an otherwise depressing day.

"Okay, here it is," Sydnee said. "We're going back into Clidepp space."

"We already figured *that* much, Syd," Caruthers said. "Now give us the whole story. W*hy* are we going back into the middle of a civil war zone?"

"It turns out that the package we picked up had nothing to do with the bombing. He was an innocent dupe— a victim of the Rebel command who it appears was trying to involve the GA in their expanding civil war."

"Then the Rebels *were* actually responsible for the bombing of Freight-One, and they killed all those innocent people?" Weems asked.

"That's what SCI now seems to believe, in my opinion. Anyway, we have to return the package to his planet because he is innocent." Sydnee then broke the news about the satellites.

"Are you serious?" Caruthers asked. "It could take *years* for one small ship to clandestinely position satellites around every inhabitable planet and moon in the entire Clidepp Empire."

"We don't have years, so we're going to do it in just one. But— it could take as long as two. That's a rough estimate, of course, based on a calculation of the travel time between the designated locations and allowing a reasonable amount of time to actually place the satellites in orbit around each planet or moon and verify each is working properly. And it doesn't include any time at all for nasty little surprises like we experienced on the last mission."

"Two years is probably a more accurate estimate," Caruthers muttered. "And that'll be two years of almost constant duty."

"It's an important job that has to be done as expeditiously as possible," Sydnee said, "so we've been allocated twenty-four crewmember slots for this mission. The ship is already prepped and supplied. If we can fill all positions, we'll leave within three days. Jerry, you'll be my first officer for this miss—"

"Whoa, wait a minute," Caruthers said, interrupting. "I have seniority. I should be first officer."

15

Like Sydnee, both officers held the rank of lieutenant(jg), but when rank conflicts arose, time in grade was usually used as the deciding factor. She experienced the urge to roll her eyes but managed to suppress it and embellish her response with flattery. "Pete, you're the *best* CPS-14 pilot aboard this ship, and I *really* want you— no, I *need* you— at the helm of the *Justice* for all of the important tactical situations. However, if you don't want to be our chief pilot, I'll give you command of the third watch. Take your pick."

"Third watch command? Why not first officer?"

"Jerry volunteered for the mission first and I've already assigned him to that position. Your choices as the second to volunteer are mission chief pilot on first watch or third watch commander."

"Oh, okay, I'll be first watch pilot. It's bound to be more interesting than third watch."

"Good. We have our first watch team basically settled now with Lt.(jg) Caruthers on Helm, Lt.(jg) Olivetti on Navigation, Lt.(jg) Templeton on Tac, and Chief Petty Officer Lemela on Com. All we need is an Engineering officer. We'll also have three Engineering noncoms this trip instead of one. Everyone must be a volunteer, so let's put our heads together and decide who we should invite to the party."

◆　◆　◆

At 2200 hours, Sydnee presented her crew list of volunteers to Commander Bryant on the bridge. Bryant nodded as he looked at the names on the viewpad, then said, "You're going to be leaving us considerably shorthanded here. You're taking some of our best people."

"I felt the mission was sufficiently complex and important enough to require the very best we have."

"It is. And I have no objection to giving you these people for this mission. Good luck, Syd."

"Thank you, sir."

"Uh, did anyone turn you down?"

"Just one, sir. Chief Petty Officer Mateski. His wife is expecting their first child in a month, and he said it would drive him crazy if he had to wait for a year or more while we were in com blackout before he could learn if she and the baby were okay. I knew it would be a real distraction, and I need people who have their heads in the game. I'm glad he informed me and rejected the offer."

"I see. His reason is certainly valid. Carry on, Syd."

"Yes, sir."

◆ ◆

After arising the next morning, Sydnee contacted Major Burrows and established a meeting time and place for the SCI briefing.

At 1000 hours, Sydnee was sitting in the meeting room when Commander Knight of SCI entered the room. She immediately jumped up.

"At ease, Lieutenant. I'm Commander Knight."

"Yes, ma'am."

"Sit down, Lieutenant."

As Sydnee sat back down, Knight placed a holo-disc on the table. When she touched a contact point on her control pad, a three-dimensional image of space rose to fill the area above the table.

"This represents Clidepp space," Knight said. "The yellow dots are suns, the red dots are occupied planets, the green dots are occupied moons, and the blue dots are space stations. We've prepared a flight path that provides the most efficient use of time."

When Knight touched another contact point on the control pad, an orange line began at Yolongus and zigzagged its way through the maze of solar systems until all of the red, green, and blue dots were connected. It ended at the border with GA space.

"Just follow that path and you'll be back here within two years."

"*Two* years?"

17

"I said *within* two years. Naturally we can't know what kind of delays you're going to encounter."

"Delays?"

"Yes, delays."

"Such as a short-circuited temporal generator with no re-placement?"

"A temporal generator can break, be struck by a micro-meteorite while the ship is stopped in space, or even short-circuit when the storage chamber becomes waterlogged. Such things happen. I read your ship's log and mission reports, and viewed the bridge videos from your last trip into Clidepp space. I was impressed by your performance under the most difficult of situations. I'm sure you'll do an excellent job with this mission. That harrowing mission worked out the kinks with the CPS-14 you commanded and helped Space Command tremendously on two fronts. As a result of your unfortunate technical difficulties, modifications have been scheduled for all previously manufactured ships, and become part of the manufacturing process and inspection testing on new ships."

"And if we break down while in Clidepp space this time, can we at least count on Space Command to send someone to assist us?"

"Naturally, I can't promise anything like that."

"So we're on our own."

"Anytime we venture into the hostile space of another nation, we're pretty much on our own. SCI can make no guarantees to any of our agents or mission commanders and crews that they will survive a mission. It goes with the territory. That's why all participants must be volunteers."

"So SCI understands that sometimes an agent or a commanding officer may have to take certain liberties with Space Command regulations?"

"Space Command and SCI always take the circumstances into consideration when reviewing reports where such liberties were taken on a special mission. Just don't start a shooting war with the Clidepp Empire. It would be better if you, your crew, and your ship were lost than to do something like that."

"I see."

"The computer aboard the *Justice* has received a copy of this projected course. You may have this holo-disc so you can view the course in private any time. The image size is adjustable, so you can enlarge it to fill a room or even an entire shuttle bay to improve the image clarity."

"I understand, Commander."

"Good luck, Lieutenant."

◆ ◆ ◆

Over the next two days, Sydnee spent most of her awake hours either aboard the *Justice* or in the DS habitat containers that would be attached to the CPS-14 once it left the shuttle bay. The initials CPS stood for Central Propulsion Ship because the over-sized space tug formed the nucleus of a mini Scout-Destroyer assembled from various components, depending on the mission.

The term 'habitat container' was a real misnomer, but to disguise their true purpose or function, regulations required that all containers be referenced only in that way. While a percentage of the habitat containers were genuinely devoted to living quarters, others were used to hold military cargo, conceal Marine aircraft, and even house the deadly weapons platforms that helped protect the CPS-14 when it was on a mission. When required, cleverly concealed hatches on containers holding the ship's weapons could be opened remotely by the tactical officer. Laser cannons or missiles could then be fired or launched within seconds on command from the captain or watch commander.

From the outside, the black containers all looked alike and appeared to be quite innocuous. Eventually, space denizens would learn just how lethal the CPS could be, but they would never be able to determine from its appearance if they were facing a ship with the firepower of a mini destroyer or that of a reclamation vessel. For any military organization, the goal should be to make their enemies fear their weapons and resolve but also to have both their enemies and their friends understand that they would never use their weapons unless provoked beyond the limits of their government's established laws and policies.

While the containers were attached to the keel of the *Denver,* they could only be entered via shielded access tubes that extended down into the container. While in the tube, a person was weightless because he or she was shielded from both the gravity plating in the *Denver* and the deck plating in the habitat. Sydnee needed to be sure that all systems were at one hundred percent and that every piece of equipment intended to be aboard the ship or in any of the habitat containers was actually there before the *Justice* deployed.

The CPS-14 was also designed to accommodate up to four MAT-14 shuttles that attached to the hull, two on either side. The MAT designation of the shuttles stood for Marine Armored Transport, and the newest model was the 14. During the first mission, two enormous DS water storage tanks that allowed the *Justice* to hide at the bottom of a lake had occupied the lower shuttle attachment points on either side of the ship, but for the new mission, the *Justice* would have four shuttles. The sheathing of all components attached to the CPS-14 preserved its ability to travel at Light-9790, and the naturally black coloration of Dakinium was perfect for surreptitious military operations.

Each evening Sydnee returned to the *Denver* in order to enjoy her assigned quarters for as long as possible. The captain's living quarters aboard the *Justice* were cramped and smaller than those assigned to a Petty Officer aboard the *Denver.* Since she would be unable to communicate with family and friends while outside GA space, she spent her last evenings aboard the *Denver* sending vid mails to family and friends informing them that she would be on an away mission that would prevent communications for as long as two years, and that she would notify them as soon as she was back.

Sydnee almost bumped into Colonel Dennier, literally, while she was checking out the Marine FA-SF4 fighter aircraft in one of the habitat containers the day before they were scheduled to deploy. Each fighter naturally had its wings folded back in a parking position to fit inside the container. At the time of launch, a support platform holding the fighter in a nose-out position would extend from the container. Once the fighter was completely outside the container, docking clamps were retracted and the aircraft floated free, at the same time allowing the pilot to engage maneuvering thrusters. The fighter was too small to have FTL capability, but with its oh-gee and sub-light engines it was as much at home in space as it was in atmo. When entering the atmosphere of a planet, the pilot would simply unfold the wings and switch to oh-gee propulsion, although the main engines were always available when extreme speed was needed. When docking with a vessel, the procedure was simply reversed. Upon reaching the ship, the pilot used the fighter's maneuvering thrusters to properly position the fighter on the platform so the docking clamps could be reengaged before the platform was retracted.

Sydnee had just finished discussing the maintenance condition of the fighters with the head mechanic, and as she turned to leave, she came within inches of contact with Dennier. She stopped in time, took a step back, and braced to attention. "I'm sorry, Colonel."

"It's my fault, Lieutenant. I came up behind you. I was wondering what you were discussing with my chief mechanic."

"I was checking to make sure he had received everything he needed before we deploy."

"Very efficient of you. But if he hadn't, I would have informed Captain Lidden."

"Yes, ma'am. But I'm the commanding officer of the *Justice,* and, as such, I have final responsibility for our mission. In the future, please send all such requests to me and I will forward them on to the proper authority."

"You would have been sent a copy of the request if we needed anything we didn't have."

"As the commanding officer, it's *my* responsibility to ensure everything we need for this mission has been requested and received. With all due respect to you and your rank ma'am, you and the chief aircraft mechanic are now part of my command. I've been told you've been briefed in that regard and have accepted the fact that I'm the senior officer aboard the *Justice* until we return to the *Denver*."

Dennier smiled. "I've heard you're a regular little firecracker. It appears to be true."

"Colonel, I do appreciate that reporting to an O-2 is going to be difficult for you, and I will endeavor to ease that as much as possible. I fully expect the Wing to operate somewhat autonomously under your command while assigned to my ship, but on those few occasions where command protocol dictates a standard reporting structure, it must operate without regard to official rank. I hope you will accept my orders without hesitation. In time, you might even come to respect my abilities."

"That was a nice little speech, Lieutenant. Have you been practicing for this little confrontation?"

"I think we both knew it was bound to happen sooner or later, Colonel."

Dennier nodded. "Yes. And as you've said, I've been briefed about the command structure and agreed to it when I accepted this all-volunteer mission. Also, as you've said, it's difficult for a senior officer to report to a junior officer. I've been told you've earned the respect of everyone who has ever come under your command, both Space Command and Space Marine personnel. If that was not the case, I doubt you would have been entrusted with command of this sensitive mission. From now on, I think I'll address you as Captain, since you are technically the captain of the *Justice*. Perhaps that will make it a little easier on my ego."

"Thank you, Colonel. I'll do everything I can to make the situation easier for both of us."

◆ ◆ ◆

The next day, the *Denver* arrived at the point in Galactic Alliance space where the *Justice* would depart from the destroyer and then head for the border with the Clidepp Empire. As the ship came to a stop, Captain Lidden ordered the DATFA envelope cancelled and the airlock-style access tubes to the eight habitat containers sealed for separation from the hull. Meanwhile, the *Justice* was preparing to leave the shuttle bay.

The Marine personnel assigned to the mission were either aboard the *Justice*, in one of the four shuttles that would dock with it, or in one of the sealed containers that would be attached to its keel. The Space Command crew consisted of twenty-four Space Command officers and enlisted, plus Sydnee. Marine personnel included Marine Captain Blade and his eleven Special Ops noncoms, First Lt. Kelly Mac-Donald and a platoon of Marines from the *Denver*, Lt. Colonel Dennier and her Wing of seven pilots, the thirty-three enlisted personnel who performed maintenance and flight operations support functions, and a staff of cooks and mess attendants for the Marine mess hall. The package being returned to Yolongus had been delivered by one of the shuttles. Since the ship would be away until their mission was complete, it had been loaded with everything they should need for the extended voyage, including two spare temporal envelope generators and enough firepower to start a sizable war. On the previous mission to Yolongus, an officer had been killed and a Chief Petty officer seriously injured because neither had personal armor. For this mission, Sydnee had insisted that personal armor be compulsory for every individual aboard ship, other than the package.

Sydnee was acutely aware that in Space Command history there were no instances where a vessel having a crew of seventy enlisted and officers had officially been placed under the command of a junior officer before the mission commenced. She supposed that if the original mission had not been simply to take the Clidepp minister back to Yolongus and return she would not have been offered the command. At the very least, the mission commander should be a Space Command lieutenant and more probably a lieutenant commander. Despite what Dennier had said, Sydnee knew she was going to have problems if she had to give Dennier an order the colonel didn't wish to follow. She had expected the last mission with Blade to be bad given his more senior rank, but she expected this trip to be worse— much worse— and it would go on for a much longer period.

◆ ◆ ◆

Lt.(jg) Caruthers was at the helm of the *Justice* when it was time to leave the docking bay aboard the *Denver*. On command from Sydnee, he raised the small ship up on a cushion of oh-gee waves, turned it around, and moved it to the temporary airlock area in front of a hatch in the outer hull. The airlock fit was tight, but he was experienced enough that he was able to properly place the small vessel within the alignment markers on the first try. When the bay's alignment-verification system confirmed the ship was properly aligned, all lights on the alignment-warning display on the bridge console went to green. Caruthers then carefully lowered the ship to the deck and sent the command to lock it down to keep it from moving while the air in the temporary airlock was evacuated. Since Dakinium wasn't magnetic, the airlock's semicircular skid clamps rolled up over the skids, then recessed slightly to lock the ship firmly in place. Once the ship was immobile, the temporary airlock walls swung down from the overhead area to seal the ship in an airtight chamber against the outer hull. The oxygen in the airlock was then sucked out and pumped into containment bottles for temporary storage.

The *Justice* deployed from the *Denver* as soon as the outer hatch had opened fully to allow his departure and the indicator light on the console showed that the skid clamps had rolled completely back into the deck. Once the ship was sitting a thousand meters away, the four MAT-14s left from a different bay and linked with the *Justice*. It only took minutes to get them properly aligned with the linkage systems. Automatic systems then activated, and all four small ships were pulled tightly against the *Justice*. Creating an airtight seal around the access hatch was the final step.

While the pilots aboard the MATS were shutting down their systems, small, unmanned tugs began ferrying the habitat containers to the *Justice* where they would be attached using a modified version of the Lewiston container link.

The Lewiston was the standardized linkage system used by all freighters in Galactic Alliance space. It normally allowed up to four full-sized, forty-meter-long cargo containers to be locked together, forming a single section. Abutted end to end, they extended one hundred sixty meters in length when complete. The entire section would then be added to a freighter's cargo load and increase the length of the ship by twelve meters— ten meters for the container and two additional meters required for the linkage. The modified link for the CPS-14 was only one-eighth as long and only held one twenty-meter-long container, but it formed the same type of airtight tunnels on the top surface that allowed full access to every attached container.

While freighter containers were attached to the stern of a vessel, the CPS-14 habitat containers were attached to the keel. Once the eight containers were connected, the assembly hanging beneath the small ship would be twenty meters high and twenty meters wide. Like the full-sized Lewiston links, the modified links added twelve meters for each container, so the habitat group would extend ninety-six meters from bow to stern. It would actually be almost three times longer than the CPS-14 itself.

As the habitat units were locked into position against the keel, automated systems completed all mechanical, electrical, and electronic connections. Engineers aboard the *Justice* supervised all work, then tested and certified connections and seals. When the work was complete, the containers were as much a part of the ship as if it had come out of the shipbuilding yard that way. Marines who had traveled over in the MATs walked through the *Justice* and descended the stairs into the tunnel created by the linkage system, then floated down into the appropriate habitat container via the access tubes.

It took just thirty-eight minutes to fully prepare the *Justice* for deployment from the time it departed the shuttle bay. Anyone seeing the enormous configuration of the assembled ship would never guess it could have been launched from the *Denver*.

CHAPTER THREE
~ November 13th, 2286 ~

"Captain," CPO Lemela at the communications station said to Sydnee who had been occupying the command chair during the deployment operation, "the *Denver* is asking if we're ready to depart."

"Engineering, are we a go?" Sydnee asked Lt.(jg) Galli at the console on the starboard side of the bridge.

"The ship is secure and all power systems are in the green. Engineering is good to go, Captain."

"Navigation, is the course plotted and laid in?"

"The course is plotted and laid in, Captain," Lt.(jg) Olivetti said. "Navigation is a go."

"Tac?"

"The DeTect is clear," Lt.(jg) Templeton said. "All tactical systems have been tested and are ready. Tac is good to go, Captain."

"Helm?"

"Standing by and ready to build our envelope on your command, Captain," Caruthers said.

"Com, inform the *Denver* we're ready to build our envelope and depart."

Seconds later, CPO Lemela said, "The *Denver* wishes us a safe journey."

"Tell them to keep a light burning," Sydnee said. "Helm, build a double envelope."

"The double envelope is built, Captain," Caruthers said two minutes later.

"Engage the drive to Light-9790."

27

The image on the front monitor immediately shifted from real-time vid to the simulated view created from sensors on the hull as the ship was instantly at maximum speed. To anyone aboard the *Denver* who was watching, the *Justice* seemed to simply disappear. Since travel was inside a temporal envelope, there was no sensation of acceleration to the crew of the *Justice*. And since it was a double-envelope, which put the ship slightly out of phase with normal space, the chances of impacting anything, such as a planet, moon, asteroid, star, or even another spaceship, were virtually nonexistent.

Lt.(jg) Olivetti at the navigation station said, "We're away, Captain. Expected time to Yolongus orbit is twenty-nine days, sixteen hours, twenty-two minutes, and— eight seconds. We'll cross into Clidepp Empire space in roughly— fifty-two seconds."

Fifty-two point six seconds later the *Justice* entered the space of the Clidepp Empire.

"Tactical, anything on the DeTect screens?" Sydnee said.

"The DeTect screens are still clear, Captain."

"Excellent. Perhaps we'll have an uneventful trip to Yolongus. We know the intruder detection systems of the Clidepp Empire warships can't see DS ships, so it should be clear sailing all the way."

◆　◆　◆

"I was surprised when I learned you'd accepted this mission," Lt. Kelly MacDonald said after supper the first night out. She and Sydnee were sitting in the captain's office, enjoying a cup of coffee and talking about the mission ahead.

"Why?"

"It's just that you seemed so burned out after the last mission. By the time we got back you looked— haggard."

"Then it was an accurate representation for how I felt. You know what pressure I was under. And the injury I sustained just compounded the situation in every way. When we got the temporal generator back into the proper hands at SHQ, all I wanted to do was climb into my rack and not climb back out for a month."

"I felt the same way, and I didn't have anywhere near the responsibility you'd had on your shoulders. But mine was a *quick* month. It lasted just three days. By the fourth day I couldn't wait to begin this new mission."

"Yeah, well, by the second day after we got back, I couldn't even stay in bed if I didn't drift off to sleep immediately. I was so keyed up from being in command of a mission that seemed to go south every time my attention was diverted for a second that I found myself either on the jogging track every few hours or simply wandering around the decks of the *Denver*. So, I decided I might as well do what's right and take the Clidepp minister back home. I figured this mission should be an easy run and I'd be able to fully unwind during the travel. When we get back to the *Denver*, I should be back to my old self."

"We've got a larger crew this time out, and we've worked out the bugs with the *Justice*, so things *should* be a lot smoother. Perhaps by the time we get back, Lt. Aguilo will have the new combat range ready for use."

"That would be great. I never truly realized how much I'd miss it until we no longer had it."

"I know. Martin promises that the new range will make the old one seem like a run around the jogging track and will definitely be worth the wait."

"There's nothing more fun than running around like a madwoman shooting bad guys for a couple of hours where no one ever gets hurt unless it's a bruise, pulled muscle, or sprain." Sydnee punctuated her testimonial with a wide grin, followed by a laugh when Kelly started it off.

◆　◆　◆

The trip to Yolongus *was* totally uneventful. Although the *Justice* passed within DeTect range of a number of ships while en route, the CPS-14 came and went so quickly that none probably would have been able to detect their presence even if the *Justice* hadn't been invisible to all Clidepp forms of ship detection electronics.

Having three full bridge crews meant the bridge was always staffed by alert personnel at the start of each watch. It also meant that, as Captain Lidden had said, there was a lot of downtime for those not on watch. It was normally impossible to find the twenty-meter corridors in the habitat containers *not* being used as running tracks, so Sydnee had to establish a sign-up list and schedule.

Everyone aboard ship was feeling good as they neared Yolongus twenty-nine days later because the first part of their task would soon be done. But the mood died a quick death for those on the bridge.

◆

"Captain, the DeTect is showing a significant number of ships in orbit around the planet," Lt.(jg) Templeton said with a clear sense of urgency in his voice.

"How many?" Sydnee asked, matching his intensity.

"Over a hundred vessels."

Sydnee, already on edge because they were approaching a potentially hostile situation, began issuing orders to her bridge officers in rapid fire. "Helm, do not approach the planet or cancel the envelope as planned. Maintain maximum speed on this course until I amend this order. Tac, eject a sensor buoy as we pass the planet. Nav, find us a nice quiet place to park a few billion kilometers from here."

"Aye, Captain," all three officers said when she paused to take a breath.

"Captain," Olivetti at Navigation said as quiet again pervaded the bridge, "I have a location well off all shipping lanes where we should be okay to stop for a while."

"Send it to Helm. Helm, take us there."

"Aye, Captain. Sent."

"Helm has it," Caruthers said. "Making for that location at Light-9790."

"The sensor buoy was launched as we passed the closest point to the planet, Captain," Templeton at Tac said. "We should begin receiving data any second."

"Excellent work, everyone. Now let's see if we can find out what's going on at Yolongus. Good work, Olivetti, finding a location for us so quickly."

"I had a location already prepared, Captain, in case we needed to find a place to stop and think."

"Excellent. Tac, can you tell us yet what we were facing back there?"

"The computer is estimating the presence of a hundred seventy-two warships in orbit around the planet through extrapolation from verifiable data received from the sensor buoy. Virtually all of the observed ships are Clidepp *Bernouust*-class destroyers. The sensor buoy has also identified one battleship, three cruisers, and a handful of freighters in orbit."

"A hundred seventy-two warships? That must be close to their entire fleet."

"According to our database, their fleet is presently composed of two hundred eleven active-duty warships and roughly four hundred lightly-armed support vessels, not including quartermaster vessels and small craft such as diplomatic courier ships, tugs, reclamation vessels, and shuttles. Most of their warships are destroyers and almost all are *Bernouust*-class. I guess when they start producing a design, they stick with it. This fleet probably represents every available Clidepp warship within a month's travel time at their top speed."

"So the question is: What are they all doing here? I'm pretty sure they weren't expecting a vessel from the GA to arrive today."

"Well," Caruthers said, "they *are* embroiled in a deadly civil war."

"Yes, but the Rebels don't have a fleet of warships that could   threaten the Clidepp home world— unless they've managed to steal a few more or perhaps turn the crews."

"Perhaps the Empire *is* worried about the GA attacking," Templeton said. "Or maybe one of their other neighbors has shown signs of invasion. The Triumvirate is not very well liked either within the Clidepp Empire borders or without."

"They know the GA would never attack unless provoked, and their other neighbors have never made any threatening moves that I'm aware of."

"Perhaps they've called all their ship captains in to have a conference regarding some new proposed action to deal with the Rebels, Captain," Chief Petty Officer Lemela said.

"It's possible, Chief, especially if they feel their encrypted communications aren't secure from Rebel eavesdropping and so have ruled out fleet-wide conference broadcasts. For the present, I guess all we can do is sit here and observe." Prefaced with a grimace, Sydnee said, "We certainly can't sneak in and drop off our package or plant our listening satellites while almost the entire Clidepp military is parked in orbit around their world."

◆ ◆ ◆

"I just received a message from Sydnee," Captain Lidden said to Commander Bryant when the XO arrived at Lidden's office for their daily briefing. "She says they've arrived at Yolongus on schedule but haven't been able to approach the planet to drop off the package because the entire Clidepp Empire warship fleet is camped out around the planet."

"The entire fleet?"

"Sydnee says they didn't stop because the DeTect system showed an enormous number of ships in planetary orbit, so she ordered a sensor buoy be dropped as they moved through the solar system. Using data received from the buoy, the *Justice's* tac computer has since identified a hundred seventy-six warships, almost exclusively destroyers. The *Justice* is presently sitting about five billion kilometers away while they monitor ship movement around Yolongus."

"Just what we need— another botched mission by a junior officer entrusted with responsibility far above her pay grade."

"Botched?"

"Uh, I didn't mean to imply that Sydnee is in any way at fault. I was just stating the way it's going to be described by people who have an agenda of making us look bad."

"You're still afraid people will start associating the *Denver* crew with the undeserved reputation that was hung on the crew of the *Perry*? That we're nothing but a bunch of screw-ups who can't perform even the simplest task without getting our tails caught in a ringer?"

"Aren't *you* fearful of that? Many of the senior officers who resolved personal issues by having their *problems* transferred to the *Perry*, hoping they'd never see or hear about them again, are still around. People like that have long memories."

"I've started to believe those days are behind us, Bry. The crew of the *Perry* performed admirably under fire. And a lot of the credit for our improved image has to go to Sydnee. What that young officer did while stranded on Diabolisto and cut off from command, and then as commander of the incursion mission into Clidepp space, was nothing less than spectacular."

"Don't forget that she simply gave the temporal generator away to someone masquerading as a Space Command officer."

"Be honest. Would you have checked a very senior officer's credentials and verified their identity if they approached you in uniform while *inside* an area requiring a verifiable top security clearance?"

"Well— probably not. And it wouldn't have done much good anyway since someone had tampered with the computer files to allow him access initially."

"I've sent a copy of Sydnee's message off to SCI at SHQ. Perhaps *they* know why the Clidepp fleet is sitting in orbit around Yolongus. I don't have a clue. In any event, they'll understand that the package hasn't been delivered and that the *Justice* hasn't begun seeding the satellites in Clidepp space."

"Why don't you instruct Sydnee to forget about the package for the present time and begin the second phase of the mission?"

"She's requested to do exactly that. I just don't know if the package's return might be tied to some other action or event I'm unaware of, and I haven't wanted to change the chronology unless SCI first approves."

◆ ◆ ◆

"How much longer are we going to sit around out here polishing the seat of our uniforms while there's a job to be done, Captain?" Marine Captain Blade asked Sydnee in a conference held in the Marine mess hall. Sydnee's office was too small to accommodate more than three people, so she was holding the requested meeting in the Marine mess hall between mealtimes. Attendance was limited to senior crewmembers. Sydnee, her senior bridge officers, Marine Captain Blade, Lt. Colonel Dennier, and First Lieutenant Kelly Mac-Donald, were the only ones in attendance. The cooks and mess attendants had been sent outside for a smoke— not literally, of course, but the age-old expression was still used in dirt-side operations and space operations alike.

"I wish I knew, Major. Although our DS shuttles are black, there's no guarantee they can sneak past the entire Clidepp warship fleet surrounding Yolongus without risk that someone will spot them. A visual identification is very possible when flying between the planet and an entire fleet of orbiting warships. If there were only a dozen ships in orbit, it would be very likely that our shuttle could reach the surface without being spotted, but with almost two hundred warships out there, the odds drop considerably. My orders are to not make our presence known to the Yolongi."

"How far away from Yolongus can we receive messages from that sensor buoy?"

"The range is only limited by the required timeliness of the data. We're presently about five billion kilometers from Yolongus, and the farther out we go, the longer it takes to receive telemetry reports. Transmissions on the IDS band travel at eight-point-zero-niner billion kilometers per second, so it presently takes less than a second for a transmission to reach us."

"So we *could* begin the satellite seeding part of the operation, and when we discover that the Clidepp fleet has left orbit we could come back here and complete the first part of the mission."

"Yes, we *could* do that. And I would *like* to do exactly that. *But* my orders are very specific. We drop the package off, *then* deploy the satellites. I *can't* change the orders and leave to begin distributing the satellites unless we get permission or an emergency arises."

"I'm sure we can come up with an emergency that will allow us to be more efficient."

"Just so we're perfectly clear, I will not deviate from my orders unless permission is given for such deviation or a *genuine* emergency forces me to alter the orders. Several weeks ago, I sent a request to Captain Lidden that we be allowed to make better use of our time by beginning to deploy the satellites and come back here when the fleet moves away from the planet. I haven't received a reply, but I expected he'd have to clear it with SHQ and SCI. Now, was there anything else you wished to discuss today, Major?"

"No, I think you've pretty well covered it all."

"Colonel Dennier, was there anything you wanted to bring up for discussion?"

"Negative. I'm fine, Captain. My people are ready to do their job when you deem the time is correct."

"Very good. For the record, I'm just as anxious as everyone else to complete our mission here and head home. Just as soon as we get permission to proceed, I'll notify all of you. If there's nothing else, this meeting is adjourned."

◆ ◆ ◆

"I've just received a response from SHQ regarding Sydnee's request to alter her orders so she can begin deploying the satellites until the Clidepp Fleet moves away from

Yolongus," Captain Lidden said to his XO during their daily meeting in the captain's office.

"What do they say? Do they know why the Clidepp fleet has remained in orbit?"

"SCI believes the fleet has been recalled to protect the home world from attack."

"Attack? From whom? From us?"

"SCI doesn't know. Reliable intel about the Empire has been difficult to come by lately, so it's all conjecture at this point. SCI says they've received a few limited-scope reports from previously reliable informants that the Clidepp Empire has perpetrated terrorist acts against the Aguspod, the Kweedee, and the Blenod. Those attacks were purportedly similar in nature to the attack on Earth's Freight-One space station."

"So they were terrorist acts. They're saying civilians were targeted in each of those three bordering nations?"

"Apparently. We've never had formal diplomatic relations with the Blenod, and our relations with the Kweedee are minimal at best because they've avoided outside contact with all of their neighbors, so the information is naturally sketchy. But the Aguspod have reported to our ambassador there that the Clidepp Empire is indeed guilty of attacks in all three nations."

"Could it be the Rebels— doing what they did to us in an effort to drag us into their conflict?"

"It's possible. But SCI believes it's also possible that the Empire has been behind *all* of the attacks. They feel the government *might* have come to the realization some time ago that they can't end the Rebel threat because so many planets in the Empire are clandestinely supporting, supplying, and hiding the Rebels. The Empire might be trying to have us and the other nations go after the Rebels for them, or at least break off all ties with the Rebels, especially when it comes to cutting off access to food and weapons."

"So SCI has changed their mind, again, about who was really behind the bombing of Freight-One?"

"Let's just say they're no longer positive it *wasn't* the Triumvirate. By refusing to help us originally, the Clidepp leadership almost guaranteed we'd get involved. They knew the GA wouldn't just sit on their hands while the guilty party or parties remained free."

"So where does that leave us? Is deployment of the eavesdropping satellites still part of the *Justice's* mission, or do they have something else in mind now?"

"More than ever, SHQ needs the information those satellites can provide. It might help them piece together the facts and identify who is really behind the terrorist acts. SHQ also suspects that the Blenod may now be using the attack against them as an excuse to lay claim to part of the Clidepp Empire territory along their common border— sort of as reparations for the attack in their territory. I guess it would be like the buffer zone Admiral Carver set up in formerly unclaimed space after the first attack by the Milori."

"Except that we're not talking about formerly unclaimed space this time. The common border between both nations has existed for the better part of a century. If the Blenod move into that area, they're essentially invading Clidepp space. Uh, how much territory does SHQ believe the Blenod are claiming?"

"SHQ *thinks* they might try to grab as much as a forty-parsec swath along their *entire* common border. And that area happens to contain some of the most valuable mining operations in Clidepp Empire space."

"Forty parsecs? That's over a hundred twenty light-years into Clidepp space and represents probably five percent of the Empire's territory. The Empire will never stand for that. That will most definitely drive the Empire to war with the Blenod."

"The Blenod may believe the Triumvirate is so busy with the Rebels that they'll either have to accept the loss or lose the civil war. And if the Empire loses the civil war, that will leave it ripe for a takeover of even more territory, possibly from the other nations that border them, sort of like what the

THUG pact attempted after we defeated the Milori. Except in our case, the Milori had already surrendered and ceded all its territory to the GA, so the THUG pact was technically attacking *us*. And any way you look at it, a war between the Clidepp Empire, the Blenod, the Aguspod, and the Kweedee could be a disaster for everyone in this region of space— including the GA."

"Maybe Sydnee was right when she suggested Admiral Carver should just annex the Clidepp Empire space and restore peace. It would probably be the first peace the various planets there would know since space travel allowed the Yolongi warlords to conquer their neighbors and create the Empire."

"We both know it isn't that simple, Bry. While Space Command could prevent extra-planetary warfare and protect the region's borders from encroachment by outside nations, the government of each planet would still be responsible for all activity within the planet's sensible atmosphere. The GA taking that region is no guarantee that the citizens would enjoy peace. The GA is forbidden to get involved in the internal affairs of member planets unless they violate GA law."

"Yes, but it would make each planet responsible for its own governance instead of forcing the people to bow to dictates coming from a planet hundreds and even thousands of light-years away. The Yolongi Triumvirate and their predecessors have been systematically pillaging every planet in their Empire for a century, killing anyone who resisted. It's something of a miracle the people on those planets have managed to survive this long."

"I suppose that's why the Rebels were able to gain so much support. If they *are* responsible for the terrorist attacks in other nations— and I tend to believe they are— they won't be much of an improvement over previous rulers should they prevail and come to power. But that seems to be the way it is all too often with civil wars. Big promises made to the general population to gain their support are quickly ignored when the war is over and the bureaucrats take up the reins of power."

"Just like with the politicians following an ordinary election."

"Yeah. Just like."

CHAPTER FOUR

~ December 19th, 2286 ~

"I've received new orders from SHQ via Captain Lidden," Sydnee said to the senior officers assembled for a meeting in the Marine's habitat container mess hall. "We're to begin distributing the satellites and only return to Yolongus for the package delivery when I feel we have a reasonable chance of returning him safely."

"About time," Blade said.

"For this mission, our FA-SF4 fighter aircraft have all been equipped with special Dakinium-surfaced chambers inside their keel, so when the bomb bay door is opened the ship remains hidden from radar. A special, satellite ejection rack attaches to the missile rack so one SF4 can release all required satellites in one pass around a planet, moon, or space station."

"It's a shame they can't make the missile casings from Dakinium so the enemy would never even know what hit them."

"They've done the next best thing," Colonel Dennier said. "Our new missiles now have an extremely thin outer skin made from Dakinium splinters."

"Dakinium *splinters*?" Blade said. "What the heck kind of weapon is that? We need to destroy an enemy we're bombing, not make him run in search of a needle and a pair of tweezers."

"The splinters aren't the weapon, Major," Colonel Dennier said with a chuckle. "That's just how the developers refer to the way the extremely thin outer skin is constructed. What they call splinters are extremely narrow strips of Dakinium foil that remain in contact with one another to present a continuous covering until detonation. When we fire the missile, enemy radar can't detect it because its surface is Dakinium. As the weapon reaches its target and detonates, the silicon-like adhesive bonding the foil-like splinters to the missile casing disintegrates, at which time the splinters simply fall away. Since the Dakinium foil isn't one piece, it can't dampen the explosive effect of the weapon at all, as would be the case if the missile housing itself was made from Dakinium. I heard the idea was taken from weapons developed back in the twenty-first century called cluster bombs. The outer casing on such bombs would be ejected over a target, releasing numerous bomblets. The area below would then be carpeted with those small explosive devices. They would explode on contact with the terrain and would effectively carpet an area with death and destruction. The payload of our new missiles doesn't break into small explosive devices, and I only repeat that example to explain how an outer-covering material can be used on missiles for different reasons. The enemy never detects a missile with the Dakinium splinter covering and therefore never has a chance to react to the weapon coming at them. Another benefit is that their radar can't track the trajectory and identify the location of the ship that fired it. And since the coating is made of thin, foil-like splinters that flake off at detonation, no enemy can collect chunks of Dakinium for their scientists to use in reverse engineering efforts."

"Having the tiny spy satellites also sheathed with Dakinium," Sydnee said, "means the fighters will remain completely cloaked from electronic surveillance as they carry out their part of this operation. Of course, visual identification is always a potential problem, but their size and black color negates most of that. Colonel, you already have a copy of the satellite distribution, positioning plans, and documentation. Do you have any questions?"

"Negative, Captain. My only comment is that I'm delighted we're going to begin this stage of the operation."

"As are we all," Blade said. "I don't know why it took SHQ so long to make the decision to deviate from the original schedule, but I'm tired of sitting around on my six. I'm glad

41

we're going to be working towards the completion of this mission even if my team won't have an active part."

"Be careful what you wish for, Major," Sydnee said. "You might get more than you want. We are pretty far out, so I'm sure the message transmission time was a primary factor in hearing from the *Denver*. I'm as pleased as everyone else that we'll be busy again. SHQ indicated that we should give priority to positioning our satellites around Yolongus as soon as an opportunity presents itself. I'm sure the information they'll potentially collect from those satellite locations will be of far more value than from any other planet in the Empire, but I've hesitated to undertake that part of the operation until the fleet moves away from the planet. With so many warships in orbit, there's a high chance of visual identification, so we'll depart this area in just under one GST hour and be on our way to the first of our other designated planets. Are there any questions?"

Sydnee glanced around the table, but no one gave voice to any issues. Mostly they just shook their heads as she made eye contact.

"Okay. Dismissed."

◆

"Navigation, is our course plotted?" Sydnee asked.

"Aye, Captain," Lt.(jg) Olivetti said, adding, "And it has been forwarded to Helm."

"Very good. Helm, is the course laid in?"

"Aye, Captain. We're ready to go as soon as you give the order to build our envelope."

"Very good. Engineering, is everything go?"

"Aye, Captain. All systems are operating at peak efficiency."

"Very good. Tac, is the DeTect board green?"

"Negative, Captain. A ship has just appeared on the De-Tect screen."

"Well, it doesn't really matter. We'll be within a double envelope, so if they're in our path we'll pass right through them without them ever being aware of us. Uh, is it a warship?"

"Negative. It appears to be a large shuttle."

"A large shuttle? Out here? Is it heading towards a larger ship?"

"It appears to be headed directly towards us."

"No one should be able to see us."

"And I believe that's still the case because they haven't slowed or altered course. If they could see us, they would have taken one action or the other by now."

"Helm, build the double envelope."

"Aye, Captain. Envelope building."

"Tac, how long before the approaching ship reaches this location?"

"Approximately four minutes eighteen seconds at their current speed."

"We're fine then. They'll pass right through us."

"Aye, Captain."

Two minutes later, Lt.(jg) Caruthers, manning the helm, said, "Our double envelope is built, Captain. Engage?"

"Negative. Hold at this location. I want to see if the approaching shuttle stops or alters course. If someone can see us with an electronic system, I want to know about it."

"Aye, Captain."

"The ship is altering course, Captain," Lt.(jg) Templeton said.

"So they *can* see us?"

"I believe it was just a slight course correction to better facilitate their approach to Yolongus. They will still pass just inside of a hundred meters of us. That's closer than any ship wants to come to another ship while traveling at its maximum sub-light speed."

"Good. Let's see what they do."

All eyes were glued to the front monitor as the small ship passed the *Justice* with just ninety-two meters to spare.

"Tac, give us a single frame image of that shuttle."

"Aye, Captain."

A second later, the shuttle image appeared on the large monitor.

"That ship has sure seen better days," Sydnee said.

"I'm amazed it's still flying," Caruthers said. "Are those weapons-fire holes in the hull?"

"It sure looks like it," Templeton said.

"The shuttle is named the *Patoosch*," Com Chief Lemela said. "They just requested clearance to land on Yolongus and received it without delay and without being required to give any special recognition codes."

"So they must be frequent visitors to the planet," Sydnee said. "Tac, can you determine their destination?"

"They haven't landed yet, but if our single sensor buoy is in a position to see, we should be able to identify their location once they do."

"Great. And how about determining where they came from?"

"I'll see what I can learn from the data. There's no guarantee I'll be able to tell you with any certainty."

"I understand. Just give us your best assessment."

"Aye, Captain."

"Helm, cancel the envelope. We're going to remain here a bit longer."

"Aye, Captain," Caruthers said.

"Everyone can stand down. We won't be departing right away after all."

"Captain," the tac officer said a few minutes later, "their point of origin appears to be somewhere on the planet Nugowlo."

"Nugowlo? Is that in this solar system?"

"Yes. It's the sixth planet from their sun. According to the database, there are a number of mining operations on the planet."

"What do they mine?"

"The database doesn't contain that information."

"Okay. Good work, Tac. Anything on that landing site yet?"

"Not yet, Captain, but from their approach, it appears it will be on a part of the planet we can't see."

"Keep watching just in case they change course."

"Aye, Captain."

"Engineering, what would it take to give one of our shuttles the same radar footprint as the *Patoosch*?"

"Our shuttles are sheathed in Dakinium, Captain. We can't make them appear like that old rust bucket."

"Even if we paint the hull?"

"Uh, I guess it would depend on what we used to paint the hull. Since Dakinium absorbs all electronic signals, the paint would have to have properties that cause the electronic signals to bounce off the surface rather than passing through the paint. I suppose it might work, if we had a space dock handy with all the right equipment— and, most importantly, with the right paint."

"Navigation, how far to the nearest planet where we can safely land to work on painting one of our shuttles. A breathable atmosphere isn't necessary as long as the other factors of temperature, gravity, stability, and a lack of dangerous indigenous life forms are within tolerances."

"I'll have to perform a search, Captain."

"And try to ensure it's not too far away. We might be limited to single envelope travel once we cover the Dakinium on the shuttle."

"Aye, Captain."

◆ ◆

"We won't begin deploying the listening satellites as early as I thought," Sydnee said to the senior officers in a special meeting later that day.

"Problems with the ship?" Blade asked.

45

"No, the ship is fine. As we were about to depart, an old shuttle passed us on its way to Yolongus. It wasn't stopped by the fleet and didn't even have to offer any special recognition code after identifying itself. We don't know where it landed exactly, but we have a rough idea. I'm proposing we wait until that shuttle leaves Yolongus, then have one of our shuttles assume its identity and deliver the package before we leave to begin the satellite drops."

"I think anybody who accepts one of our MAT-14s as being a Yolongi shuttle has to either be blind or crazy," Blade said.

"We'll naturally have to alter its appearance a bit so it shows up on Yolongi radar. A coat of paint ought to solve that problem. Hopefully, if we can give it a similar radar footprint, no one will look too closely. And if we can give it a flight path that maximizes the distance from all fleet ships while not looking suspiciously distant, we might have a chance. The Yolongi military has apparently been sitting out here for quite a while, so things might be getting a bit lax aboard those ships by now."

Sydnee sat back and let the officers think about the idea for a few minutes. Finally, Lt. Colonel Dennier said, "It's damned audacious, but it just might work."

"Does paint adhere to Dakinium?" Lt. MacDonald asked Sydnee.

"I don't know. My engineers haven't found anything in the ship's database regarding efforts to *paint* DS surfaces, although I heard that colorizing the material was a stated primary goal. I also seem to recall *hearing* that paint wouldn't adhere to the original Dakinium formulation, but I've also heard rumors that Space Command engineers keep tinkering with the formula in an effort to improve it. I guess we'll just have to try it and see."

"Why would Space Command want to change the color?" Blade asked. "It seems they'd want everyone to immediately know they're dealing with an almost indestructible ship and should not start something Space Command will finish."

"I suppose there are other occasions where they wouldn't want to intimidate folks, such as with diplomatic ships or perhaps Quartermaster ships, but would still want the protection and speed that properly formulated Dakinium offers."

"Where will we make this disguise attempt?" Blade asked.

"We've identified a planet twenty-four light years from Yolongus where the conditions are suitable. We can be there in about six hours with double-envelope speed, but the return trip may be limited to Light-480 in a single envelope because the Dakinium on the altered shuttle will be covered with paint."

"Does paint make that much difference?" Kelly MacDonald asked. "It's still Dakinium beneath the paint."

"We really don't know yet. Again, that data wasn't available in the database. A double envelope is owed to the resonance the temporal generator establishes within the Dakinium, not just on the surface. I hope the paint doesn't prevent it, but there's no reference to anyone having tried it. Perhaps, as the Major just implied, no one thought a deployed DS warship would ever want to cover a black, radar-absorbing surface with paint that might destroy its lethal appearance, not to mention its stealth capability."

"We've already wasted so much time sitting out here, I say we give it a try," Dennier said. "Another month won't make much difference, given the length of the mission ahead, and it would be great to have a key part of our task complete."

"It's too bad this isn't a Scout-Destroyer," Blade said. "They have a shuttle bay large enough to accommodate two shuttles. The work could be done without leaving this part of space and the shuttle would be inside the ship so the painted surface wouldn't affect the Scout-Destroyer's travel speeds."

"Yes, that would be great. But we have to work with what we have."

"You're the ship's captain," Blade said to Sydnee. "The decision is yours."

"To save time, we're already underway to the planet where we believe we'll be able to prepare the shuttle for a surreptitious insertion into the Yolongus atmosphere. I wanted to hear your ideas before I fully committed us to the plan, so if anyone can present a convincing counterargument for why this is not a good idea, I'll reevaluate my decision before we finalize our plans."

"Do we have enough paint onboard for the effort?" Kelly MacDonald asked.

"No, but my selection of the planet was made after a review of the information contained in our ship's database and discussion with our four engineers. They're confident we can produce a sufficient quantity of *something* having the general properties of paint by mixing the reported natural elements available at our destination with the lubricants and other chemicals we do have on board. The final result may not be pretty, but the *Patoosch* certainly wouldn't win any awards for appearance."

"Surely the *energy* trail of our shuttle isn't even close to that of the Yolongi shuttle," Dennier said.

"No, but we've computed a possible approach vector which will minimize use of the shuttle engines as we approach the planet and enter orbit. Once the MAT is ballistic, there's no energy trail from its engines. Like us, the Yolongi use Deuterium thrusters for simple maneuvering, so that works to our advantage."

"What's the worst case scenario?" Blade asked.

"Worst case scenario is that the shuttle has to abort the attempt and return to the *Justice*. If that happens, we may be required to intercede since shuttles are limited to Sub-light speeds while the Yolongi destroyers have FTL."

"That would give away our presence in Yolongi space," Dennier said.

"Yes, it would. But as Major Blade knows, I won't abandon our people."

"We could postpone delivery of the package as SHQ suggested," Dennier said, "until we're confident the delivery effort is reasonably safe."

"As I mentioned at our last conference, SHQ has stated we should give priority to positioning our satellites around Yolongus," Sydnee said. "We can combine part of that task with delivery of the package by having the shuttle drop several units as it approaches the planet. The satellites are pre-programmed to maintain a precise position relative to geographical coordinates on the planet. They operate off solar energy amassed by their Dakinium sheathing and produce Deuterium from collected hydrogen. The production process is slow, and it could take weeks for the satellites to produce the Deuterium needed to maneuver to their programmed locations using tiny thrusters. But in the meantime, they'd still be collecting data and retransmitting it in encrypted bursts to SCI. SHQ has covered our asses by including the word 'safely' in our orders, but I'm sure they'd prefer to have communications data coming in ASAP. Since our shuttles have double-walled Dakinium plating, they're impervious to all laser fire. Torpedo strikes could possibly damage them, depending on the explosive force of the torpedo used, but even that is unlikely from what we know of the Yolongi weapons. Does anyone think the effort is too dangerous to attempt at this time?"

As Sydnee glanced around the table, everyone shook their heads when she made eye contact.

"Very well. We'll continue on to the chosen planet to see if we can give one of our shuttles a radar footprint like that of the Yolongi shuttle *Patoosch*. Dismissed."

◆ ◆ ◆

Six hours later the *Justice* was approaching the selected planet. The SC database identified it as Vucoppi.

"Helm, all stop," Sydnee said from her command chair. "Tac, any ships on the Detect monitors?"

"Negative, Captain."

"Any natural phenomena that presents a danger?"

"Negative, Captain."

"Any evidence of activity or habitation on the planet?"

"Negative, Captain. It appears that we're the only ones out here. It seems to be as dead as Earth's moon before we started building bases there."

"Navigation, do you have a landing site selected, or do you want us to circle the planet while mapping it?"

"I have a tentative site selected, Captain. The planet is reputed to have no fauna larger than ten centimeters in size but abundant flora. Empire mining syndicates have declared that extraction of mineral resources here would be more costly than the value of the resources they could recover. The SC database contains a number of excellent topographical maps and mineral survey reports, but the latest scan is sixteen years old. There're no inhabited planets or moons in this solar system, so it's unlikely we'll run into anyone out here."

"Very good. Send the location information to Helm. Helm, cancel our envelope and perform a flyover to examine the area before we commit to a landing."

"Aye, Captain. Envelope cancelled. I have the location information. We should arrive over the site at an altitude of ten thousand meters in seven minutes."

"Very good, Helm."

Sydnee sat back and watched the front monitor as the image changed. Until then they had been traveling FTL, so the image had been created from sensor data. The new image showed significantly more detail because it was provided by the ship's exterior cameras.

◆

"There it is, Captain," Caruthers said from the helm chair.

"Navigation, please tell me you haven't selected a volcano for our landing site."

"I haven't selected a volcano for our landing site, Captain."

"It sure looks like a volcano. The last one we used as a hiding place erupted, and we barely got away with our lives."

"It's not a volcano, Captain. It's a meteor impact site. The database lists the impact date as being roughly two thousand years ago."

"That can't be right. Look at the vertical rise in the walls."

"That has to be because of the soil composition density and the fact that there's limited atmosphere on the planet, which means erosion is almost non-existent. It's probably looked the same way for all of those two thousand years."

"But the planet is almost green. How does the flora survive without rain?"

"I don't know, Captain. Perhaps there's a very high water table and the plant-life has deep roots."

"Okay, Nav. We'll accept your word that we aren't going to burn up in a fiery explosion."

"I can't guarantee that another meteor won't land in the same place while we're here, although the odds of that happening are so remote as so be absurd, Captain."

"Have there been an unusual number of meteor strikes on this planet?"

"No more than any other world with limited atmosphere. Without a decent atmo, even the tiny ones get through to the surface since they don't burn up on the way down."

"Are there any records of annual meteor showers on this planet?"

"There's nothing in the database."

"Make a note in the duty log that I want all navigators searching the sky during their watch since they won't have any other assigned tasks during that time."

"Aye, Captain. I'll enter that note in the log."

"Okay, Helm, set us down nice and gently."

"I'll touch the ship down so lightly you won't even know when we're on the surface, Captain," Caruthers said with a smile.

CHAPTER FIVE
~ December 20th, 2286 ~

"Aye, Captain," Lieutenant(jg) Galli said during a meeting with the Engineering staff before they deployed to begin their camouflage efforts, "I suggested to Lt. Olivetti that she select a meteor crater for our landing site. A meteor disrupts the surface and may fling hundreds or even thousands of tons of surface matter outward from the impact spot. I hoped that might have exposed more minerals than we're likely to find on the undisturbed surface. If we don't find what we need at the lowest point in the crater, we'll next search the walls. We'll move outside the crater last if we still haven't found what we need by that time."

"Good thinking, Lieutenant. I hope your idea proves out. Are you ready to begin?"

"Aye, Captain. My people are anxious to get to it. We know what we have in the ship's storage lockers, so we have an idea what to look for. We're hoping to find enough to allow us to produce something like white paint with enough metallic flakes mixed in to reflect a solid radar signal. I have a couple of Marine volunteers grinding down a spare piece of equipment— nothing we'll ever miss— to produce the metal filings."

"I really hope it's something we won't miss. It's not a temporal generator, is it?"

"No, ma'am. It's an air circulation pump. We have a spare in the *Justice* and in the engineering section of every habitat, which means we have nine spares on this voyage. They almost never break within their estimated lifetime so it's unlikely we need more than one spare."

"Very good. Go to it, Lieutenant."

"Aye, Captain."

On their previous trip into Clidepp space, the *Justice* hadn't had any of the oh-gee carts used in maintenance bays aboard most ships, so when a problem arose with the temporal generator they'd had to improvise with an oh-gee robot. Owing to those maintenance difficulties during the previous voyage, Sydnee had requisitioned two of the collapsible carts for this trip, and they were stored in the access corridor of one of the two weapons habitat containers beneath the ship. All weapons chambers were still fully accessible, but several meters of that corridor couldn't be used as a running track on this trip. The two-meter by three-meter carts that, once opened, resembled the rear of a flat-bed truck with a meter-high railing, were self-propelled and would allow the engineers to reach any exterior part of the ship, as well as using them for basic transportation in and around the crater while searching for the paint-making ingredients they lacked. Colonel Dennier had immediately agreed to Sydnee's request and assigned four of her aircraft mechanics to assist in the operation. There would be two teams consisting of two engineers and two mechanics in each cart as they searched the crater and surrounding area for the minerals and plant-life they needed to make the paint.

◆ ◆ ◆

After almost a week of effort, the teams had amassed enough raw materials to begin production. They had rigged a crude pile-driver to smash the rocks collected and an equally crude cooking chamber using laser weapons for a heat source since there wasn't enough oxygen for a fire outside the ship and Sydnee wouldn't agree to preparation of the paint inside the ship because of the danger of possible toxic fumes. While outside the ship, the workers were encased in EVA suits with independent oxygen supplies.

When the collected materials were ready, the engineers mixed a sample batch with the lubricants, metal filings, cleaning materials, and cooking supplies taken from aboard ship.

The first effort adequately covered the flat rock chosen for the test, but the paint cracked and peeled off as it dried, and so began days of effort to find the right formulation from the collected and assembled materials.

◆ ◆ ◆

"How goes it, Syd?" Kelly MacDonald asked as she sat down in one of two available chairs in Sydnee's tiny office.

"The engineers are hard at work. They still feel confident they'll be able to come up with a paint that will hold up during travel through the cold of space on our return to Yolongus and also withstand the journey through the atmosphere there."

"Have they tried to paint over the Dakinium yet?"

"No. They want to wait until they have a paint formula down for the first problem. Then they'll work on the second."

"If the paint doesn't stick, the first part of the effort is wasted."

"Yeah, but I'm letting them make the call on this one. If their efforts fail, we'll just fall back on the plan to go seed space around the planets on our list with the communication satellites."

"Ya know, Syd, I half expected to face some emergency after we landed on this planet. I mean, like wild vegetation that could attack anything that moved or some hidden form of wildlife like those things on Yolongus that come out only at night to grab you and coil around your body, crushing the breath from your lungs."

"I know what you mean. So does Blade. His offer to have some of his Special Ops people stand sentry duty on our perimeter probably came from his memories of the situation on Yolongus. So far everything has been quiet. And since our people have to wear EVA suits when outside the ship and they go through the standard decontamination process in the airlock every time they reenter, I feel confident we're not bringing any dangerous pathogens aboard. We'll just have to continue as we've been doing and respond to any situations as they arise."

◆ ◆ ◆

A few days later, Lt.(jg) Galli reported that they had finalized the formulation for the paint insofar as the basic requirements were concerned and that they were about to begin testing to see if the paint would adhere to Dakinium.

◆ ◆ ◆

All initial tests failed. The paint would not stick to the Dakinium sheathing on the shuttle section chosen for the initial attempt.

"No luck again today, Captain," Lt.(jg) Galli said as he sat across from her in her office. "We're going to put our heads together after dinner and try to come up with a solution."

"There may not be one," Sydnee said.

"Perhaps, but I'm not ready to give up yet, unless you order us to stop our efforts."

"No, I'm not ordering you to stop— yet. Let's agree that one more week will mark the end of this attempt. Either you find a solution by then or we terminate the proposed mission. Okay?"

"Okay, Captain. We'll work on this for one more week and then call it quits if we haven't found a solution."

◆ ◆ ◆

Six days later an excited Lt.(jg) Galli entered Sydnee's office with a huge smile on his face. "I believe we've found a solution, Captain. We've added more metal filings to the paint formula we developed."

"And how do extra metal filings make the paint better adhere to the Dakinium?"

"By themselves, they don't. But everyone knows that Dakinium absorbs energy like a sponge and that the absorbed energy actually causes the Dakinium's structure to change at a cellular level, making it more resistant to outside forces. In fact, it doesn't just absorb available energy, it's more like it actively sucks it in. When Admiral Carver originally discovered the material on Dakistee, the energy not being used to enhance the physical structure of the Dakinium was just being dissipated. These days, with Dakinium sheathing on all of our newest ships, the excess energy is routed to our graphitic-crystalline storage cells. Anyway, we managed to glue a tiny conductor wire to the surface of the Dakinium hull using a tube of experimental glue Space Command has distributed to Colonel Dennier's ordnance people. They have it because they're responsible for maintaining the new missiles where Dakinium strips have been glued to the missile casing. Then we pushed a small electrical charge through it as we painted over a small area of the shuttle's outer skin. During all past attempts, the paint immediately flaked off. But this time the paint stuck."

"Interesting. Do you believe the paint will stay in place during flight operations?"

"Yes, I do. I tried to peel it off and was unsuccessful. The Dakinium is holding onto it like a starving man would hang onto a loaf of bread."

"How much energy will be consumed by the process?"

"Virtually none. The charge sent through the connection is absorbed by the Dakinium, which then returns any excess to the storage cells. It's like a perpetual motion process so the loss of energy is negligible."

"And where is the power connection point on the shuttle? Will it interfere with building a double envelope while the shuttle is attached to the *Justice*?"

"I'm not sure if the paint will prevent a double envelope or not. It shouldn't interfere with the establishment of resonance in the Dakinium, but only an actual test will show us whether it does. As for the power connections, I'd suggest several, but they will not interfere with envelope creation. We'll tap off energy connections in hull-mounted sensors. The wire will be glued to the hull so there will be no gaps between the hull and wire. The envelopes should follow the outside contours, as always."

"How soon can we be ready to head back to Yolongus?"

"Two days max, Captain. My people are ready to make the electrical connections and paint the shuttle hull as soon as you give the approval. We've computed where we have to paint and how much coverage is required based on the metal content of the paint to give a radar footprint similar to the one that Yolongi shuttle has."

"Excellent work, Lieutenant. You have a go."

"Aye, Captain. We'll get started right away."

◆ ◆ ◆

Two days later the *Justice* lifted off from Vucoppi and was on its way back towards Yolongus. Their stay on the planet had been uneventful. No volcanoes erupted, no meteors hit the part of the planet where the *Justice* had landed, and no dangerous animals tried to chow down on crewmembers as the engineers and mechanics went about their work.

"Chief," Sydnee said to the com petty officer, "We're still receiving a constant feed from the sensor buoy we dropped at Yolongus, aren't we?"

"Aye, Captain. It apparently hasn't been discovered yet."

"I'd like you to put together a report that lists all identifiable arrivals and departures of shuttle flights to and from the planet other than to or from ships in orbit. I need the date and time of each contact. Possible?"

"I should be able to produce a list based on communications and clearances if they're not encrypted."

"Good."

◆

An hour later Sydnee was in her office scanning the list prepared by Chief Petty Officer Lemela as she planned the upcoming mission to the planet. In case new trespass safeguards had been installed at the minister's home since he'd been abducted, he wouldn't be returned directly there but would instead be dropped off at a place where he could contact someone to come pick him up. The communications satellites to be dropped by the shuttle as it entered the planet's exosphere and reached a point about thirty-five thousand kilometers above the surface had been tested for proper operation and programmed to seek and then maintain specific assignment locations via terrain identification while they continued to record interplanetary communications traffic and retransmit the data in high-speed, encrypted bursts toward GA space.

"Captain," Sydnee heard in her CT, "we've just received a Priority-One message from the *Denver*."

57

Touching her SC ring to activate a carrier, she said, "Put it in my queue, Chief."

"Aye, Captain."

"Marcola, out."

Sydnee opened her message queue and selected the newly arrived video message. She had to lean in so the computer could perform the required retinal scan, then sat back to learn what was important enough to justify a Priority-One classification. An image of Captain Lidden appeared almost instantly.

"Hello, Sydnee. I've just received a briefing from an SCI officer. This information is so sensitive they didn't even want to send it to me through normal Priority-One communication channels, but they understand we must use this system now to communicate the data to you. According to SCI, an undercover agent has reported that he has new information regarding the attack on Freight-One and believes he has discovered the secret identity of the Rebel leader who, until now, has been known only as Citizen X. The communication system he was using isn't secure enough so he couldn't send the information directly. They want you to take whatever steps are necessary to recover that agent from Yolongus as soon as possible. So stop your distribution of satellites and get back to Yolongus. This mission must be completed as quickly as possible, even if the entire Yolongi fleet is still in orbit around the planet. Perhaps you can combine the delivery of the package at the same time, but if not, recovery of the agent and his information takes priority over everything. You must recover him at all costs. The full details are attached in text form. Good luck, Sydnee."

Sydnee took a deep breath and sighed. The original mission had been to simply drop off the package and return. Then SCI added the requirement that they deploy satellites all over Yolongi space. Then the crew of the *Justice* learned that the entire Yolongi fleet was parked in what seemed like permanent orbit around the planet. Now an additional layer of difficulty had been added, i.e. rescue an undercover agent at all costs. And the newest layer involved the greatest risk of all. It reminded her of the last mission to Yolongus where they had to meet a contact who might be able to get them a necessary part to repair the ship. The Special Ops team had been lucky to complete that task without the Yolongi Intelligence Service crashing the party, but they'd killed three members of the Yolongi Secret Police in doing it.

Sydnee hadn't reported that they'd never begun the satellite distribution process, so Lidden probably believed they were far away from danger, not back on danger's doorstep and just one brief step away from more potential trouble than they had so far faced.

"Major Blade," Sydnee said after activating a carrier with her ring."

"Blade here, Captain."

"Would you join me in my office? And if Colonel Dennier isn't busy, ask her to join us as well."

"Will do, Captain. Blade out."

"Marcola out."

Sydnee was reviewing the text included with Lidden's message when Blade and Dennier arrived.

"Come in and take a seat," Sydnee said. "We have a lot to discuss."

When Sydnee had related the mission revisions, Blade asked, "So do we deliver the package and then pick up the SCI agent during our return to the ship?"

"No," Sydnee said. "We have to assume that once we deliver the package, the Yolongi government will possibly be alerted to our presence in the area."

"Possibly?" Dennier posed.

"There's always the possibility they will believe the minister was away voluntarily, such as for an extended love tryst."

"For so long?"

"They might believe he intended to make it permanent but things didn't work out. But I'm going to assume the worst case scenario, which is that they'll believe everything he says and start hunting for us immediately. We know there's no guarantee the agent will be able to make a scheduled rendez-vous, so until the SCI agent is recovered, we'll keep the package in our possession."

"So when do we go in?" Blade asked.

"I've reviewed all the communications since we first ar-rived and dropped a sensor buoy. No one should take notice of a change in schedule for the shuttle we're going to simulate because it appears to have no schedule. The danger is that the real *Patoosch* will show up while our MAT is on the planet. So we want to get in, get our agent, and get out. Once the *Jus-tice* reaches the location where we parked following our ini-tial arrival in this system, we'll send a message via laser beam to the sensor buoy so there's no chance of anyone getting a fix on our location. The buoy will then relay it to the agent. The buoy is so tiny that it's unlikely the Yolongi fleet could ever identify where the signal came from. As soon as the SCI agent sets a timetable and location for the pickup, we'll com-mence the operation."

"So the order is to be ready on a moment's notice," Blade said. "We can handle that. Just my Special Ops team?"

"That should be more than adequate for this operation. This is a simple pickup."

"Nothing ever seems to be simple when you're in hostile space," Dennier said.

"True," Sydnee replied. "But I always live in hope that this time will be different."

"Don't get too hopeful, Captain," Blade said with a chuck-le.

◆ ◆ ◆

An encrypted response from the SCI agent arrived the next day. It included the proper recognition code and identified a date, time, and coordinates for the pickup.

Sydnee selected Jerry Weems, her second in command, to pilot the small ship because of his experience on the previous mission. Where piloting skills had been in short supply on the first mission to Yolongus, that wasn't a problem this time. Fifteen of the officers on the mission were certified for MAT-14 operations, so she also named one of the officers new to Clidepp space to function as copilot for the brief trip. Lieutenant(jg) Alfonso DiRoma had a reputation for both being an excellent pilot and being dependable in tough situations.

The shuttle separated from the *Justice* just after 0645 GST. Their destination on the planet had slipped into darkness several hours earlier, and most families in that time zone had finished their evening meal and settled into their midweek nightly routine.

Weems followed the same flight path observed by the *Justice* crew when the *Patoosch* had passed their location on its trip from Nugowlo. When challenged, Weems identified the *Justice*'s shuttle as the *Patoosch* and requested permission to land on Yolongus. Permission was granted, and Weems proceeded on course.

When the shuttle reached the point where the communications satellites were to be launched, the shuttle was traveling ballistically. The launching had to be performed manually since the shuttles didn't have the special deployment harnesses mounted in the keel of the Marine FA-SF4 fighters. Weems gave the word and an engineer wearing an EVA suit in the airless starboard airlock opened the outer hatch and pushed three of the tiny satellites out into space. After sealing the hatch, he reestablished atmo in the airlock and reentered the rear cabin. Since the MAT had already identified itself as the *Patoosch*, opening the hatch didn't betray their presence in the area.

Aboard the *Justice*, the flight crew watched the telemetry provided by the sensor buoy as the shuttle descended towards the surface unmolested.

◆ ◆ ◆

"Al, check the nav computer and tell me when we're about to descend below the planetary radar defense grid," Lt.(jg) Weems said to his co-pilot.

61

"We should reach that point in about two minutes, Jerry. The nav computer says we're right on the preplanned course."

"Good. Once we're off their grid, we'll duck down as low as we dare go and head for the rendezvous point. With luck, there won't be anyone around to see us land except the contact."

"What if he's not alone? I mean, what if this is a trap?"

"We'll make contact, ask for an explanation, and set a new meet time for when he's alone if we believe the others with him are planetary or military security forces. Then we find a place to park and ask for instructions from the captain. She's the boss. We're certainly not going to land and invite planet security forces into the shuttle."

"Jerry, I know she's been officially designated as the captain, but I still feel a little funny having a lieutenant(jg) in full command of the mission and the ship. Do you ever feel that way?"

"No, never. Not with Syd. She's as sharp as they come, and I'd trust her judgment any day. But then I've worked with and for her for quite a while now, including our last mission into Clidepp space. I can't think of a single person aboard the *Denver* whose judgment I trust more. Or on any other ship I've been on."

"Including Lidden?"

"Captain Lidden has my full faith and confidence, but no more so than Sydnee. You ask anyone who served on our last mission to Yolongus. I bet they'd tell you the same thing."

"I have— and they have, but hearing it from you puts my mind a little more at ease. Hey, we're coming up on the grid boundary."

"Tell me when we're beneath it."

A few seconds later DiRoma said, "We're below the defense grid boundary, Jerry. They can't see us anymore."

"Okay, we'll go a bit lower just to make sure we're well away from it before I alter course. I'm reading just over three thousand meters AGL. I'll level off at one thousand and head for the rendezvous point. That'll put us well above any civilian oh-gee vehicles and below normal air traffic."

The sun had been down for hours, but they were able to get a feel for how fast they were traveling as the street and house lights flashed past below them. Their oh-gee movement was completely silent, and the forward-looking radar showed no obstructions ahead so there was no need to slow down.

CHAPTER SIX
~ January 17th, 2287 ~

Nine minutes later, DiRoma said, "Coming up on the RP, Jerry. We should slow a bit or we'll overshoot it."

"Slowing," Weems said.

"Okay, it's just a little over ten kilometers now."

"The RP marker just popped up on my nav map. Time to destination, eighteen seconds. Slowing."

"It's dark out here."

"That's the best kind of rendezvous point there is. No civilians around. On our last mission to this planet, we had to hide at the bottom of a lake."

"Really?"

"Yeah. It was the only way to remain completely hidden."

"There're no lakes around here. It's just mountains and high desert."

"Send the code, Al."

"Sending."

"Six seconds to RP."

"I'm receiving a response. It's valid."

"Okay, I'm taking it down. There appears to be a nice open area there. It's hidden between two mountain ridges, but we have an easy exit ahead or behind if we need it. Notify the Major."

"Major," DiRoma said into the com headset, "we're there. We'll be on the surface in a few seconds. The contact has replied with the valid code."

As the shuttle touched down, the flight deck door opened and Blade entered.

"Anyone other than the contact here?"

"Only one warm body on the scan," DiRoma said.

"How about movement? They could be wearing thermal protection."

"Nothing registering," Weems said.

"Okay, I guess we'll know in a few seconds. My people are all wearing armor, but we may need to beat a hasty retreat if this is a trap. I wish we could have arrived earlier and sent in a recon team."

"We're all wearing DS armor and the ship is Dakinium sheathed as well. If there's a problem, just pile back in. We can lift off in seconds."

"Roger."

◆

As the large hatch opened in the rear compartment, and before the ramp had been extended, the Marines jumped to the ground and took up defensive positions around the shuttle. There was only one warm body on their thermal scans, so most of the Special Ops team devoted their full attention to scanning the surrounding area for signs of trouble as one member of the team advanced to make contact.

"Contact appears legit," Blade heard, so he began moving towards the cloaked figure. As he reached the individual, he said, "Show yourself."

The cloaked individual pulled back the hood that had been hiding his features.

"You're Terran?" Blade said.

"Of course."

"I was expecting a Yolongi."

"Were you told to expect a Yolongi?"

"No. I just thought that only a Yolongi would have access to the kinds of information SCI would be looking for."

"I didn't have access to the inner circles, if that's what you mean, but I have contacts who do and who aren't happy with either the current government or the one that wishes to replace them."

"Fine. We'd better get going. The sooner we're off this planet the sooner you and your information will be safe."

"I'll get my people."

"Whoa. Hold it. Your people?"

"Yes. Many people have risked their lives to get us the information we need. I promised them we'd take them to safety."

"Many? How many are you?"

"There are thirty-six of us here, and forty-nine at the other site."

"Thirty-six? And forty-nine more? We can't take that many. Look behind me. That's a shuttle, not a passenger liner."

"The members of this small group have risked their lives to get us the information SCI wants, and I fear the government may have discovered their identities. If they remain here, they and their entire families might either be captured and tortured or simply killed. We owe them. Big time. The information I have is worth a thousand times what I promised them."

"It's not a question of how valuable the information is. This shuttle can't hold thirty-six more people, much less eighty-five."

"We'll just have to make multiple trips. We owe these people."

"We've risked *our* lives for this one special trip. And even if we could get everyone up to the ship, the ship isn't built to handle that many more people. We're about maxed out just with crew."

"We don't need fancy accommodations. We'll be perfectly fine in a hold for the trip to GA space. And no one will complain. A hold will be infinitely better than the caves we've been living in."

"Our ship doesn't have any holds."

"What? What kind of warship doesn't have any holds?"

"Warship? What were you expecting?"

"Only a Dakinium-sheathed ship could sneak into Clidepp Space without being detected. I figured a destroyer. Or a Scout-Destroyer at the very least."

"Well, I'm sorry to disappoint you, but all we have is a tug."

"A tug? You came all this way in a tug?"

"Yes, and every single berth is already assigned to crew-members. Most of us are living in a shipping container."

"So you're pretending to be a space tug on a recovery or reclamation trip?"

"No. The tug is Dakinium sheathed."

"Space Command would never waste Dakinium sheathing on a tug."

"I guess you've been away for a while. Dakinium production continues to increase because the uses for the material and needs of the military are endless. You'll have to come with us to see for yourself."

"I'm not going anywhere without my people."

"I'm ordering you to comply."

"You don't have that kind of authority," the SCI agent said, looking for some sign of rank on Blade's armor. Finding none he said, "What are you? A Staff Sergeant?"

Blade bristled at the question. "I'm a Marine captain."

"And I'm a Space Command lieutenant commander. I out-rank you, Captain."

"We still can't take your people. We don't have room. Even squeezing in the thirty-six may be impossible."

"They don't take up much space. Most are children."

"Children?"

"This was our safest hiding place. The other is less secure, so we decided that this site was best to house all children under thirteen years of age."

"We don't have room for thirty-five Yolongi children."

"Most are Terran."

"Terran?"

"They're the children of Terran slaves."

"Yolongi and Terrans are biologically incompatible. Yolongi can't produce Terran children."

"The Yolongi have male Terran slaves as well. After their regular supply of Terran slaves from the Raiders was severely constrained because of Ensign Carver, the Yolongi began breeding programs to grow their own. Then, when that Space Command lieutenant(jg) shot an ambassador aboard a Yolongi diplomatic ship and proved that the Yolongi were keeping Terran slaves, virtually all access to slaves from GA space ended. The Clidepp Empire really stepped up the breeding programs after that."

Blade grinned. "You'll never guess who our ship's captain is."

"Carver?"

"No. Carver's a four-star now out in Region Two."

"A four-star? Last I heard she was just a captain at a base at the edge of Region One."

"I guess you've been undercover for a long time. That was more than a decade ago."

"Yeah, well, we don't get much news about the GA here."

"You heard about the Milori attacking the GA, didn't you?"

"Yeah. I heard we whipped them— twice."

"That was Carver. She was in command as a brevetted one-star when they attacked the first time and as a brevetted two-star in the second invasion. The GA Senate unanimously approved her permanent promotion to full admiral in '81. She'd already been the youngest one-star and the youngest two-star in Space Command history. Now she's the youngest four-star, and there's talk she'll be the youngest five-star. The bookies have been taking bets for a year."

"I'd heard about the attacks, but I hadn't heard that Carver was in command. We aren't in the GA, and I think the media has orders to never talk about it. So who's the captain of your ship?"

"It's the other one. Marcola."

"The one who shot the ambassador because he was abusing one of the Terran slaves he had on board?"

"The very same."

"Then I know *she's* not going to leave the slaves here, or the children of slaves."

"No matter how much she wants to take them all, we don't have enough room, enough food, or possibly even enough air. Air recycling processes have limits."

"Then talk to her because I'm not leaving unless we take every one of the slaves and the Yolongi who risked their necks for us. Plus their families."

Blade exhaled loudly in frustration and turned back towards the shuttle. After climbing aboard he walked to the flight deck and said to Weems, "He won't come."

"What? Won't come? After all we went through to come get him?"

"He has eighty-four people he insists on bringing. I told him no way, and he says he won't go without them."

"We can't take eighty-five extra people with us. This is just a MAT-14."

"I'm not the one you have to convince. Can you contact the *Justice*?"

"Possibly. The planet has turned slightly since we left the ship so we can't send a direct transmission, but we might be able to relay a message through the sensor buoy as we had the SCI agent do, or perhaps one of the communication satellites we just dropped."

"Give it a try."

"Okay. I'll have to record the message and send it as an encrypted burst. Give me all the facts."

After hearing everything Blade knew, Weems organized his thoughts and recorded the message. Blade nodded in agreement when the message was ready to be sent. "Three tenths of a second," Weems said, then touched the contact point on his console to send it to the *Justice*.

"Now we wait," Weems said.

"I'll be in the rear cabin."

◆ ◆ ◆

"Captain, we just received a message from Lieutenant Weems. It was encrypted and sent in burst form through the sensor buoy."

Sydnee, sitting in the command chair on the bridge, said, "Play it over the speaker, Chief."

As the message began to play, Sydnee struggled to maintain an impassive expression. As the message ended, all bridge personnel looked in her direction briefly, then turned back to their consoles.

"Any reply, Captain?" Chief Lemela asked.

"Not just yet, Chief. Olivetti, you have the bridge. I'll be in my office."

"Aye, Captain."

As Sydnee left the bridge, Lt.(jg) Olivetti moved to the command chair while Caruthers remained at the helm station. Sydnee had been alternating the command time so all WCI graduate officers got a chance to sit in the 'big' chair.

"I suspected *something* would go wrong with this last-minute assignment," Sydnee said aloud after closing her door, "but I never figured on anything like this. Eighty-four additional passengers, many of whom are children? I wonder if SCI knows about this and just didn't bother to tell us."

Sydnee knew she could try to order the SCI undercover agent to come to the *Justice* alone, but if she did and he called her bluff, she might appear to have lost control in the eyes of the crew. And besides, she didn't want to leave any Terran slaves or the children of slaves on Yolongus. After mulling the problem over in her head for at least ten minutes, she touched her Space Command ring and said, "Lt. Galli, report to my office."

She heard the engineering officer say, "On my way, Captain."

Galli had been on the bridge and knew the situation. He reached her office in about ten seconds.

"I need to know how many additional people this ship can support. I'm talking mainly about oxygen and environmental conditions."

"Well, environmentally— meaning temperature and humidity— the main ship can easily support eighty-five additional Terrans by itself. Water and oxygen are also no problem because we recycle both. So the main ship could handle the extra people on its own, and if there was a problem, any of the habitat containers could take over and stand in for the systems on the ship. The lowest level in every habitat design I'm familiar with is dedicated to engineering functions. Their environmental systems could fully support the habitat for years if it became separated from a ship, and with eight habitat systems on this voyage, we could support virtually any unanticipated demands. If one or more of the systems should break down, the systems in the other containers would automatically adjust to support the malfunctioning systems— for as long as the habitats are connected. So all those needs are not even a consideration. Food is probably our only concern. We have plenty right now because we were supplied with enough for an extended mission in mind, but I don't know if it would be enough for all the additional mouths if our mission remains unchanged. It all depends on how much the passengers consume and how quickly we can complete the satellite distribution. Sleeping accommodations are another weak point. There are definitely not enough berths. And, naturally, no warship is built with children in mind. It would be impossible to lock them out of certain areas where they just shouldn't go, so we'd have to have Marines on security duty 24/7."

"I estimate we have enough food to last our crew of seventy-seven for twenty-eight months. So, with an additional passenger complement of eighty-five, many of whom are children, we should have enough for fourteen months."

"I concur. And we'll have to restrict all passengers to below deck locations, Captain."

"You mean the areas in the habitats?"

71

"Yes, Captain."

"I agree. Visitors must understand that the children are not permitted even in the link section tunnel."

"The weapons habitat containers are sealed and can only be opened by you or me, so we have no problem there. The FA-SF4 fighter hangers can also be secured, Captain, as long as no one gets sloppy and leaves one unlocked."

"We also have to restrict use of the access tubes, or we'll find them filled with children every time we try to use them. Having grown up in a dirt-side environment, weightlessness will be a new and exciting experience to them."

"Aye, Captain. Even adults who haven't experienced it before can get a little carried away at times."

"I just had a thought. Berths are our biggest concern right now. The seating in the rear cabin of the shuttles can be converted to beds. We can lock the flight deck so the children can't get in, but we might have to post a guard at the access hatches of each ship so the children can't slip into the main ship."

"No matter how I look at it, Captain, it's going to be a major headache."

"Yes," Sydnee said in agreement, "a fourteen month headache."

◆　◆　◆

"The captain says we can bring all thirty-five members of your group up to the ship if we can squeeze them into the shuttle," Blade said to the SCI agent. "By the way, what should I call you?"

"Call me— Winston."

"Is that your first name or your last name?"

"Neither. It's just something you can call me since you need a handle. What about the other group?"

"There's no way we can fit forty-nine additional people into the shuttle. We'll have to make a second trip. And probably a third."

"Okay, we'll load you up, and then I'll go to the other site and prepare the rest."

"No, the captain says you come this trip or nobody comes."

The SCI agent stared at Blade for about ten seconds before responding. He was trying to read Blade's determination to enforce the captain's orders. "If you return without me, SCI will have your heads."

"SCI requested that we pick you up. We're here, right now, just waiting to give you a ride off the planet. If you refuse to get aboard the shuttle, it's not our responsibility. We've put our necks on the line just coming down here to get you."

"I'm not coming."

"Fine by me. I wish you luck finding another ride." Talking to his team via Com 1 while the external speaker on his armor was still active, Blade said, "Okay people. Get on board the shuttle. We're pulling out."

The SCI agent stood impassively, watching as the Marines climbed back into the shuttle. He waited until Blade was about to step through the hatchway before shouting, "Wait, Captain. I've decided to come after all. I'll get my people."

Blade nodded, and when the SCI agent turned away, he smiled. *Marcola played that one perfectly,* he thought. He watched as the man who had chosen the name Winston walked towards the mountains on one side of the wide ravine and disappeared into an opening in the rock wall.

◆

It took over half an hour for the SCI agent to return with the thirty-five people who had remained hidden in the cave until then. Only four— all women— were adults. The rest were children, three of whom were infants. Three of the children were Yolongi, while the others and the four women were Terrans.

Every seat in the rear cabin was filled when the shuttle finally lifted off, with some seats having two small children strapped into it. The women were holding the infants. Blade had never taken his eyes off the SCI agent, believing he might try to make a break for it after the shuttle was fully loaded, but Winston took his seat and glared at Blade before twisting to talk with one of the women.

The shuttle again identified itself as the *Patoosch* as it climbed through the planet's atmosphere and received an immediate clearance to depart the planet.

When the shuttle reached the *Justice,* half the children were screaming or crying and had been since the small ship had climbed through the planet's atmosphere. Blade had removed his helmet after the shuttle lifted off but put it back on and turned down the audio because his head was already splitting by the time they reached the halfway point. He reminded himself over and over that he had definitely made the right decision when he chose never to marry and have a family. He had made the decision because he never knew if he would return from the next mission, but now he realized that he didn't have the patience for fatherhood if it meant listening to screaming children on a regular basis.

As the docking procedure was completed and the shuttle's hatch was opened, several of the Marines practically knocked one another over trying to get out and away from the noise. Sydnee was standing off to the side of the corridor with Lt. Kelly MacDonald and a staff sergeant as Special Ops personnel rushed past them on their way to the access tube that would take them down to the quiet of the Marine habitat container.

"In my office," Sydnee said to Blade as he emerged from the shuttle. MacDonald and the staff sergeant were there to see that the newly arrived passengers all remained aboard the shuttle until Sydnee okayed them to exit the small vessel.

"Rough trip?" Sydnee asked as the door to her office closed.

"Those kids didn't stop screaming the whole way. And I mean the *whole* way, Captain."

"The smaller children probably haven't been taught how to equalize the pressure in their ears. The babies definitely haven't."

"Yeah, that's probably it. I didn't think of that."

"Did the SCI agent give you any difficulties about not retrieving the other group right away?"

"Yes, and you were right. Winston refused to come with us until I told him that if he didn't come, nobody else would."

"Winston?"

"That's the name he wants to use. It isn't his real name. He says he's a lieutenant commander in SCI."

"Did he give you the location of the other people?"

"No, and I didn't ask. We couldn't handle any more than the one group."

"Okay. I'm glad that was the most serious problem we've had to face on this assignment."

"Are you going to retrieve the others?"

"If we can. I just don't know how many times we can pass ourselves off as the *Patoosch* before the Yolongi fleet wises up. Perhaps we've already used up all of our free passes. Thank you, Major. Would you ask Winston to come in?"

"Do you want me here also?"

"No, go take some aspirin and relax. He may want to speak alone. You know how these SCI types are."

Blade nodded and left the office. A few minutes later the computer advised Sydnee that an unidentified person was at the door.

"Computer, in the future refer to that individual as Winston."

"Information recorded."

"Open the door."

CHAPTER SEVEN
~ January 17th, 2287 ~

As the door slid open, the SCI agent looked into the office and said, "Is this your office or a clothes locker?"

"It's my office and my private quarters, and yes, it's smaller than a Petty Officer's sleeping quarters on a warship. Come in, Winston."

"That's not my name."

"What is your name?"

"Uh, just call me Winston."

Sydnee resisted an urge to roll her eyes. "Okay, Winston. Come in and have a seat."

"What about my people?"

"I'm sure they'll be perfectly comfortable now that the Marines are out of the shuttle. They should have plenty of room."

"I'm talking about the ones still on the planet."

"That's a more difficult question. We disguised that shuttle for one surreptitious visit to the planet in order to accomplish our mission here. We've now used that one visit to rescue you, and we haven't accomplished our original mission. We got away with it once, but the risk increases exponentially if we try it again. All it takes is for one Yolongi to note that the real shuttle named the *Patoosch* never landed at the proper location on its last flight and then also left much too quickly. The obvious deduction is that it wasn't really the *Patoosch*."

"Are you saying *I* wasn't your original mission?"

"Until a few hours ago I had no idea you were on the planet. Your rescue was assigned to us because we were already in the neighborhood preparing for a different mission to the surface. Now we have to devise a way to make at least one

76

more secret trip, and possibly three. I don't know how long it will be before we can recover your people, or even *if* we can recover them. You became our top priority when I received orders to get you, but my original mission has top priority again now that we've recovered you."

"What is your mission?"

"Sorry, it's need to know, and you don't need to know."

"I knew I shouldn't have gotten aboard that shuttle."

Sydnee knew she had to make Winston believe she would have stood behind her threat, even though she knew she would have ordered the shuttle to bring the group from the cave even if he had refused to come along, so she said, "If you hadn't gotten aboard, you and those thirty-four passengers would still be on the surface. Because of you, more than a third of your people have been rescued."

"I can't believe you would have left helpless Terran children behind if it was so easy to save them. Aren't you the same Lieutenant Marcola who shot the ambassador aboard a diplomatic ship because he had a harem full of Terran slaves?"

"I've never shot an ambassador. I wish I knew how that rumor got started. I did shoot the ambassador's guards, and the ambassador *thought* I was going to shoot him next, but I never did. And I was acquitted of all charges regarding shooting the guards because the recorded data from my helmet cam proved they were reaching for their weapons before I reached for mine."

"You pulled your weapon and shot two guards *after* they started reaching for their weapons? Impressive."

"They were torturing a female slave in my presence, so my adrenaline was peaking. But that's old news."

"Are you saying you don't intend to rescue the others?"

"Tell me something, Winston. Did you fill that cave with just women and children because you believed it would be harder for us to leave them behind and not because it was the safer of your two locations?"

"It *was* the safer of our two locations. The remoteness made it ideal because it can be difficult to quiet very young children when they're scared or hungry. Are you going to rescue the rest of my people now that I yielded and came aboard?"

"I already answered that question when I said we have to figure a way to make as many as three more trips. Naturally, I can't make any promises about the others on the surface. For instance, they may be discovered before we can reach them."

"If you had come in a destroyer, you could have forced your way through the Yolongi Fleet perimeter. They're no match for a GA destroyer."

"As I said, you were not our mission. We came in a ship best suited for our original goals. But for the record, the entire Yolongi fleet is no match for this ship either. However, SHQ doesn't want anyone to know we were ever here, so forcing our way through a planetary blockade is out, regardless of the size and armament of the vessel."

"What exactly is this ship's designation and armament? It's far too small to be a Scout-Destroyer."

"It's a CPS-14. Think of it as a tug on steroids."

"Blade said it was a tug. I didn't believe him."

"It's not like any standard tug, not even a space tug. But like a tug, this ship is mostly power plant. It's been designed to be the central component when assembling a ship for a specific mission. While the crew space inside the CPS is limited, we can attach up to four shuttles to the larboard and starboard sides, and up to eight customized twenty-meter-long containers to the keel. Our armament consists of missiles and laser cannons, and we currently have an Air Wing of Marine FA-SF4 fighters on board. The hull is Dakinium-sheathed and we can achieve Light-9790. When configured like this, we're *sort* of like a mini Scout-Destroyer."

"So you've got the protection of Dakinium and all the firepower you need to withstand an attack by the Yolongi fleet?"

"As I said, my orders are to not let anyone know we're here or ever were here. Shouldn't you be preparing a communication to SCI?"

"Actually, what I want to do is to send a communication to my people still left on the planet. I'm sure they're wondering where I disappeared to and may be considering leaving their current hiding place if they fear I've been arrested and will crack under torture and reveal their location."

"I'll arrange for you to send a short message. Can they handle a burst transmission?"

"No, but we have an encryption computer system."

"That will have to do. You'll have to record it rather than send a live message. That way we can work to make it as brief as possible and relay it through a sensor buoy we dropped near the planet. We want to conceal as much of our operating methods as possible from the Yolongi military and security forces. I want you to tell your people to remain where they are and stay hidden until they hear from you again. Tell them we'll pick them up as soon as possible, but if they're not there when we arrive, we can't return for a second try. We will only make one attempt to get them."

"Tell me something, *Captain*— how did a lieutenant junior grade come to be in command of a powerful mini-warship like this one? Especially one with a mission this vitally important."

"The junior officers aboard the *Denver* all drew straws," Sydnee said drolly.

"And that's how you won command?"

"No, I lost. Damn my bad luck."

"You're joking."

"Yes. We never actually drew straws. We played musical chairs."

"Now I *know* you're joking."

"I was offered this volunteer mission by my captain."

"And you wanted to prove yourself?"

79

"No. Someone had to do it, and I was the only Space Command officer aboard the *Denver* who had previously commanded a clandestine mission to Yolongus."

"You've commanded other such missions to Yolongus?"

"This is not my first."

Winston chuckled. "And that's how you got a Marine captain to report to you?"

"Winston, I'm the duly appointed captain of this vessel, an appointment which has been fully endorsed by SHQ *and* SCI. You can verify that when we get back. For now, know this. This is *my* ship for the duration of this mission, and *everyone* aboard reports to *me*. If you really are a lieutenant commander in Space Command you know that both Earth's maritime laws and the GA extraterrestrial laws establish that the duly appointed captain of any military vessel is the master and commander of all persons aboard said vessel. That is unequivocal unless a person having a superior military rank and guilty of disobeying a command from the captain can prove that the appointed individual was either operating outside their orders or was mentally incompetent. My appointment gives me the same authority as if I held the Space Command rank of Captain. That authority extends over all Space Command and Space Marine personnel who have volunteered for special duty and been assigned to this vessel— including Marine Captain Blade and his Special Ops team, a platoon of Marines from the destroyer *Denver*, Lt. Colonel Dennier, who is my Air Wing commander, the officers of the Wing, and anyone else who comes aboard, such as lieutenant commanders from SCI. When this mission is over and we've returned to GA space, you will outrank me if you really are a lieutenant commander in Space Command. But until this mission is over, I'm in command, and you will obey my orders or I will have you confined to the brig. Are we perfectly clear on that point?"

Winston nodded and said somberly, "Of course, Captain," then turned towards the office door.

"One last thing, Winston. Do you really have the vital information you claimed to have, or was this all a ruse because you needed transportation for the eighty-four people?"

As he touched the small control plate that would open the office door, Winston turned back slightly and gave Sydnee an enigmatic smile. "I'll prepare that message for my people still on the surface."

As the door closed behind Winston, Sydnee scowled. Whether his claim was a ruse or not, she had received orders to rescue Winston, so it didn't really matter if he had the information he professed or not. Taking her seat behind her desk, she turned her attention to devising a new plan to deliver the package. The first trip to the planet had worked flawlessly, but she was loath to push her luck with another such mission. Unfortunately, the options seemed severely limited. And she knew that as soon as the package was delivered, it would become even more difficult to penetrate the Yolongi defenses. Despite what she said to Winston about the importance of conducting their original mission next, she knew that if they were to have any hope of rescuing Winston's forty-nine people still remaining on the surface, they must do that before dropping off the package.

◆ ◆ ◆

Sydnee listened to the prerecorded message Winston created for his people on Yolongus before she allowed it to be sent. Even though it would be encrypted before going out, it contained a number of special code words and phrases. Winston said they were necessary so that the people receiving the message knew it hadn't been faked. In a message that seemed to be sent to Yolongi parents, he told his mother that he had to leave town unexpectedly on business, but that he was okay and expected to return very shortly. He told her not to take any long trips because he expected to have very good news when he returned and he was anxious to celebrate with her. The phrases could have very different meaning from what they seemed, but Sydnee had no way of knowing what they might really be communicating.

81

"Good," Sydnee said. "You kept it very brief. I'll have the Chief send it right away."

"How soon can we leave for the surface?"

"I'm still weighing options, but in any event, you can't go."

"What do you mean? I *have* to go."

"Have you written and filed a full report that contains the information you claimed to have when you reported to SHQ?"

"I'm not writing that report until my people are safely aboard. It's the only leverage I have."

"You don't need leverage, Winston. What you need is a friend. And you're not improving your position by refusing to cooperate. Let me put it like this. Right now you are the only one with the information you claim to have gathered, so I can't allow you to leave this ship and possibly be captured or killed. However, if you prepare a complete report with all the information you've promised, it will no longer be necessary to restrict your movements. You'll be able to return to the surface and help bring your people back to the ship."

"If I prepare the report, you will no longer be anxious to help me rescue my people."

"That's incorrect. I'm not anxious to help *you* at all. But I do want to rescue any slaves, their children, and others who have risked their lives to provide us with the information SHQ wants. That's my only motivation in your regard. I already have you onboard, so whether you send SHQ the information to prevent it from possibly being lost if I allow you to return to the planet or I keep you up here and simply return you to SHQ when our original mission is complete won't really matter to SHQ. Either way they get the data you've collected. All you'll accomplish by not filing your report is to ensure you don't leave the ship before we return to GA space."

Winston scowled and said, "Okay, Captain, you win. I'll prepare a full report for SHQ."

"Good. Once that's done you'll be free to participate in the mission to recover the people still on the surface."

"And when will that be?"

"One step at a time, Winston. I'm just as anxious to be done here and leave the solar system as you, but I have to find a way to rescue your people *and* complete my original mission without exposing our presence to the Yolongi. For now, just get your report filed."

♦ ♦ ♦

"Captain," Lieutenant(jg) Templeton, the first watch Tac officer, said to Sydnee the next day as she sat in her command chair on the bridge, "I'm picking up a ship on the De-Tect system. It's heading this way. It seems to be on the same course as the *Patoosch* the first time we encountered it."

The *Justice* hadn't used any exterior lights since entering Clidepp space, and the Dakinium didn't reflect radar signals, so Sydnee said, "Helm, build our double envelope so the *Patoosch* doesn't accidently hit us. Also, turn us so our starboard side is facing them so they can't get any kind of radar reflection from the shuttle surface we modified."

"Aye, Captain," Lt.(jg) Caruthers said as he touched several spots on the helm console in front of him. "Envelope forming, and I'm using thrusters to turn the ship."

"Com," Sydnee said, "monitor the *Patoosch* communications and tell me if they do anything different than the last time they approached Yolongus."

♦

After the *Patoosch* had entered orbit and descended to the surface of Yolongus, Chief Lemela said, "No change, Captain. They requested and received permission to descend to the planet and were cleared without any delay and without giving any recognition code. The signals picked up by one of the new satellites we put into orbit allowed me to identify their destination when they requested landing permission at a shuttle port named Magomca."

"Tac?" Sydnee said.

"One second, Captain. I'm checking." After a slight pause, Templeton said, "Yes, here it is. It's a small shuttle port that's registered to the Nugowlo-3 Mining Cooperative."

83

◆ ◆ ◆

Following breakfast the next day, Sydnee held a briefing in the Marine mess hall. Only Blade, Dennier, Winston, Mac-Donald, and the flight officers involved in the shuttle operations had been invited.

"I've decided we'll try to pass ourselves off as the *Patoosch* one more time," Sydnee said. "We got away with it once, so we might be lucky again. We know the real *Patoosch* is presently still on the surface. The communication records during our time in Clidepp Empire space show that the shuttle has remained here anywhere from one day to four days and has returned anywhere from two days to ten days after departure. Obviously, there are no scheduled arrival or departure times. We estimate that their flight time to Nugowlo is about ten GST hours, so we'll begin our next operation one full day after the shuttle departs. As before, Weems and DiRoma will take the modified shuttle, designated as Shuttle One, and fly to the new location where the Terran slaves are waiting. Winston has given us the coordinates, and that information has been loaded into the flight computers. Because the number of people waiting to be picked up exceeds what one shuttle can accommodate, we'll need two shuttles. Caruthers and Burns will take the second shuttle, designated as Shuttle Two, and follow in the exact flight path ten seconds later. Shuttle Two will be invisible to radar, and anyone spotting its dark shape will hopefully assume it's the *Patoosch*— or a reflection. On the way down to the planet, both shuttles will have an engineer suited up in an EVA suit and waiting in the stern airlock. On command, the engineers will simultaneously open the outer hatch and deploy the remaining communication satellites.

"Arriving at the pickup location, Major Blade will deploy with his people and secure the ground area while Winston makes contact with the people waiting there and brings half of them to Shuttle One. Shuttle Two will hover nearby and watch for approaching craft. After loading its passengers, Shuttle One will rise and hover while watching for approaching craft as Shuttle Two lands to pick up the remaining passengers. Our Marines, led by Lieutenant MacDonald, will deploy and secure the area as the remainder of the people are loaded. The package will be in Shuttle Two, and when the pickup is complete, Shuttle One will return to the *Justice* while the package is taken to the drop point. Shuttle Two will then return to the *Justice*. Any questions?"

"Why can't we load both shuttles simultaneously?" Caruthers asked.

"Winston says there isn't room for two shuttles in the narrow canyon outside the cave where the people are waiting. And the nearest clearing is too far to walk even during daylight hours."

"What's this package you mentioned?" Winston asked.

"That was our primary mission until we were ordered to recover you. It's need to know, and you don't need to know more than that."

"Is there a role for my people in this?" Colonel Dennier asked.

"I hope not, Colonel. I'm hoping we can do this without a fight. But I wanted you to be aware of what was happening in case we need your help."

"Is that all?" Blade asked after a minute of silence.

"There's one more thing. The four adults and children we picked up have been sleeping in Shuttle One until now. We have to move them out so we can use that ship. Space is very limited, but we have to find space in one of the habitat containers. We have six units to choose from. Any suggestions?"

"We're shoehorned in pretty tight as it is," Dennier said. "The only open space is in the corridors, and our people use those as exercise areas."

"I agree," Blade said. "There's no unused space in the habitat units."

Sydnee looked around the table. "We have one option, but it'll require quite a bit of work. We can move the satellites stored on one level of a habitat container to another level, then use that cleared space for the children and the others coming aboard. Presently, the satellite containers are only piled one layer high on each level, but they can be stacked right up to the overhead. The cases are strong enough to support the weight. I suppose they had so much space in the container that there was no need to economize.

"If Major Blade and Colonel Dennier can have their people take responsibility for moving those satellites, we can preserve the corridors as exercise areas."

Sydnee waited for protests that never came. Both officers just looked at her for a few seconds and then nodded.

"Okay, it's decided then. We add the satellites on the top level of the container to those on the lowest storage level and use the freed space for the newcomers. My engineers and the Colonel's mechanics can supervise to ensure that the satellites are moved with the utmost care."

"What do we use for bedding?" MacDonald asked.

"That's a problem. We don't have any extra mattresses and only a few extra blankets. We just weren't prepared for passengers."

"Tugs usually carry gravity-shielding pads so the tug operators have a place to sleep on long hauls." Winston said. "Don't you have any of those?"

"I say this ship is like a tug on steroids because the main ship is almost entirely devoted to the power plant, but it's not actually a tug. We have twenty-four regular berths, and all are assigned to crewmembers. We have no gravity-shielding pads in our stores because we didn't anticipate a need for them."

"My people can sleep on the deck until we get back to GA space. They'll use their extra clothing for bedding. At Light-9790 it should only take a month to get back to GA space."

"Except we can't return to GA space until we complete our mission here."

"How long will that be?"

"SCI told me it could take as long as two years."

"Two years? Two *years*? GST years?"

"Yes."

"What kind of mission takes two years?"

"It's those satellites I was just talking about. SCI came up with a plan to seed communication satellites around every occupied planet, moon, and space station in the Clidepp Empire."

"Good Lord. That sounds like the crazy plan Captain Hellman dreamed up a decade ago."

"I don't know who initiated it. All I know is that we've been assigned to make it a reality. In any event, the extra mouths mean we'll only have enough food for fourteen months, so we may have to cut the mission short."

"I want to send a request to SHQ that this ship be recalled to GA space immediately to unload all passengers."

"You have my permission to make such a request, Winston, but let's complete this mission before we begin making other plans. Is there anything else to discuss? Anyone?"

After looking around the table and not receiving any answers, Sydnee said, "Okay. This meeting is adjourned. Our first task is to move those satellites."

CHAPTER EIGHT
~ January 20th, 2287 ~

Sydnee was alerted when the *Patoosch* left Yolongus a few days later. Its course as it left orbit indicated it was headed for Nugowlo. She immediately established a schedule for the final operations on Yolongus and authorized Winston to send a message to his people so they would have the precise timetable and be prepared for evacuation from the planet.

Fully one-quarter of the small satellites in one of the habitat containers beneath the *Justice* had been moved, clearing an entire nine-by-twenty-meter area for the children and four adults who had been staying in Shuttle One. The pintsized occupants were less than overjoyed at surrendering their comfortable beds in the shuttle, but the older children understood the reason and looked forward to seeing their parents again. The shuttle's rear cabin area was rearranged for seating only, and the small ship was made ready for departure. The lowest level in the habitat container used for storing the satellites was now half-filled with crates containing satellites, and Sydnee hoped they wouldn't have to access any of the bottom row until they had been able to reduce the number of satellites through the seeding process.

At the designated time, Blade and his Special Ops team entered Shuttle One while Lt. MacDonald and two of the *Denver*'s fire teams assigned to the *Justice* entered Shuttle Two. The 'package,' released from his special holding area for the first time since coming aboard the *Justice*, was placed in Shuttle Two. An opaque hood covered his head so he wouldn't see his surroundings and no one other than his guards could later recognize him. Although his movement aboard ship had been restricted to the special brig and his guards weren't permitted to converse with him, he had been well fed and was in the best of health. He had been provided with a

88

viewpad that contained an enormous collection of music, books, and videos from Yolongus to keep him entertained, but he hadn't received any news regarding the situation on his home world since being abducted by the Special Ops team on the first incursion by the *Justice* into Clidepp space.

As each shuttle prepared for departure, an engineer suited in EVA gear entered the airlock at the back of the rear cabin. Several of the tiny DS satellites, programmed with their location coordinates and ready to be deployed, had already been placed in each of the airlocks. After ejecting the satellites and closing the hatch, the engineers would move back into the rear cabin, remove their EVA suits and don their personal armor, as required by Sydnee to help avoid the kind of problems they'd experienced on the previous mission while performing tasks outside the scope of the original parameters. Winston, aboard Shuttle Two, was without personal armor, as was the 'package' aboard Shuttle Two. All personal armor had to be custom-fit to the wearer's body, so there was no extra aboard the *Justice*.

Shuttle One left on schedule, with Shuttle Two exactly ten seconds behind on the same course. Sydnee was seated in her bridge command chair when Chief Lemela reported that Shuttle One had been cleared to enter the planet's atmosphere. No alarm was raised, suggesting that Shuttle Two had either not been observed or that the ruse of having it seem to be either the approved flight or merely a shadowy reflection of the approved flight had worked.

◆

Once a ship entered a planet's troposphere, only the ship's oh-gee capability was used for flight, except where massive propulsion was required to respond to an emergency condition. Shuttle One gently touched down at the coordinates provided by Winston a few seconds before Shuttle Two arrived overhead and assumed a stationary position a hundred meters above ground level. Floating overhead on a cushion of opposed-gravity waves, Shuttle Two had a perfect view of the narrow ravine where Shuttle One rested.

As Shuttle One came to a complete stop, the Special Ops team deployed in seconds and took up positions in the ravine. They were in unknown territory and therefore on high alert as Winston sauntered out of the ship as if on holiday and began walking away. It was already dark on this part of the planet, so the SCI agent was using a tiny flashlight to light his path. The people wearing armor had the benefit of infrared and thermal imaging in their helmets, so the time of day made no difference to them.

"Winston," Blade called abruptly, and the SCI officer stopped and returned to where Blade was standing. "What's your plan now that we're down?"

"I'm going to get my people and bring them to the shuttles."

"How many men do you want to accompany you?"

"None. It will only frighten my people until they get used to those black-on-black suits of protective armor. You look pretty intimidating because the secret police on Yolongus all wear black uniforms."

"We're only here to provide protection."

"I know, but my people don't. You have to realize how oppressive and repressive the government is here. Let them get used to the idea that men in black armor aren't here to hurt them before you storm into their presence."

"Okay. We'll wait here. Contact me via CT when you're ready to return."

"I don't have a CT. It was removed before I first went undercover on this planet in case I was ever captured and medically examined for espionage technology."

Reaching into a pouch on his belt, Blade produced a small earpiece. After depressing a tiny raised dot on the side, he held it out to Winston. "Put this into either ear. I'll be able to hear you through my CT, and you'll be able to hear me."

"Can it pick up the voices of others?"

"If they're close enough to you. It will pick up all conversations within a roughly three-meter range."

Winston took the small device and looked at it. "Can I accidentally deactivate it?"

"No. It's always on once activated and can only be deactivated by a tech with the proper tool. But no one else will be able to hear me while you have it in your ear."

Winston looked at Blade skeptically, then placed the small earpiece in his left ear. It was virtually invisible. "Can you hear me in your CT?" he asked.

"Five by five," Blade said.

"Okay, I'm going to get my people. They probably don't know we've arrived because the camp is so far inside the mountain. It's an abandoned mine shaft leading to an enormous natural cavern."

"We'll be waiting, and we'll load them aboard the shuttle as they arrive. Don't bring more than twenty-eight in the first group. That's the most adults we can take. After the second shuttle is able to land, I'll notify you to bring the rest."

"Got it. Be right back."

Blade heard Winston's respiration noises for perhaps a minute, and then the signal terminated. He was tempted to go see what happened but held off because Winston had been so adamant about him not interfering.

"Lt. Weems, are you picking up anything from the earpiece I gave to Winston?"

"Negative, Major. The audio terminated a minute or so after Winston began walking towards the cavern."

"How about the tracking signal? Is that still coming through strong?"

"Negative. That ended at the same time the audio signal stopped."

"Damn."

◆

Another ten minutes passed without a sound from Winston or any indication that everything was well. Blade was about to take four of his people and go search for Winston when three Terran women, who appeared to be in their late teens or early twenties, suddenly appeared on the path Winston had traveled. Like Winston, they each had one of the tiny flash-lights.

The women appeared leery of the armored soldiers and halted but then approached slowly. Until then, the image on Blade's faceplate was blank, but he changed it to show his true image. Once they realized he was a Terran, the women seemed less frightened. "Please step into the shuttle and take seats, ladies," Blade said through the speaker in his chest ar-mor, but the women didn't appear to understand, so he set the translator output to Yolongi. When he repeated the message, they nodded and moved towards the ramp.

Another five minutes passed without anyone else appear-ing. Blade heard Weems say over the CT command frequen-cy, "Major, what's happening? We've only had three women come aboard."

"I don't know any more than you, Lieutenant. Winston told me he had to do this alone. Wait, I see more people coming."

"Friendlies?"

"They appear to be. I see light weapons, but none are be-ing held in a threatening manner."

A total of eighteen people filed past Blade and entered the shuttle, then another six appeared a couple of minutes later and entered the shuttle. Of the twenty-seven who had entered the shuttle, all were Yolongi except for the first three.

"Major, what's going on?" Weems said. "I'm looking at the monitor that shows the rear cabin, and all I see are Yolongi except for the first three girls. I thought we were here to res-cue Terran slaves."

"I'm as much in the dark as you, Lieutenant. We'll let the captain straighten it out."

"We can only take one more adult passenger. Tell Winston to come back so we can lift off and let Shuttle Two land to pick up the rest."

"I'll try, but he appears to be out of communication range."

Blade then called to Winston repeatedly, but received no answer.

Suddenly, Caruthers, aboard Shuttle Two, half shouted, "We've got numerous oh-gee craft headed this way."

"How many, what configurations, and how far?" Blade said calmly.

"It looks like about twenty, but could be as many as thirty because they're so tightly clustered. The computer says they're APCs, heavily armed, and the mounted weapons are too powerful for our personal body armor. They're just five minutes out."

"I'm going for Winston," Blade said. "Team Alpha, you're with me. Everyone else hold position, but be prepared to get aboard and bug out on my command."

Five of the Special Ops Marines hurried after Blade as he ran along the trail where he had last seen Winston, but he was suddenly confronted by five different cave openings. His helmet's infrared heat sensors indicated that tracks in the dirt at all five openings had been made by the recent passage of numerous individuals. "Great," he muttered. He then began calling to Winston using his body armor's external speaker at full volume, but he still received no responses.

"The APCs are just three minutes out," Caruthers said. "We have to get out of here, Major. Now! Those were the captain's orders if any Yolongi military showed up."

Blade cursed and ran back to the shuttle with Team Alpha. The rest of the Special Ops Marines climbed aboard behind them.

Weems lifted off even before the hatch was fully locked. Shuttle Two was already climbing skyward vertically. Weems lifted the small cover that protected the electrical current to the outside surface of the ship from being accidentally disengaged and pressed the button. Instantly, the electrical circuitry that had kept the special metallic paint stuck to the hull was disabled. The paint immediately flaked off the Dakinium and fell away like a miniature snowstorm, rendering Shuttle One as invisible to radar as Shuttle Two.

As both black shuttles climbed through the moonless night sky, no one could visually or electronically mark their path. The officers in the APCs were confused to see the hard contact just ahead appear to simply disintegrate in front of them. When they landed and looked for signs of wreckage, the only unusual things they found were tiny flakes of what seemed to be white paint.

As the two shuttles left the vicinity of the planet at the maximum velocity capable with the oh-gee engines, there was no indication that their travel had been noticed by the Clidepp fleet in orbit around Yolongus. As per orders, Weems did not attempt to contact the *Justice* until the shuttles were well away from the planet and could establish a laser communication link. He would only be permitted to violate that order if they came under fire or were faced with a situation they couldn't resolve.

The identification signal going in the approximate direction of the *Justice* was wider than the actual communication link would be, but once received and acknowledged by the *Justice*, both ships would have a precise transmission direction fix, and the laser relay connection would hardly be wider than a human hair. Interception by other parties was virtually impossible. And the signals were naturally encrypted as well, making eavesdropping efforts a waste of time. The signals between the *Justice* and the shuttles would be sent by and received by Shuttle One, but the laser signal would be immediately relayed to Shuttle Two, who also had the ability to transmit through the established relay link.

"Captain," Weems said after he had made contact with Sydnee, "we've lost Winston. He went to round up the refugees and hadn't yet returned when we detected two to three dozen APCs headed directly towards us. I have twenty-four Yolongi and three Terrans on board."

"Did a confrontation occur?"

"No, I dropped the reflective paint and we bugged out with all hands and an almost full load of refugees about a half minute before the APCs arrived at the ravine."

"Did you get any final messages from Winston?"

"We never received any messages from him at all. Blade gave him a communications earpiece, but he never used it as far as I know."

"What's the status of the package?"

"The package is still aboard my shuttle," Caruthers said from Shuttle Two.

"Return to the ship."

"Aye, Captain. Shuttle One and Shuttle Two returning home."

While the shuttles headed towards the distant *Justice* at maximum sub-light speed, Weems settled into his chair and thought about the botched mission.

♦

In the Marine mess hall, Sydnee listened as everyone involved was debriefed and they told what they knew of the rescue effort. Colonel Dennier had also been invited to the meeting. The package had been returned to the special brig, while the refugees were still in the shuttle pending Sydnee's decision regarding their status. All refugee weapons had been confiscated and would remain in the ship's armory locker, located in the Marine habitat container, while the visitors were aboard the *Justice*.

Sydnee never asked a question until everyone had reported their information. "Major," Sydnee finally said, "you said Winston never communicated with you at all once he left you at the shuttle. He never even reported his progress with a simple statement like, 'I'm entering the cave'?"

"Not a single utterance, Captain. I did hear some nasal sounds like breathing for a very short time, but even that stopped after about a minute. It was as if he turned off the earpiece, but that's supposed to be impossible without the proper tool."

"May I interject something here, Captain?" Dennier asked.

"Go ahead, Colonel."

"Perhaps the composition of the cave walls was responsible for blocking the signal. Did anyone perform a basic analysis of the rock?"

"There was no time," Blade said. "As per Winston's wishes, we waited at the shuttle until we learned that military APCs were headed our way. We only had five minutes' warning. As I've reported, when we ran to where we expected to find the cave entrance, we found five entrances, all recently used. We didn't even have time to search the caves, much less perform a metallurgical analysis of the cave walls. We had to either get back to the shuttle and get off the planet or engage the Yolongi military in a fight. Our standing orders were to avoid all contact with military or police forces."

"You took the proper action, Major," Sydnee said. "The question now is— where do we go from here? We can abandon Winston, drop off the package, and then resume our efforts to seed all of Clidepp space with satellites or forget everything else in favor of finding Winston or at least trying to learn of his current situation. Once we drop off the package, the Yolongi military will probably go on high alert, so we have to hang onto him if we're not leaving Yolongi space."

"Why is the number of Yolongi refugees so disproportionate to the number of Terran slaves?" Dennier asked. "I expected many more slaves."

"I expected the same thing," Sydnee said. "Perhaps Winston sent the Yolongi ahead because their lives would be more at risk if any were caught. The escaped slaves will probably be returned to their owners and possibly receive a beating, or worse, for running away, while the Yolongi might very well be executed for treasonous actions or activities. We may learn more when we interview them, but I wanted to have this meeting first."

◆

Sydnee conducted the interviews of the twenty-seven new people in the mess hall. Blade and Dennier sat in while two Marines stood outside in the corridor, sending the rescued people in one at a time when the previously interviewed person reemerged. None of the twenty-seven appeared to speak Amer, or at least failed to respond to any questions posed in Amer. And Sydnee received little information other than names and previous addresses. They all said Winston was still in the cavern when they left. It was he who decided who would go on the first shuttle and sent them out to find their way to it. None had any idea what had happened after they left. When Sydnee asked them to speculate, all just shook their heads and professed ignorance again.

As the interview of each refugee was concluded, they were escorted to the habitat level that had been cleared in the container where the spy satellites were stored. Sydnee received reports from the Marines that many of the children were delighted to see the refugees, although they were anxious about the fate of their parent or parents.

◆

"We're no further ahead now than we were before the interviews," Sydnee said to Blade and Dennier after the last of the refugees had been questioned and escorted out of the mess hall.

"Allow me to sum it up," Blade said. "We have no idea where Winston is, who has him, or even if he's still alive. The people who might have helped are here with us and obviously can't return to the planet because they'll be killed on sight. It's unlikely anyone else is going to help. We have no access to information sources and certainly no access to the inner circle of power players. As far as we know, Winston was the only SCI agent on the planet, so this situation is a hundred times worse than the time we found ourselves stranded on the planet without a workable temporal envelope generator."

"What was that last part about being stranded without a temporal envelope generator?" Dennier asked. She hadn't been briefed on the specifics of the last mission to Yolongus.

"Sorry," Blade said, "I momentarily forgot that you weren't with us on the last mission."

"But I'm here now. And knowing what happened previously might enable me to better contribute."

Blade looked at Sydnee with raised eyebrows that furrowed his brow.

"I guess it can't hurt," Sydnee said. "We've already exceeded the expected mission parameters by a parsec or two. Go ahead and brief her. But, Colonel, what you hear doesn't leave this room."

"Understood, Captain."

"While you brief the Colonel, Major, I'm going to see if there's any hot coffee available."

◆

"I couldn't find any hot coffee, so I brewed a pot," Sydnee said when she returned to the table ten minutes later. She was carrying a tray with a pot of dark liquid, several cups, plus jars containing milk, sugar, and what appeared to be honey.

Dennier looked up at Sydnee with a strange look on her face as she said, "When we first met, I mentioned that I'd been told you've earned the respect of everyone who has ever come under your command. From the sketchy accounts that were related to me in my initial briefing, what I've witnessed since coming aboard, and now with what the Major has told me about his personal experiences, I begin to understand why that is."

"I just do my job," Sydnee said as she prepared her coffee. "Now, what are we going to do about Winston?"

Blade looked at Dennier and said, "I told you."

Dennier grinned and said, "Yes, you did."

"No suggestions?" Sydnee asked.

"Drop off the package, leave this area, and begin the satellite-seeding mission," Blade said. "Winston is lost to us."

"I agree," Dennier said, "for all the reasons mentioned earlier, Captain."

"We can't give up so easily," Sydnee said. "There must be something we can do. We just need a starting point."

"I told you," Blade said to Dennier.

"Again with the 'I told you's'?" Sydnee said to Blade. "Just what did you tell the Colonel while I was making the coffee?"

"Among the mission events I related, I told her that the words 'give up' and 'surrender' have never made it into your personal dictionary."

"I wouldn't go *that* far."

Blade looked at Dennier and said, "I told you."

"Okay, okay," Sydnee said with a grin. "Enough with the 'I told you's.' Yes, I've been called tenacious at times because I don't give up easily. And I'm not going to give up easily on this new problem. Space Command and the Space Marines never leave a man or woman behind unless we're absolutely sure there's no way to recover them. There has to be a way to get Winston back. Or at least find out what happened to him."

"I'd be willing to bet a month's pay that at least one of those Yolongis you interviewed knows a lot more than he's admitting," Blade said.

"Yes," Dennier said. "They're probably scared and believe that if they offer to help, we'll ask them to return to the planet and participate in the effort."

"Okay," Sydnee said. "How do we find out which one, or ones, we should lean on?"

Taking the viewpad on the table that contained the names of all refugees and their statements, Blade scrolled down through the list, highlighting a few names as he recalled the interview in his mind. When he was done, he handed the viewpad to Dennier, who examined the list and highlighted a few more before handing the viewpad to Sydnee.

Sydnee nodded as she examined the list and highlighted one more herself. "That makes eight of the Yolongis who we feel might be concealing information. Let's begin a new round of interviews with just these people, but this time we'll put a bit of pressure on them to reveal information they might have kept secret."

CHAPTER NINE
~ January 21st, 2287 ~

"I swear, Captain," Sydnee heard via her CT, "I don't have any idea what happened in the cave after we left."

The small translator on Sydnee's belt, set to Yolongi, was sending the Amer signal directly to her CT rather than broadcasting it to the room. Blade and Dennier were likewise wearing personal translators linked to their CTs, while the Yolongi was wearing an earpiece connected to a translation device sitting on the table. The individual being interviewed, Broqupio by name, was the third Yolongi to be questioned of the selected eight. So far, the three *Justice* officers hadn't learned anything they didn't already know.

"Tell us again what happened in the cave after the first of my shuttles landed in the ravine."

"As I said before, Captain, a sensor near the entrance to the cave alerted us to the fact that someone was approaching, so the men with weapons took up defensive positions while the unarmed people moved as far back into the recesses of the cavern as possible. There are a lot of large boulders and outcroppings there that offer protection from weapons fire. We were expecting Cornwallis, so no one at the entrance would fire unless they were absolutely sure it wasn't him."

"Cornwallis? You're referring to the Terran to whom you were providing information?"

"Yes."

"Why have you been supplying information about your government? Was it just to get a seat on a ship headed into Galactic Alliance space?"

"No. We love this planet and would dearly love to stay if we could live a decent life here. Do you have any idea how difficult it is to leave your home and everyone you've known and loved all your life, knowing that you can never return? We despise the Triumvirate, and our tiny group from the capital was hoping that the information we could provide might result in the downfall of an evil and thoroughly repressive government. Originally, we held out hope that the Rebellion might be our savior, but lately we've learned that the Rebel leaders have revealed themselves to be just as vicious as the Triumvirate, and we certainly don't want to see one evil government replaced by another after all the heartache and suffering that's been endured during this civil war. We've actually been hoping they'd kill each other off because it's the only way we'll ever have an opportunity to replace them with a government that has the interests of its people— all its people— as its main priority. There's almost no chance of a civil uprising to replace the government because private ownership of guns was outlawed decades ago. The government at that time said they simply wanted to reduce crime and murder among the populace. The people, believing the military would protect them from any concerted threat, willingly surrendered their weapons. But we later learned, once the government had all the guns, that their control of the population was complete. The military leaders backed the politicians, who were then able to end all pretense that they cared about anything except enriching themselves and attaining more power."

"But the Rebels have managed to acquire weapons."

"In very limited quantities. We've heard rumors that their weapons were purchased through large, off-planet arms dealers and smuggled in through legitimate freight operations. And there aren't nearly enough Rebels and weapons on Yolongus to overthrow the Triumvirate and the fanatical militarized legions that support them. Besides, the weapons most of the rebels have acquired don't come close to the deadly arsenal the government controls. They have armored vehicles with cannons, automatic weapons, grenades and other explosives, and much, much more. There are only enough weapons in the hands of the Rebels to keep this civil war raging on the other planets until one side or the other surrenders. No matter which side wins, the people lose."

"But your people in the cave had weapons, and your group had weapons when you reached this ship."

"Small arms only. A few were stolen from police property rooms after being confiscated from local criminals, and some were actually purchased from the large criminal organizations that supply weapons to their own confederates. But they're certainly nothing like the advanced energy weapons the military has. It's rumored that the criminal organizations are actually far better armed than the local police, but they won't sell those weapons to us because they want to maintain their own power over the citizenry. That's why the local police rarely venture into some parts of the large cities. In any event, there're certainly not enough weapons available for the populace to stage an uprising and overthrow a thoroughly corrupt and despotic government. And if an ordinary citizen is actually caught carrying a weapon, that person is executed on the spot— unless the individual belongs to one of the criminal organizations who pay the police hierarchy to look the other way."

"So what happened after Cornwallis entered the cavern?"

"He announced that two shuttles were waiting to take us off-planet and bring us to a freighter ship that would take us to Galactic Alliance space. He said that only one shuttle at a time could land in the ravine because it was so narrow. Then he began separating us, with Yolongi in one group and Terrans in the other. He announced that only twenty-eight could go out on the first shuttle and everyone remaining would go on the second shuttle. He then told the twenty-eight to gather their things for the trip, including their bedding because we would be living in a shipping container until we reached the GA. Three young Terran slaves immediately picked up all their personal belongings and bolted from the cave. Rather than trying to catch them and force them to come back, Cornwallis trimmed the size of the planned group by three, but then an argument broke out because he was separating a husband and wife. After a lot of screaming and shouting, he pulled the wife out of the first group and told us, the remaining twenty-four, to gather our belongings and go. He then addressed the second group, telling them to remain calm because a second shuttle was already waiting to land and everyone not on the first shuttle would simply board the second ship. I was in the first group, so I don't know what happened once I left the cave. I'm afraid that's all I know."

"At least on the topic of what happened in the cave."

"I don't understand."

"It's simple. We need to find out what happened to Cornwallis. We know that between twenty and thirty armored personnel carriers were en route to the ravine. The two shuttles left the area less than a minute before they arrived in the vicinity. My people were under orders not to engage or even risk a confrontation with the military. We have to assume that Cornwallis was captured and taken *somewhere*. We need to ascertain where that somewhere is."

"He could be almost anywhere. There are military bases all over the planet. And it might not even have been the military who took him. The secret police also have APCs. It could have been the Metawasa, the Riwaxgo, or even the Qummuc."

"There are three *different* secret police agencies? And they're completely separate?"

"Completely. They even battle among themselves at times for jurisdiction. And if a prisoner is released by one agency, it's not unusual for another to pick him up and begin the torture all over again as they try to learn why the other agency was questioning him. They never share information with one another because they're all trying to make their organization the most powerful of the three. Each agency reports to a different member of the Triumvirate."

"So each of the three most powerful people in the Empire have their own private police agency?"

"Yes."

"And which of the three did you work for?"

"None of them. I was in the Capital Budget & Accounting department. But in my position as an auditor I got to see it all— the bribery, cronyism, incompetent misallocation of funds, and outright theft. The three members of the Triumvirate have more money than they could spend in a thousand lifetimes, and they always want more."

"It's like that on many planets. On some they've been able to enact strict term limits so politicians don't become too firmly entrenched in the theft and graft games."

"Perhaps that's possible where you have free elections, but certainly not in the Clidepp Empire. As long as the Triumvirate is generous towards the top military leaders and the citizens remain virtually unarmed, things can never change. The Triumvirate keeps the citizenry under control by immediately squashing any signs of discontent."

"Let's get back to the issue at hand. How can we find Cornwallis or at least learn what happened to him?"

"If you could find a witness who saw the markings on the APCs, you would have a starting point."

"The area is pretty remote, so I imagine it'll be difficult to find anyone who witnessed the arrival of the APCs."

"Yes, and anyone who happened to be in the area would most likely have been taken for questioning as well."

"How many of the second group in the cavern were Yolongi and how many were Terrans?"

"I believe there were only seven Yolongi. The rest of the group— about eighteen— were Terran slaves, all of whom were females. Male slaves are almost always sent to the mining colonies off-world as soon as they're purchased."

"Do you have any contacts that can help us?"

"As far as I know, all of the people providing information to Cornwallis were in the cave. I didn't have any trustworthy contacts outside of them."

"Do you have any idea how the military or secret police discovered your location?"

"None. We had been waiting there for weeks. Cornwallis had promised that someone from Galactic Alliance space was coming to pick us up."

"Is there anything else you can think of to help us in this effort?"

"Nothing."

"Very well. Please let me know immediately if you do think of something else."

"Certainly, Captain. Uh, might I ask when we'll be leaving this system?"

"Not until we've established that Cornwallis is definitely lost to us."

"I see."

"Thank you for your help, Mr. Broqupio. That will be all."

After Broqupio had left the mess hall and the door had closed, Sydnee said, "Well, we have a little more information. But it makes the task ahead of us seem even more impossible."

"There's no way we can identify the markings on those APCs," Dennier said. "The shuttle crews only knew the APCs were coming because they saw them as distant electronic blips on their scanning equipment."

"There's been something nagging at me in the back of my mind about all this, and I've finally realized what it is," Blade said. "Broqupio said that their entire group was in that one cavern and that they had a sensor system at the entrance to warn of anyone entering. When I ran up the ravine to the cave entrance area with my Alpha One team to see what was taking so long, we discovered there were five entrances leading into the mountains. There were three on one side of the ravine and two on the other side. I also saw infrared heat indications that all of the caves had seen visitors very recently. So if all the people we were there to rescue were in just one cave, who was going into or out of those other four caves?"

"Could it have been Cornwallis, or rather Winston?" Dennier speculated. "Perhaps he got confused as to which entrance was the correct one."

"I suppose that's possible," Blade said. "But what if he knew exactly where he was going and it was someone else making those tracks?"

"Then we might have that witness we need," Sydnee said.

"Assuming that whoever took Winston and the Terran slaves didn't also grab anyone else they might have found in those other caves. I'd like to return to that ravine and check it out. How soon can I leave, Captain?"

"I think we have to be concerned that the military, or the secret police, might have left someone behind in case anyone returns."

"What I want to know," Dennier said, "is why the military or police chose that exact time to raid the cavern."

"They might have intercepted and decrypted Winston's message that he was coming to pick up the people in the cave," Sydnee said.

"Or there might be a spy in the group who relayed a message to— whoever," Dennier said.

"Which means that the spy is possibly aboard the *Justice* now," Sydnee said, "because I doubt if the spy would have been one of the Terran slaves."

"We can't rule that out though," Blade said.

"No, not entirely," Sydnee said in agreement.

"If a spy has gotten aboard, he might try to activate some sort of tracking device, like the earpiece the Major gave to Winston," Dennier said. "I'm sure the Yolongi would love to identify the GA ship coming to free slaves."

"It won't work," Sydnee said. "The Dakinium shields all radio signals. Both in and out. All communications can only go through the com chief on the bridge. The same is true aboard the shuttles. CT signals are routed through the flight deck com system, but nothing else gets through. There's also the possibility that the spy was one of the four Yolongi who were taken out of the first shuttle group, in which case we'll probably never see him again."

"We need more information, and the only place we can reasonably expect to find it is on the planet," Blade said. "Do I have your permission to go back down?"

"I don't see any other alternative if we're to get those people back. You should probably get some rest and have a meal first."

"The meal part sounds great. We haven't done anything so exhausting that we require rest."

"Okay, let's interview the other five Yolongi before we move on your request. After that, I'll have the cooks come in and prepare some food."

◆

After each Yolongi was interviewed, he or she was temporarily taken to a separate area so no comparison of stories was possible with the people who hadn't been interviewed yet. The other people more or less verified Broqupio's account of what happened in the cave, as well as the political situation on the planet.

When the interviews were over, the mess cooks were allowed to return and begin preparing a meal. Sydnee left the mess hall so she could think about the situation and consider possible future actions in the peace and quiet of her office. Everything had gotten too complicated, too quickly. It reminded her of the last mission in that respect. While they had expected that mission to be dangerous, it had begun with very straightforward goals. But with each passing day, the current situation had grown progressively more complex, as well as more dangerous. Fortunately, no one had been killed this time. "At least, not yet," she murmured. "But we're far from done, and it's déjà vu all over again. I'm under orders not to engage the Clidepp military or civilian authorities, but how do I rescue our SCI agent, if that proves necessary and possible, without engaging whoever is holding him? What a mess."

After preparing a cup of coffee in her office's beverage synthesizer, she leaned back in her chair and focused on the problems at hand.

◆

Sydnee's concentration was interrupted by the computer advising her that Marine Captain Blade was outside her door.

"Open," she said.

"Not hungry, Captain?" Blade asked as he stepped into the small office.

"I can eat later, Major. I've been sitting here going over everything concerning Winston since he first came aboard. I suppose it's a little like what you said earlier about there being something in the back of your mind that was nagging at you."

"And have you had a revelation?"

"No, no epiphanies, but I can't shake the feeling that there's something I've missed."

"Any clue at all to what's troubling you?"

"No, just the thought that I've missed something."

Blade nodded thoughtfully before saying, "My people have eaten and are ready to deploy to the surface. With your permission, we'll search those caves for anyone who can give us a clue about the identities of the people who took Winston and the Terran slaves."

"I suppose that's the only hope we've got. We can't use the subterfuge of being the *Patoosch* again. Weems correctly released the metallic paint to hide your departure from the surface."

"They can't see us on radar, so the chances of being spotted are small."

"Yes, but it's currently daylight down at the part of the planet where the cave is located. We should wait until it's dark there to avoid being spotted visually. That'll be in nine hours. You can leave then."

"We'll be ready, Captain."

"Thank you, Major."

After Blade left, Sydnee resumed her rumination. The thought that she had missed something was so predominant in her mind that she couldn't shift away from it to consider other matters.

◆

Two and a half hours and six cups of coffee later, Sydnee suddenly sat bolt upright in her chair and addressed a question to the vocal computer interface in her office.

"Computer, read me a copy of the message sent to SHQ by the crewmember known as Winston."

"Unable to comply. That message was marked most secret. It can only be viewed visually on a monitor."

"Then display it on my monitor."

"That message was marked most secret. It can only be viewed by the captain of the ship."

"Computer, I *am* the ship's captain. Show me the message."

"A retinal scan is required."

Sydnee leaned in towards the computer monitor and said, "Then scan me."

"Scanning. Scan approved."

"Then display the message."

"The message is already displayed."

"All I see is a page heading."

"The full message is displayed."

Sydnee sat back in her chair as she tried to figure out why the message only contained a heading. Her first thought was that Winston had sent it that way just so he could say he sent a message. After a few seconds she sat back up again, having remembered an old trick used in her school days to hide messages from unwelcome eyes.

"Computer, display all background layer information in light blue and all text in black."

"The message is displayed with the new colors."

109

Sydnee could see a patchwork of black marks and globs on a field of light blue.

"Computer, is there a foreground overlay?"

"Affirmative."

"Move the foreground overlay to a separate screen area."

"The message is displayed."

Sydnee could see text, but it was just a jumble of strange symbols and characters.

"Computer, is the message encrypted?"

"Affirmative."

"Decrypt it."

"Enter the encryption algorithm."

"Did the individual named Winston enter any encryption algorithms into his account directory?"

"Affirmative."

"Computer, use the first algorithm."

"The message is displayed."

It was still just a jumble of strange symbols and characters.

"Computer, use the next algorithm."

"The message is displayed."

"Use the next algorithm."

"The message is displayed."

The message was still just a jumble of strange symbols and characters.

"Computer, use the next algorithm."

"There are no more algorithms in the Winston directory."

"Did Winston delete any encryptions?"

"Winston ordered all other personal encryptions deleted."

"Are they still in his recycle directory?"

"Negative, he deleted his recycle directory."

"Computer, is there a backup of the recycled files?"

"Recycled files are retained for thirty days unless other-wise ordered by the ship's captain."

"Examine the recycle directory and tell me if Winston's encryption algorithms are there."

"There are six encryption algorithms bearing Winston's file ID."

"Computer, copy the six algorithms into my personal directory area and label them WE1 through WE6. Then show me the message using the first."

"The message is displayed."

It was still just a jumble of strange symbols and characters.

"Computer, use the next algorithm."

"The message is displayed."

"Use the next algorithm."

Finally the message was partially readable as Sydnee scanned the document, but she could only read every third character in a text message without any breaks that indicated word parameters.

"Computer, apply the next algorithm only to the text you cannot equate to alphanumeric characters, or symbols, found in your Amer dictionary."

"The message is displayed."

Sydnee could now read most of the characters and guess where spaces should be to separate words. "Computer, apply the next algorithm only to the text you still cannot equate to alphabetic or numeric characters, or symbols found in your Amer dictionary."

"The message is displayed."

Sydnee's eyes grew wide as she looked at the message. It was now almost entirely readable, and from what she saw, she knew that Winston had been right to go to the extremes he had to conceal the message. She had only been able to decrypt most of it because Winston may not have been aware of the triple redundancy of computer files aboard a Space Command warship. There were always backups on top of backups on top of backups with properly designed government computer systems. Or perhaps he knew but also knew only the captain of the ship could authorize early deletions from the recycle level. He knew the message was ultra secure aboard the *Justice* and that all encryption codes in the recycle file would disappear after thirty days anyway, so he may not have requested that Sydnee delete his codes because he didn't want her trying to determine what he was hiding. Even so, he had added additional protections, such as an overlay and background layer matching the text color, to confuse anyone trying to read it. Anyone intercepting the message in space, even if they managed to remove the foreground and background layers, would never be able to decrypt enough of the message to read it. Only when it was passed on to the appropriate section at SHQ-SCI could it again be properly decrypted for reading.

Sydnee cleared her computer so no one else would be able to read the report sent to SCI, then went to stretch her legs. She believed the report provided a major clue to the identity of the forces responsible for the abduction of Winston and the Terran slaves. But knowing the probable perpetrators and actually recovering Winston and the slaves, if they were still alive, was another issue entirely.

Sydnee knew that the obvious one to talk to was Broqupio, so she headed towards the cargo container level where the Yolongi were being housed.

CHAPTER TEN
~ January 21st, 2287 ~

When Sydnee reached the corridor on the uppermost level of the habitat container previously used only for satellite storage, the two Marine guards on duty there braced to attention.

"As you were," Sydnee said. "Sergeant," she said to the higher ranking of the two Marines, "I'd like to talk to Mr. Broqupio. Would you ask him to please step out here?"

"Aye, Captain," the sergeant said before turning and entering the living quarters space previously used to hold spy satellites.

Once Broqupio had emerged from the housing area, Sydnee handed him a portable translator. "Walk with me, Mr. Broqupio," she said once he had inserted the tiny earpiece into his ear. Broqupio nodded and walked alongside as she headed towards the end of the corridor where the access tube rose towards the main ship. As they reached the tube, she stopped and faced the Yolongi.

"Mr. Broqupio, I have a few more questions I'd like to put to you. First, can you tell me which of the three secret police organizations reports to Gustallo Plelillo, the Premier of the Clidepp government? Is it the Metawasa, the Riwaxgo, or the Qummuc?"

"The head of the Qummuc reports directly to Plelillo, and takes orders only from him."

"I see. And do you know where the Qummuc headquarters are located in the capital?"

"Of course. I can show you on a map of the city."

"And do you know where the Qummuc normally house prisoners being held for interrogation?"

113

"There are several locations around the capital where they take prisoners initially, depending on the crime the prisoner is suspected of committing. Then there are the two long-term holding facilities."

"If the Qummuc took the slaves from the cavern, do you know where they would take them?"

"The slaves? Probably to the holding facility at Bewqussio Raxo."

"Is that another city or town?"

"No, it's a street name."

"How confident are you about that location?"

"It's where slaves have always been taken when first purchased from Raiders and traders because it maintains the central registry for the Empire. The Raiders and traders are never allowed to run their own auctions or sell slaves directly. If a slave owner is found to possess a slave who has not been properly registered, the government seizes all his or her assets and the owner may receive a jail sentence that includes a hard labor recommendation. The Raiders and traders could only sell their slaves directly to the government on Yolongus, but once registered, the slaves can be sent anywhere in the Empire and can be bought or sold by anyone at anytime. Since the government controls the initial sale, it always gets its cut immediately, but these days the number of slaves being brought into the Empire by Raiders is probably less than a thousand per annual. However, slave owners from all over the planet bring many slaves they wish to dispose of to Bewqussio Raxo because there's a big auction there each month."

"What about the newborn children of slaves?"

"All must be registered by their first annual, or the slave's owner must pay a steep fine and is at risk of being jailed."

"Would the Qummuc take Cornwallis to the same facility?"

"Only if they assumed him to be an escaped slave and didn't check his fingerprints immediately with the registry. Most likely they did check and knew he wasn't a slave. Non-slave Terrans are rare on Yolongus, but are tolerated because the government deals with the Raider organization and most representatives are Terran. If the police knew or suspected his true identity, they would probably take him to one of the intelligence sections of headquarters."

"Do you know of an accurate way to determine where Cornwallis has been taken?"

"No."

"You don't know anyone inside the intelligence section of the headquarters who can simply tell you whether he's there or not?"

"No. I'm sorry, Captain. I don't have a single contact inside any of the secret police organizations. Most of those people are fanatically dedicated to their superiors. Some say they've been brainwashed into believing in their 'cause.' Most are recruited just after birth, raised and trained in isolation, and taught never to doubt the word of a superior on any issue at any time. They live in virtual isolation, or with their fellow officers, and never associate with the normal population."

Sydnee sighed. "But you do know where all the various secret police headquarters and holding facilities are located?"

"Yes. I think a lot of people know where *most* of them are, but because of my job in the capital I had access to information that showed where *all* of them are out to a distance of perhaps a hundred kilometers from the capital. Every government facility naturally has to be maintained and supplied, so an auditor in the Capital Budget & Accounting department sees everything. He or she has access to much more information than certain departments would prefer to share, but we're considered the final eyes on everything. The people at the highest levels know that even the secret police have to be closely watched."

"Okay, that information will have to do. Please come with me so you can identify all locations on our maps."

◆　◆

"The Major has proposed that he and his team return to the cavern site and search for any clues to the whereabouts of our missing SCI agent and the Terran slaves," Sydnee said to the officers seated around the table in the otherwise empty mess hall. Everyone who would be involved in the ground operation or could possibly be called upon to assist had been invited to attend.

"I had approved the special ops mission for this evening, but there was something I felt had been overlooked in our efforts to find and recover Winston. I finally realized what was nagging at me. I had never reviewed the mission report he sent to SHQ-SCI. If he hadn't gone missing, the contents of his report would have remained sealed because it really wasn't any of my concern. However, his disappearance added new importance to learning what he had been involved in. Upon accessing the report, I was shocked to read a few highly interesting— facts and assumptions. I regret I can't share them with you. Suffice it to say that if the information in the report is accurate, and if it were made public on Yolongus, it would be most embarrassing for Gustallo Plelillo, who is the Prime Minister of the Clidepp government. Since the Qummuc special police organization allegedly works for and reports directly to Premier Plelillo, I'm working on the assumption that the Qummuc is responsible for the attack on the cavern. They may have learned of Winston's investigation and what he had learned, and were there to capture him."

"And how do you intend to proceed?" Colonel Dennier asked.

"One of the people we rescued has identified the locations of all detention and interrogation centers within a hundred kilometers of the capital. Here's the map. I'm open for suggestions on how we should proceed."

Sydnee pressed a spot on a small remote control and the large monitor on the bulkhead illuminated with an aerial image of the capital city and surrounding area.

"The white dots indicate where every military base is located, and the blue dots show where the detention facilities are located. As you can see, there are many."

"Many?" Blade said. "There must be a hundred."

"You're close," Sydnee said. "There're actually ninety-one." After she touched another spot on the remote, the image changed slightly. "The blue dots identifying Qummuc facilities have been changed to green in this image."

"Eight different facilities?"

"Yes. That's an accurate number according to Mr. Broqupio."

"So you believe that Winston *must* be at one of these facilities?" Dennier asked.

"I feel that these are the most likely locations. This is strictly guesswork on my part."

"And you can't tell us what you learned from the report so we can provide additional suggestions?" Blade asked.

"I'm sorry, but no. I understand the frustration you might be feeling, but I can't share that information with anyone who might be captured themselves during our recovery efforts."

"I don't expect that I'll be in any danger of being captured, Captain," Dennier said.

"I can't rule that out entirely. We might need the assistance of you and your Air Wing if things get out of control."

"Uh, are you saying you might attack the Clidepp fleet and planetary defenses?"

"I'm keeping all options open at this point because I have no idea if this operation will go smoothly or completely fall apart."

"Exactly what are you proposing, Captain?" Blade asked.

"We'll start with the operation you proposed and visit the cavern site to see if there's anyone there who can verify my hypothesis or perhaps point us in a different direction. Once that phase is over, we should have a better idea of which direction we must proceed in."

"Captain," Dennier said, "I agree that we should never leave our people behind, but a proposal that we take on an entire planetary police force and the planet's military fleet without having any intelligence information is foolhardy."

"I understand your position, Colonel, but we must at least make an initial attempt to perform a rescue and see where it leads us. If things begin to spiral out of control, we'll pull back and leave the system. Okay?"

"You're the captain. It's your call."

"Okay. Anything else?"

When no one spoke up, Sydnee said, "Shuttles One and Two will separate from the *Justice* and head for the caverns area on Yolongus at 1430 GST hours. That will be two hours after sundown in that part of the planet. Shuttle One will contain the Major and his Special Ops team. Shuttle Two will contain Lt. MacDonald and the two fire teams she selects from the *Denver* personnel. The bridge teams will be the same as on the last mission. Since we can no longer pretend to be a Yolongi shuttle, we'll go in fast until we reach atmo, using the natural coloration of the Dakinium and the darkness of the umbra to conceal our presence. Once we're between the fleet and the planet, we'll slow sufficiently to prevent a pressure wave building along the leading edges. We don't want the MATs to light up like a meteor while they descend through atmo. We'll operate under the assumption that we haven't been spotted as we near the planet surface unless we learn something to the contrary. The *Justice* will naturally be monitoring all military and police communications via the sensor buoy and communication buoys we've placed. That's all. Dismissed."

◆ ◆

At exactly 1430 GST both shuttles detached from the *Justice* as planned and headed for the shadowy umbra created when Yolongus blocked light from its sun. At maximum sublight speed, the shuttles should enter the planet's shadow just twenty-three minutes after departing from the *Justice*. The shuttles would still have a significant distance to travel, but

Sydnee wanted them in the planet's shadow long enough to guarantee that no one should be able to see their approach. Upon entering the umbra, the two small ships would have an additional six minutes of flight time before they reached the planet's exosphere.

◆

The pilots were confident that no one had seen their approach as they reached the ravine where Winston had last been seen. Shuttle One set down as before, while Shuttle Two established a stationary position overhead. Their sensors registered no warm bodies or movement in the area.

As the main hatch of Shuttle One opened, the Special Ops Marines leapt out and took defensive positions around the craft, then relaxed slightly when no fire came their way. Except for a few insects, nothing was stirring.

"Team Alpha, you're with me," Blade said as he began hurrying up the ravine in the direction of the cave entrances. Five of the Special Ops noncoms left their positions and hurried after him.

Arriving at a point where all five cave entrances were visible, Blade examined the ground using his helmet's infrared and thermal imaging capabilities. It was obvious that people had very recently entered or left four of the five caves.

"There are five cave entrances," Blade said on Com 1 so everyone, including the shuttle pilots, could hear. "Beginning with the first of three on the left, I'm numbering them one through five in a clockwise order. The ground in front of all but Cave 4 shows recent activity, so we'll begin there to eliminate it from further consideration.

"Symons," Blade said to a staff sergeant, "Remain out here and cover our six. The rest of Team Alpha will go with me. "Fannon, you take point. Let's move out."

With Fannon taking the lead, the five Marines entered the cave now designated as 4. There was absolute silence in the cave except for a few sounds of dripping water at various points. The darkness was complete once the Marines had walked a few meters from the entrance, but the electronics in their helmets allowed them to see well enough to keep moving. The Marines proceeded carefully, searching the ground and walls for signs of explosives or other traps.

About ten meters into the cave, Fannon stopped and said, "Concealed electronic device. Left wall. Investigating."

After several minutes Fannon said, "It's safe. Just a motion detector. But it's active, so if there's anyone in here, they now know they have company."

"Keep moving," Blade said.

No more devices of any type were found as the Marines continued to advance into the cave. After close to a hundred meters into the mountain, the tunnel suddenly turned left and then widened into an enormous cavern after a dozen meters.

"This might be the cavern we were told about," Blade said. "Spread out and look for any signs of recent activity. Check the walls to make sure there are no additional tunnels."

After a thorough search, Blade said, "If there were people living in here, someone did a good job of removing all evidence. They either moved somewhere else or they were moved." Switching to Com 2, the com channel reserved for special communications by noncoms and officers, Blade said, "Shuttle One, are you receiving this?"

"Five by Five," Weems said.

"So that means we should have been able to hear everything Winston said the night he disappeared, unless there was some kind of electronic dampening device in here which has now been removed. We're proceeding to Cave 5."

Cave 5 was located in the same mountain as Cave 4, but upon entering, the tunnel's direction quickly turned away from Cave 4 and headed downward with a roughly fifteen-degree slope. There were recent signs of foot traffic at the entrance to Cave 5, so the Marines moved even more slowly than they had in Cave 4 as they scanned the area for any signs of life. Their sensors could detect the heartbeat of a mouse from ten meters away, so if there was anyone in Cave 5, they would be found. But as they moved ever further from the entrance, they detected nothing ahead.

"Captain, I can't go any further," Fannon said.

"The way is blocked?"

"Uh, sort of. There's an underground lake here and no way to walk around it."

"I'm on my way."

When Blade arrived where Fannon was standing, he was amazed by the sight of a lake that seemed to stretch into the darkness for thirty meters at least.

"Anyone feel like a swim?" Blade asked.

"It's deep, Captain," Fannon said. "According to my helmet sensors, it's real deep. I wouldn't recommend that anyone get in there unless they have a safety line around them. And we don't have any idea what kind of marine life they might encounter. It might be the type that eats everything it can get its jaws or tentacles around."

"I don't see any indications of a boat having been here," Blade said, looking for scars on the floor of the cave where it disappeared into the water.

"No, sir." Pointing to a sack against the cave wall, Fannon added, "The only thing here is this backpack with some kind of grain in it."

While their backs were to the water, a noisy splash was heard. If it was marine life, it had to have been big.

"Did you see anything?" Blade asked Fannon.

"No, sir. I was looking down at the sack."

"Let me see it."

Fannon picked up the large backpack and held it out towards Blade.

While Fannon continued to hold the pack, Blade lifted the flap, peered in, then reached in and pulled out a handful of grain. "It looks and feels fresh. I wonder why someone would have left this here. I wonder if we surprised someone who was in here."

"If we did, there's no place for them to have gone except into the water, and I don't see anyone swimming."

Blade tossed the handful of grain into the water. Immediately the water began churning and a few large fish jumped clear before falling back.

"There's the answer," Blade said. "The grain is to feed the fish. Perhaps they farm them for food. It's doubtful there's anything larger or the fish wouldn't be hanging around here looking for a meal."

"But what happened to the farmer?"

"Maybe there's an underwater exit to another chamber. Or perhaps it wasn't feeding time when the sack was brought in here. It doesn't matter. We're done here. Let's head to Cave 3."

The tunnel in Cave 3 was similar to the others in construction. After carefully working their way close to sixty meters into the tunnel, Fannon said, "Dead end, Captain. I've reached a solid wall."

"Check the ground around you. Any signs of foot traffic?"

"None."

"Then we must have missed something because there were definite signs at the entrance. Everyone begin looking for a hidden opening in a side wall. Maybe someone blocked the entrance to avoid detection when we arrived."

After fifteen minutes of searching, one of team members said, "Captain, I've found something here. It looks like it might have been an entrance to another tunnel at one time, but it appears to have collapsed at some point. However, I'm able to move a large boulder at the base without bringing down the rest, so it might be a disguised entrance."

"Stop right there," Blade said. "I'm on my way."

After examining the wall, Blade said, "I think you're right. Let's try to push it back."

Prepared for a strenuous task, the Marines were surprised at how easily a number of piled rocks near the bottom moved back as one piece once they put their backs into it. But as soon as the pile was out of the way, someone opened up with small arms gunfire from inside the new tunnel. Their personal armor prevented any injury to the Marines who were struck by the bullets. Their Dakinium armor would hold up against anything short of a grenade in their lap or a direct strike by an RPG. Laser strikes only made the armor stronger and more impervious to damage.

"Lead projectile firearms," Blade said to himself. "Whoever's in this tunnel sure isn't part of the military or secret police."

"Hold your fire," Blade announced in Yolongi with the speaker on his chest plate set to maximum volume. "We're looking for someone, and we mean you no harm. You can't harm us, and we won't harm you— unless we're forced to return fire."

On Com 1, Blade said, "Fannon, crawl in there. So far all we've seen is gunfire from small arms. It appears they don't have anything that can penetrate our armor."

"Roger, Captain."

A few seconds later, Fannon was wriggling his way through the opening. Fire from the other side intensified briefly, then stopped. Perhaps whoever was firing finally realized they were simply wasting ammunition and inviting return fire.

As two more members of team Alpha crawled through the small opening, Fannon was heard to say, "You'd better come in here, Captain."

"On my way," Blade said as he got down on all fours, then got down on his belly and began slithering to get past the low overhang. As he reached the other side of the wall he stood back up, only then discovering he was in another, even larger, natural cavern than the first one. The roof wasn't quite as high as the one in Cave 4, but the area was significantly larger at ground level.

As Blade scanned the interior of the cavern, he muttered, "Holy Moly."

◆　◆　◆

"I can't stop thinking about the change to Sydnee's orders," Captain Lidden said to Commander Bryant during their daily briefing session.

"The first one where she was required to plant spy satellites throughout the Clidepp Empire, or the second change where she was ordered to pick up an SCI agent?"

"She accepted the first change before she even left the *Denver*, so I'm not as focused on that one, although it was sort of a dirty deal to change the mission orders after she had agreed to perform the voluntary task of dropping off the package. Once she had accepted the initial mission, a refusal would have looked bad when the orders changed. I had Burrows tell her it wouldn't be held against her if she refused, but by then SCI already knew she had accepted the initial mission and it had probably been recorded in several reports before Sydnee was even made aware of the expanded mission parameters. But it bothered me a lot more later when I had to order her to forget all previous orders for the moment and rush to rescue the SCI agent."

"It was just a simple pickup."

"When you're hiding in what I would define as enemy space and the planet is surrounded by practically every warship that belongs to the Empire, the planet's defenses are probably on high alert, and your new mission is to breach those formidable obstacles and make a surreptitious trip to the surface and return, there's no such thing as *simple*."

"Looking at it like that, you're right. But I think Sydnee is up to it."

"I hope so. But I won't stop worrying until I hear she's completed the mission at Yolongus and resumed the satellite seeding part of the operation. I've sent a message to Admiral Clereborg at SCI HQ outlining everything Sydnee's done in the past and is now doing for SCI. I requested he support her early promotion by the AB. She deserves that extra half bar more than anyone I could possibly name. I don't understand why the Admiralty Board hasn't given it to her."

"Well, if they don't promote her early, she'll be eligible for normal promotion long before she returns from this mission. She graduated in '84, so when the PRB convenes this fall, her name will undoubtedly be included for consideration."

"Yes, but that's not the point. Early promotion is something that stands out on your record for your entire time in the service. She's done enough to deserve it three times over, and I want her to have it."

"I understand— and agree. Since we're so shorthanded, at least we know there will be an open slot if she *is* approved for early promotion."

"Every ship in Space Command is shorthanded."

"Changed your mind about possibly losing her if she makes the promotion list?"

"I know of at least one other ship's captain who would grab her in a heartbeat if he could."

"Commander Galeway of the *Missouri*?"

"Yes. He's already said he'd love to have her on his ship if he had an open slot. And as you said, everyone has open positions these days."

"But the *Missouri* is just a Scout-Destroyer. Sydnee wouldn't leave a destroyer to transfer to a small ship like the *Missouri*. Would she?"

"Back when we were still aboard the *Perry*, I told her I'd approve her transfer to another ship if someone wanted her and she wanted to leave. I'm sure there are a number of captains these days who would take Sydnee if she wanted to transfer. Her name is becoming quite well known. When the SCI officer was here to brief me on the expanded mission, he didn't need reminding who Sydnee was when I mentioned that she had volunteered to take the new mission."

"But our situation has changed so much since we were aboard the *Perry*. You don't think she'd actually want to leave the *Denver*, do you?"

"I sure hope not. I wouldn't stand in her way, but I would hate to lose her. She's a fine officer and will go far in Space Command, unless something really catastrophic happens."

"Such as starting a war with the Clidepp Empire?"

"Don't even suggest that outside this office. But, yes, that would be such a catastrophic event."

"You're really worried that might happen this time though, aren't you?"

"It's a possibility. As you well know, Sydnee never does *anything* halfway. She's been ordered to retrieve an SCI agent from Yolongus, and she will do everything humanly possible to complete that mission. It's amazing she managed to avoid starting a war when she was sent to kidnap that minister and was left on her own to find a way to get back here."

"That risk was only because of the mechanical problems with the ship. It would have gone very smoothly but for that."

"Yes, but it so easily could have all fallen apart for a dozen different reasons at a dozen different times. I wish we were closer and that I hadn't had to place restrictions on communications. I'd sure love to know what's going on over there in Clidepp space."

CHAPTER ELEVEN
~ January 21St, 2287 ~

"Captain," CPO Lemela at the communications station said to Sydnee as she entered the bridge, "we've just received a message from Shuttle One. It's returning to the *Justice*."

"So soon? And Shuttle Two?"

"Shuttle Two is also returning."

"Did they give any more information than that?"

"No, ma'am. When I asked if that was all, they said they'd report when they got back."

"Thank you, Chief. Carry on."

Lt.(jg) Olivetti had been in command of the bridge while Sydnee was occupied with other duties, so she stood up and returned to the navigation console as Sydnee resumed command. As Sydnee took her seat, her mind began reviewing the mission objectives as she tried to develop possible reasons for the early return.

◆

Sydnee was waiting at the airlock hatch where Shuttle One had docked when the connection was certified and the hatch was opened. Major Blade was the first one out. The cheering noise behind him was almost too loud for Sydnee to hear when he said, "Captain, you're never going to believe this story."

Although she wanted to see what was going on in the shuttle, she needed to hear Blade's report first. "In my office."

◆

As the doors closed behind Blade just seconds later, Sydnee turned and said, "What was going on in that shuttle? Did you find Winston and the Terran slaves?"

127

"Uh, no. Not exactly. The cavern where Winston and the Terran slaves had been located was deserted. And it had been picked clean. There wasn't even any bodily waste left in there. It was as if no person had ever been in there before."

"The Qummuc cleaned up the latrines?"

"I thought that perhaps the inhabitants might have been re-cycling the bodily waste to use as fertilizer for growing food."

"I heard a lot of voices in the shuttle."

"Uh, yes. I'm getting to that. After the first cave had been checked, we moved to another. All we found was a subterra-nean lake. Or maybe it should be called a sub-yolongun lake."

"Subterranean communicates the idea. What else?"

"That was all we found, except for a large pouch contain-ing grain. We decided that someone had been feeding the fish in the lake to use them as food. Then we searched the first of the caves across the ravine. Initially we reached a dead end, but when we examined the walls, one of my people found what appeared to be a side tunnel that had collapsed. He dis-covered it might be a disguised entrance when he was able to move a large boulder at the base and nothing fell from above. My people pushed it out of the way and we entered what we thought was a tunnel. But there turned out to be an enormous natural cavern on the other side of the cave wall. We drew fire for a few minutes, but when we told the shooter, or shooters, that while we meant them no harm, we would begin returning fire if they didn't stop, the shooting ceased. When I crawled into the cavern, I was almost without words."

When Blade stopped momentarily, Sydnee said, "Why were you without words?"

"Uh, Captain, I tried to do what I thought you'd want me to do, so I brought back some people we found there."

"Out in the corridor it sounded like you brought more than a few. Are they all Yolongi?"

"Uh. No. Actually, all are Terrans. They're all former slaves."

"Then you took the correct action, Major. How many are there?"

"Well, I spoke to Lt. Weems and asked him how many each ship could handle. He said that with the current passenger count, meaning my people and Lt. MacDonald's people, we could take only twenty-eight more in each shuttle. I asked him what the maximum load could be if not everyone had a seat. He said that because the trip to the *Justice* was so brief, I could take everyone I could squeeze into the ship and seal the hatch."

"Why didn't you simply take your twenty-eight and then let Shuttle Two take the rest?"

"Uh, Shuttle two is packed from airlock to flight deck as well."

"Packed? How many did you bring up?"

"Uh, all told we brought back a hundred twenty-two Terran slaves."

"A hundred twenty-two? All Terran slaves? You managed to cram sixty-one Terrans into each shuttle, in addition to the Marines?"

"Well, there are also a lot of Terran children. If they had all been adults, we might not have gotten that many in."

"And Winston knew of these former slaves?"

"According to the woman who's their elected leader, Winston knew. He had told them that if he mentioned the full number to the captain of the Space Command warship, the captain might refuse to take any of them. That's apparently why he tried to make sure the second trip contained all of the Yolongis. He feared that the captain— you in this case— would refuse to take the Yolongi if they were not already aboard the ship when he told the captain how many Terran slaves were still on the ground. The first trip, the one with the children, seemed intended to tug at our heartstrings so we'd agree to pick up more. If all of the children had been at that first site, we wouldn't have found so many at the new cavern."

"He played us. So do we have everyone now?"

"We still don't know what happened to Winston. I didn't have time to interview the new Terran group we found. And, uh, there are still Terran slaves down there. I promised we'd be back as soon as possible."

"More? How many more?"

"Uh, as I understand it from what their leader said, they've been running a sort of Underground Railroad for some time."

"You're referring to the white population who helped runaway black slaves on Earth reach freedom in the Northern U.S. before slavery was finally abolished there by a law passed in 1865?"

"Exactly. The caverns were the final destination. They call the main cavern Sanctuary. The people have been growing their own food there and farming fish in the Cave 5 subterranean lake. That's why the first cavern was so pristine. They use all the bodily waste as fertilizer for growing mushrooms. You have to see that place to believe it, Captain. It's like a small city. They have a waterfall and pool that they use for bathing, and they built a waterwheel to generate electricity."

"You're stalling because I'm not going to like the answer, right? How many more are still down there?"

"Uh, well, as I understand it, there are four hundred eighty-three more."

"Four-hundred eighty-three!" Sydnee exclaimed. After taking a deep breath, she said, "I can understand why Winston didn't pre-announce *that* fact. Four-hundred eighty-three plus the hundred twenty-two you've just brought, plus the twenty-four Yolongi and three Terrans from the second trip and the original thirty-five makes six hundred sixty-seven. And we still don't have Winston or the original Terran slave group aboard. We definitely don't have enough food to feed all those additional mouths."

"Perhaps we can raid their food stores in the caverns."

"And put it where?"

"Uh, yeah. That could be a problem."

"This small ship just cannot support six-hundred sixty-seven passengers indefinitely."

"So what are we going to do? I didn't think you'd want to leave them."

"No, I don't *want* to leave them. How long do you think they can survive where they are?"

"Perhaps indefinitely. That's assuming that whoever grabbed Winston and the others doesn't get them to talk and reveal there are more than six-hundred slaves still hidden in the caverns."

"I'm beginning to believe that if it wasn't for bad news, we'd have no news at all."

"So what are we going to do— just leave the remaining four hundred eighty-three Terrans down there?"

"No, we can't do that. I don't know how we're going to survive with almost seven hundred additional people crammed into the habitat containers, but I couldn't live with myself if I didn't make the effort to save them from their Yolongi masters. Let's herd everyone down to the satellite habitat space we freed up and then prepare all four of the shuttles to make another trip. We have to act fast in case any-one noticed you on the way down or the way up."

"I'm on it, Captain."

As Blade left to help empty the shuttles, Sydnee contacted four additional crewmembers who were certified to fly the shuttles and had them report to her office. After briefing them, the four shuttle pilots headed for Shuttles Three and Four to begin their pre-flight check operations.

As the newest passengers were being escorted to the habi-tat container, Sydnee was briefing all available staff. The top level of the satellite container had been cleared, but there were still three more levels being used to store satellites. Sydnee ordered all of her conscripted workforce to begin moving the small satellites from the upper two levels to the lowest level. Fortunately, the satellites were stored in foam-padded protective cases— six to a case— so there was little chance of damaging them during the move if care was taken.

◆

Less than two hours after Shuttle One and Shuttle Two returned, the four shuttles separated from the *Justice* and departed for Yolongus. Two hours later they were back, packed from airlock to flight deck with former Terran slaves and their children. The shuttles were quickly emptied and prepared for another trip.

"Where's Major Blade and his people?" Sydnee asked when the shuttle was empty and Weems came out into the corridor.

"He stayed on the planet, as did Lt. MacDonald and all the Marines. Blade said it left more room for slaves. We were able to squeeze thirty-two more in on this trip than we would have if the Marines had come back."

"I hope nothing happens while you're gone. Get back down there as quickly as you can."

"Aye, Captain. I just have to make a quick trip to the head and then I'll be ready to leave again."

"What's wrong with the head aboard the shuttle?"

"Uh, two of the slaves were put in there because room was so limited. The Marines were packing people in like the conductors do on the Tokyo trains at rush hour. Anyway, one of the women got airsick, and then the other got sick when the first one couldn't hang onto the contents of her stomach. The automatic system cleaned up the mess after they left the ship, but the aroma is still lingering. I don't want to risk getting sick myself. The air filtration system should see that the smell is gone by the time we reach the planet again."

"Okay, Pete. Make it quick. We don't know how much longer our window will last."

"Aye, Captain."

Ten minutes later the four shuttles were detaching from the *Justice*.

◆

When the shuttles returned, they were again packed with Terran slaves. Sydnee watched as the slaves timidly entered the ship— at least as timidly as they could with the other shuttle passengers behind them pressing them to move.

As the last of the former slaves disappeared below, Blade approached Sydnee. "That's the lot of them, Captain. It was a tight squeeze, but we wanted to limit the number of trips we had to make."

"Any problems?"

"A few wanted to bring their possessions, but I told them they either left them behind or we couldn't take them because all available space had to be devoted to people. After the ships were loaded, I stockpiled the things people dropped as they entered the shuttle against the cliff wall. With your permission, I'd like to make one more run to get everything the people had to leave behind. They didn't have much to begin with, and now they have nothing. We also packed up as much of the food as we could. If we return, we can fill any remaining space with that. I think it will really come in handy."

"Where will we put it?"

"It's mostly fresh food, so a lot of it will disappear into stomachs in a very short time. I know it will go quickly with the number of mouths we have now. We can store the rest in the Marine areas that aren't already filled with equipment and satellite crates."

"I don't know if we should risk another trip."

"The extra food will really help, Captain. As you know, we really don't have enough food for all these additional mouths."

"Did you see any indication that you were being observed at any time?"

"None. And I had all of my people standing guard and watching for any sign of danger while your Marines assisted in the move."

"I hate to approve this additional trip, but you're right that we're going to need as much food as we can get. And it would be nice if these people could get their few possessions. All right, Major, I'll tell the pilots we're making one more trip. If there's anything else you need to do, do it on this trip because I expect this will be your last opportunity."

"Aye, Captain. We'll wrap it up with this trip."

Sydnee relayed new orders to the shuttle crews and everyone began preparing for a final trip to the ravine.

◆

The final trip was no more eventful than the earlier trips, but the shuttle crews never let down their guard. They knew they were pushing their luck with every additional trip, and they were anxious to get loaded and get out.

When the shuttles lifted off, the cargo areas beneath the ships and the rear passenger compartments were filled to capacity. All of the Marines on this final run were in one ship so the Special Ops Marines had used their rappeling ropes to rig a sort of spider web of rope to protect the forward area of the rear compartment from cargo at the rear in the event the ship stopped short. That wasn't likely, but better safe than sorry. The other three ships were so loaded that the two-man crews would have to wait until their shuttle was at least partly emptied before they could leave the flight deck.

Although each of the levels in the former satellite habitat were just under sixty meters long by nine meters wide— a meter of width on every level in every container being dedicated to a corridor that ran the full length of the container— there didn't seem to be a spare bit of space anywhere. Sydnee toured each of the three container levels once the new arrivals had settled in. As soon as word spread that she was the ship's captain and responsible for their salvation from the oppression on Yolongus and the Clidepp Empire, the adults all wanted to touch her and thank her for taking them home. Most of the older women cried as they told her of their capture and separation from parents and loved ones at the hands of the Raiders, and then of the indignity and humiliation they suffered during decades of slavery at the hands of their owners. Sydnee told them she was ecstatic they were now free and that she was delighted to be able to bring them home. She told them that in the following days, each would be interviewed so Space Command could locate and contact their relatives in the GA and tell them the good news. She told them that each person would be allowed to record a brief message that would be sent once the ship began the trip home. When asked when that would be, she would simply say, "Soon. Very soon."

After completing her tour and ensuring that the rescued Terrans and Yolongis were as comfortable as was possible on the crowded ship, Sydnee returned to her office to think. She had known when approving Blade's repeated trips to rescue the people in the caverns that the satellite-seeding mission was over. The food they had on board, even when supplemented with the food brought from the caverns, would not feed the number of people on board for more than six weeks at most. Since it would take almost thirty days to reach GA space, they could not remain where they were for long. They still had no idea where Winston or the slaves he'd intended to bring to the *Justice* had been taken. Sydnee had just begun recording a message to Captain Lidden informing him they would be returning to GA space without completing their mission when the door annunciator declared that Major Blade was at the door.

"Come," Sydnee said as she cancelled the message she had just begun.

Blade opened the door with a huge smile on his face. "I have a present for you, Captain," he said as he stepped aside to allow an older woman to enter before himself.

"Hello, Captain. I'm Anese. Once upon a time, on Earth, I was known as Sharon Gilbreth. We met a short time ago."

Sydnee smiled at her and said, "I remember, although you didn't tell me your name at the time."

"I'm sorry. I was too overcome with emotion. I've been praying for someone to rescue us for over forty years. I couldn't find my voice when you visited us in the habitat. My throat sort of constricted."

"I understand perfectly. You're safe now. I promise you we'll get you home."

"Home. It sounds so welcome, and yet— so foreign."

"I realize it will take time to adjust to your new situation. Why don't you go relax and try to remember all the good things about Earth and the GA?"

"I can't relax just yet. There are others on the planet who must be rescued."

"I'm afraid we're filled to capacity. Actually, we're well over our capacity, so we can't take anyone else on board. Once we get to GA space, you can tell the senior officers there and they will decide if additional ships should be sent to pick up slaves. I'm sorry because I'd love to take every single slave back home. But it's just not possible. Our food stores are finite."

"I'm not talking about rescuing a group our size— just the ones who were supposed to be in the first wave with Cornwallis."

"You know where they are?"

"As I was just telling Captain Blade, I have a lot of contacts in the Moonlight Brigade."

"Moonlight Brigade?"

"That's what I call it. In Yolongi, it's Aleoxlene Reqoppl. A more direct translation is Darkness Flows. But I like Moonlight Brigade."

"I see. And do you know where Cornwallis is now?"

"Not exactly. We only know that he and the others were taken by the Qummuc. We barely had time to get our people in and cover the tunnel entrance. The Qummuc are not as clever as your people, so once we had closed the entrance we were safe. It still might be possible to recover him if I can contact the Aleoxlene Reqoppl and request they try to learn where he's been taken."

"You're welcome to use our communications."

"No, I can't. The Aleoxlene Reqoppl can only be contacted in face-to-face meetings. I know a woman who can put us in touch, if she hasn't been arrested."

Sydnee looked at Blade for a second, then back to Anese. "So you're saying you need to go back to the planet?"

"Yes. We can hardly expect the Aleoxlene Reqoppl to come here."

"How soon do you want to go?"

"It's morning there right now, so we should wait until dark."

"My people and I will be ready, Captain," Blade said.

"No," Anese said, "I can't approach the Aleoxlene Reqoppl with armed people wearing those hideous black uniforms."

"We'll wear a standard Yolongi cloak over our uniforms and stay back a short distance."

"Well— okay."

"So we're on for departure nine hours from now," Sydnee said. "Good luck to both of you, and to all of us."

◆ ◆

Just after nightfall on the part of the planet they intended to visit, Shuttle One and Shuttle Two separated from the *Justice* and headed for Yolongus. Sydnee had decided to send Shuttle Two as backup. They would either hover nearby or land in a secluded area from which they could respond to a call for assistance. Sydnee knew that sending two shuttles into a populated area increased the chances of having one or both shuttles being spotted, but time was short, both for their ability to remain in Clidepp air space and to recover Winston before he died under torture or was killed for being a spy.

◆

After determining that the roof of a deserted factory building on the outskirts of a town named Porgwuq should be able to support its weight, Shuttle One, running dark, silently touched down. But Weems didn't allow the full weight of the shuttle to rest on the roof. The shuttle was actually floating in position. If the entire building beneath it suddenly collapsed, the shuttle would remain in exactly the same place.

Porgwuq was the town where Anese believed she could make contact with a woman known to her only as Merlooa. The Aleoxlene Reqoppl organization was a typical cell structure in which most members only knew the names of three other members, usually the escorts or either brought runaway slaves to a safe house or picked them to continue their journey to Sanctuary, and a district coordinator. If anyone was caught and tortured to reveal names, the maximum information they could surrender was limited. This gave the organization a little time to help the members most in danger escape the authorities, perform damage assessment, and patch the hole so they could resume operations. Only the district managers knew everyone in their district who worked for the organization.

The contact Anese believed could best help them was only one lowly individual in a large operation, and Anese only knew her because she had helped Anese reach the relative safety of the cavern. But the woman might provide a chance to locate the Terran Anese knew as Cornwallis.

Anese left the shuttle in the company of Blade and Team Alpha. All were dressed in the oversized grey cloaks worn by most of the population on the planet. The distance to the house was over a kilometer, and Blade had feared they might have to carry the woman most of the way. But Anese proved to be surprisingly resilient and had no difficulty keeping up with the Marines.

"That's the house there," Anese said as they approached a modest cottage that was in need of a bit of repair. "There's a secret stairway to a basement area where we waited until the time was right to move to another location closer to the cavern."

"There are lights on inside, so it's a good chance someone is there."

"I'll go to the door alone. Merlooa may be frightened if she sees someone she doesn't know."

"No. You haven't been here for a while. Merlooa may be long gone and the person inside might not be friendly towards an escaped slave. You can do the talking, but I'll accompany you."

"I'd prefer to go alone."

"You're the contact person, but I have to insist. The captain will have my hide if I lose another person."

"Lose another person?"

"Winston, or rather Cornwallis, insisted that he had to go to the cavern alone. I let him. And that's the last we ever saw of him. I'm not losing anybody else. If you don't want me to accompany you, we go back to the ship."

"Very well, but stand a meter behind me."

"Deal. Let's go."

As Blade and Anese walked towards the cottage, Team Alpha blended into the surrounding area and in seconds was invisible to anyone in the cottage.

Reaching the door, Anese pulled a rope lanyard lying flat against the doorframe. A bell sounded inside the house, then a woman of advanced years opened the door slightly and stared at the two cloaked figures. "What is it?" she asked.

"Hello, Merlooa."

"Who is that? I can't see with your hood pulled down so far."

Anese pulled the hood back to reveal her face.

"You're a Terran slave. What do you want here?"

"You helped me a long time ago. I need your help again."

"I don't recognize you. I never helped you with anything."

"It was a long time ago. You helped me reach Sanctuary."

The expression on Merlooa's face reflected her growing anxiety as she stared at the figure of Blade. "I don't know what you're talking about. I don't know about any place called Sanctuary. Who's that behind you?"

"A friend, as you were once. Are you alone?"

"Uh— no. I have company. Go away."

"I can't. We need you to help another who works for the movement."

"I don't know about any movement. Go away."

"The movement is the Aleoxlene Reqoppl."

"I don't know what that is. Now go away."

"Please Merlooa. We have nowhere else to turn."

CHAPTER TWELVE
~ January 22nd, 2287 ~

"I've told you I can't help you," Merlooa said. "Now go away."

"I once asked you why you'd risk your life to help escaping slaves. You said that no sentient life form should ever be enslaved, and that you had dedicated your life to freeing the slaves on Yolongus. Have you lost that zeal?"

Merlooa appeared to be weakening. If not, she probably would have already slammed the door closed. "Who's that behind you?"

"A friend, like you. He's working to free the slaves on Yolongus."

"I want to see his face. Hey you, pull back your hood."

As Blade reached for his hood, he used his eyes to select an animated image that would appear on his helmet's faceplate so the woman wouldn't be frightened by the blank appearance. It wasn't an image of his face, but it would appear that way, and no one could ever really identify him after seeing it.

"He's a Terran also," Merlooa said as she studied the image. "We can't stand out here. Someone might see us. Come in."

"What about your company?" Anese asked.

"There's no one else here. That was a lie to get rid of you."

As Blade closed the door behind him, he saw they were in a hallway with several doors, all of which were closed. Merlooa immediately reached out and pulled Anese towards her, embracing the Terran with genuine affection.

"I really thought you didn't recognize me," Anese said as she returned the embrace.

141

As they separated, Merlooa said, "I have to be careful in case someone is watching. But how could I ever forget you? You were here for almost a month because the Triumvirate managed to identify and arrest several escorts. That was a difficult period. The operation ground to a halt and you were stranded here with me. I expected to be arrested any day, but I guess the escorts died without revealing my name."

"I've never forgotten you or the kindness you showed me and the many others who have passed through this house."

"Where have you been all these years? Did you get recaptured?"

"No, I made it to Sanctuary. I've been there ever since. But now a ship has come from the GA to take us home."

"A ship from the GA? Really?"

"Yes. We were aboard until about an hour ago. Over six hundred former slaves and their children are now safely aboard the ship and Sanctuary is empty— at least until new escaping slaves arrive. We had to take a lot of the food stores to the ship because they weren't expecting such a large number of slaves, but there's enough left for new arrivals at Sanctuary to survive until the hydroponics gardens produce again. And the fish pool is well stocked."

"Then this Terran male isn't an escaped slave?"

"No. The Major is a Space Marine assigned to the Space Command ship."

"I'm so happy for you. For all of you. But why have you come back?"

"As the first group of slaves were preparing to leave for the ship, the Qummuc attacked."

"No!"

"Yes. Half the first group of slaves had made it aboard a shuttle, but the small ship had to leave quickly as the Qummuc armored ships approached. So the rest of the first group was unfortunately left stranded on the ground. The shuttles returned after the Qummuc was gone, but so were the slaves, and we don't know what happened to them. We were fortunate that the main group was still well concealed in a different cavern so the Qummuc never discovered us. I was hoping your contacts might be able to find out where the re-captured slaves were taken."

"You surely can't believe that an attack on a Qummuc compound would be successful."

"The people who have come for us can do amazing things. They might be able to work something out. In any event, they want to try."

"If they can raid a secret police compound and rescue the slaves there, it would be the most glorious day for us in the Aleoxlene Reqoppl since the ambassador's ship was boarded in GA space and a Space Command officer shot him and his security guards because they were abusing one of the ambassador's Terran slaves. With that, the GA finally had verifiable proof of Terran slavery in the Empire."

"I've heard about that from other slaves. How did you hear about it?"

"A freight-hauler told a shipper and the shipper told some-one in the movement. The story then spread through our net-work around the planet. I can't wait to pass along that a GA ship has finally come to take you away from the misery of Yolongus."

"Yes, but first we need to know where they took the slaves and the Terran male who arranged for our ride home."

"There's another member of the Aleoxlene Reqoppl in town. He coordinates the movement of slaves so he always has far more information than me. He may not know what you want, but he might be able to find out. I'll learn what I can."

"Should we wait here?"

"Yes. Remain in the hallway so you won't be spotted through a window. And don't open the door for anyone or even answer it. Let them think I'm not home." Taking her cloak from the rack in the hallway, Merlooa wrapped it around herself and pulled the hood portion over her head. "I'll be back as soon as possible." Pointing to a door on one side

143

of the hall, she said, "Stand in that closet while I leave so you're not seen when I open the front door. After I unlock the door on my return, I'll pretend the door is stuck to give you a chance to get into the closet again." With that, she waited until Blade and Anese were inside the roomy closet before opening the front door. Blade and Anese heard the sounds as she stepped outside and turned the key in the lock.

◆

As soon at the front door was closed and locked, Blade opened the closet door and moved out into the hallway. Shifting his gaze to the external speaker control in his helmet, he winked his right eye. The movement immediately deadened the speaker. With another wink at a different control, the com to Team Alpha was activated and he said, "Alpha-One this is Sierra-Leader. Have two of your people tail the woman who just left the house, but make sure she doesn't know she's being tailed. I want to ensure she's contacting a member of the Aleoxlene Reqoppl and not the military or the secret police."

"Roger, Sierra-Leader. Should we take out the female if her contacts are military or police?"

"Negative, Alpha-One, unless they present an immediate threat to you and you can perform the action without notice. Just report when contact is made."

"Roger, Sierra-Leader. Alpha-One out."

"Sierra-Leader, out."

Blade shifted his eyes to the external speaker control and it was re-activated.

"I sent two of my people to watch Merlooa."

"What?" Anese said. "Why?"

"I know she helped you once, but people have been known to turn. Sometimes the secret police have a loved one in custody to use as a lever, and other times it's simply a personal choice because some event altered their previous loyalties."

"But she saved my life."

"I understand, and my people will only observe from a distance to ensure she's not alerting the secret police."

"And if she is?"

"Then they'll notify me and we'll be gone from here before they can reach here and surround the house."

"And Merlooa won't be hurt?"

"Not by us. Not unless she physically tries to stop us from leaving."

"I'm sure you're wrong, Major."

"There's no wrong or right. My action was simply a preventative measure. Sort of like insurance. You buy insurance with the hope you'll never need it."

"What if we can't rescue Cornwallis and the others?"

"We're going to do our absolute best to get them back. I imagine you know most of the slaves that were taken away?"

"I— I know them all. I don't know the Yolongi very well— the ones who were waiting to board the second shuttle because they had only recently arrived and they remained in the one cavern— but I hope you can free them as well. Many Yolongi have risked their lives to help us and they shouldn't rot in one of the Qummuc prisons. Cornwallis assured us that we would *all* be rescued, but he insisted on not telling whoever was coming to get us that there were many more of us still in the main cavern. He said he had to wait until the first group had been transported to the ship. He said that once a large group was already aboard the Space Command ship, it would be easier to convince the captain to take everyone. We held a lottery to see who would go in the first group. I was the leader at Sanctuary, and most wanted me to be among the first group to leave, but like the old tradition of the captain always going down with his ship unless everyone aboard is first safe, I refused. However, I asked that one of the young slaves be allowed to go in my place. I expected to see her when we got to the ship, but she wasn't there. One of the Yolongi told me she had been among the slaves who were to board the second shuttle. She must have been recaptured and taken by the Qummuc. I was devastated when I learned."

"She's someone special to you?"

"They're all special, but she's— she's— she's my daughter."

"Your daughter?"

"I was among the first slaves to be bred on the planet. I was impregnated through artificial insemination. I never met the man who provided the sperm, but my daughter was allowed to remain with me until she was nine. She was then sold to another master. I never saw her again until she showed up at Sanctuary. We all change so much as we grow to adulthood that I suspected the only way I would ever be able to recognize her was by a distinctive birthmark like mine on the side of her neck." Anese pointed to a spot on her own neck before continuing. "But it was she who recognized me first. It was wonderful to be with her again, but we only had six months together before the rescue began."

"We'll do our best to save your daughter. We'll save all of the slaves *and* their daughters if we can. Captain Marcola never gives up without doing everything possible. I've seen her do things that I, with all of my experience, believed to be impossible. Unfortunately she's under strict orders not to let the Empire know of our presence here. That makes the quickest and most effective action— a direct frontal assault— impossible."

"So what else is there?"

"Some kind of surreptitious attack where the enemy doesn't know you're coming and isn't even sure who was responsible after you're gone. That sort of military planning is where the captain shines."

"It sounds like you've known her for a long time."

"This is only my second mission where she's been the ship's captain. And I admit to having been apprehensive at the start of my first mission with her when I learned someone of such a young age had been entrusted with such an important role, but she's proven herself to be not only a very capable Space Command officer, but to actually be superior to the best I've served under. By the end of that first mission under her command, I regretted ever having doubted her. Following that first mission, I had an opportunity to read the reports of her military missions before I became part of her crew. The outstanding success of every situation where she was in command, as well as the medals and commendations she's received, are proof of her abilities. Your friend Merlooa mentioned an incident aboard an ambassador's ship where a Space Command officer protected one of the ambassador's slaves by shooting him and his guards. Do you know the name of that Space Command officer?"

"No. I've heard the story repeated many times, but no one has ever known who the officer was."

"It was Lieutenant Sydnee Marcola, the present captain of the ship that will be taking us back to GA space."

"Really?"

"Really. She's an amazing officer. You can rest assured that if we can locate Cornwallis, the missing Yolongi, your daughter, and the two dozen missing Terran slaves, Captain Marcola will move heaven and Yolongus to rescue them. All of them."

"Sierra-Leader, this is Alpha-one," Blade heard in his com as he stood waiting in the hallway with Anese.

"Go ahead, Alpha-One, this is Sierra-Leader."

"The subject has arrived at a private home. A man answered the door and then stepped back to allow her to enter. He seemed nervous and stepped outside to see if anyone was watching."

"He didn't spot you, did he?"

"Negative, Sierra-Leader."

"How many bodies are you seeing in the house?"

"Thermal imaging only shows two people in the house."

"Roger. Maintain surveillance and report any changes."

"Roger, Sierra-Leader. Alpha-One out."

"Sierra-leader out."

◆

Some eleven minutes later, Alpha-One contacted Blade again.

"The subject is on the move. She appears to be returning to her house, accompanied by the Yolongi male from this house. That assessment is based solely on height and estimated body size since both are wearing cloaks with a hood. Thermographic scans indicate no weapons on their person."

"Is anyone tailing them?"

"Just us."

"Roger, Alpha-One. Maintain surveillance. Sierra-Leader out."

Turning towards Anese, Blade said, "It appears Merlooa is on her way back here. She's with a person who seems to be a Yolongi male. We should get into the closet again."

The two Terrans waited until they heard the key turning in the lock before closing the closet door. Less than a minute later, the closet door was opened by Merlooa. Blade and Anese stepped out as a Yolongi male pulled back the hood of his cloak.

"Major, Anese, this is Golwoggin. He's the coordinator in this district for the Aleoxlene Reqoppl organization. You can trust him. Golwoggin, this is Anese, one of the Terrans we've successfully helped escape from slavery in the past. And this is the Major. He's from the GA ship that's come to take them home."

"How do you do?" Golwoggin said. "Merlooa has told me of your mission. Major, I'd like to speak with you alone."

"Give me a moment to shutter the windows in the parlor and you can use that for your discussion. Anese and I have a lot of catching up to do while you talk."

Several minutes later Golwoggin led the way into the shuttered parlor. Turning to face Blade after the hallway door was closed, he said, "Please remove your helmet. I like to see who I'm talking to."

"Sorry. I can't do that. Space Marine regulations forbid me from removing any part of my armor while I'm in hostile territory or any potentially dangerous situation."

"I insist."

"And I refuse."

"I promise I'll never tell your superiors."

"You wouldn't have to. I would have to tell them myself. Following that I would be court-martialed and reduced in rank, or possibly even lose my commission."

"But if you don't speak of it, no one would even know."

"I'd know. And you would know. So it's not going to happen. If that's a requirement for speaking to us, you've wasted your time by coming here."

Golwoggin scowled before saying, "You're very stubborn, Major. Very well. Leave it on."

Blade merely nodded.

"Have a seat," Golwoggin said, gesturing towards a couple of chairs. "That is, if you're allowed to sit."

As Blade sat in one of the chairs, he said, "As long as I don't remove any part of my armor, I can do practically anything except eat."

"You must get awfully hot and thirsty inside that armored shell."

"No, not really. The armor is extremely lightweight and is designed to help protect the user from outside temperature extremes. Under most situations, it can actually maintain the wearer's body temperature within several degrees of optimal. It has its own air supply and recycling system, although the air is primarily intended for relatively short-duration situations. And there's a small water supply I can access from a tube in the helmet. It's refreshed from recycled sweat and urine."

"Sweat and urine. Sounds delicious."

"It's not malted liquor, but it sounds worse than it is. It actually doesn't taste bad at all. And once you get used to it, you don't even think about it. Now, let's get down to business. Do you know where Cornwallis has been taken?"

"Yes, I know where he was taken."

"And the others? The Yolongis and the Terran slaves that were taken at the same time. Do you know where they are?"

"Uh— yes."

"Why the hesitation when you answered."

"We do know where they were taken— but we can't confirm they're still there. We do our best to keep track, but we have no one on the inside, and prisoners are moved around all the time."

"What's the last date you *can* confirm their presence?"

"As I said, we know where they were *taken*. We *don't* know if they're still there, or how long after their capture they remained there. Except for Cornwallis, that is. There have been no transfers from that facility, so we know that this morning he was still at the same facility where he was taken for questioning. We don't know if he's still alive. We only know he hasn't been transferred from the facility."

Blade sighed. "Is there any way we can get more up-to-date information?"

"Not from our network. We know that the criminal organizations have people watching all of the secret police facilities, just as we do, but we don't have anyone inside the Qummuc, and we certainly don't have any contacts inside the criminal gangs. We've tried to get people in place with the secret police, but the Qummuc and the others are all fanatics of the highest order and our people haven't been able to pass the entrance tests."

"Why not? What does the entrance test consist of?"

"The only way you can become a full-fledged member of the Qummuc order, or the Metawasa and Riwaxgo orders, is to behead at least five people in licensed and televised state executions. The executioner must use a ceremonial sword and completely separate the head from the body on the first attempt. If you can do that, you're in."

"Good Lord. They televise that butchery?"

"Lord? Who's that? One of your gods?"

"Yes."

"I thought so. We use the expression Great Lullelian. Our religion teaches us that Lullelian created the universe and our people."

"I guess most cultures have their own Lullelian."

"Yes, the government televises all brutal punishment sentences because they believe it keeps the people cowed. And it is fairly effective. We have crime, but most of it's not violent crime in the streets. It's illegal drug distribution, gambling, black market trading, and the like. If a young person joins a group of thugs and they actually harm a taxpaying citizen, the secret police track down that gang and publicly execute every single member over the age of six, even if that person didn't participate in the violence. There isn't even a trial when the crime involves a gang. As a result, few adolescents are stupid enough to join gangs. And those who are so foolish— usually die quite young. It's brutal, but highly effective. There's no recidivism in gang violence. However, if the act happened in one of the few depressed areas where the regular police don't patrol, and citizens have been warned to avoid, all the government does is stop the press from even mentioning it. You take your life in your own hands when you go into those well defined areas because the police will never be there to help you out. So what will you do now?"

"Can you identify on a map exactly where each of the prisoners was taken?"

"Yes. They were all taken to one of three locations. And the facility where the Yolongi were taken is very close to the facility where the slaves were taken."

"The slaves aren't taken directly back to their owners?"

"The Triumvirate never misses an opportunity to collect a fat fee for services rendered. The return of a slave requires the owner to pay a thousand Yolcreds. Only the wealthiest owners will normally have that much on hand. It usually takes at least a few days for the owners to produce the fee. So the longer it takes to retrieve the slaves, the less likely you are to get them all."

"Great."

"Why?"

"Uh— just an expression. It means the situation is not great."

"I see— I think."

"You can't always take Terrans literally."

"We're the same, such as how we also invoke the name of our deity when feeling frustration."

"I've noticed that in many cultures, but Terrans are not so very different from Yolongi. Except we despise slavery."

"As do most Yolongi. Only a small part of the population supports it, but it's the wealthiest and most powerful segment made up of elitists and politicians. The rich want unpaid servants to cater to all their needs or to work on their farms and in their factories. The government gives them what they want because the Triumvirate skims money for themselves from every transaction involving slavery, and the rest is passed down to the upper political levels and the military leaders. I'm sure the Triumvirate would put the entire population in chains if they could."

"It sounds like your population is already in chains. You just can't see them or hear them when you move."

"Yes, that's true. And there doesn't seem to be any way out. Most of the population has been thoroughly brainwashed from the time they first enter school to accept things as they are, rely on the government for absolutely everything, and not direct resentment towards the government for anything. The central government makes sure that all children are taught from a common set of educational syllabi that establishes these core beliefs. The core beliefs keep people undereducated and unaware of the true problems facing our society, while the government actively works to keep people resentful, jealous, hateful, and mistrustful of their fellow citizens, basing that anger on income levels, birth history, age, gender, and even career choices. With so much resentment in people for most other people, it's impossible for anyone to organize a successful movement against the government. Those who try quickly become victims of the fanatics trying to earn an entry position with the Qummuc or one of the other secret police groups. It's not surprising that most of the Rebels in the civil war are off-worlders."

"Off-worlders?"

"There are three main sentient species under the thumb of the Clidepp Empire. The government hasn't been as success-ful with brainwashing the other species as they have with our species on Yolongus."

"I sympathize. I wish we could help."

"You can. The GA is a very powerful nation, much more powerful than the Triumvirate could ever hope to be because their power base is so intentionally disjointed. Only your na-tion can help set us free. The Rebels promise that, but we've learned recently they are as corrupt as the Triumvirate. If we support the Rebels, we'll only be exchanging one cruel master for another. And please don't suggest the people rise up and overthrow the authorities and ruling class. Aside from the problems of organizing in the face of widespread peer con-flicts, we have no weapons with which to rise up. They were taken from us decades ago under the guise of protecting us from one another. Many believe the fatal attacks of that time were all staged to convince the people that getting rid of all weapons was the only way to stop the random violence. So we turned over our weapons willingly and forever lost the ability to fight back and defend ourselves against a thorough-ly corrupt government. We know now that the political lead-ership had pressed for the weapons ban so that no one could ever contest their control of the population. Most attempted overthrows have been coup d'états within the government. After it happens, the state media releases stories that the pre-vious leaders have retired to a warm climate. We need the GA to set things right here."

"Retired to a warm climate? Hell is rarely described in such a pleasant way. Look, I certainly can't speak for my nation. I'm only a Marine officer."

"Yes, but you can tell your commanding officers that we need their help. And they can tell their commanding officers that we need their help. We'd love to become part of the GA, and we would welcome any assistance you can offer."

"I'll pass your request on to my superiors. That's all I can promise."

"I understand, and I'm most grateful. Tell them that if they fail to free us, they will also be failing to free hundreds of thousands of Terran slaves."

"Hundreds of thousands?"

"Perhaps millions. No one except the government really knows."

"Millions? You're saying there are millions of Terran slaves on this planet?"

"I'm saying there are millions of Terran slaves in the Clidepp Empire. Remember, Terran slavery exists throughout the entire Empire. I doubt if there's a single occupied planet that doesn't have Terran slaves. We do know that slave owners have been breeding slaves for many years now. The total population of the Yolongus citizenry is estimated to be about three billion, so the estimate of a million slaves may actually be very conservative. That would mean there was only one slave for every three thousand Yolongi, which seems quite low. The women are mainly used in factories and as household servants while the men are used in mining and other physically demanding jobs in space."

"Okay," Blade said as he removed a viewpad from the pack he was carrying, "I'll pass that along. Right now I need you to mark the location of the three facilities on this map."

Golwoggin took the viewpad as Blade held it out. After a cursory look, he said, "I don't know how to operate this technology."

"It's easy. Here, I'll show you."

CHAPTER THIRTEEN

~ January 22nd, 2287 ~

Alpha-One reported in after following Golwoggin back to his residence. The Yolongi had neither stopped anywhere else nor engaged anyone in conversation along the way.

"Merlooa," Blade said following a lull in the conversation between the two women as Anese and Blade were preparing to leave, "thank you for your hospitality and assistance. The information supplied by Golwoggin requires that we move quickly if we're to act on it. Anese, we must leave now."

"You're most welcome, Major. I hope the information enables you to save the people the Qummuc have taken. Will you be returning to Yolongus after taking your passengers to the GA?"

"That's up to our superiors."

"I understand. I only ask because now that Sanctuary is empty, we can begin escorting escaped slaves to that location again. We had slowed the process because they had almost reached the estimated maximum capacity of the caverns and food sources."

"You might want to delay or even avoid using that location again. We still don't know how the Qummuc learned of it. The location might be compromised."

"But you said they never found the hidden cavern."

"True, but they might have set up spotters watching for foot traffic to that location expecting the Aleoxlene Reqoppl to either set up operations there again in that cavern where they found Cornwallis, or even using other nearby hidden locations."

"I see. What about the numerous other Sanctuary locations around the planet? Can you help them?"

"Do you have their location information?"

"No. For security reasons, only the coordinators and a few escorts in each district have that information."

"Then there's nothing we can do. We can't search your planet for hidden locations that even the Yolongus secret police organizations don't know about."

"On the way back to my house, Golwoggin said he hoped the GA would step in and help restore a formal democracy on Yolongus. He said your technology is far superior to anything the Clidepp Empire possesses, and you could annex our space very easily."

"I can't speak for the GA Senate, but I know that the GA normally doesn't interfere in the internal affairs of member planets. The GA only serves to protect the nation from outside attack or protect the planets from criminal activity that occurs outside each planet's atmosphere. They would almost never send in troops to alter a planet's government because we don't believe we have a right to subvert the will of the people. The rights of the individuals to be free from government control and oversight are paramount, so the GA refuses to climb onto the slippery slope of interfering in internal planetary matters."

"Even if the people have no free will and are being subjugated by an oppressive government?"

"Even then. The only possibility is where the government is violating GA law. Slavery is outlawed in the GA, so the Senate would take action to free all slaves, but they would not replace the government unless the government first attacked GA forces or threatened planetary neighbors."

"So there's no hope?"

"Well, there is one bright spot."

"Which is?"

"The fact that Cornwallis, as you know him, was here undercover to investigate the slavery issue is a positive action. It hasn't been that many years since slavery in the Clidepp Empire was mere conjecture in diplomatic circles. Without proof positive, nothing could be done. Terrans and other GA citizens have never been welcome here. The government tolerated diplomatic members because they had to, but they always followed them when they left the embassy and prevented them from wandering too far from the embassy compound. When the Clidepp Ambassador's ship was attacked by your Rebel factions while in GA space, an opportunity arose for Space Command personnel to enter the ship. Space Command was restricted from involving ourselves in the slavery issue there because the interior of the ship was considered Clidepp territory, but it proved the slavery issue was more than just speculation. And when the slaves from that ship were later recovered following a space battle between the diplomatic ship and Rebel forces in GA space, their presence at a news conferences on Earth was broadcast to the entire GA. We learned of their ordeals and misery at the hands of their Clidepp owners, and that information could finally be adopted as fact by the GA governments."

"How does that help us?"

"It's a beginning. With proof that the enslavement of GA citizens is a reality, people have started addressing the issue. And when we return with hundreds of more slaves, it will be the main topic in the news for weeks, at the very least. That should ensure that the subject will finally become a major political issue in the GA Senate. If the GA decides to order an end to slavery in the Clidepp Empire, it would first have to order a takeover of this part of space."

"But you say that the GA won't replace the government. So how does that help us?"

"The end of slavery would no doubt send the Yolongus economy into free-fall because the rich would no longer have free labor for their companies, factories, and mining operations."

"But how does that help us here on Yolongus?"

"History shows us that when economies fail, the suffering imposed on the populations give them a rallying issue that unites them and spurs them to take action against a government who has ceased to be responsive to their needs. That would offer a prime opportunity here for the people to unite and rise up as one to overthrow the triumvirate. People will only accept being trod on for so long. I'm not saying it will happen soon, so all I can say is— be patient. Things are bound to heat up."

◆

As soon as Anese and the Marines were safely aboard Shuttle One, the small ship lifted off and rendezvoused with Shuttle Two at the remote location where the second ship had waited. Blade, Lt. MacDonald, and the four pilots held a conference in the rear cabin of Shuttle Two, while Anese remained in Shuttle One with the Special Ops team. Lt. MacDonald's fire teams were outside, watching for uninvited guests.

"Here're the three locations we're concerned with," Blade said, pointing to the image being projected on the large monitor mounted on the bulkhead between the rear cabin and the flight deck. "We want to perform a flyover and record as much detail as possible. It will allow us to properly plan the operation. If the first pass doesn't provide adequate image quality, we'll have to perform another, but I'm hoping that won't be necessary. We can tempt fate just so many times before it bites us on the ass. We have very detailed images of the entire planet back at the *Justice,* but they're several years old. We just have to know what changes have been made since then so we take them into account."

"Are you recommending a full assault on these prisons, Major?" Lt. MacDonald asked.

"No, Space Command has ruled that out by ordering the captain not to reveal our presence here, so I know she'll never approve such an attack. But I'm hoping she'll allow a stealth operation where we sneak into the three locations to free Winston and the others."

"How soon do we go in, sir?" Lt.(jg) Weems asked.

"That'll be up to the captain, and first we'll need to complete our surveillance so we're able to plan our operation. We have to move quickly. Every minute we delay means that some of the people taken from the cavern might be hurt, killed, or— in the case of slaves— returned to the owners who claim them. So let's get those images and hustle back to the ship. Anything else?"

When no one spoke or seemed to be considering a response, Blade said," Okay, let's get everyone aboard and get this first step done."

The two ships lifted off in complete silence within five minutes. There was no moonlight to speak of, and the black, Dakinium-sheathed ships would only use their oh-gee engines until leaving the planet's lower atmosphere. Invisible to Clidepp radar, the ships should be able complete their tasks without being noticed. The only time they might be seen was as a visual identification of a black shadow as they climbed through the upper atmosphere and passed through the fleet of ships circling the planet.

◆ ◆

As soon as the two shuttles were away from the planet, Blade transmitted an encrypted message to the *Justice*. It contained all of the imagery they had just shot and a brief outline of a plan for a rescue attempt. It was unlikely any other ship would intercept the narrow directed-beam laser transmission.

Sydnee was immediately notified of the message's arrival and began reviewing the data as soon as it was forwarded to her office computer.

◆ ◆

"I believe we have an opportunity to get Winston and most, if not all, of the people taken by the Qummuc," Blade said at the start of the conference in the mess hall, "but only if we act quickly. By quickly I mean tonight. There are still seven hours before dawn in the capital."

The mess hall actually seemed crowded for this conference. In addition to the senior ship's officers, which included the eight pilots who would fly the four shuttles, the Special Ops team, the *Denver's* Marines, and all flight officers from the Marine Wing were present.

Sydnee sighed before saying, "I hate the idea of going in without being sure the people are still there. We don't even know for sure if they ever were."

"Golwoggin seemed pretty confident about his information. And while I can't know if we should trust him implicitly, I think this is the best we'll get in the time required." Pointing to the image on the large monitor, which showed the basic attack plan, he added, "If we don't try something like this now— tonight, we might as well pack up and leave the area."

"The facility and the immediate surrounding areas are very brightly lit," Sydnee said. "It's going to be impossible to get inside without setting off every alarm there. The second you begin your operation, every military unit and police unit on the planet is going to know. Remember the situation at the minister's home when the alarms were activated? Within minutes there were police vehicles headed towards his house."

"Yes, I remember. And I remember you derailed all of them with a shuttle they never saw, giving us ample time to get away. We can do the same here."

"This is different. The three facilities are right in the heart of the capital. You'll have support vehicles flooding in from every direction."

"It appears the only solution to that is a major diversion," Dennier said. "A power blackout that knocks out every last bit of energy in the city might do the trick."

"I'm sure the prison facilities and major government buildings will have emergency generators," Sydnee said.

"Yes, but it will cause chaos elsewhere and slow down the arrival of reinforcements overall."

"For all we know," Sydnee said, "the entire Qummuc force lives at the three facilities. We just don't have enough intel."

"And we never will since we're on a world hostile to Terrans," Blade said.

"True," Sydnee said. "So it appears that a city-wide assault is the only possible solution. We must black out the city as Colonel Dennier recommends, then hit them with everything we've got."

"I wasn't actually suggesting we do it, just that it's the only way to accomplish the goal. Haven't you said that such action was contrary to your original orders, Captain?" Dennier asked.

"Yes, but I'm not simply going to sail away and surrender those people to the Qummuc. The order to get Winston arrived after I was given our original orders, so one might say it supersedes our previous orders. The new orders say nothing about not revealing our presence to the Yolongi. And— I believe this is the only way to quickly and safely accomplish that mission. My revised orders stated that I was to take whatever steps are necessary to recover that agent from Yolongus as soon as possible. I was still hoping to mask our presence here and satisfy the original orders while also getting Winston, but it appears that is no longer possible, so we'll do whatever is necessary to recover Winston."

"If the Clidepp Empire's Triumvirate learns it was us, they might declare a state of war exists between the Clidepp Empire and the GA."

"Yes, so we should try to make it seem like a Rebel attack," Sydnee said. "If they don't actually see us arriving and leaving the planet, they'll have to assume the attack was from forces already on the planet and possibly even in the city. They'll probably tear the place apart looking for clues after we're gone, so we must leave absolutely no trace of our involvement. Our original orders didn't place any limits on what we could do here. They only said we must not reveal our presence to the Yolongis. So let's make sure no one can prove it was us."

"That means we'll have to permanently dispatch all Qummuc guards."

"We're not dealing with innocents here. These are the nutcase fanatics who each earned their membership in the

Qummuc Secret Police by cutting off the heads of living people. Correct, Major?"

"Yes, that's what Golwoggin said."

"Admiral Carver once said that when you meet an enemy who is totally ruthless, you must be *just* as ruthless if you ever hope to defeat them. We may not like what they force us to do, but we cannot shirk from unpleasant actions when it's the only way. I have no problem with letting these Qummuc butchers meet their maker and explain to him or her why they did what they did."

"Aye, Captain. Neither do I."

"Colonel Dennier, are your people ready for a little action?"

"Aye, Captain. We're all tired of sitting around on our sixes with little to do. We'd love an opportunity to get some payback on behalf of the Terran slaves who have suffered in this nation for so many decades."

"Then your Wing will take the lead and knock out every power generation and distribution station in the city. Major, as soon as the air attack starts, your Special Ops team and the Marines from the *Denver* will simultaneously hit the three facilities. No pussyfooting around. Hit them and hit them hard. The Special Ops team should hit the facility where Winston is reputed to be a prisoner. Free everyone you find imprisoned there and give them whatever weapons you find so they can defend themselves. I'll leave the other details up to you. Lt. MacDonald will take one of the secondary targets and can name a senior noncom to lead the third attack."

"What if we find other Terrans besides Winston and the slaves?"

"Bring as many Terrans back as you can fit in the four shuttles— if they want to come."

"Wouldn't you want to come?"

"Yes, I would. But there may be extenuating circumstances, such as spouses and loved ones on the planet. Don't force them to come if they don't want to. That doesn't include Winston, naturally. I want him back here even if he doesn't want to come. Tie him up if necessary. He gets no voice in this."

"You think he may not want to come?"

"I'm still unsure why we lost contact with him so quickly that first night he went to retrieve the slaves. That earpiece you gave him couldn't have failed on its own so quickly. He has to be responsible. He seems to have his own agenda, and I don't know if it extends beyond the slaves we found in Sanctuary. But I want to know what it is."

"Aye, Captain."

"I suggest you rappel from the hovering shuttles onto either the roofs or into their prison yards, as was done at the minister's home. I'll leave that decision to you. The shuttles will then wait while you begin your assault of the facilities. I'm sure you won't waste time trying to bypass security systems rather than just blasting your way through. The shuttle pilots will use the ship's limited weapons to prevent any interference from outside forces and then pick up everyone when it's safe to do so. After destroying the power stations, the FA-SF4s will patrol around the city and *delay* any assistance that might be headed in your direction. Isn't that right, Colonel?"

"Aye, Captain," Dennier said. "It will be our pleasure."

"As has been our custom lately, we'll make a stealthy approach to the planet through its umbra. We don't want to alert the Clidepp forces before the fireworks start on the planet. The rest is your baby, Major. So take over."

Blade stood and began assigning tasks to Lt. MacDonald and the Marine noncoms. Like Sydnee, Blade would have liked to have much better intel, but that wasn't possible, so they were going to have to wing it. His Special Ops people were all well trained and experienced, but he was fearful that Lt. MacDonald's people were going to be in over their head. There was no choice though. They would have to go with what they had and hope their Marine training got them through. The near indestructibility of their personal armor gave them at least a ten-to-one edge over any Qummuc special police they would encounter. Blade decided that Lt.

MacDonald should lead the assault against the facility where the Yolongi prisoners were reported to be, and her senior noncom would lead the attack on the facility where the slaves were being held.

◆ ◆

Less than an hour after the conference ended, the four shuttles were detaching from the *Justice*. At the same time, the Marine SF4s were being deployed from their customized habitat containers. Since leaving the *Denver*, the Wing's mechanics had spent their workdays checking and rechecking every engine component and every electronic system on every ship.

Neither the shuttles nor the FA-SF4 fighters had FTL, but the proximity of the *Justice* to the planet made it unnecessary. The sub-light speed capability of the ships would allow each of them to be in attack position on Yolongus within the hour. The shuttles would approach the Yolongi capital first and take position near the targets. Once everyone was in place, the fighters would begin their attack runs.

The ships were slightly spread out and followed slightly different flight paths to the capital to minimize the chances of someone visually spotting a large attack force descending on the planet. But all ships were cloaked in the planet's umbra for their approach, and black ships flying in an almost moonless sky or against a planet wrapped in nighttime darkness always gave the crews confidence that their approach would be unobserved.

◆

Sydnee sat on the bridge looking at the chronometer. She sighed deeply, wishing she were with the forces currently approaching Yolongus. She always felt guilty sending others into harm's way when she wasn't there herself to support their efforts. As captain, her place was on the *Justice*, but that didn't lessen her guilt about being safe while others were in extreme danger as they carried out her directives. She wished she could at least receive regular reports and offer advice for unanticipated problems. There were *always* unanticipated problems, but she would just have to sit quietly until the teams returned. Since there was nothing she could do to help once the operation started, she turned her thoughts to what she was going to tell Captain Lidden when he learned she had seemingly ignored the original orders and possibly dragged the GA into a war with a neighboring nation. She also wondered about the lecture she would receive when she returned to GA space without planting a single spy satellite around any planet other than Yolongus. The number of civilians on board, and the limited food supplies, meant that they would have to return to GA space as soon as they recovered Winston and the other people taken from the cavern by the Qummuc. Needing to do something other than think about things over which she had no control, she got up to get a cup of coffee.

◆

When the MAT-14s were in position, Blade gave the order to commence the operation. Simultaneously, the four shuttles moved over their designated buildings. Two of the shuttles hovered over the facility where the slaves were reputed to be warehoused. As the Marines began rappelling down ropes to the roofs, the nighttime sky over the capital suddenly illuminated from a series of brilliant flashes. While the ground shook from the explosions, huge swaths of lights all over the city began to wink out and fires were burning at many power generation and distribution locations. The darkened city made the fires seem even larger and brighter.

Blade's team was the first to have boots on the roof of their target, and they immediately started taking fire from the lone guard tower on a perimeter wall. As the team secured the roof, they began to reciprocate and poured a torrent of deadly laser fire into the guard tower. Within seconds, the fire from the tower ceased. Infrared scanning showed the single occupant of the guard tower to be down and unmoving.

"One down, hundred to go," Blade said. "Let's get that roof door open."

One of the Special Ops team slapped explosives against the door and yelled, "Charges placed. Take cover."

As Blade yelled, "We're clear. Blow it," the door began to open. The noncom who had placed the charges flicked the detonation switch and the door closed again in the blink of an eye. The bent, broken, and twisted door and frame wreckage then continued inwards, crushing the two guards who had been about to exit onto the roof in response to the city-wide attack. When the first Marine poked his head into the large opening to assess the danger, he grimaced and said, "Two down, hundred to go. We're clear."

The 'hundred to go' slogan was an axiom of Blade's. It meant they had no idea of the force size they were facing but were prepared to take on any they encountered. Blade and the team members climbed over the door wreckage, including the bloody pulp that used to be two bodies, and disappeared down the stairs.

CHAPTER FOURTEEN
~ January 23rd, 2287 ~

A noncom on the roof of their assigned building with Lt. MacDonald's team tried the handle of the door, but discovered it was locked. As he waited for one of the Marines to attach explosives, the door suddenly opened outward. The guard might have been sneaking out for a smoke or perhaps hoping to see the situation in the city from a rooftop perch. Whatever his intent, he suddenly found himself staring into the barrels of a dozen laser rifles. He was immediately thrown to the ground and checked for weapons. After being relieved of a pistol and stun stick found on his body, he was stunned with his own weapon and left on the roof to sleep it off.

As MacDonald's team penetrated the building, they split into four pre-designated groups and began moving to their assigned floor in the stairwell. The plan was to begin the attack on the three floors simultaneously. Two fire-teams would clear the top floor and work downward in support of the others as the floors were cleared. The lights appeared to be on throughout the building.

On a signal from MacDonald, all teams opened the doors on their designated floors and rushed into the corridors. Guards on duty reacted quickly to the sudden appearance of the Marines and pulled their weapons, but most died before they could fire a shot.

The top floor of the building was dedicated to offices, and three of the Qummuc guards didn't even have a weapon on their person. They meekly threw up their hands in a gesture of surrender. MacDonald, coordinating the mission from the roof, had the three guards brought to her.

"I want to know where the Yolongi are that were captured at the cave a few days ago."

167

When none of them spoke, she checked to make sure her external speaker was on and the translator was set to Yolongus. They were.

"Last chance," she said pointing her laser pistol at the guard whose facial expression made him appear to be the one least likely to talk. "Where are the Yolongi who were captured at the cave a few days ago?"

Three seconds later she pulled the trigger, and as the Yolongi guard crumbled to the floor, she pointed her weapon at a different guard and asked the question again. This time there was no hesitation. He answered the question immediately. MacDonald then relayed the information to the team on the second floor before assigning two of her team to bring the remaining two Yolongi guards to the roof and stun them.

"We've got them, L.T.," the team on the second floor reported. "They've been tortured and badly beaten, but they're alive."

"Take them to the roof."

"We've found a couple of Terran males, L.T.," the first floor team reported. "It looks like they've been here for a while. They're on their last legs."

"Bring them to the roof. Carry them if you have to."

"What about the other Yolongis in the cells?" another team leader asked.

"Set all of them free and let them take the guard's weapons. But don't bring them to the roof. We can't take them with us. All teams return to the roof."

MacDonald was waiting on the roof when the team who found the Yolongis arrived. The report had been accurate. The Yolongis had been tortured so badly that they could barely walk.

"Wait a minute," MacDonald said as it became apparent that all of the Yolongis from the cave were not on the roof. "I was told there were seven in the cavern. Where's the other one?"

"He was an informant," a young Yolongi male who was limping on injured feet spit out. "It was he who alerted the Qummuc about the ship coming to pick us up. He was released almost immediately after he identified himself to the Qummuc."

"I see. Well that explains a lot." To the Yolongi male who had just spoken, she said, "We have to prepare to leave here and I need someone to guard these three Qummuc until we go. Do you think you could handle the job?"

"What do you intend to do with them?"

"We have to find a way to make sure they can never identify who attacked the building. I'm sure my captain can suggest a way to ensure that."

"Yes, I can guard them."

"Okay, here's a laser pistol."

MacDonald turned and had just started walking towards where the shuttle was setting down when she was called back by the Yolongi. When she returned, he said, "I'm sorry," with no regret or sadness. "I guess I'm not familiar enough with this weapon. It seems to have discharged several times as I held it. At least we don't have to convince them to keep silent now."

The three Qummuc prisoners who had been stunned now had a neat laser burn hole directly between their eyes. Since they had been sleeping, they never consciously felt a thing.

"I understand. No problem. I'd better take that back though."

As the Yolongi handed her the pistol, his smiling face reflected the satisfaction he felt. MacDonald was glad he had understood the situation and acted.

As MacDonald climbed into the shuttle, the pilot said, "Lieutenant, we're needed over at the third facility."

"Sitrep."

"They have too many slaves to transport."

"But they have two shuttles."

"Aye, Lieutenant. And each of them is already so full they had trouble closing the hatch. It's standing room only in the rear cabin. And the airlock and head are already occupied. The two ships have lifted off to keep people from getting hurt while trying to climb onto the exterior of the ship. And our Marines are still down on the roof with more slaves."

"How many more slaves?"

"They estimate about two hundred twenty more."

"Two hundred twenty? More?"

"The slave pens were filled to overflowing. I guess they were having a big auction in a few days."

"There's no way we can transport that many slaves to the *Justice* with four shuttles."

"We can't just leave them there, Lieutenant. And your people are still out on the roof as well."

"We may have to leave most of them there. We've got to be away from this city before the Yolongi get their forces organized. I'll contact the Major."

◆

"Sierra-Leader," Blade said in response to the call from Mike-Leader."

"We have a serious issue, sir. Facility Three was overflowing with Terran slaves. The shuttles are packed and about two hundred twenty still remain on the facility roof. My people are also on the roof and the shuttles have lifted off to stop slaves from trying to climb aboard the exterior of the ships any way they can."

"Good Lord. We can't transport that many, and we have to vacate this city— *now*."

"Yes, sir. My team is ready to leave this facility. Should I proceed to Three and pick up my Marines?"

MacDonald heard no response for several seconds, so she repeated her message.

"I heard you. I'm thinking. Mike-leader, pick up your people and as many slaves as you can squeeze into the shuttle.

My team is done here at One. We'll proceed to Three and fill up also."

"Wilco. Mike-Leader out."

"Sierra-Leader out."

◆

"Captain, we've just received a message from Sierra-Leader," Sydnee heard in her CT from the com chief. "The shuttles and fighters are returning."

Activating a carrier she asked, "Is everyone okay?"

"They report there were no fatalities. That's all they said."

"Okay, Chief. ETA?"

"About six minutes."

"Thanks, Chief. Marcola out."

Sydnee breathed a sigh of relief as she leaned back in her office chair. She had begun to worry because the force was over an hour late. Without the ability to contact them on the planet, all she had been able to do was worry.

◆

The fighters were instructed to complete their docking maneuvers first. Once all ships were back inside their container bays, the four shuttles were allowed to dock with the *Justice*. Sydnee was standing by when the hatchway to Shuttle-One was unlatched and opened. Blade was the first one out.

"I'm getting real tired of standing on shuttle flights," he said as saw Sydnee.

"You stood? Why?" she asked.

"We folded the seats to their cargo transport storage positions and made everyone stand so we could get as many people on board as possible."

"I'm not going to like this, am I?" she said. "First, I assume the mission was a success. Second, there were only supposed to be about twenty-five people to retrieve."

"The mission was half successful. And there were a lot more slaves than we had counted on."

171

"How many more?"

"A *lot* more."

"But you were able to bring them all back with you?"

"We brought as many as we could— but we had to leave a lot behind on the planet. We just didn't have the capability to bring more, or I would have. As it was, the air was getting really thin in Shuttle-One. There were too many people breathing the limited air in the rear compartment for the ship's systems to accommodate, even with supplemental oxygen pumped in from the reserve tanks."

"You're saying there are over sixty people in the shuttle?"

"About seventy-two when you count the pilots."

"Seventy people in a rear cabin intended to hold no more than forty?"

"Only sixty-six were in the cabin. We squeezed two people into the rear airlock, and two in the head."

"So how many did you bring in total?"

"Two hundred fifty former Terran slaves, two Terran male freighters who had been arrested on charges of entering Clidepp space without a visa, and six Yolongi. The freighters were hands aboard a Clidepp freighter who had hired on in GA space after a few Yolongi deserted while in port."

"And how many people did you leave behind?"

"About two hundred thirty-five slaves, all from facility Three. Apparently there was a big slave auction scheduled for this week. The slave pens were filled."

Sydnee sighed. "It's a shame you had to leave anyone behind, but you brought all you could. It doesn't sound like you could have fit even one more aboard."

"No, we couldn't— but…"

"Save it for the briefing. You and I, the Colonel, and MacDonald will meet in the mess hall as soon as we get our new passengers squared away."

"Aye, Captain."

◆

Once the new passengers had been subjected to a prelimi-
nary interview to record their names, they were taken to the
habitat container being used to house the people rescued from
Yolongus. The senior officers then convened a conference in
the mess hall.

"Colonel, your people did an excellent job," Sydnee said.
"I think the Yolongi capital city is going to be dark at night
for many months. The broadcasts from the planet are blaming
the attacks on the Rebels. We don't know yet if the Triumvirate honestly believes that, but I suppose we'll learn in time.
Based on the reports filed by our interviewers here aboard the
Justice, only six of the Terran slaves from the group recaptured by the Qummuc and six of the seven Yolongi taken at
that same time are now on board. And we still have not seen
Winston. Major, where's Winston?"

"He wasn't at facility One where he was reputed to be. We
were told by one of the dying guards that he escaped two days
ago. The facility was actually undermanned because they
have squads of Qummuc special forces out looking for him."

"So it was a wasted effort. And we might have dragged the
GA into a war for nothing."

"I wouldn't call it a wasted effort," Blade said. "We recovered six of the Yolongi taken from the cavern and identified
an informant inside the Aleoxlene Reqoppl organization. I'm
sure Golwoggin will take care of that little bugger when he
learns of it. How are the Yolongi who were tortured?"

"Our medic says all will heal physically, although there
will be scars. He's not trained in psychiatry. Were there any
Qummuc left who could identify our people?"

"None that we know of. Most showed a preference for
fighting to the death, so we accommodated them. Then, after
downloading everything we could get from their computers,
we destroyed all video equipment, recorded images, and blew
the computer centers in every facility into tiny little pieces
just for good measure before setting fire to the places."

"Good."

"What are we going to do about Winston, Captain?" Dennier asked.

"I don't know that there's anything we can do. If he did really escape, he could be anywhere on the planet. He's been undercover here for years so I'm sure he has numerous contacts. At this point, he's probably not willing to reveal himself to anyone other than the people he trusts most. I guess we'll have to accept that and take our cargo of people back to the GA."

"What about the other slaves?" Blade asked.

"The ones you had to leave on the planet?"

"Yes."

"By now the Qummuc have probably moved them to a different facility and we have no idea where that is. We can't perform another attack to rescue them, even if we knew where they were. I was only able to justify this raid because it was combined with a search and recovery effort for Winston."

"Uh, I guess I never finished giving you all the facts about the slaves we left behind," Blade said. "I couldn't leave them at the facility, only to be taken again, and we wanted to burn that place to the ground anyway."

"And?" Sydnee said.

"I decided that we could move them to the cavern that hadn't yet been discovered by the Qummuc. The flight was only twenty minutes each way, and we had four shuttles. We should have been able to move everyone in just two trips. The Colonel could have stayed near the facilities and provided protection in case the remaining people came under attack while we made the first run."

"So the slaves you left behind are at the cavern?"

"Uh, no. After a few minutes of reflection I decided that since the Qummuc knew about the one cavern, it might not be completely safe."

"So where are they?"

"I took them to our embassy compound in the Capital. It was only two air minutes away from the facility. Although our ambassadors have been recalled because of the civil war, the embassy is still technically GA territory, just as Clidepp ambassadorial ships are considered Clidepp territory when in GA space."

"Major, that points a finger directly at the GA as being responsible for the attack tonight."

"I realized that, Captain, so I put them all down in the underground bunker where no can see them."

"There's an underground bunker at the embassy compound?" Sydnee asked in surprise.

"As far as I know, all of our GA embassies have underground bunkers— even those built on planets in the GA. Where embassies are required to be located in major cities, they're normally built at the very outskirts where the excavation can be performed without damaging the foundations of other major buildings. The GA Senate prefers to build down into the ground rather than above ground where the building makes an easy target in air strikes or from space. That's why most embassies are only two stories high. On Yolongus, the embassy compound is enormous, covering almost three hectares, and the underground complex is about two-thirds as large. It's also five levels deep and nearly indestructible."

"Do the caretakers have access to that area?"

"No. The caretakers have their own quarters on the grounds and have done an excellent job of keeping vandals out of the embassy compound, but they don't have access to the below-ground levels. I learned there's a tremendous amount of emergency food rations stored in the underground bunker on Yolongus. My special access code allowed me to open the bunker and get the slaves settled in on level B2. There's a shuttle and vehicle bay on B1, so we were able to enter the underground with the shuttles. No one ever saw the slaves when they left the ships."

"How do you access the underground bay?"

"The tennis court in the yard behind the embassy rolls back to reveal part of the bay. Once below ground, almost the entire B1 level is available for shuttle parking. There's a diplomatic shuttle down there, but the flight deck is all pulled apart. It appeared it was being worked on when the embassy was closed and the ambassador was recalled. After the slaves were settled in, I took out enough of the food stores to last them for several weeks. I assumed that by then you'll have decided how to proceed."

"I left four of our fire teams to protect the embassy from intrusion by Yolongi or other forces," Lt. MacDonald said. "But they have orders to remain out of sight."

"I didn't know there were massive long-term food stores at the embassy," Sydnee said.

"I didn't either," Blade said. "One of the caretakers who has worked at the embassy for two decades told me about it. He doesn't have access to the bunker, but he'd been down there when the embassy was active and knew of the storage areas."

"We could really use some of that aboard the *Justice*. How much is left?"

"I'd estimate there's enough stored there to feed the embassy staff for at least ten years."

"How many would be fed?" Sydnee asked.

"I'd guess the full embassy staff for that location, including the Marine protection detail, would be at least fifty."

"Enough food to feed fifty people for just five years would get us back to the GA without cutting rations and worrying that anyone would have to go hungry. We need those supplies."

"There's another issue," Dennier said. "Do we take the slaves who are down in the bunker now or leave them there until someone else comes for them? There's plenty of food to support them."

"I'd prefer to take everyone on this one trip. But we need those food supplies even more."

"If we remove all of the support equipment normally contained in the underbelly cargo area of the shuttles," Dennier said, "we could fill it completely with food stores. Two trips with all four shuttles should be enough to bring all the slaves and the food here."

"The real problem now is that we've reached a point where our presence might be known to the Yolongi authorities. Despite their black coloration and the blackout of the city from our attacks on the power plants and distribution network, someone might have witnessed our shuttles operating in the area where the three Qummuc facilities are located."

"The distrust and contempt the people have for the government might make them hesitant to report anything," Blade said. "The real danger is that a government employee or informant saw us during the attack."

"Our embassy compound is on the outskirts of the city, not in a remote location, so it's also possible our ships have been spotted landing and taking off from the embassy grounds. Someone might put two and two together."

"I don't see where we have a choice if we're to recover the slaves and get the food we'll need for the voyage," Blade said.

"You might be right. I'm just trying to consider all relative issues. Okay, when do we do this?"

"We've still got three hours of darkness left now," Blade said. "I suggest we go right away while the capital is still without power and everything is in confusion."

"I suggest my Wing provide protective cover," Dennier said. "If the military or secret police show up, I'm sure we can dissuade them from getting carried away."

"Okay, Colonel, you're in. But let's not start shooting unless there's no alternative. In fact, have your Wing remain outside the atmosphere where you won't be spotted. You can be down at the capital in short order if you're needed."

"Aye, Captain."

"Time is short. Is there anything else?"

When no one responded, Sydnee said, "Okay, that's the plan. Everyone make your preparations. We have to be underway within sixty minutes or we won't be able to complete our task before dawn."

◆

Every able-bodied person not manning an important post was recruited to clear the cargo bays of the shuttles. Much could be removed through a hatch in the deck of the shuttle, but larger items had to wait until the shuttle had undocked so the equipment could be removed via exterior hatches. Marines in EVA suits clearing the holds would just pull or push the equipment out. It would be tethered to the *Justice* after the shuttles moved away from the ship. The Marine mechanics were a little grumpy because they didn't have a chance to complete a full check of the SF4 fighters before their second deployment of the day, but no problems had been reported with any of the spacecraft and there just wasn't time for the usual protocols.

The convoy left the *Justice* behind just sixty-three minutes after the conference ended. With luck, this would be the final trip to the planet for a while.

As Sydnee sat in the command chair on the bridge, she thought about the overall mission so far. Like the last mission in Clidepp space, everything had seemed to go wrong at some point. The surreptitious trips to the surface had been the one bright spot. She hoped their luck held for just one more round trip.

CHAPTER FIFTEEN
~ January 23rd, 2287 ~

"I want the heads of whoever was responsible for this attack!" Gustallo Plelillo, Premier of the Clidepp government, screamed. The only other people in the room were his two Triumvirate partners. "Was it the Rebels or that damned Aleoxlene Reqoppl group?"

"It's too early to know," Weislis Danttan, the Minister of Intelligence said. "They were ruthless, so that points to the Rebels. But they also freed all the slaves, and that points to the Aleoxlene Reqoppl. The Rebels wouldn't have bothered with the slaves, so that lets them out. And the Aleoxlene Reqoppl have never been ruthless in their efforts to end slavery, so that sort of excludes *them* as well."

"So you're saying you have no idea who is responsible. You're the Intelligence Minister. What's the use of having an Intelligence Minister if he can't even figure out who attacked my police compounds?"

"Perhaps the Rebels are running low on funding and took the slaves to sell them, or maybe the Aleoxlene Reqoppl have decided they'll never see the abolishment of slavery if they don't get ruthless," Kurrost Mewaffal, the Minister of Public Information, offered.

"No, the Aleoxlene Reqoppl would never go from a group of pacifists to a band of assassins overnight," Danttan said. "Perhaps…"

"Perhaps what?" Plelillo asked after waiting a reasonable time for Danttan to complete his thought.

"Well, I was just thinking— what if it's the Blenod?"

"Impossible," Plelillo said. "Impossible. They could never have gotten past our fleet. The entire planet is ringed by our warships. And if the Blenod were anywhere in this solar system, we would have been alerted by our distant defense warning system."

"Yes, unless they've found a way to cloak themselves from our detection radar. Perhaps they've developed a cloaking system that completely hides them."

"An invisibility cloak? Have you been drinking again during work hours? They may have powerful warships, but they're not *that* advanced."

"Then who is that advanced? No one spotted any ships over the capital, but we know the attack on the power systems came from the skies. Perhaps the Blenod were already here when we assembled the fleet around the planet and they've just been waiting for the right moment to attack."

"And what made this the right moment?"

"Our guard was down because the Blenod never arrived to attack the planet as we expected. That message we intercepted, and had begun to believe was a ruse, may have been instructions to Blenod already in place."

"How could they possibly have remained hidden this long?"

"Perhaps the Rebels are supporting them by hiding them and getting them food."

"The Rebels wouldn't do that. It would be like inviting someone to take over the role you want for yourself."

"Is it possible our own fleet attacked the city from space?" Mewaffal asked. "Perhaps one of our admirals has joined the Rebel movement."

"No," Plelillo said. "Someone would have gotten word to us if that was the case because we have numerous spies spread throughout the fleet. We also know the Rebels don't have many ships, and the ones they do have are mostly freighters or small luxury yachts they've stolen."

"Then who has the kind of ships necessary to pull off a raid such as this?" Mewaffal wondered aloud.

"No one— except..." Plelillo paused as he thought.

"Except who?" Mewaffal asked impatiently.

"During the attack, hundreds of slaves were taken from their pens, right? Who wants to see slavery end other than the Aleoxlene Reqoppl?"

"The Rebels have announced they will end slavery in the nation," Danttan said.

"That's just propaganda to win over the Aleoxlene Reqoppl and its supporters. The Rebels would never end slavery. It's too profitable."

"Then who?" Mewaffal asked again.

"I can think of only one. The Galactic Alliance."

"The GA!" Danttan exclaimed. "How could the GA pull off a raid like this? They pulled their ambassador and his staff out when the Rebels began making small attacks in cities around the planet."

"Yes, they *notified* us they were pulling their ambassador and the staff out— but what if the GA staff never really left? The embassy has Yolongi caretakers living on the grounds, ostensibly guarding the compound to protect it from looters, but what if the GA is simply putting a Yolongi face on the staff? Do either of you doubt that those Yolongi are probably more loyal to the Terrans than to us?"

"But GA ships would have been seen if they tried to reach the planet."

"Not if the attackers came from the embassy compound."

"There're no warships parked in the embassy compound. If there were, they'd show up on satellite reconnaissance imagery."

"Not if the ships are kept underground. We know that when the embassy was built, they created an underground bunker as a place to hide if there was ever an attack on the embassy. What if they made it large enough to hold fighter planes? They could roll back a part of their gardens and launch those fighters, then hide them again after the attack was over. And the reason I say the Terrans are not gone is because my Qummuc picked up a Terran this past week. He was found with a bunch of escaped slaves in the Ciprotiq mountain range. He was obviously aiding them in their escape."

"And you're just informing us of this now? We must interrogate this Terran prisoner immediately, force him to tell us where he was taking those slaves, and learn if the GA is behind this," Danttan said.

"We can't. He somehow managed to kill two guards and escape."

"Did he have help from outside?"

"We don't know for sure since we can't interrogate him, but the video records show him leaving the facility alone. If he did have help, it had to be the GA. During the attacks last night, every single guard at each of the three facilities was killed and the surveillance systems and computers were all destroyed before the facilities were burned. Whoever attacked knew what they were doing.

"So the Terran was helping slaves to escape?" Danttan said. "Escape to where? There's nowhere on the planet where escaped slaves would be safe from recapture."

"Exactly."

"What does that mean?"

"It means that there's no place on the *planet* where escaped slaves would be safe from recapture. According to the official reports, hundreds of slaves have mysteriously disappeared over the years. We require that every slave owner report when one of their slaves has gone missing. Where have they gone? They must be somewhere. But where?"

"If we knew where they were, we could recover them and earn a healthy fee for returning them to their owners," Mewaffal said.

"But we can't recover them if they're not on the planet."

"There's no way they could have gotten off-world," Danttan said. "No way at all."

"Not by themselves, no. But if they're being assisted by the GA, they could be long gone. And that's why so many have been able to avoid recapture. They're not hiding; they've managed to get off the planet. There's another indication of GA involvement as well."

"What is it?"

"I managed to get an informant deep into the Aleoxlene Reqoppl. Recently, he learned that a group of slaves and traitors were waiting to be picked up by a GA ship. My man was able to join that group on the evening the pickup was scheduled to happen. When he signaled my Qummuc that the pickup was imminent, my patrols moved in. They didn't arrive in time to prevent most of the traitors from being picked up, but I don't doubt that the GA was behind that effort. We did manage to recapture a couple of dozen slaves that night."

"Did you get positive identification of the ship picking up the slaves and traitors?"

"My forces said that as they approached the area, the ship was clearly visible on their radar. But as they got close, it simply disappeared."

"Disappeared? You mean it vanished?"

"Yes. Before they got close enough for visual identification."

For the first time since they had gathered for this meeting, the room was as quiet as a tomb while the three men considered the possibility that the GA was involved.

After a lengthy silence, Danttan said, "So if the GA was behind the slave escapes, then they must have been behind the attack on the power systems."

"Obviously," Plelillo said. "They used that to distract attention away from what they were doing and mask the escape."

"And they're then responsible for the deaths of all the Qummuc guards."

"Also correct."

"And it was, in effect, an act of war."

"Yes."

"But why now?" Mewaffal asked.

"Because they know we're somewhat distracted by the Rebels, and we've been expecting an attack on our home world by the Blenod. So the GA figured we'd never suspect them of the attack. It was the perfect time for them to hit us."

"But we haven't attacked the GA and they never attack anyone who hasn't attacked them first," Mewaffal said. "That's why we haven't been concerned about them. They always give their enemies enough warning that the enemy can be well prepared to strongly resist the assault."

"But they *were* attacked by Yolongi and even lost one of their destroyers."

"That Yolongi warship wasn't under orders to attack a GA ship. It wasn't even commanded by a Clidepp Empire crew. It had been stolen from the repair yard by Rebels, and they were responsible for all those attacks in GA space. The GA hasn't accused us of being involved."

"The GA may feel that we were ultimately responsible because we *allowed* the Rebels to steal two warships from right under our noses and failed to stop them from attacking ships in their space. And we refused to devote any resources to assist their investigation regarding that attack on their space station. By not accusing us, they might expect we'll not point a finger at them when we're attacked by unknown forces."

"But the only ship that was actually attacked in GA space was a Yolongi diplomatic ship, and we were refused permission to enter their space to provide an escort," Mewaffal said.

"Don't forget the stolen destroyer that was eventually commandeered by an elite Space Command commando group who then went on to attack the other stolen destroyer and the Yolongi freighter. We've always believed the attacks in GA space to be the act of an insane Rebel officer consumed by his own arrogance. But what if it was all part of a carefully orchestrated plot to involve the GA in our internal affairs?"

"It's brilliant," Danttan said. "The Rebels have never really had a hope of taking the Empire by force. They only chance was a win through attrition. So they might have hoped to get the GA and our other neighbors to fight their war for them, expecting that when the shooting ended they would be able to pick up the pieces. Brilliant."

"Stop calling those fools brilliant. They're mad. Right now I see our great empire crumbling from within and without. If the Aguspod and Kweedee follow the lead of the Blenod, they'll gobble up our empire between them. There won't be anything left for the Rebels to inherit. If I had this Citizen X here right now, I would strangle him with my bare hands. I gave my youngest son the use of my yacht and told him to find out who this Citizen X is and where he can be found. He can travel anywhere in the empire with that ship and yet he hasn't been able to learn a thing about the Rebel senior command and their leader."

"If we have to fight the Blenod, Aguspod, and Kweedee, we certainly can't simultaneously fight the GA," Danttan said.

"We can't begin to fight the GA even if we don't have to fight the others," Mewaffal said. "They are far too powerful. They would destroy us within months. If one of their ships could disappear before the very eyes of the Qummuc patrol, it means they have an invisibility cloak. So what do we do, Gustallo?"

"If I knew that, we'd already be doing it."

"We should contact the GA ambassador and register a formal complaint," Mewaffal said.

"Haven't you been listening?" Plelillo said with disgust. "There *is* no GA ambassador on the planet. At least not officially."

"Oh yeah. That's right."

"If we assume that the GA was responsible for the attack on the city to misdirect attention away from the slave auction pen," Danttan said, "then we should also assume they don't want to go to war with us."

"What's your point?" Plelillo asked.

"Just that we shouldn't look for an excuse to start a war with them if they're obviously trying to avoid one with us."

"You think they fear us?"

"Not for a second. I think they only want their people freed, and this might be the opening salvo of that effort. Perhaps they hope we'll run to them for help and promise to free all slaves if they help protect our nation from the others. Whatever we do, we must keep the attacks from escalating."

"If they don't want a war, that gives us diplomatic leverage. But first we need proof they were really responsible for the attack."

◆ ◆ ◆

As Sydnee ordered, the Marine Wing remained outside the planet's atmosphere. And by remaining a bit spread out, the small ships didn't block out a large cluster of stars from planetary view and shouldn't be noticed by anyone since the Dakinium sheathing didn't allow them to be seen on Yolongi radar.

As the four MAT-14s approached the planet, they also remained spread out to minimize possible sightings. The city was still in near-complete darkness, except for those buildings that had emergency generators. All streetlights were off, but they could see the headlights of oh-gee vehicle traffic moving in the traffic corridors. The GA embassy had emergency generators, but all exterior lighting in the compound was off. As the tennis court began the slow process of rolling back to allow the shuttles to enter the underground, the lights in the shuttle bay likewise shut down so no light would be seen from outside. Once all four shuttles were below ground, the tennis court rolled back and the lighting in the bay was restored.

Time was short, so the pilots and the Marines aboard the ship jumped into action. Elevator load after elevator load of food was brought to the bay level and loaded into the cargo holds beneath the ships until there was no more space available.

When Blade emerged from the elevator on B2, he received a standing ovation. The slaves had originally been a bit disoriented as they were herded aboard the shuttles, but as slaves they had been trained to do what they were told without argument. Since arriving at the embassy, they'd had time to think about things, talk among themselves, and evaluate their situation. The promise of soon-to-be-realized freedoms in the GA now appeared as a reality.

"Okay," Blade said, "thank you, but time is short and we have to get you aboard the shuttles. It will be very crowded, and you will all have to stand until we reach the ship that will be taking you all to the GA. But the trip isn't that long and you will all be fed and provided with a place to sleep once we get there. All of the other slaves from the facility are already up there. We didn't have to leave anyone behind. If any of you were in the Sanctuary caverns, you'll be pleased to know that everyone from the second cavern are also already aboard the ship. Before we leave…"

Blade paused to take a message from one of the Marines on duty in the security room. "Sierra-Leader."

"Major, about three dozen armored personnel carriers just took up positions around the embassy's outside walls. The gates into the compound are closed and locked, but that won't stop oh-gee vehicles. Should we activate the Automatic Perimeter Defense System?"

"What are the APCs doing?"

"Just sitting outside the wall, sir. I guess they're watching for any sign of activity inside the compound."

"Did it appear like they were passing by and merely paused for some reason?"

"No, sir. It seemed like the embassy was their destination. They might be waiting for orders before attacking."

"Okay, activate the APDS. And let me know immediately of any changes. Sierra-Leader out."

"A number of Yolongi military vehicles have arrived outside the walls of the compound," Blade announced to the former slaves. A number of women grew fearful and began crying because they saw their new freedom slipping away.

"There's nothing to worry about," Blade said. "This embassy is considered GA space, and if they enter the grounds, it'll be recognized as a formal act of war against the GA. So I want everyone to relax. We won't be leaving as quickly as I thought, but there's absolutely no danger. Even if they were able to breach the perimeter walls, there's no way they can reach us down here. We have plenty of food and water, and this bunker is as secure as the GA could make it. We could remain here for many years if necessary, but I assure you that won't be necessary. Your days as a slave in the Clidepp Empire are over. You're free."

The former slaves immediately began talking among themselves as Blade walked to the elevator. He wanted to get eyes on the situation so he went to the second floor. From there he could walk up to an observation post on the roof.

The observation post allowed Blade a view of the entire compound and surrounding wall. He could have simply looked at the monitors in the bunker's security room, but he wanted to see the situation with his own eyes. There were armored personnel carriers just outside the wall on all sides of the compound. Each APC had what appeared to be a 40mm chain cannon mounted in a turret.

After watching the APC's for a while, Blade sighed and returned to the bunker. The DS shuttles were completely impervious to laser fire, and Blade doubted that a 40mm round from an APC would even mar the surface. So the problem wasn't one of fearing the Yolongi weapons. The problem was that if four shuttles left the embassy while someone was watching, it could confirm that the embassy wasn't as empty as the Clidepp Triumvirate had previously believed, which in turn could support the idea that the GA was behind the attack on the city. Blade knew it was far better that the government on Yolongus not have any proof of recent embassy activity. That meant the shuttles couldn't leave while the APCs surrounded the compound.

As Blade exited the special elevator on B3, he headed for the security room. Once there, he composed a message for Colonel Dennier and another for Sydnee. The burst-mode encrypted messages would be directed at one of the spy satellites that had been placed in orbit around the planet and then retransmitted to the appropriate parties. The laser transmission beam would necessarily be a little wider than the narrow laser messages sent previously when communicating with the *Justice* because they didn't have an exact location for the Marine Fighter Wing, and the *Justice* wasn't currently in line of sight, so the satellite would relay that message from satellite to satellite until one had a direct line of sight to the *Justice* and identification had been confirmed.

◆　◆　◆

Sydnee was working in her office when she received a call from the Com Chief.

"Message from Sierra-Leader, Captain. It's coming through satellite network retransmission."

"Send it to my queue, Chief."

"Aye, Captain, you have it."

Sydnee called up the text message, decrypted it, and then sighed when she had read it. She knew things had been too good to last and that they were pressing their luck with the most recent trip to the surface. But it had been a necessity. Though she had wanted to get all the slaves on board, the food was even more important.

"Well, at least we'll have two hundred thirty-five fewer mouths to feed, plus the Special Ops team and half our Marines from the *Denver*."

She had been procrastinating sending a status report to the *Denver* because so much had been happening, and she had wanted to wait until she could report matters with some certainty, but it was time now to compose a long report for Captain Lidden. It would be a vid message, but first she needed to organize her thoughts. Using her official ship's log for reference, she began preparing notes on everything that had happened since her last report. She hadn't realized just how much she hadn't reported until she finally finished and organized her list an hour later.

Since Yolongus was roughly eight hundred four light-years from the border with GA space, the message to the *Denver* would take just under eleven days to reach the ship *if*

189

the *Denver* was near the border. And a reply couldn't be expected for perhaps as long as twenty-four days. It could be days longer if Captain Lidden had to send a message to SHQ/SCI and wait for a reply.

Sydnee rose from her chair and checked her appearance in a mirror before sitting back down to record the message. She dreaded reporting the events of the past weeks and could only imagine what Captain Lidden was going to think when he viewed it.

Sitting up straight and holding a viewpad with all her organized notes, she began. "Priority One message to Captain Anthony Frederick Lidden, commanding officer of the *Denver,* GSC-DS2026, in Region One, from Lieutenant(jg) Sydnee Marie Marcola, commanding officer aboard the GSC-CPS14 *Justice.*

"Sir, I apologize for the tardiness of this report but a great deal has happened, and the outcome has been very uncertain..."

◆　◆　◆

"The commander of the APC unit sent to watch the GA Embassy compound reports that everything there is quiet," Danttan said in the Triumvirate's first meeting of the day. "They arrived an hour before dawn and surrounded the compound. They saw a couple of bodies moving around inside the walls, but that's all."

"What kind of bodies?" Plelillo asked. "What race?"

"It's impossible to know from simply seeing an infrared image and thermal imagery. All you see is a large yellow blob from the body heat. You can't identify the race. Since the sun came up, all they've seen is the embassy's Yolongi caretakers tending the grounds."

"Damn. I know the attacks were made by the GA. I feel as sure about that as I am sure that the sun will rise again tomorrow."

"Should we enter the embassy compound?"

"Of course not. That's GA territory. We can't enter unless invited. To do so would be an overt declaration of war. But if we can get proof that they were behind last night's attacks, we'll make that declaration without hesitation."

"You would *really* declare war on the GA?" Mewaffal said. "I thought you were only posturing."

"We can't allow an enemy to attack us and not retaliate with all the force at our disposal. If we let anyone get away with something like that, we're finished. No one will fear or respect us. And when it comes to nations, you may want other nations to like your nation, but they never really do and never will. People can like other people, but nations never like other nations. Only sophomoric idiots believe that's even possible. Their diplomats and politicians may pretend to like your nation, but that only lasts as long as they are getting what *they* want for *their* nation. If that ends, the so-called friendship vanishes faster than a free lunch at a public gathering. The only guaranteed way to have other nations *like* your nation is to let them tread on you. They still won't really like you, but they'll like being able to use you as their doormat.

"Fear is different. Fear is honest. Fear is intrinsic. Fear is— intestinal. It's far more important that other nations fear your military might. When nations fear one another they show proper respect for each other and actually get along *much* better because no nation needs to constantly prostrate itself in a ridiculous effort to have the other nations *like* it. Respect is what all nations should seek from other nations."

"But if we attack the GA," Danttan said, "*they'll* retaliate against *us*. And nations that attack the GA quickly get destroyed and absorbed by them. Remember the massive empires controlled by the Milori, the Tsgardi, and the Uthlaro? They're all gone now. Well, not gone exactly. The star systems and people are still there. But the territories have been completely absorbed by the GA. And all because they foolishly attacked the Galactic Alliance. The Milori actually attacked them twice. After being defeated and sent packing the first time, the Milori stupidly attacked them a second time. That left the GA with no choice but to decimate the Milori forces and take over their former empire. I understand Carver just about destroyed the Milori home world in the second war. The lesson here is that you don't attack the GA unless you want Admiral Carver to come here and do the same to us."

"I don't care how big or how powerful they are. We cannot afford to appear weak in their eyes. They must respect our military might, even if they don't like us, and even if they are more powerful."

"I usually agree with you, Gustello," Danttan said, "but in this matter I have to go along with Kurrost. While I will order our people to attack GA ships if you tell me to, I believe such an attack would be a serious error. I doubt that they would ever fear our military might."

"So you recommend that we merely allow them to come here and destroy our cities whenever they feel like it?"

"We could always abolish slavery and establish friendly relations with the GA," Mewaffal said. "They wouldn't attack us if they didn't have the major grievance of our Terran slaves. It would also rid us of the Aleoxlene Reqoppl. With no slaves to free, they would disband."

"Are you insane? Where do you think most of our personal wealth has come from? Slavery is the most profitable cash crop in the universe."

"Gustallo," Danttan said, "we all have more money than we can spend in our lifetimes. Perhaps it's time to step back a little and enjoy life."

"You can resign your position if you want and go retire to a warm, comfortable villa somewhere on the planet, but I'm not resigning. It took us a long time to reach this level in the government, and I like my life as it is. And don't tell me you don't enjoy your position. When was the last time you missed watching a beheading at your police-training academy? I've seen the expression on your face and the glint in your eyes when you cleave the air with your hand to signal the executioner to proceed."

"I have my weaknesses. Yes, I enjoy the power. Perhaps I've enjoyed the power even more than the wealth we've accumulated. Which is why I don't want the GA to come here and destroy everything."

"They can't control the massive empire they have now, so they're certainly not going to annex us simply because we fought back following their attack on our capital."

"It's not certain they *did* attack us," Mewaffal said. "Our forces haven't found any sign of attack aircraft at their embassy compound, nor have they seen any sign of the missing slaves at the embassy. And the statement from your informant that the GA was taking slaves off the planet is not proof the GA was involved. Perhaps it was some rogue Terran organization that works like the Aleoxlene Reqoppl but one with some limited ability to take slaves to freighters heading towards the GA. And perhaps they're not even freeing slaves. They might be stealing slaves here to sell them somewhere else in the Empire. Or perhaps it's the Raiders. They, easier than anyone else, could get away with pretending to be Space Command. Their organization was founded by Terrans and seems to still be managed by Terrans. And they certainly have the resources to build enormous, powerful ships that are far faster and more militarily sophisticated than our own."

"You can suggest alternative identities of the attackers all day long and I will still know the GA is responsible. But the GA isn't stupid. They'll not place incontrovertible proof at our feet. But they were responsible for the attacks. I *know* they did it. And when we destroy their embassy the way they destroyed our power grid, we'll get our proof."

CHAPTER SIXTEEN

~ February 4th, 2287 ~

When Commander Bryant entered the captain's bridge office for the daily briefing, he found Lidden sitting with his chair in a reclined position and his eyes closed. The XO wondered for a second if the captain was sleeping. Bryant's position as second in command aboard the ship meant he didn't normally have to wait to be admitted once his presence at the door was detected by the annunciator system. If Lidden wanted privacy, he could order the system not to admit anyone until approved, as opposed to his established protocol that allowed his second immediate admittance whenever he approached the office door if Lidden was alone.

Bryant waited a full minute for some acknowledgement before finally saying, "Are you awake, sir?"

"Yes, I'm awake, XO. Have a seat. I'm thinking."

"Yes, sir."

After waiting in silence for several more minutes, Bryant asked, "Would you like me to come back later, sir?"

"No," Lidden said, touching the button that would raise his chair to a standard work position. "I received a Priority One message from Sydnee an hour ago while I was in the shower."

"And— you're upset because it wasn't really an emergency?"

"Oh, it's an emergency alright. We may soon be at war with the Clidepp Empire."

"What? No."

"Yes. But it hasn't come to shooting yet. Correction, the Clidepp Empire hasn't retaliated yet. We've attacked them and done plenty of shooting and bombing."

194

"Bombing? Good God, no. What has Sydnee done now?"

"She laid waste to their capital using the Wing I placed under her command."

"She destroyed their capital city?"

"Not quite— destroyed. She ordered her Wing to attack all power-generating and distribution facilities in the capital. And they performed the mission as ordered. The capital was left in complete darkness. Or nearly so because there are always emergency generators standing by in some locations. We have no idea what the loss of life is."

"Lord no."

"I'm afraid so. She confirms that she gave the order and is personally responsible. She says that neither Colonel Dennier or Major Blade should be held accountable at all. She says they were only following her orders."

"Have they come under attack by the Clidepp fleet?"

"No. As far as we know, the Clidepp Fleet doesn't even know the *Justice* is in their solar system."

"I don't understand. How can we be at war if they don't even know one of our ships is there?"

"The Yolongi secret police, at least one of the secret police groups— there are three— have surrounded our embassy in the capital."

"But there's nobody there except for a few Yolongi caretakers."

"That *was* the case."

"Who's there now?"

"A few hundred or so Terran slaves, Blade and the Special Ops team, and four of our Marine fire teams."

"But they haven't been attacked yet?"

"Not yet. Here, I'll play the Priority One message to bring you up to speed."

After the message ended, Bryant stood up and walked around the office several times. "What a mess."

"It gets worse."

"Worse than being at war with the Clidepp Empire?" the XO asked as he retook his seat.

"Only on a personal level. I've just received word that Sydnee is one of the handful of Space Command officers approved for early promotion. Lieutenant(jg) Sydnee Marcola is to receive a half stripe and become Lieutenant Sydnee Marcola."

"Why is that worse? You've been lobbying for that promotion for some time now."

"I know. It's just that she might see it disappear before she even has a chance to change her uniform's rank insignia."

"You mean if we *are* at war with the Clidepp Empire and she's charged with being responsible for it?"

"Yes. Of course, I might suffer along with her. I'm the one who passed on the orders to find and recover the SCI agent at all costs. It's the 'at all costs' that might be my downfall."

"But you must have supporting documentation that shows SCI ordered you to send those instructions."

"Nope. My briefing was face to face and was not recorded. I was told the matter was so secret they couldn't even send a Priority One message ordering me to do it. Normally that suggests that someone doesn't want there to be any record whatsoever of the order. They knew the only way I could convey that instruction was via a Priority One message to Sydnee, so they were forced to approve that, but the only fingerprints on any of this so far are mine."

"You don't think they'll stand behind you?"

"I honestly don't know. What I do know is that if this situation worsens, someone is going to be left holding the dirty end of the shit-stick. I'm afraid that might be me. I've been there before, if you remember. That's how I wound up on the *Perry*. Someone under my command got a little lax with established procedures during a freighter interdiction, and when the axe fell, my neck proved to be the only one under the blade."

"So what are you going to tell Sydnee?"

"I'm going to tell her she's been officially promoted to the rank of Lieutenant. Let her enjoy the promotion for as long as she can."

"No, I mean about the other. They're just sitting there waiting for something to happen on the planet. In the meantime, a shipload of former slaves are eating their way through the ship's limited food stores. What of her request that we resupply them as soon as possible?"

"I've been forbidden to send any support vessels as I did when she got stranded just over the border on her last mission into Clidepp space. And I hate to tell her to abandon the former slaves in the embassy and return to GA space ASAP to offload her passengers, but I know of no way for her to surreptitiously acquire more food if they remain where they are. And even if she cut rations and left Yolongus space today, they will most likely run out of food long before reaching GA space. The only way we could avert that disaster would be to send a CPS-14 loaded with food that would meet them halfway. Raiding the long-term emergency food stores from the embassy was inspired, but that's impossible while the Yolongi secret police is surrounding the compound. If the shuttles leave the embassy, the Triumvirate will have proof that a GA ship was in the area and could have been behind the attacks."

"There doesn't seem to be much choice. She has to cut rations and head back immediately. The people in the embassy bunker should be safe from attack by the Yolongi. I'm sure that bunker can withstand almost any attack the Clidepp Empire can make, short of completely destroying their own capital city. And, as you said, they have plenty of food down there."

"Even cutting rations, they won't have enough food to make it back here once they receive my message eleven days from now. I think it's time I practiced a little CYA."

"How are you going to accomplish that?"

"I've pretty much decided to send a Priority One message to SHQ/SCI and inform them that while following orders issued by them, the commanding officer of the auxiliary ship involved in the special mission was required to commit actions inconsistent with normal protocols."

"That seems pretty general, sir. How does that cover your ass?"

"It'll be on record that I ordered a subordinate to perform an action following orders SCI directed be passed along verbatim. The lack of specifics, other than the date I send the message, is necessary owing to the top-secret nature of the orders. Granted it's a one-sided avowal, and it could be argued that it pertained to another mission entirely, but the significance of the message won't be lost on SCI."

Bryant shook his head slightly and said, "And God help our people on the *Justice*."

◆　◆　◆

Sydnee considerably underestimated the time a response from the *Denver's* commanding officer would take. Thirty-six days after sending the message, a Priority-One message finally arrived from Lidden. Sydnee was asleep at the time, the message arriving at 0328 GST, but she jumped out of bed when informed by the watch commander that it had been sent to her queue.

After rubbing the sleep from her eyes, Sydnee leaned in so the computer could verify her identify with the required retinal scan. Once satisfied with the identity of the recipient, the computer began to play the encrypted vid.

"Hello, Sydnee," the image of Captain Lidden said. "To begin, I want to apologize for putting you in this position. As you know, when I offered you the mission the task was simply to return the package. SCI then altered it to include placing satellites all over Clidepp space. You accepted the additional task, but I felt like we were taking advantage of your acceptance of the original mission. Then when SCI altered it again to have you recover one of their agents on Yolongus, I had no choice but to pass on their orders.

"The narrative you provided about having had their agent on board and then allowing him to return to the planet to recover slaves drew criticism from the SCI, but they were gratified you required him to send his full report before allowing him to leave the ship. They also acknowledge that his superior Space Command rank put you in an extremely awkward position when you tried to deny his request. They have received his report, by the way, and I understand they were very enlightened by the information it contained. They also acknowledge that once their agent was captured by the secret police, it became most imperative he not remain in their custody because he might be forced to talk about his mission on Yolongus and the information he had collected. I haven't been privy to the information contained in that report so I'm unable to share it with you, but I understand it's worth everything you've been through and far more. Should the diplomatic status between our nations worsen, I believe— or at least hope— the SCI will stand behind us. They have also said they want you to take whatever reasonable risks you deem appropriate to again recover the agent you referred to as Winston in your message.

"I regret I'm unable to provide any support for your current food situation. Space Command has adamantly refused to allow another ship to enter Clidepp space, especially in light of the current situation there following the attack on the capital city. I practically begged them to send a Scout-Destroyer loaded with food that would also bring back the slaves you've freed, but they say a second ship might make war inevitable. I regret this might mean that, at this point, they will disavow your mission and put the entire blame for your unauthorized presence in Clidepp space squarely on your shoulders should the situation deteriorate further. Your intense disapproval of the slavery situation in the Clidepp Empire has been well known since the incident aboard the Clidepp diplomatic ship. Since I'm forbidden from sending supplies, you must start back immediately. Reduce meal portions to stretch the remaining food supplies as much as possible. Other than that advice, I'm afraid you're on your own. But I know that in spite of the difficulty confronting you, the fate of the *Justice*, his crew, and the former slaves couldn't be in better hands than those of one of the newest lieutenants in Space Com-

199

mand. Congratulations Lieutenant, the Admiralty Board approved early promotion a few weeks ago and you've been appointed to fill a vacant O-3 command position here aboard the Denver. You are now entitled to wear two full bars on each shoulder. The usual promotion celebration will naturally have to wait until you make it back to GA space, but I'm confident you'll be with us shortly.

"Anthony Frederick Lidden, Captain, Commanding Officer of the *Denver*, GSC-DS2026, in Region One. End of message."

Sydnee, her mouth hanging open in shock, sat back in her office chair and stared at the Space Command logo that signified the end of the vid. She desperately needed food for her crew and passengers, plus help recovering the people still on the planet, so she had been counting on support from Space Command. But instead they gave her an extra half bar for each shoulder and a pay raise. She wasn't ungrateful for the promotion, but she needed that mission support far more than she needed new rank insignia.

With food levels now reaching critical levels aboard the *Justice* and the embassy stores completely out of reach, Sydnee knew that even on reduced rations they would run out of food before they were even halfway back to GA space. She had waited too long for the APCs to leave the embassy compound in the hope that she could recover her people while securing the emergency food supplies. She would now have to find an alternate source of food on her own. The problem was further exacerbated by having all four of her shuttles parked in the underground bay at the embassy compound. The slaves had been growing their own food, so they would probably be adept at foraging in the wild. But even if the *Justice* could reach a planet where they could acquire food, they had no way of transporting it up to the ship. The Marine FA-SF4s had returned to the *Justice* after the attack on the capital city, but the sleek aircraft were designed for slicing through the dense atmosphere of a planet at supersonic speeds, not ferrying passengers or supplies. And while equally adept at flight in the vacuum of space, every cubic centimeter not allocated to cockpit space or propulsion functions was devoted to armament.

The message from Lidden made Sydnee feel as if her ship and crew had been abandoned by Space Command. She supposed military ships and personnel were always labeled as expendable when on a clandestine mission behind enemy lines, undercover in hostile territory, or just outside the borders of their home nation, but she'd like to think they would endeavor to recover them if possible, just as she was ordered to recover Winston.

Well, if Space Command isn't going to help us, she thought, *we'll just have to save ourselves. And we'll let the chips fall where they may.*

Since the day of the attack on Yolongus, she had been receiving a message from Blade each morning. Initially it was a full status report, but after the first week it was usually just the same two words— 'still here.' It wasn't meant to report that the former slaves and the Marines were still at the embassy. It was to report that the Qummuc APCs were still on the perimeter of the compound with their weapons pointed at the embassy. Pointing their weapons at the embassy was a useless act, probably intended solely for public consumption. The embassy's APDS would prevent any APC barrage from seriously damaging buildings inside the compound.

Sydnee had been thinking about the problem of food shortages for weeks, as with each passing day the food supplies dwindled. Most plans had to be discarded because they required at least one shuttle. She wished she had held one back as reserve, but the attack plan on the capital might have suffered without dedicating the full resources of the ship to a quick resolution. There was no way she could have known the number of rescued slaves would be so great and all four shuttles would be required to transport the slaves and food from the embassy.

Without a shuttle, there was no way they were going to get food from Yolongus. Sydnee had composed a message to Blade weeks ago informing him that the ship was leaving the solar system to find food and that they would return when they could. The people in the embassy were safe where they were, so she had to think only about the people aboard the ship now. She sent the message to the com station on the bridge with instructions to send it on. It would be forwarded to the nearest com satellite, routed around the planet to the com satellite having the best line-of-sight with the embassy, and then sent directly to the embassy.

With the task complete, she returned to her bed. In the morning, she would have the navigator plot a course to a distant point she had selected from the space charts. The hundred-thirty-two-light-year trip would take almost five days to complete, and there was no guarantee they would find food there, but they had to try something, and Sydnee felt this had the greatest chance of success since there would be no food coming from the GA.

Once back in bed, Sydnee tossed and turned. She realized how much she had been counting on receiving some form of support from Space Command, even if it was just another CPS-14 such as *Lifeguard* bringing habitat containers filled with food, possibly a couple of MAT-14 shuttles, and providing additional habitat space for rescued slaves.

◆ ◆

After sleeping on it, or at least trying to sleep on it, Sydnee showered and dressed, then walked to the bridge. She was early, and when the watch commander, Lt.(jg) Ming, started to stand to yield the command chair, she waved him down. Instead, she paced around the bridge, thinking of all the reasons why she shouldn't do what she was considering doing. She would have preferred to walk around inside her office while she thought, if it had been large enough to walk around in. She could think of a dozen reasons why she *shouldn't* do what she was fairly sure she was about to order, but only one reason why she should. The reason in favor of the action— the desperate need for food— eventually won out. She believed if she didn't take the action she was contemplating they would run out of food completely within eight days. Being a month from GA space meant that she would have to order the four shuttles beneath the embassy to load up and leave the planet. If they did that, the Yolongi Triumvirate would essentially have proof the GA could be responsible for the attack on the planet and most probably declare war. Even worse, the Clidepp Empire would immediately know that the Dakinium-sheathed ships couldn't be tracked with their radar. They would then blame the GA for every event they couldn't explain, such as what happened to the ship in the ravine that suddenly disappeared.

"No," Sydnee mumbled to herself, "I can't order the ships to leave the embassy while it's a certainty they will be seen. Better not to give the Yolongi something else to think about, especially if it's also something they can use to declare war. At the very least they would learn their radar is useless where our DS ships are concerned."

◆

Just before the watch was due to change, Sydnee took command from Lt.(jg) Ming. The usual briefing for commanders when the watch changed took just seconds. The ship had been parked in the same basic area of space since the camouflage work on the one shuttle had been completed and they'd returned from that planet, and aside from minor issues occurring inside the ship, there was nothing to report.

Following the watch change, Sydnee called Lt.(jg) Olivetti to her chair.

"Plot a course to this location," Sydnee said as she handed Olivetti a viewpad.

Olivetti looked at the viewpad information for a second, then asked, "We're leaving Yolongus, Captain?"

"Yes. Just as soon as you have a course plotted."

"Aye, Captain. This destination is at least a hundred twenty light-years from here."

"Actually, it's about a hundred thirty-two light-years from here. Plot the course, Lieutenant."

"Aye, Captain."

The entire bridge crew naturally heard the order to plot a new course, but Sydnee didn't offer any explanations.

Before the shuttles had left to pick up the slaves and food supplies at the embassy, they had disgorged the contents of their underbelly storage. The items had simply been tethered to the *Justice's* hull at that time, but when it became clear that the shuttles would not be returning right away, the tethered items had been brought inside though one of the SF4 hanger doors. Their presence there would prevent a launch from taking place, but there were still seven other SF4 aircraft available.

◆

When it appeared that Olivetti was done, Sydnee asked, "Navigation, is our course plotted?" Sydnee asked.

"Aye, Captain," Lt.(jg) Olivetti said, adding, "And it has been forwarded to Helm."

"Very good. Helm, is the course laid in?"

"Aye, Captain. We're ready to go as soon as you give the order to build our envelope."

"Very good. Engineering, is everything go?"

"Aye, Captain. All systems are operating at peak efficiency."

"Very good. Tac, is the DeTect board green?"

"Negative, Captain," Lt.(jg) Templeton said. "A ship has just appeared on the DeTect screen. It appears to be that mining company shuttle again, the *Patoosch*."

"That won't interfere with us. Helm, build the double envelope."

"Aye, Captain, building the double envelope."

As the helmsman waited for the envelope to complete, Chief Petty Officer Wilson Lemela said, "Captain, the Clidepp fleet has asked the *Patoosch* to provide today's identification code. Now they're acknowledging the code and allowing the *Patoosch* to approach the planet."

"I guess someone had their head handed to them after the attack and they've tightened security," Sydnee said with a grin.

"The envelope is built, Captain," the helmsman said.

"Engage."

"Aye, Captain," the helmsman said as he tapped a point on his console and the image on the large bridge monitor changed from a visual image via bow cameras to a computer image generated from the ship's sensors.

"We're away, Captain," the helmsman said.

Sydnee relaxed in the command chair and watched the front image until she grew bored. She then turned watch command over to Lt.(jg) Olivetti and left the bridge.

Sydnee went down to the habitat container where the former slaves were housed and looked for the elected leader of the group. When she located her, she invited her to step into the corridor where they would have a little privacy.

"Anese, I need to inform you of something," Sydnee said.

A worried look immediately came over the former slave's face. "Is it about my daughter?"

"Your daughter is fine. All of the former slaves are being cared for. They're getting enough food and sleep, and their work assignments are light. They're only asked to work at daily cooking and cleaning chores for the benefit of the group as a whole, just as the former slaves do here. They are perfectly safe where they are."

"That's a relief. Your expression made me think you had bad news."

"I wanted to tell you so you can inform your people that we have left the vicinity of Yolongus. We've been unable to recover the other slaves from the embassy because, as you know, the Qummuc have surrounded the compound. I've been waiting for the Qummuc to tire of waiting for something to happen and leave the area, but they remain outside the walls. I'd continue to wait here except that our food supplies are getting very low. It's important that I take steps to replenish those supplies, and we can't do it while we're in the Yolongus solar system."

"Is that the only reason?"

"Yes, and it's a pretty important one."

"And we'll return to get the others when your food issues have been resolved?"

"Of course. Please don't worry about them. They're fine. We rescued everyone who was in that Qummuc slave facility, and as I've told you previously, that included your daughter."

"Thank you, Captain."

"I want you to pass that information on to the others. We just left the Yolongus solar system, and I'm sure the word will reach everyone down here before too long. I want them to understand we are not abandoning the others."

"I'll tell them, Captain. Thank you again for everything you've done for us." A few tears wound their way down the face of Anese. As she wiped them away, she said, "For so long we prayed that someone would free us from slavery. The Aleoxlene Reqoppl freed us from our masters but had no way to get us back to the GA. You are our real angel. You are the one who will take us home. We trust you completely and know that when it's possible to recover the people at the embassy, you'll do it."

CHAPTER SEVENTEEN
~ March 4th, 2287 ~

When the *Justice* arrived at its established destination, Sydnee asked Colonel Dennier to join her in her office.

"Thank you for coming, Colonel. Coffee?"

"I'm fine, thanks."

"I'm sure you've noticed that a number of food items are no longer available in the mess hall."

"Of course. The selections have been getting smaller and smaller."

"That's why we've left the Yolongus solar system and traveled a hundred thirty-two light-years. We desperately need food. I'd hoped that either the Qummuc would cease their vigil around the embassy and we could recover our people and the food stored at the embassy or that Space Command would send us supplies, but neither has occurred, so I've had to take matters into my own hands."

"And you're going to do that how? As I understand it, we're out in the middle of nowhere."

"As you understand it?"

"From talk in the mess hall. You can't keep something like this secret from the crew."

"Of course," Sydnee said, nodding slightly. "Anyway, the secret is about to be revealed. We're going to become pirates."

"Pirates?"

"Pirates," she said in acknowledgement.

"And who are we going to attack?"

"No one, I hope. We're going to attempt to stop freighters and assess their cargo to see if they're transporting any food-stuffs."

"And then we're going to just take it?"

"In a manner of speaking because I won't allow them to re-fuse our— request. Every ship sent out by Space Command carries a certain amount of cash based on its mission, intend-ed degree of travel, and the time it's expected to be away from normal supply lines. I'm going to pay for any food we take with GA credits. We were supposed to be in another nation's space— hostile space— for a period of up to two years, so the amount of credits I have in my safe would put some small banks to shame."

"And if the ship we're taking the food from refuses to ac-cept payment in GA credits?"

"I've heard that GA credits are actually far preferred over Clidepp credits here in the Empire, but if that's not the case, then we take the food anyway. We have no choice."

"And I assume my Wing will be used to perform an— in-terdiction-like inspection?"

"Perhaps. I'm hoping we can convince a freighter to sell us food without using any force or even boarding their ship."

"I formally protest, Captain. This is outside our mission."

"Yes, it is, and your formal protest is noted. I take full re-sponsibility for the action so you're covered. If we don't do this, we'll probably be completely out of food within a week. We've already exhausted the chemicals required by the food synthesizers to produce most foods, and all of the normal foodstuffs have been consumed. In less than a week, all of the emergency rations will also be gone."

"It's that bad?"

"Yes. I've sworn the cooks and mess assistants to secrecy, but I'm sure some of the crew know the truth. As you touched on a minute ago, you can't really keep any secrets on a ship this size, especially since so many of the former slaves are working in the mess hall helping to prepare meals."

"I'm sure you realize the freighters will be traveling FTL. How do you propose to stop them?"

"I've had some small experience in that regard. We pick a likely freighter and order them to heave-to. If they refuse, or if they simply don't acknowledge the order, we threaten them with the use of force. And if they still refuse or still refuse to acknowledge the order, we have no choice but to perform an envelope merge and stop them. We want to avoid hurting anyone, but we must do whatever is necessary to get food."

"*Whatever* is necessary?"

"Yes. If they fail to stop on their own, the only way I know to stop them is with an envelope merge. But we must be careful not to hit any occupied parts of the ship. We will only target their propulsion systems. I don't want anyone harmed."

"A dangerous maneuver at best and deadly at worst."

"True, but if they refuse to stop, it's the only alternative. Since freighters have their temporal generators mounted on their bow of their ships, the danger of a serious collision is lessened considerably compared to stopping a military ship with their temporal generator mounted on the sail area because that requires us to perform an envelope merge so we can fire our lasers at the generator. All we have to do with a freighter is match their speed, then slide over in front of them and let them run into us. This ship won't be damaged, but their temporal generator will be crushed and their envelope will be cancelled. I'm hoping that once they realize they'll be dead in space in the middle of nowhere if they fail to stop, they might come around and be cooperative."

"And if they fire on us?"

"Non-military vessels in Clidepp space are restricted from carrying offensive weapons by the Clidepp government."

"You mean like that Clidepp freighter you destroyed after they fired two missiles at the Clidepp destroyer you commanded?"

"That was an exception. The freighter was controlled by the Rebels and merely disguised as an innocent freighter."

"You do realize we have no authority to stop ships in another nation's territory."

"Yes, but I'm already in this so deep it probably won't make much difference. The worst they can do is kick me out of the service."

"Actually, if you start a war with another nation independent of authorization by the GA Senate, they can confine you on Saquer Major for the rest of your life."

"Stop trying to cheer me up, Colonel. Listen, if we don't get food, none of us may live long enough to be locked up for life."

"Okay, Captain. It's your call. We'll support you in whatever action you order."

◆ ◆

"Captain, the DeTect system has identified what appears to be a freighter," Lt.(jg) Templeton announced the next day.

"How far, how big, and on what course?"

"It appears to be about five kilometers in length. The DeTect system indicates the ship is roughly three-point-six billion kilometers from our present position. Its current course will probably take it to the Olimpood home world."

"Lt. Olivetti, establish a course that will take us alongside that ship and send it to the helm."

"Aye, Captain."

"Helm, when you receive the course, take us there."

"Aye, Captain," Lt.(jg) Ming said.

Traveling at Light-9790, the *Justice* closed the distance to the freighter in mere minutes. It then had to cancel its double envelope and build a single so it could slow to Light-120 to match the speed of the freighter. The hull sensors scanned the freighter from a distance of five kilometers and the results appeared on the bridge monitor.

"Unlikely they have much food, Captain," Lt.(jg) Galli said as he reviewed the data. "They appear to be loaded down with unprocessed ore. Of course, they'll have the food for the crew."

"No, that won't even make a dent in what we need. I guess we struck out this time. Maybe the next freighter will have what we need."

◆ ◆

Three more freighters were scanned and rejected over the next couple of days. Sydnee's brilliant plan was shaping up to be a monumental failure. With little more than a day's worth of food left on the ship, Sydnee had cut the half rations to quarter rations and the crew was getting restless. Desperation had set in and Sydnee had reached a point where she was pre-pared to do something she had told herself she would never do. When another ship, any ship, came by, they would stop it and take some of the crew's food.

She was sitting in her office when she received a message that another freighter had just come into view. She jumped up and rushed to the bridge in time to see the scan data appear on the large monitor.

"Looking good, Captain," Lt.(jg) Galli said. "No mining ore containers at all according to the scans. And they're nearly maxed out with cargo containers."

"We just have to hope they're not traveling empty," Lt.(jg) Olivetti mused.

"It's the best chance we've had since we arrived here," Sydnee said. "Bring us alongside, Helm." Once the *Justice* had matched speed and come alongside the freighter, she said, "Com, hail them. The name on the freighter appears to be *Diutomis*."

A few seconds later, Com Chief Lemela said, "They want to know who we are and why we're calling them."

"Tell them we need food and we're willing to pay for it."

After sending the message and listening to a reply, Lemela said, "They say they're not running a grocery store."

"I'll talk to them, Chief. Patch my CT into the connection."

After touching a few spots on his console, Lemela said, "Go ahead, Captain. You're tied in."

211

"This is the Captain of the ship off your larboard side. I want to talk to your captain."

"You are talking to the captain. I'm Captain Serwooth."

"We are desperately in need of food. We wish to purchase some of whatever you're transporting."

"We're freighters, not food merchants."

"And we're desperate enough to destroy your ship and take the food if you won't sell it to us."

"You wouldn't dare."

"Are you willing to bet your life on that?"

"You wouldn't dare attack us."

"Is that your final answer? And is your will up to date?"

"You wouldn't dare attack us."

"We're getting nowhere. After I destroy your temporal generator you might be more amicable."

"You wouldn't dare attack us."

"You keep saying that, but you obviously don't understand what hunger can drive people to do. After we destroy your temporal generator, I'm hoping you will stop. If you attempt to continue with sub-light speeds, we'll destroy your larboard engine. And if you fail to stop after that, we'll destroy the starboard engine. Then we'll start cutting your ship into little pieces. I suggest you recall everyone from the cargo section before we reach that point. Call me back whenever you want me to stop firing on your ship. And we're monitoring all frequencies, so I warn you not to attempt to call for help or send any communication messages at all regarding my order to stop. Captain Ahab out."

After terminating the connection, Lemela said, "Ahab, Captain?"

"Yes," Sydnee said with a smile. "It was the first name that popped into my head that described my frame of mind. He was the insane captain of a whaling ship in the book *Moby Dick* by Herman Melville. I decided to use that instead of

Captain Kidd, although a pirate's name might be a little more appropriate.

"Helm, line us up with their bow so we can destroy their temporal generator."

"Captain, we're not really going to attack that freighter, are we?" Lt.(jg) Templeton asked.

"Only if they refuse to yield, Tac."

Templeton tapped a few points on his console before saying, "Aye, Captain. I'm ready to fire on the sub-light engines whenever you give the command."

"Helm, take your time lining us up. I want to make the captain believe we're *really* going to destroy his temporal generator and that it's taking us extra time to guarantee the destruction. Perhaps the extra seconds will allow him to understand I'm not bluffing."

"Aye, Captain."

A few minutes later the helmsman said, "We're in position, Captain. I can't delay any longer. If we're going to do this, I only have to nudge us a little bit closer."

"I guess he's not going to chicken out," Sydnee said. With definite determination in her voice, she added, "Well, neither are we. Move us in and destroy their generator."

"The captain of the *Diutomis* is calling Captain. He wants to talk."

"Helm, back off. Okay, Chief, patch me in again."

"You're in, Captain."

"That was close, Captain. I had just given the order to complete the destruction."

"Captain Ahab, you can't be serious about this."

"I'm very serious, Captain Serwooth. If you're not going to stop, we'll stop you. And there will be no more chances to stop the attack, so cancel your envelope."

"Our sensors say you have no weapons."

"Our weapons remain hidden until we need them."

"That sounds quite suspicious."

"We're traveling FTL, Captain Serwooth, so I can't fire my weapons and prove their existence unless we destroy your generator and then destroy some part of your ship."

"Okay, Captain Ahab, I surrender. I'm going to stop. Please put a little space between our ships so we don't accidently collide."

Everyone on the bridge was watching Sydnee. She nodded to the helmsman and he returned his gaze to his console, then touched a few control points. When he looked up, turned slightly, and nodded, Sydnee returned her attention to the com link.

"Okay, Captain Serwooth, we're in a safe position."

"I'm canceling our envelope, Captain Ahab."

Sydnee waited until the freighter suddenly disappeared behind them before telling the helmsman to return to where the freighter had stopped. With the return to sub-light speeds, normal video communications that allowed use of the large bridge monitor was possible, and both parties got a look at the other. Captain Serwooth was a Mydwuard, one of the three main sentient species in the Clidepp Empire.

"A wise decision, Captain," Sydnee said. "I want this transaction to be peaceful and equitable. Starting off by destroying part of your ship would have made pleasantries impossible."

"How is it that a Space Command ship is so far from the GA?"

"I see you recognize our uniforms."

"Yes. I suspected you might be Space Command. The Clidepp military would have identified themselves before issuing such orders, and Raiders would have fired first and talked afterwards. What is a Space Command ship doing so far from GA space?"

"It's a long story and one I'm not at liberty to discuss anyway."

"Do you really have weapons? And would you have really destroyed my temporal generator?"

"Yes to both questions. Obviously we're not a battleship or even a destroyer, but even small GA space tugs like this one have weaponry sufficient to defend ourselves. And it can also be used offensively when absolutely necessary. I would have used it most regretfully— if you had not agreed to stop. I have no choice, Captain. My back is against a wall. I know this is highly unorthodox, but I need food supplies *desperately*, and I believe you might be able to accommodate us. It's that's simple. Now, I would like you to send us a copy of your ship's manifest so we can select what we need."

"I'm going to get in a lot of trouble when the deliveries come up short."

"You'll be well compensated for all missing supplies with enough GA Credits to more than satisfy the intended food recipient. And with enough to pocket some for yourself. Now please transmit the ship's manifest."

◆　◆

As soon as the manifest was received. Sydnee took the information to the mess hall and had the cooks review the available food lists. Her instructions were to get enough to last the crew and passengers for six months.

"Six months, Captain? That's a lot of food, and this is a small ship."

"I'll have Lt.(jg) Galli and his engineers standing by to consult with you after you've had a chance to review the list. He'll be able to tell you if we can take on what you select. Dried foods like pasta that take a minimum of uncooked space and expand when cooked would be best, but we'd also prefer a varied diet with vegetables, if possible. The most important task is to acquire enough food that we don't have to do this again. I'm sure that when we're done here and the freighters tell their story, the Clidepp military will speed to this area and begin searching for us. I would very much prefer not to have to return here for more food."

"Yes, ma'am. We'll do our best to make this just a one-time shopping trip."

"Very good, Staff Sergeant. Contact me when you've made your selections."

◆ ◆

The freighter captain was anxious to resume his voyage, so he kept calling Sydnee every fifteen minutes until she was able to give him a list of the food she wanted. After he'd had a chance to examine the list, he called her again.

"Captain, this is an enormous amount of food for such a small ship as yours, and it could take days to assemble it all."

"I'm sorry, Captain. We're a very long way from home and my cook believes we need everything he listed. I must insist you supply what we need so I'm not forced to stop other freighters on our return trip. You're pulling almost ten kilometers of shipping containers, and they contain ten thousand times the amount of food we're requesting. And you'll be able to give each of your crew a nice bonus for the extra work we're asking you to perform. As soon as you have the cargo container filled, send it over using a robotic tug and we'll begin emptying it. If we work together instead of complaining or commiserating, we can complete this transaction more quickly."

"Aye, Captain. My people are already hard at work filling a quarter container in the maintenance bay. I'll contact you when we're ready to send it over."

◆ ◆

Two hours later, the first part of the shipment, loaded into a standard forty-meter-long quarter-sized shipping container, was coming alongside the *Justice*. A dozen Marines in EVA suits were standing on a launch platform usually used to launch and recover a Marine SF4. The Fighter had launched and was holding position over the *Justice*. By necessity, it would remain outside the ship until all of the food had been received and stored inside the ship since the *Justice* had no storage holds accessible via a hatchway in the hull. When the SF4 platform with its gravity set to one-sixth normal was filled, it would be retracted into the habitat container and the area would be re-pressurized. A long line of waiting Marines and Space Command officers and enlisted would then unload the platform, passing the food into crew accommodations, engineering spaces of the ship, corridors, and any available space in the habitat containers. The process would be repeated over and over again until the ship was crammed full with food. As each platform was unloaded, the items were marked off against the list of requested food.

◆ ◆

It didn't take days to transfer the food, but it did take just over sixteen hours. Aboard the *Justice*, everyone who had worked to store and secure the food was so exhausted they didn't even want to think about food, which was just as well because the cooks and their assistants had helped with the unloading and storage and were just as beat.

Sydnee had had the cooks estimate the cost of the goods at the time they'd prepared the list, so she was ready when Captain Serwooth sent an invoice for the food to the *Justice*. She contacted him and requested he return her call in private. When he called, Sydnee could see he was in a small area, probably his office.

"I've reviewed the invoice, and I see that the prices you've quoted are about four times the cost of the food at wholesale."

"Captain, I assure you that the price is fair. We had to perform a lot of work to get the supplies out of the shipping containers. Everything had to be tracked down and then either brought up through access hatchways or the container had to be detached and brought to a maintenance bay so the end doors could be opened."

"I understand, Captain. And for what I've put you though, I'm adding an additional fifty percent over the amount you've requested."

"Fifty percent additional? You're not much of a businesswoman, Captain."

Sydnee smiled before saying, "No, I'm a military officer who is grateful that you were able to accommodate our needs and that we were able to conclude our business peacefully.

Should you desire to do so, the extra money will allow you to give your crew a nice bonus for working so hard today."

"Thank you, Captain. I'm sure they'll appreciate that."

"If you wish to thank me, don't mention that we forced you to stop. Our situation is difficult enough in Clidepp Empire space. I don't want the diplomats getting involved and all worked up over this issue, then starting a small war. If you must identify us, just say that Captain Ahab of the *Pequod* needed food for the crew and beseeched you to sell us enough to last on our return voyage to the GA. You agreed to stop and sell us what we needed in a humanitarian gesture of good will towards a neighboring nation."

"Done, Captain. You contacted us and I agreed to help you out in a spirit of cooperation with a neighbor."

"Very good. Now allow me to take care of the accounting because I must account for every last credit I distribute from the ship's funds. I'm going to state the details of the transaction, and I would like you to also state the amount, date, and reason for the expenditure. This video will become part of the ship's log."

Sydnee stated the information, and Serwooth repeated and confirmed the transaction details.

"Very good, Captain. I'm going to place the GA credits into a sealed pouch and have one of my people attach it to the robot sled used to deliver the last food container. Once the sled has returned to the *Diutomis* and you've had a chance to count the credits, please confirm that you've received them and that our business is concluded. We'll then both be on our way."

When Captain Serwooth called again, he was smiling. "I'm very satisfied, Captain," he said. "I wish the Empire forces were as fair with freighters and as pleasant to work with as Space Command captains. I wish you and your crew aboard the *Pequod* a safe journey back to GA space. And I will do everything I can to keep this transaction a secret. Another war— or even just an unpleasant diplomatic squabble— would not be in the best interest of either freighters or the people of this nation. The war with the Rebels is causing enough problems and grief."

"Thank you, Captain. I wish you a swift and safe journey as well. Good-bye."

As both ships departed the area, Sydnee went on a tour of the ship. Everywhere she walked there were boxes and crates lining the walls and bulkheads from deck to overhead. Each item had a new code stamped on it indicating the location so the cooks would be able to find what they needed when they searched for supplies. There didn't seem to be a spare meter of space anywhere in the entire ship, but food would not be a problem for many months to come.

With the most important problem facing her command resolved— that of starvation— Sydnee could concentrate on other matters. As she returned to the bridge, an idea that had come to her while she and the *Justice* had been playing 'chicken' with the captain of the *Diutomis* began to replay and expand in her brain. With enough food now on board to allow the *Justice* to remain in the Yolongus solar system for up to five more months without anyone experiencing hunger, Sydnee was determined to recover the people housed at the embassy. And it would happen without allowing the Qummuc to see the shuttles leaving or even providing any proof they had ever been there.

CHAPTER EIGHTEEN
~ March 10th, 2287 ~

Arriving back at what Sydnee had come to think of as their station, Sydnee sent a simple message to Blade. It read, 'We're back. Enough food for six months. We'll have you out before it becomes an issue again.'

She then began conducting a series of meetings with the former slaves and the Yolongi rescued from the planet. Everyone had been interviewed thoroughly after coming aboard the *Justice*, and she used those records now as her starting database. She picked the brains of each person to learn any tidbits of information that would later help her refine her plan. Sydnee knew that the former slaves and the Yolongi who had helped them trusted Anese implicitly and wouldn't hold back vital information if she were there, so she always had the leader from Sanctuary sit in on all meetings.

The interviews would consume weeks of time, but Sydnee was trying to acquire information the slaves might not even realize they knew. When the interviews were over, a database of slave information that might even surpass the database of the Qummuc in certain respects would reside in the *Justice's* computer system. The computer already contained the entire slave registration database, downloaded from the computer at the government facility where the slave auctions were held. Sydnee was adding a new subset that contained the name, basic physical description, and last known owner and location of every slave with whom each of the freed slaves could remember ever having had contact during their lifetime. An associated database contained the names and descriptions of every Aleoxlene Reqoppl contact person the former slaves had met, knew of, or had even heard of. Finally, the records also contained a list of all locations where slaves had been housed while awaiting processing or sale, the names and addresses of every slave owner, the slaves they owned, and every address where slaves had been assigned to work, both domestically and in factories. Sydnee pressed the people she interviewed to mention every fact they could remember and then asked them to return should they remember anything else afterward. She impressed upon them that even the smallest tidbits of information would be useful when the time came to end slavery in the Clidepp Empire because the completed database would contain not just information about the slaves on Yolongus, but also information about slavery on the home worlds of the Mydwuard and the Olimpood, and every other planet where former slaves aboard the *Justice* had worked or traveled to with their owners. Once the information had been collected, the computer system on the *Justice* was able to manipulate it to not only answer virtually any question that could be ascertained from the collected data, but the computer could also hypothesize innumerable other situations, including tactical choices for an attack.

◆ ◆ ◆

"Have you read this report from our man aboard the freighter *Diutomis*?" Plelillo asked his two Triumvirate associates in a private meeting.

"The one where our undercover agent reported the freighter provided food to a Space Command vessel?" Danttan asked.

"Yes."

"Yes, I saw it."

"I didn't see it," Mewaffal said.

"A Mydwuard-registered vessel stopped in space and gave supplies to a tiny Space Command vessel."

"How tiny?" Mewaffal asked.

"Here, read it yourself," Plelillo said, sliding a viewpad across the conference table.

"So what?" Mewaffal said after reading the report from the agent. "They gave supplies to a space tug that was low on food. I see it was transporting eight small containers."

"So what?" Plelillo screamed. "So what? Are you brain dead? We have a freighter giving supplies to a ship from another nation that's operating inside our borders. And not just *inside* our border but more than eleven annuals of travel inside our border."

"It's not eleven annuals of travel for Space Command vessels," Danttan said. "GA passenger liners are reported to be four times faster than our fastest civilian ships, and their military ships are reported to be at least four times faster than our fastest warships. In fact, we've been hearing unsubstantiated rumors that they've made enormous advances in light-speed travel. One report has even declared they've broken the theoretical boundaries of FTL through something they call double-envelope FTL. Space Command will neither admit its existence nor deny it."

"This was just a tiny, little, insignificant space tug," Mewaffal said. "A ship that could be swatted away by any of our warships. It wasn't even close to the size of their Scout-Destroyers, which are so small they don't even classify them as a warship in their military classification system. They wouldn't have put their best technology into such a nothing ship. If they had, it would simply have gone back and resupplied at the border."

"And the double-envelope nonsense is just propaganda intended to frighten anyone who is even considering fighting the GA."

"Meaning what exactly?" Danttan asked.

"Never underestimate the GA. We aren't talking about the Aguspod, who are morons compared to the GA. You say the GA would not have put their best technology into such a tiny ship. So you must believe the attack on us here had to come from a different ship— a warship. The burning questions then become: How many military ships do they have in our space? When are they going to attack us again, and in what strength? And, most importantly, how do they manage to hide from our planetary detection systems? We can identify the exact position of every one of our warships ringing the planet. Why can't we see the GA warship that's hiding out there?"

"Perhaps because there is no GA warship hiding out there to see," Danttan said.

"I've repeatedly said we can't fight the GA," Mewaffal said. "They are far too powerful. We rely on them not getting so angry with us that they decide to take over our nation. You spoke of having fear for the military ability of another nation. Well, I fear the military ability of the GA."

"The issue of *who* attacked us is already dying down as we work to restore power in the capital," Danttan said. "The issue has now become one of *why* they attacked and why they chose this way to attack us. Some people are blaming the Blenod, while others are blaming the Rebels. Some are also saying the Aleoxlene Reqoppl was behind it, and it's time to end slavery forever in the Empire. I've ordered my best people in my disinformation department to focus as much blame on the Rebels as possible because the attack has inconvenienced such a large part of the population. Early data-gathering by information agents has shown that people are accepting the Rebels as being responsible, and their anger with the Rebel cause is increasing."

"Don't be fooled by what people are saying aloud in public," Plelillo said. "They may believe the Rebels are responsible for the attacks, but they're blaming us for not protecting our planet."

◆　◆　◆

"Sir," his first deputy said to the Rebel leader, "I've had all of our unit commanders contacting their people, and I've been able to ascertain with reasonable certainty that none of our units were responsible for the attack on the Yolongi capital. And— no one knows who *is* responsible."

"I believe I know who is responsible," the leader said from his relaxed position on a sofa.

"You do? Then why did you have me contacting people to find out if any of our people were responsible?"

"It was the only way I knew to verify my assessment was correct. There was always a chance I could be wrong and that some Rebel commander had taken it upon himself to attack the capital. If that was the case, we had to know because that act would alienate our followers and supporters. But now that we know it wasn't us, we can honestly deny it to all of our followers. And I'm reasonably certain I know who did attack the capital."

"You know who did it? How could you possibly know that? The Prime Minister has said even *they* don't yet know."

"I believe they know. It's really very simple. Whoever ordered the attack is incredibly powerful. They simultaneously brought the capital to its knees, destroyed the entire garrison at two separate Qummuc facilities, and did the same at a slave pen containing hundreds of slaves. And all without losing a man, apparently. To solve the riddle, all you have to do is ask yourself— who would steal slaves during a bombing attack? Do you realize how difficult it would be to transport hundreds of slaves through the streets without anyone seeing them? The first thing people do when their electric service fails is go outside to see if anyone else is without power. Combine that with explosions throughout the city and you know that virtually the entire population of the city was outside their homes or work locations. And yet, while people certainly heard the explosions, nobody saw or heard the attackers or the missing slaves.

"We know it had to be someone from outside the Empire because we are the only force within the Empire who could have managed something even close to this. So that leaves us with just five possibilities. The Aguspod and Kweedee are so busy with other problems that they haven't yet initiated any action against the Empire for the bombings in their nations. And the Blenod seem to be content with commandeering part of the Clidepp Empire along our common border. And none of these three could have pulled off an operation like this where there are absolutely no witnesses. That leaves just two other possibilities. The Raider organization is one. They have the people, the knowledge, and the support infrastructure to have done this, but it doesn't ring true because they're business partners with the Triumvirate. That leaves just one other possibility— the Galactic Alliance."

"The GA? But there's been no formal declaration of war."

"Yes, that's true. It appears the leadership in the GA has finally changed their policy about always alerting their adversary, or their enemies, of their plans in advance. Only idiots announce their attack plans in advance because it gives their adversary information they can use to prepare. It's about time they got smart."

"But if it's the GA, they may be intending to annex the Empire."

"That's not why they're here. If it were, Carver would have come here and issued ultimatums herself. No, I think they're just sending a message at this time. They don't want this part of space. They just want all of the Terran slaves released and returned to the GA."

"The Triumvirate will never agree to that."

"I know," he said with a smile.

"So what happens next?"

"We'll have to wait and see what the GA does. This should be interesting."

"But what if the GA decides to annex the Clidepp Empire?"

"Trust me, they won't."

◆ ◆ ◆

"Captain?" Com Chief Lemela said when Sydnee entered the bridge the following morning for the watch change.

Sydnee stopped, then walked to the com station. "You're here early, Chief. What is it?"

"I relieved Chief Lasotta a little early. Yesterday I picked up a strange stream of radio communications from what appears to be a single source. I've been trying to decrypt it but haven't had any success."

"We know decryption isn't always possible, Chief."

225

"Yes, ma'am. But the strange thing about this transmission is its origin."

"Why is it strange?"

"It's strange because, according to all the charts, there's nothing out there in that direction— no planets, moons, or space stations."

"Then it must be coming from a ship."

"Yes, ma'am. But it hasn't moved. It's like us. It appears to be parked in a remote location where no space traffic is likely to encounter it."

"That *is* interesting. You say you've been monitoring it? How long?"

"I noticed it early yesterday. I was intrigued by the regularity of transmissions that weren't from a planet or a satellite, so I had the computer monitor it all night. In more than twenty hours, the source was broadcasting fairly regularly for about seventeen. Do you suppose someone else has seeded satellites in Clidepp space and we're picking up what they're rebroadcasting?"

"Are the transmissions in burst mode?"

"No, ma'am. They seem more like normal conversations."

"And you believe you've got a reasonable fix on their bearing?"

"Uh, yes, ma'am. It's a reasonable fix— but may not be precise. I'd need help from the tactical officer for that."

"Maybe we'll go investigate after the watch begins. Keep monitoring them, Chief. Good work."

"Yes, ma'am. Thank you, ma'am."

◆

Once the first watch had reported in, Sydnee instructed the tactical officer to lock onto the radio transmission signal and forward a course to the helm so they could follow it to its source. The *Justice* then left its parked location and headed towards whatever was generating or relaying the signals.

After just a few seconds of travel, the helmsman said, "The signals have stopped, Captain."

"Chief, confirm."

"Confirmed, Captain. They've stopped broadcasting. At least for the moment."

"Continue on the previous heading, Helm."

"Aye, Captain."

"Captain," the Tac officer said, "I've got a small ship dead ahead on the DeTect system monitor."

"Helm, all stop."

"Aye, Captain, all forward progress is halted."

"Tac, can you identify the ship?"

"Based on size and assumed configuration, it appears to be a space yacht, Captain," Templeton said.

"Assumed configuration?"

"At four billion kilometers, we're still too far away for more detailed images of such a small ship. I'm basing the assumption on apparent size alone."

"That's not always a good indication of lethality, as is proved by our small size," Sydnee said with a grin, "but let's assume that for now. If it *is* a space yacht, we have to wonder what a space yacht is doing this far out while transmitting to someone on the planet when they could just as easily go to the planet. They can't simply be broken down or someone would have arrived to tow them to Yolongus long before now."

"Perhaps they're smugglers contacting their buyers and making arrangements for delivery. If so, they can't simply arrive, land on the planet, and go through customs," Olivetti offered from the navigation console.

"True. Or perhaps they're no more welcome on the planet than we are," the Tac officer said.

"It must be something like that," Sydnee said. "Perhaps they're gunrunners supplying the Rebels. Tac, alert the Wing. I want two SF4s ready to launch and perform a fly-by investigation of that ship. Helm, take us to twenty-five thousand kilometers and keep the SF4 launch platform hidden from the contact so they don't get a radar hit when the hatch opens."

"Aye, Captain."

A few seconds later the com chief said, "Colonel Dennier's aide says the Colonel would like to speak with you, Captain."

"Put her through to my CT, Chief."

"Aye, Captain, making the connection."

"Good morning, Colonel."

"What's up, Captain?"

"There's a space yacht parked out in space beyond DeTect range from the planet. We believe it's been conducting extremely heavy communications with someone on Yolongus for the past twenty-four hours. We've moved to within twenty-five thousand kilometers. I'd like you to have a couple of your pilots perform a fly-by and look it over."

"What do you suspect?"

"Nothing specific. I'm just wondering why a space yacht would be parked out here in space instead of parking in orbit or landing on the planet."

"Aye, Captain, we'll launch two SF4s within sixty seconds. Dennier out."

"Marcola out."

After watching the SF4s deploy, Dennier headed to the bridge. She entered just as the fighters arrived in the area where the space yacht was parked and reported in.

"Lima-Five reporting. It's a space yacht alright, and a fancy one at that. It's definitely a luxury model. Wait a second, *Justice*, they're raising their temporal generator."

"On an RF band, warn them to stand down and heave to," Sydnee said. RF band communications were rarely used in space simply because the signals traveled so slowly compared to the S-band transmissions that traveled in hyperspace, but they were still used frequently in ship-to-ship communications where a laser protocol hadn't been established. By the time a low-power RF signal traveled the billions of kilometers back to Yolongus, the parties would probably be long gone.

"They're not responding, Captain."

"Warn them that if they don't respond within sixty seconds, you'll destroy their generator."

"No response yet," the pilot said after fifty seconds. "I'm locked onto their generator."

"Fire," Sydnee said. A few seconds later, a small explosion flared briefly where the temporal generator had been raised on the sail area of the ship and then winked out.

"They'll not be going anywhere FTL for quite a while," the pilot said.

"Maintain your surveillance, Lima-Five."

"Aye, Captain."

After a few more minutes, the Lima-Five pilot said, "They've fired up their sub-light engines."

"Their direction?"

"They're headed away from the planet, Captain."

"Lima-Five, return to the ship."

"Aye, Captain. Lima-Five and Lima-Six breaking contact and returning to the *Justice*."

"We know they can't see either us or the SF4s with radar," Sydnee said aloud, "so they can't know we're here. But if they were legit, they'd be heading towards Yolongus for help just as quickly as their sub-light engines would take them. Helm, as soon as we've recovered our fighters and closed the outer hatches, follow that yacht. Match their sub-light speed and remain near the edge of our DeTect range. To minimize the chance they can catch a glimpse of us between them and the sun in this solar system, make sure it's never behind us."

"Aye, Captain."

◆　◆　◆

"That ship had to be GA," the Rebel leader said to the ship's officers in a hurriedly called meeting.

229

"I was told no one ever saw a thing, so it could have been anyone," the first officer said.

"No. A Clidepp Empire pilot never would have destroyed the temporal generator on a luxury yacht without first getting permission from the Triumvirate. And that would have taken much more time. By the time they got approval to fire, we'd have been long gone."

"Why haven't they pursued us after we engaged the sub-light engines?" the first officer asked.

"What makes you think they haven't? The ship that destroyed the temporal generator didn't register on radar."

"But we've been scanning the area around us visually using the cameras mounted on the hull. There's nothing out there."

"They're out there," the Rebel leader said. "Their ship is probably painted black. All Space Command warships are painted black these days. Without radar you can't see a black ship in space unless there's a sun or moon behind it."

"Then we should maneuver so the sun will be behind us. If they're following, we'll be able to spot them."

"They're not fools," the Rebel leader said. "They're not going to let us catch a glimpse of them. I don't know the purpose of this game, but I know they're back there. They only destroyed our generator to make sure we didn't get away."

"Get away? If it's the GA, they can fly circles around us. This tub has trouble doing sixty times the speed of light."

"They prevented us from going FTL because they can't fire on a ship while it's traveling faster than light. This way we're at their mercy. They can take us down anytime they wish."

"What are we going to do?"

"I don't know yet. I need to think. Leave me alone so I can concentrate and plan a way out of this."

◆ ◆ ◆

"I wish we had access to the Clidepp Empire ship registry files," Dennier said as she stood next to Sydnee's command chair.

"That would be nice," Sydnee said. "The Space Command ship registry file has a good number of Clidepp registrations in it because every ship that's ever stopped in a GA port would have had its description and owner information recorded. However, that ship wouldn't be registered. It's so slow it would take twenty years to reach the GA. I doubt it can even approach the Light-75 restriction in effect in the Clidepp Empire for all civilian ships. And it probably wouldn't do much good to learn who it's registered to anyway. It's most likely stolen. The only reasons I can think of for the ship remaining billions of kilometers out in space while they carried on almost a full day of non-stop conversations with Yolongus is that they are either smuggling contraband or at least one of the people aboard is wanted by the Yolongi or Clidepp governments. We know the ship wasn't disabled until we destroyed their temporal generator."

"Captain, does this little side-trip have anything to do with recovering our people from the embassy?"

"Suppose you were a senior politician who had an extremely angry populace blaming you for allowing someone to destroy their power grid, leaving them without power for weeks. Now suppose you learned the whereabouts of a notorious smuggler *and* that he was someone who could be put on public display and blamed for all the power problems in the capital. What would you do?"

"I'd probably mobilize all my forces, arrest him, then put him on display in a big fancy trial."

"Yes, that's what I was thinking. It would take a substantial burden off your back, even in an oligarchy. Wouldn't it be nice if all the Qummuc APCs were suddenly withdrawn from around the embassy because they were needed to track down and arrest that very elusive smuggler and close down his operation?"

"Do you really think such a person is aboard that yacht?"

231

"I don't know. But I do know that whoever is aboard that yacht was trying to avoid having certain people know he or she was out here. I also know that yachts like the one we're following cost many millions of credits and only major businessmen, celebrities, or criminal kingpins can afford something like that. And I also know that of the three types, only the criminals would be afraid of having the authorities know they were nearby."

"So what now?"

"Now, we reel in the big fish we've been tailing and weigh him to see if he meets the requirements of a legal catch. If he screams for help from the Clidepp authorities, we'll know I made a mistake and we'll have to quickly lose ourselves in the blackness of space. But if he doesn't scream for help, we'll know we might have a real trophy on our hands."

CHAPTER NINETEEN
~ April 7th, 2287 ~

"Sir, we're being warned again. This time they say to cut our sub-light engines and perform something called 'heave-to.'"

"Who's giving the orders?"

"We don't know. We can't see any ships out there. But they're still using the old RF frequency, so we know they're close."

"And if we don't comply?"

"They haven't identified what they'll do. I suppose they'll threaten us with destruction. This yacht has no weapons that will help us in a ship-to-ship battle. All we have are dirt-side weapons."

"They're useless if that ship blasts us out of existence. But if we can get them to board us, we might be able to capture some of them and use them as hostages in negotiations."

"Do we cut our engines?"

"We seem to have no choice."

"Does that mean yes?"

"Of course it means yes," he said angrily.

"I'll go give the order."

"You do that," he said as he began to pace around the luxurious stateroom trying to figure a way out, but he knew he had no real options. He would have to allow them to board the yacht. He had thought that no one would ever dare question a luxury yacht in Clidepp space. He decided that his best response would be to play the role he knew so well, that of a rich dilettante who was merely out for a cruise in his birthday present. As he paced, he worked to immerse his mind in the persona he was attempting to portray.

"We've stopped," the ship's captain reported via intercom. "Now they're saying we must go over to them rather than them boarding us."

"They don't want to search our ship for contraband? That's unusual. Have they identified themselves yet?"

"No. They say they will tell us where to take our shuttle once we leave the ship."

"So they haven't identified me by name?"

"No."

"That probably means they don't know who they've stopped. Okay, tell them our shuttle only carries two. Tell them they'll have to pick us up if they want all of us to come to their ship."

A few seconds later the ship's captain called again and said, "They say to send over our two top people. And they added that if our shuttle suddenly develops problems during launching, we should get into escape pods and eject because they're going to destroy the ship."

"So they're willing to play rough— unless it's all bravado. Okay, tell them we'll be over just as quickly as we can launch our shuttle."

◆　◆　◆

"What appears to be a shuttle has been launched from a bay on the starboard side of the ship, Captain," the Tac officer said.

"Com, give them a course heading to the *Justice*."

"Aye, Captain, sending them the course on the same RF frequency we've been using," the com chief said. A few seconds later, he added, "They acknowledge receipt of the course heading."

"The shuttle is headed directly towards us," the Tac officer said.

"Com, when they reach us, direct them to the larboard, upper airlock amidship."

"Aye, Captain."

As Sydnee stood up she said, "Lt. Templeton I need you at the Tac station, so although you are next in the rotation, Lt. Olivetti will take command while I'm off the bridge."

"Aye, Captain," Templeton said.

"Com, notify the Marine mess hall staff I need the room for conducting interviews. Inform the senior Marine non-com on duty that I need an armed Marine fire-team at the airlock to escort our *visitors* to the mess hall. The visitors are to be considered armed and dangerous, so I want them checked for weapons as soon as they're aboard. Also, any electronic gear should be confiscated. Their images are to be recorded as they enter the ship and checked against our Space Command facial recognition database during the interviews. I will interview the senior member first while the other one is kept isolated in a separate area. Once I start the first interview, the visitors are not to be allowed voice contact or even eye contact with one another until both have been interviewed. I also want the Marines to prepare two storage lockers to serve as brig cells. Nothing elaborate or large. And extend an invitation to Colonel Dennier to attend the interviews."

"Aye, Captain."

Turning to where Galli was sitting at the engineering console, Sydnee said, "Lt. Galli, once our visitors have been escorted below deck, have your people check the shuttle for weapons and explosives. Then collect all the fingerprints you can find on board. I want to compare the prints of everyone who has been in that shuttle lately with the fingerprints we have on file for persons wanted by the Yolongi government."

"Aye, Captain."

Having completed making her arrangements, Sydnee left the bridge and walked down to the mess hall to await the visitors.

◆

Some twenty minutes later, as Sydnee and Dennier sat at a table in silence, a Marine non-com stuck his head into the mess hall and said, "The visitors are here, Captain."

"Send the senior person in, Staff Sergeant."

"Yes, Ma'am."

As the Marine non-com withdrew, a Yolongi appeared in the doorway and entered the room. Sydnee gestured to a chair across from her and Colonel Dennier.

"State your name for the record," Sydnee said.

"I'm Eroclis Sleeques, the captain of the *Bluqcols*."

"Who was right?"

"What?"

"Who was right?"

"I don't know what you mean."

Sydnee touched a point on the viewpad in front of her and the words of the man calling himself Eroclis Sleeques issued from a speaker overhead in Yolongi. The translation to Amer was, "He was right."

"That was you," Sydnee said as she stared at the man. "It was recorded as you entered this ship."

"Uh, uh, I uh, was referring to my helmsman. He said that you were probably GA."

"Really? Your helmsman?"

"Yes."

"We told you we wanted the two top people to come here. Where is your boss? Why did he send you?"

"I'm the most senior person aboard the ship."

"You own it?"

"Uh, no. I'm just the captain."

"Well, I wanted to see the owner."

"Uh, he's on Yolongus."

"Then why are you out here? Shouldn't you be waiting for him on Yolongus?"

"He was afraid that if the authorities saw the yacht sitting on the ground, they might decide to confiscate it for their own use. Private property means nothing to them. He'll contact us when we should pick him up."

"How many crewmen are aboard the *Bluqcols*?"

"Seventeen."

"Seventeen? That's a lot of people for such a small ship."

"Well, they're not all bridge personnel and engineers. We have two cooks, four attendants, and two maids."

"And what contraband are you carrying?"

"We're carrying nothing that concerns the GA. You have no right to stop us or board us. This is not your nation, so such an act is considered piracy."

"So call me a pirate. Now, what contraband will we find when we search the *Bluqcols*?"

"None. And if you intend to board my ship, why did you insist I come over here first?"

"Simple. Now there are two fewer fools we'll have to kill when we board your ship because you'll be here in our brig rather than facing us with light weapons."

"You cannot board my ship," Sleeques screamed. "I'll have you arrested if you do."

Sydnee touched a couple of points on her viewpad and then asked calmly, "Do you have a brother?"

"What?"

"It's a simple question. Do you have a brother?"

"What business is that of yours?"

"I was just wondering," she said as she turned the viewpad so Sleeques could see the face, "because this individual looks amazingly like you. In fact, our computer says there's a 99.99% chance it *is* you. And we can make that 100% simply by taking your fingerprints."

Sleeques looked at the image and went pale as his mouth dropped slightly open. It was from an old reward poster from when he had escaped custody while being transported to prison on a gunrunning conviction. He couldn't believe the GA had a copy of that old poster on file.

"But I don't think we have to retake your fingerprints here again. By now my Marines have entered your shuttle and made copies of all the fingerprints found in there. I see your name is really Rodhrer Blethque. And your companion is Wydteep Hliprez, who *also* happens to be wanted by the Yolongi authorities for gunrunning. Uh, do you still want to contact the Yolongi government and prefer charges of piracy against me?"

Blethque scowled at Sydnee but said nothing.

"I thought not. So let's stop playing games. Who is the top person aboard that ship?"

"I am the top person currently aboard that ship."

"So you're not tired of playing games yet?" Sydnee said as she pressed several contact points on her viewpad.

A second later the door opened and the Staff Sergeant looked in questioningly.

"Staff Sergeant, is the other person secured somewhere other than the corridor?"

"Yes, Captain. We have him totally isolated and under guard in a food storage locker."

Sydnee smiled. "It must be kind of tight in there."

"Yes, ma'am. We managed to squeeze him in, although it was a bit difficult closing the door. Secure places where he could wait and not see or hear anything were limited because of all the provisions we picked up recently. We probably shouldn't leave him in there too long because it's bitterly cold."

"Take our friend here and put him into one of the prepared brig cells. He'll be remaining with us for a while."

"You can't hold me," Blethque screamed. "I'm a Yolongi citizen."

"We're only doing what the Yolongi will do when we turn you over to them."

"Turn me over? Captain, please, you can't turn me over to them. They'll kill me. I escaped custody once, and escapees are automatically beheaded when recaptured. You and I are on the same side. I'm part of the Rebel cause, trying to rid this nation of its ruthless dictators."

"We're not on the same side, Mr. Blethque. There are more than two sides in this particular game. Take him away, Staff Sergeant."

The Staff Sergeant had to pick Blethque up bodily and carry him away. Blethque screamed insults about Space Command, which echoed in the corridor until he was too far away to be heard.

"An escaped gunrunner? That might be someone the Qummuc would pursue vigorously," Dennier said.

"Yes, but I want whoever he's protecting."

"You really think there's someone higher up still on that yacht?"

"Yes. Possibly more than one. He said he's part of the Rebel movement, and while Blethque might be a good little Rebel soldier, he's certainly no mastermind. I want the person who pulls his strings."

"He said there's fifteen more still aboard that yacht, but I'd bet on twice that many."

"So would I. If that ship is being used by the Rebels to run guns, there might be fifteen support people, but there has to be at least a dozen Rebel soldiers aboard as well. The problem is that we'll run into massive fire if we attempt to board the ship."

"You have personal armor."

"Yes, we do. So the only thing we have to worry about personally is RPGs. The armor won't protect us from them. The second concern is capturing the top person without him or her being killed during a gunfight. The value to us falls by fifty percent if the person is dead."

"Who do you think he or she is?"

"I have no idea what their name might be but I'm hoping they're as high up the chain of command as a battalion commander. They're certainly not going to give that kind of yacht to a lieutenant."

"Why not? Space Command gave command of the *Justice* to a lieutenant(jg)."

Sydnee calmly stared at Dennier for several seconds before responding. "Yes, they did. And I've regretted accepting this mission ever since they altered it and expanded the mission to include seeding satellites throughout Clidepp space. And perhaps because of the actions I've taken to carry out my orders, this is the very last time a lieutenant(jg) will ever be entrusted with a mission this big and this important. So I'm going to do all the good I can while I *am* in command. And if the Admiralty Board wants to rescind my promotion, that's certainly within their power. I just hope I'm not kicked out of the service or jailed."

"Promotion? What promotion?"

"Oh, I haven't announced that. I've been notified that the Admiralty Board has approved early promotion for me to O-3, and that I've been promoted into a vacant position aboard the *Denver*."

"Congratulations, Lieutenant. But— you're out of uniform."

"I haven't wanted to distract anyone from their job. There's plenty of time to change my rank insignia when we get back. In the meantime, as the duly appointed captain of this ship, I'm already the senior officer. Of course, they might break me back to ensign when we return with a thousand former slaves and a ship still full of satellites."

"They won't if they're smart. You're too good."

"Thank you, Colonel, but I may have been too smart for my own good this time. If the Clidepp Empire declares war on the GA because of my actions, nothing can save me."

"Then we'll just have to make sure your plan to divert blame and draw the Qummuc forces away from the embassy is successful. What's next?"

Putting up an image of the shuttle interior taken by the engineering staff during their inspection, Sydnee asked, "How many Marines in armor do you think our new shuttle can hold, Colonel? Someone aboard the yacht said it could only accommodate two, but that's certainly not true. They were obviously trying to get us to come to them."

Looking at the image on the large wall monitor, Dennier said, "It looks kind of small. Perhaps six, including the pilots."

"Six of our people in personal armor should be able to take two dozen Rebels with light weapons, although I wish Blade and his people were here."

"The people aboard the yacht may or may not be Rebels," Dennier said.

"True. All we have is Blethque's statement to that effect."

"And he might have been trying to win sympathy for his release."

"Yes, that's possible. Let's interview the other one and then see where we stand."

When the second man was brought into the mess hall, Sydnee gestured to the chair and said, "Have a seat, Mr. Hliprez."

"My name's not Hliprez. It's Aklerroz. Stasif Aklerroz."

"And I'm Gustallo Plelillo, the Prime Minister of the Clidepp Empire. How do you do?"

Hliprez just stared at her as he settled into the chair.

"We know your real name because your associate, Mr. Sleeques, gave you up in return for his freedom and identified you as an escaped prisoner convicted of gunrunning. He's on his way back to the *Bluqcols* in his shuttle."

"You lie. Rodhrer would never do that."

"Who's Rodhrer?"

"Uh, I meant Eroclis. Rodhrer is another member of the crew."

"I see. I assume by that lie, and by your reluctance to admit your real name, you're not going to be truthful with us. Is that correct?"

Hliprez just stared at her.

"No response? You have nothing to say?"

When Hliprez continued his silence, Sydnee summoned the Staff Sergeant waiting in the corridor.

"Staff Sergeant, put this liar in the other prepared brig cell. We'll dispose of their bodies later."

"What?" Hliprez said. "You can't kill me. I've done nothing."

Sydnee turned her viewpad towards Hliprez so he could see the image from the wanted notice. "The GA and the Clidepp nations have a decades-old pact to share information about wanted felons and escaped prisoners. We know who you and Mr. Blethque are, what crimes you've been convicted of, and the details of your escape from custody. When you and Mr. Blethque exited your shuttle, my people moved in and collected all the fingerprints they found on the flight deck and in the rear cabin. We've identified six different individuals. Yours and Mr. Blethque's fingerprints and images just happen to match those associated with wanted posters we have on file. Since neither of you will cooperate, we'll just save the Empire the effort of cutting off your head."

"You can't do this. You're not the police. You're not even supposed to be in Clidepp space."

"Take him away, Staff Sergeant."

After the Yolongi was gone, Dennier asked, "Are they going to see the package?"

"No. A special holding area cell was created for the package because he isn't guilty of the acts he was originally accused of. He actually has a lot of creature comforts compared to the barren lockers where Blethque and Hliprez will be housed. In fact, his quarters are four times larger than my office and bunk area combined."

"What now?"

"As the old expression goes, it's time to stoke the fire and fan the flames."

◆ ◆

"This is the *Bluqcols*," Sydnee heard through the overhead speaker on the bridge when she attempted to make contact with the yacht.

"I told you to send your two top people. Did you really think we'd be fooled by your sending two stooges posing as leaders?"

"Where are our men?"

"They're in my brig because they refused to stop lying to me, even after I showed them the outstanding wanted posters on them."

"Wanted posters. Who *are* you?"

"I'm the captain of the warship that's going to start blowing holes in *your* little ship unless you start cooperating."

"Stand by, Captain."

Several minutes later, Sydnee heard, "Captain, who do you represent?"

"Are you the top person aboard that ship?" Sydnee asked.

"I am the owner. Now, who are you?"

"I'm the top person aboard *this* ship."

"And your name is?"

"I'm Captain Bonny. Captain Anne Bonny."

"Well, Captain Bonny, what can I do for you?"

"You can get into a shuttle and come over to my ship so we can talk face to face."

"And why would I want to do that?"

"You may not want to do it, but if you don't do it, I'm going to start blowing holes in your pretty yacht. How good are you at breathing vacuum?"

"Not very."

"Then it behooves you to comply."

"I cannot. You have my only shuttle."

"I'll send it to pick you up. One warning though— and one is all you get— if you don't come quietly, I'll destroy your ship so fast you and your people won't know what hit them."

"That doesn't sound like a very courteous invitation."

"Our courtesy ended when you tried to play me for a fool."

"I sent two of my most reliable people to function as representatives."

"That's not what I specified, and you know it. Your so-called reliable representatives lied and misrepresented themselves from the moment they arrived here."

"Regardless, I'm willing to meet with you now."

"Fine. Be ready. I'm sending the shuttle. Bonny, out."

"Bonny, Captain?" Lt.(jg) Templeton queried after the connection ended.

"Anne Bonny was a famous female pirate captain on Earth in the eighteenth century. She was an Irish woman who married a pirate named Bonny and joined him on his raids. She was only active for a few years because women rarely reached positions of authority on ships back then. Her ship was captured after the crew got drunk following a successful attack. After being tried, she was sentenced to be hanged, but she said she was pregnant. Back then they simply took the word of any woman who declared that, and the court issued a temporary stay until after she delivered. That's where the official story ends. There's no record of her execution or her escape. But it's generally assumed she got away and lived to a ripe old age."

"I see. I thought you may have been referring to Bonnie and Clyde, the famous bank robbers."

"Not this time," she said with a smile, "but who knows how many other names of famous criminals I'll use before we get out of Clidepp space."

CHAPTER TWENTY
~ April 7th, 2287 ~

Sydnee sent one pilot and two Marines, all in personal armor, to retrieve the yacht's alleged owner. On the return trip, the pilot reported in using a pre-arranged code phrase to show all was well and that they were in control.

Sydnee and Dennier were again sitting in the mess hall when the visitor from the *Bluqcols* was brought there. Sydnee looked up, pointed to the chair across the table, and then returned her gaze to the viewpad she was holding.

"Where are my men?" The visitor asked as he sat down.

"Under lock and key. They're learning it's not wise to lie to me. We knew their real names before they were even brought in here to be interviewed."

"You're Captain Bonny, I presume," the visitor said.

"I am. Who are you?"

"I'm Aderses Plelillo."

Sydnee stopped what she was doing and looked up.

"You recognize the name, I see."

Sydnee returned her gaze to the viewpad and keyed in the name, then touched the search contact point. Immediately a picture of Aderses Plelillo appeared on the viewpad. He was a few years younger in the photo, but it was almost definitely him.

"Yes, I do. I doubt that anyone in Clidepp space wouldn't recognize the name of the youngest son of the Prime Minister."

"So now you understand why I sent two of my men rather than coming myself. A pirate could claim a huge ransom fee for me. I didn't know you were GA.

"But you suspected it."

245

Plelillo said nothing.

"I know this because Blethque uttered the words, 'He was right,' as he entered the ship and saw the uniforms. He tried to deny it later, but he's a poor liar. I'm sure you could have done better for a chief aide."

"What are you doing here, Captain? I mean, what are you doing in Clidepp Space? I'm sure my father didn't invite the GA to come here and track down his missing son."

"Are you missing?"

"I know where I am."

"But your father doesn't."

"I don't always tell my father everything. For example, if you let me and my people go, I promise not to tell him that Space Command is operating in Clidepp space."

"That's not much of a deal. Other than the three of you who have come aboard, no one knows we're Space Command."

"My staff knows you're GA."

"I'd say 'suspects' is a more accurate term. The GA has been concerned for some time that things were getting out of hand here, and we've already seen indications of mass refugee relocations and ships of refugees headed towards GA space. Your civilian ships are so slow it will take years before it significantly impacts us, but it *will* impact us at some point. So we occasionally send ships to take a look at the situation and report back to Space Command."

"Ships such as this one? Black ships that cannot be detected on radar? Ships that can fly circles around anything the Clidepp Empire has in their fleet?"

"Yes."

"So we'd never even know you were out here— watching?"

"Yes."

"And you were responsible for the attack on the city. That's why no one saw anything."

"Yes."

"Uh, Captain?" Dennier said.

"It's okay, Colonel. I'm not telling Mr. Plelillo anything his father doesn't already suspect. That's why the Qummuc APCs are encircling the embassy."

"A damned waste of time. Everyone knows the GA embassy is deserted, except for a few caretakers," Plelillo said arrogantly, before the realization struck him. With awe, he said, "It's not deserted, is it? That's what all this is about. You want something to trade for whoever is in the embassy. And I'm the prize you've been searching for. You believe my father would do anything, pay any price, to get his youngest son back."

"In all honesty, I didn't know who was aboard that yacht. I suspected it was being used for gunrunning. But it seems I've landed a far bigger fish than I'd even dared hope." Touching a contact point on her viewpad, the door opened and the Marine noncom stuck his head in. "Staff Sergeant, give our visitor a separate accommodation near that of his friends."

"Captain, if you let me go, I can make you wealthier than you've ever imagined," Plelillo said as the Staff Sergeant helped him stand.

"What would I do with money? There never seems to be anyplace to spend it here in Clidepp space."

"I could give you enough to buy your own planet if you'll let me go."

"Take him away, Staff Sergeant."

After they were gone, Dennier said, "Congratulations, Captain. You've got your big fish, or perhaps I should say your golden goose. The Prime Minister will probably do anything to get his son back. You can spread some rumors that his son is being held in a house outside the capital and he'll send every Qummuc APC to rescue him. We'll be able to recover our people now."

"Perhaps," Sydnee said.

As Sydnee headed for her office, she took a side trip to where the three Yolongi were now imprisoned in three storage lockers. The ship's stores that had been stowed in the two-meter-by-two-meter lockers had been added to the stacks along the corridor wall. A Marine PFC and the Marine Staff Sergeant who had jailed the three Yolongi braced to attention when they saw her approaching.

"Staff Sergeant, I'm making you personally responsible for these three prisoners. They are not to have any contact with each other or anyone other than the people assigned to guard them. Your people are not to converse with them or update them on any issues. They are not to be released from these temporary brigs except by my express orders, and there must always be two guards present when any of the doors are unlocked."

"Yes, ma'am. Uh, it's going to get a little messy in there."

"Give them water, buckets, wash cloths, and basic bedding. I don't know how long they're going to be with us, but while they are, they're to get a change of clothes every three days. Their meals will be delivered here. Also, I want a complete blackout on their presence in this brig. You are not to talk with your fellow Marines regarding the prisoners or discuss the prisoners with other members of the crew. If anyone has any questions, refer them to me, and report anyone who tries to get you to discuss the presence, status, or intended disposition of the three prisoners after being made aware that the topic is not open to discussion."

"Yes, ma'am."

"Any questions?"

"No, ma'am."

"Carry on, Staff Sergeant."

◆ ◆ ◆

"What do you mean there's no response from Bonny?" The captain of the *Bluqcols* screamed at the com operator. "Try again."

"I've been trying every two minutes for the past hour. Captain Bonny just isn't responding."

"Dammit. I'm tired of waiting. Helm, follow the same heading the shuttle took."

"Aye, Captain. What speed?"

"Maximum sub-light."

"Aye, sir."

Some five minutes later, the yacht was circling the area where the shuttle was sitting, but there were no other ships there.

"There's nothing here except the shuttle, Captain," the first officer said.

"I can see that, dammit. Recover the shuttle and see if he's inside."

"If he was inside, he'd have contacted us already."

"Just do as you're told, dammit."

"Aye, Captain."

Under his breath he said, "How am I ever going to explain losing the Prime Minister's son? I'm a dead man."

◆ ◆ ◆

As the *Justice* resumed its usual place on station in the solar system, everyone on the bridge was aware that Sydnee was a woman filled with inner turmoil. She continually stared at the large monitor at the front of the bridge with unseeing eyes as the prevailing burdens of command consumed all of her thoughts. It was at times such as this that she most missed not having someone in whom she could confide. Having returned with Blade to get the slaves left at the embassy, Lt. MacDonald was in the embassy bunker with everyone else who had been part of that operation. Blade, often a bit brusque and outspoken but almost always honest, probably would have made a good sounding board in a discussion of her present dilemma, but he was also at the embassy. And Sydnee had never developed the kind of relationship with Dennier that she needed right then. That was most likely owed to the large discrepancy in rank. And although surrounded by crewmembers she considered friends, her circle of confidants had to remain small with regard to shipboard matters because she was the superior officer aboard ship and couldn't afford to appear weak and indecisive.

After sitting on the bridge for over an hour, she turned command over to Lt.(jg) Templeton and walked to her quarters. But rather than sitting at her desk, she climbed onto her bunk and stared at the overhead as she continued to weigh and then discard options for recovering the people at the embassy.

Sydnee was brought back from her preoccupations when she received a call from the com chief via her CT.

"Captain, we've intercepted an encrypted message on the special frequency we've been using for ship-to-ship communications since we arrived here in the Yolongus star system. It's addressed to SM. I'm assuming that might mean you."

"Send it to my queue, Chief. Marcola, out."

The message appeared in her queue a second later. It was definitely encrypted and appeared as a jumbled mass of symbols and weird characters. The only thing perfectly clear was the letters SM at the top and WC at the bottom. Sydnee was quite sure those initials didn't stand for 'water closet,' but they might stand for Winston Cornwallis.

"Computer, show me the message after applying the first encryption algorithm in the file area assigned to Winston."

The image changed but appeared just as jumbled and unintelligible.

"The message is displayed," the computer said.

"Show me the message using the next encryption algorithm."

"The message is displayed," the computer said as the confused mess seemed to get even more confused.

"Show me the message using the next encryption algorithm."

"The message is displayed."

"That's the one, computer. Leave that message up."

The message on the computer monitor read 'At home friend An/Knife.'

Sydnee assumed the message meant that Winston had made it to the home of the Aleoxlene Reqoppl member where Anese and Blade had gone seeking information. For her response, she decided to use another new name for herself so it couldn't be tied to the ones she had used previously. She would use the first four letters of her last name, with the letter 'y' appended. She would use the same name alteration for Winston.

After entering her own message that read, 'If Corny, send agreed codeword to verify. Marcy,' she used the same algorithm from Winston's file that Winston had used for his message. She then ordered the com chief to transmit the response on the same frequency.

A few minutes later, she received another message. After decryption it read, 'No code agreed. Capital you?'

Winston had never established a secret codeword for communications, but Sydnee believed that if he were being coerced by someone, he would know enough to transmit some made-up word. If he had done so, it would tell her he was being forced to send the message. That he acknowledged no codeword had been established and there was no hesitation in the response meant the sender really was Winston and that he most probably had no one forcing him to send the messages.

Sydnee sent, 'Correct twice. Marcy.'

The returned message read, 'Pickup avail?'

'Not now. Stay low. Will come. Marcy.'

'Waiting for Marcy' was the final reply.

Sydnee leaned back in her chair. It was wonderful that Winston was alive and currently safe, but it added another layer to her problems. In addition to recovering the people from the embassy and dropping the package off, they now had to recover Winston as well. If Sydnee had a shuttle at her disposal, she would send someone immediately, but since all four of her shuttles were parked in the underground bay beneath the embassy, Winston would have to wait until Sydnee had one to send. Hopefully, he would remain safe until they could get to him.

◆ ◆ ◆

Six days after arriving back on station, Colonel Dennier showed up at Sydnee's office. After being admitted, she sat down in one of the chairs without being invited to sit, but her superior rank entitled her to take such liberties.

"Captain, I was wondering if you had formulated a plan for recovering the people from the embassy now that you have an ace in the hole."

"Lately, I've done little else other than weigh alternative options for recovering our people."

"So you have a plan?"

"We can recover our people any time we want, but recovering them without providing proof to the Clidepp Triumvirate that we were behind the attack on the capital city is the problem."

"But what about Plelillo's son? I thought the whole idea in capturing him was to recover our people."

"I had expected to find some arch criminal that we could use to distract the Qummuc. I certainly never expected to find the Prime Minister's son aboard that yacht. My problem is I don't believe the Prime Minister would pull the APCs away from the compound if we attempt some sort of ransom plot. He'd want to keep it as quiet as possible, not send in all the forces at his disposal. And besides, for any kidnapping plot to work, we'd need a shuttle. We seem to be fresh out of shuttles at present."

"It's too bad this ship doesn't have a shuttle bay. We could have used that shuttle from the yacht."

"It wasn't Dakinium-sheathed. That's what's allowed us to penetrate the Clidepp Fleet defenses without alerting them to our presence."

"We could have pretended to be the *Patoosch*."

"After the attack, the Clidepp Fleet initiated a password system. We've noticed that each time the *Patoosch* has returned to the planet and requested permission to land, they've used a different code. I haven't tried to figure out the system they use for establishing the pass code, but it's probably complex and might even be something that's determined before the shuttle leaves the planet and heads home to the mining colony."

"We have the fighters. They're Dakinium-sheathed."

"Yes, but they hold the pilot, the weapons, the engines, and nothing else. There's no second seat in the SF4s."

"So what you're saying is that there's nothing we can do?"

"No, I'm not saying that at all. We do have one option."

"Which is?"

"Another attack on the planet. If we make it appear the new attack is the first step in a coordinated landing and incursion operation by Rebel forces, the APCs might forget about the embassy area and rush to where a landing by phantom Rebel ships seems most imminent."

"Phantom ships?"

"That's the way the press on Yolongus has been describing the Wing because no one saw or heard anything except the explosions. And the government seems intent on blaming the attack on the Rebels— at least publicly."

"Phantom ships. I like that. Perhaps we'll change our Wing designation to the Phantom Squadron. Too bad we can't paint an image of a specter somewhere on our ships."

"Yes, but that could increase your visibility during stealth operations."

"So where and when do we attack?"

"I'm still deciding that. I would like to avoid hurting any civilians. Casualties during the last attack were light because of the targets and the time of day, except at the secret police interrogation facilities and the slavery pens."

"Fanatical, decapitating scum who have no respect for the lives of others don't deserve any special considerations for themselves. They certainly don't extend respect to any of the innocent victims they behead."

"Yes, and I have no qualms about exterminating any members of similar rabid murderous groups we might encounter in the future."

"So where do we hit the planet?"

"When Admiral Carver attacked the Milori home world, she targeted munitions factories and telecommunication facilities first. Civilians are frequently used to make munitions and we're not at war with the Clidepp Empire, so I'm leaning towards limiting the attacks to communications facilities, which are often isolated towers."

Colonel Dennier nodded. "That sounds like a good strategy. The capital city will then be silent as well as dark. But how does that draw the APCs away from the embassy?"

"We'll also have to hit the homes of the three Triumvirate members. Or at least hit their compounds. According to the damage assessment photos taken during your attack, each of their compounds never lost power. So they obviously have their own emergency generators. Usually, emergency generators are away from the house because of the engine noise. I want to put the Triumvirate in the dark and let them have a taste of what the city is enduring."

Dennier smiled before saying, "I'm sure they'll have replacement generators at their homes before the next evening."

"Yes, but I think the initial fear for their own safety may get them to react by immediately repositioning all available military and police resources around their own compounds. Especially if they believe the Rebels are massing for a ground assault with their capture as one of the prime objectives. We only need their attention to be focused somewhere other than our embassy for a few minutes. Our shuttles can launch in complete darkness, and by restricting their escape to oh-gee engines until they're in the upper atmosphere, no one should ever hear or see a thing. It'll be a real tight squeeze inside the four shuttles, but we should be able to recover everyone in one trip."

"It sounds like a plan. All we need is a date and time. When do we shove off?"

"First we have to identify all of the communication system locations in and around the capital. Then I have to coordinate the attack with the Major. I'll set a date and time after we complete those tasks."

"Are you going to release Plelillo's son now?"

"Not just yet. He's fine where he is. It's not the luxury accommodations he had on the yacht, but he's fed three times a day and has plenty of time to relax and plot his escape."

"Plot his escape?"

"Wouldn't you if you were in his situation? It's impossible of course, but that's what prisoners do."

"But he's an innocent civilian."

"Civilian? Yes. Innocent? Not so much. He or someone on his yacht spent most of the previous day communicating with someone— perhaps many someones— on the planet rather than returning to Yolongus and contacting them from there. And the two top *representatives* he sent to meet with us are escaped fugitives convicted of gunrunning. There's a lot more to this than just an innocent playboy enjoying his daddy's wealth. Don't worry, Colonel. He'll be released at the appropriate time. That's all I can promise right now."

◆ ◆ ◆

It took several days to firmly identify all of the potential targets in and around the capital from old maps, surveillance photos, and computer records. The first priority was the military communication locations, followed by the secret police communication facilities, and then the civilian broadcasting stations, antennas, and towers. Lastly, the fighters would take down all remaining cell and microwave towers. Sydnee prepared a message to Blade in which she laid out the plan and proposed a specific date. The time of day would be three hours before dawn. She decided that time would find the most people still in their beds.

After the transmission was recorded and condensed to burst mode, it was sent. A reply came sooner than expected.

"Captain," Blade said, "we can't adhere to the schedule you propose. I haven't reported this because I didn't feel it was that important in the grand scheme, but since arriving here, we've had two births. Also, there are six more women with child who are within thirty days of delivery. The midwives tell me that the trip to the *Justice* would be dangerous for both the mothers and the babies. We can only follow your plan if we leave the pregnant women and two of the midwives here in the embassy. What are your thoughts on this? Blade."

After watching the vid message, Sydnee hung her head and sighed. She hadn't thought about the pregnancy issues when planning the attack. She should have because there had been eighteen births aboard the *Justice* since they had begun bringing former slaves to the ship. It had even been necessary to set aside an area as a nursery inside the overcrowded habitat container. The ship's engineers, with the help of the Marines, had walled off an area for that purpose so crying babies wouldn't keep the rest of the group awake at night.

The *Justice* presently had enough food to feed everyone for months, but if they remained where they were until all the pregnant women at the embassy reached full term, they could run out of food again. The number of people at the embassy meant that it was going to be standing room only in all four shuttles if they attempted to take everyone to the *Justice* in one trip, and that was not the kind of trip a pregnant woman near the end of her pregnancy could make, or should be asked to make.

But a second, later trip to recover those women from the embassy might not be possible. They had seemingly fooled the Yolongi Triumvirate once, and the second attack might fool them again, but the odds of getting away unscathed a third time dropped substantially. She didn't doubt they could execute a successful third attack with little or no damage to the ships or people. Their equipment and advanced technology almost guaranteed that. But it might be the final straw that, even without proof positive a GA ship was responsible, might drive the Triumvirate to declare a state of war with the GA.

And that could end Sydnee's career. She had told Dennier she intended to do all the good she could while in command of the *Justice,* but she knew she could do a lot more good if she didn't lose command or possibly even be dishonorably discharged from Space Command. Lieutenant Milton had once told her while they were still aboard the *Perry,* 'Don't never do no wrong'. She was about to break that cardinal rule for the second time. *But if it seems so right, how can it be wrong?* she thought.

Sydnee took a deep breath and released it slowly as she thought about the pregnant women at the embassy who were unable to make the flight to the *Justice* until after their children were born. "Two steps forward and three steps back," she said as she shook her head very slightly.

Sydnee allowed herself a full day to consider and reconsider all the options before making a final decision. There were no completely right answers because all possible solutions required sacrifices.

When Sydnee sat down to record the message to Blade, it was with a heavy heart. She composed herself, trying to appear strong and confident, then touched the record button and issued her orders.

"Sierra-Leader, we cannot delay until all women reach full term and deliver their children. I imagine other women are pregnant but are not yet at risk for such travel as will be required under the present circumstances. The Yolongi were heavily involved in breeding programs to provide a never-ending supply of Terran slaves. It's better that we recover the women who are not yet at risk or we could be delaying the recovery for many months. That's time we certainly don't have.

"The women who are unable to travel should remain in the embassy. If an insufficient number of midwives volunteer to remain behind, you will select those who must stay. The women who must remain behind are far safer than they ever would have been in Sanctuary. They'll have all the food they require, and they're well beyond the reach of the Yolongi.

They must remain in the bunker until another ship arrives to transport them to GA space.

"Provide a suggested timetable using the previously provided requirements. Juliet-Leader."

CHAPTER TWENTY-ONE
~ April 18th, 2287 ~

Working with Colonel Dennier and Lt.(jg) Templeton, Sydnee created an attack plan for the Wing. If successful, the attack would cripple communications in the capital for days, if not longer. Since few broadcast towers should be undergoing construction or maintenance in the very wee hours of the morning, any loss of civilian life should be minimal. Everything in the plan was intended to make the attack look like a prelude to a full invasion by— someone. An hour before the SF4 attacks commenced, a burst of encrypted messages would be directed towards the planet from the eight SCI satellites previously placed into orbit. Because the tiny satellites were sheathed in Dakinium, neither the Clidepp Fleet nor the Yolongi military would be able to identify the origination point of the messages, so they should logically assume there were at least eight hostile ships approaching the planet. The encryption algorithm was intentionally weak so it would be easy to crack very quickly. When the message was decrypted, the code-breakers would be able to read Rebel orders in the Yolongi language that outlined their plans to seize the three Triumvirate leaders at their estate compounds and occupy all main government buildings, although no attack times were included. With luck, when the first communication towers began to fall, the Qummuc APCs around the embassy would be ordered to leave their positions and rush to key defensive locations around the city, including the estate compound of the Prime Minister.

At the embassy, the shuttles would complete loading just as the first air strikes began. The hold beneath the passenger compartment was already loaded with as much food as it could contain. The emergency food supplies remaining at the embassy were a thousand times more than sufficient to feed the women unable to make the trip and their progeny for as long as they had to remain there, although Sydnee didn't believe the women would be there for a period approaching even five years. At least not if she could do anything to prevent that from happening. And by not risking travel in a cramped shuttle, the pregnant women would be far better off.

Blade had positioned some of his Special Ops people on the second floor of the embassy. Their assignment was to watch the APCs and make sure every single one left when the air attack began.

◆ ◆

The Wing left the *Justice* right on schedule and flew to their attack positions. The Clidepp fleet should have been on alert but seemed to be asleep as the fighters used the planet's umbra to help mask their approach and atmospheric entry. When everyone was positioned, Colonel Dennier issued the order to commence their attack runs. Within minutes, communication towers were toppling and crashing to the ground following brilliant explosions at their bases. All over and around the city, communications came to a near halt. Only landline and ground-level line-of-sight communications remained in use.

The *Justice* received an encrypted message from Colonel Dennier as the Wing left the planet behind. It contained just two words— 'mission complete.' A few minutes later, the *Justice* received another encrypted message. The later message was from Blade. It was almost as simple as the first message, but not as positive. It read— 'No movement, preparing to stand down.' The message meant that the APCs hadn't been ordered to abandon their vigil at the embassy compound and that the people aboard the shuttles would soon disembark and return to their beds.

◆ ◆

"They didn't fall for it," Sydnee said to Dennier as the two women talked in the captain's small office.

"That doesn't make sense. Could there be a spy in our midst passing information to the Triumvirate's secret police?"

"That doesn't seem very likely. The Dakinium sheathing guarantees that the only communications possible from this ship must go through our bridge communication system, so any outgoing messages would have to be sent by our com chiefs. And the embassy is fully shielded to prevent eaves-dropping, which also blocks outgoing signals not sent from the communications center. The only people allowed outside the bunker are Blade's Special Ops people. I suppose one of them could potentially transmit a message from the roof of the embassy, but that's unlikely in the extreme."

"So why didn't the plan work?"

"I wish I knew," Sydnee said. "Perhaps one of the Yolongi caretakers is a government spy or informant. Or perhaps we're not as clever as we think we are. The question is: where do we go from here?"

"Well, summing it up once again, we know that if the people at the embassy simply ignore the APCs, leaving the embassy will reveal the presence of DS shuttles there, and that means alerting the Triumvirate to the fact that we had landed in the embassy compound with ships they can't detect. That would then lead them to believe that the raids had been carried out by GA ships because we were also black and unde-tectable. I agree that we absolutely cannot allow that to happen. So, it will be far better to leave the people at the embassy where they're safe and head back to the GA. As you've said, we can't remain here for more than a few more months or we'll run out of food *again*."

"Yes, but I hate to leave people behind, even though I know they're safe and well provisioned."

"That's an admirable quality, but right now you need to think about the welfare of the almost one thousand slaves and crew we have crammed into the *Justice*. The Marines at the embassy will watch over the two hundred five slaves and their children. They'll be fine until we get back."

"You're assuming we'll be allowed to come back."

"You don't think we will?"

"We can't take anything for granted. We're operating undercover in hostile space, and we shouldn't really even be here now. And when you factor in that I may be responsible for starting a war between nations, nothing is certain. I might be sent to a ground base somewhere for the rest of my Space Command career. If there was another *Perry* around, that might have been my next destination and my final ship posting."

Dennier smiled. "I'd almost forgotten you were posted aboard the *Perry*. What did you do to earn that ship assignment, by the way?"

Sydnee hesitated before responding, but then decided to tell her. She took a deep breath and then released it before saying, "It was my first posting following graduation from the Warship Command Institute."

"That must be some kind of record. What did you do, kick the Institute Commandant high up between his legs?"

"No. I've since been told it was a clerical mix-up. Someone with a similar name, which appeared right next to mine on the Institute's Class Roll, received my intended posting aboard Admiral Carver's battleship in Region Two. I was sent to *his* intended posting aboard the *Perry*. But I don't regret my time there at all. I made a lot of great friends and I learned a great deal. Mostly I learned that many of the crew on the *Perry* didn't belong aboard a ship that had a reputation for everyone being a screw-up. They were there simply because they were a constant reminder to someone with pull of their own embarrassing actions or limitations."

"Thank you for telling me. I've been wondering why someone believed to be a screw-up had been entrusted with a mission of this magnitude and how that individual had managed to garner the support of everyone around her."

"Does that include you, Colonel?"

"Yes, it does. You've had my full support for some time. Now— what's your decision?"

"We go back to GA space and unload our passengers, and hope they allow me to come back here and finish this mission. But before we go, we have to recover Winston."

"How can we? We have no idea where he is."

"I know where he is."

"You do? How?"

"He contacted me by encrypted message. I responded and told him to remain where he is. I told him we'd come get him as soon as possible."

"But we have no shuttles."

"I have an idea for recovering him that doesn't require a shuttle."

"I can't wait to hear *this* plan."

"It's fairly simple. How much room is there in the weapons bomb bay of an SF4?"

"The rack that holds the eight missiles doesn't leave room for anything else. We'd never be able to squeeze him in unless he's lost more than a hundred fifty pounds, is as skinny as a broom handle, and is as flexible as a Boa constrictor."

"And if we remove the missile rack, how much room is there?"

Dennier smiled as she considered the question. "There should be enough to hold an adult male in an EVA suit. But it's going to be a *very* rough ride. That area certainly wasn't designed for passenger travel, so there no inertial compensation. He'll be in complete darkness once the bomb bay doors close, then squeezed like a lemon for its juice while being shaken like a mixed cocktail until we're out of the lower atmo."

"That'll have to do. I can't think of any other way to recover him. Can you have your mechanics fix us up? There will have to be some kind of harness to keep your passenger from being slammed all over the bay."

"I'll get them working on it right away. We should be ready to go in a few hours."

263

"We'll plan on a pickup time of two hours past midnight in the capital. The location for the pickup will be the roof of a deserted factory building about a hundred kilometers from the city and one kilometer from where he's in hiding. I'll get the coordinates ready and notify Winston of the pickup time and place."

◆　◆　◆

Ten minutes after sending an encrypted message using one of Winston's algorithms, a reply arrived addressed to Marcy from Corny. In the message, the sender acknowledged the pickup time and place.

◆　◆

Colonel Dennier and three of her Wing arrived at the pickup location right on time. There was no indication that the Fleet surrounding the planet, or anyone else, had noticed their flight. Three of the SF4s hovered on cushions of oh-gee waves while the Colonel landed her ship on the roof. Within seconds of Dennier cutting power, Winston stepped out of the shadow of a roof stairway housing and walked towards the ship.

"What's this?" he exclaimed as Dennier sat looking down at him from the cockpit. "Where's the shuttle?"

"You're looking at it. The other shuttles are unavailable. But fear not, Winston. I'll get you safely to the ship."

"How? There's only one seat in that bucket."

"I never said you'd be seated during the trip."

Dennier reached down and pressed something that caused the ship's bomb-bay doors to open. After climbing down from the cockpit, she reached up into the belly of the ship and freed something. As she returned to face Winston, she was holding the lower half of a bulky EVA suit.

"You're kidding, right?" Winston said.

"Never been more serious. If you want off this rock, this is the only way that's going to happen."

"This is Marcola's idea, right?"

"Yep. I can't claim credit for this one. The captain came up with the idea."

"I knew it. That woman hates me because I pressured her to let me return to the planet. She's purposely trying to humiliate me."

"Winston, that woman has agonized over every detail of this entire mission. She's trying to make sure we accomplish all of our mission objectives and that we all get home safe. She is not trying to humiliate you. This is the *only* way we have to get you up to the ship."

"Where are the shuttles? There are four of them, aren't there?"

"Yes, but they're not available to us. Look, it's a long story and you'll hear it all when we reach the *Justice*. Now either start putting this suit on or I'm leaving you here, and I can guarantee no one else will be coming to get you. Make up your mind."

"Okay, calm down, Colonel. I guess I have no choice."

"You can choose to stay here."

"That's not a choice. It's an epitaph."

◆ ◆

"Thank you for coming up, Anese," Sydnee said as she welcomed the woman to her office. "I wanted to speak to you about your daughter."

"Oh my, is she okay?"

"Yes. She's fine. She's still safe in the underground bunker of the GA embassy on Yolongus."

"Then why have you asked me to come up here?"

"I'm afraid we're unable to recover the people in the embassy at this time. It's complicated, but basically we have to conceal our involvement in the freeing of the slaves. Presently, the Qummuc forces have surrounded the embassy and are watching to see if the GA still has an active presence there. So our people must remain out of sight. As soon as the Yolongi tire of watching the embassy and leave the compound area, we'll recover our people. I promise you you'll see your daughter again, but not right away."

"I trust you, Captain. If you say she's safe and will be with me again, I believe you and will look forward to the day you reunite us. God bless you, Captain. My family owes you a debt we can never repay."

◆ ◆

Sydnee was waiting outside the FA-SF4 habitat hanger when the four ships returned and began their docking. She entered the hanger when the ramps had retracted, the outer hatch had closed, and the atmosphere had been restored. She watched as Dennier opened the bomb-bay hatch beneath her ship and one of the mechanics climbed under the ship and began loosening straps. A few seconds later two legs in an EVA suit appeared as they hung down towards the deck. And after a few more seconds, the lower part of a torso became visible. The upper half still had to be unstrapped before it could move away from the ship.

As Winston got clear of the ship, stood up, and removed his helmet, the smell of vomit was immediately noticeable. He held the helmet in front of him and spewed a bit more into it before wiping his face with the back of his hand. The mechanic who had freed him handed him a clean grease wipe and took the helmet away to be cleaned and disinfected.

"Rough trip, I guess," Sydnee said to Winston as he approached her.

"Ever tried it?" he asked.

"No, I've always been in the cockpit."

"You haven't lived until you've made a trip into space while strapped into a bomb bay. They should have a ride like that at amusement parks."

"I'll pass. And I apologize, but all of our shuttles are stranded on the planet. This was all we had available."

"Stranded? Tell me about the shuttles."

"Why don't you go get cleaned up first? It smells like you could use a shower and a gargle."

"Okay, but then I want to hear what's been going on since I was captured."

"You won't believe half of it," Dennier said as she approached from behind Winston.

"I want to hear it anyway."

◆ ◆ ◆

"You're saying we still don't know who was responsible for the second attack?" Gustallo Plelillo screamed at Weislis Danttan, the Minister of Intelligence.

"It was like the first attack. No one saw a thing except the explosions. We know that an hour before the attack, a massive number of messages were intercepted that, after being decrypted, showed plans for a ground assault on the capital. They specifically stated that each of our three residential compounds would also be attacked."

"What? When did we learn this?"

"Not until eight hours after the attack was over. When the communications systems went down, the com center couldn't transmit anything to my Intelligence Center. So the messages sat at the com center until they could be hand-carried by courier. Since everything was so confused during the air attack, the couriers were all swamped with deliveries. Then when we did finally receive the data, we had to break the encryption before we could read the messages."

"So it took nine hours to read of the enemy plans when we already had the data? I told you a wireless intelligence network was a bad idea. I said it was too easy to interrupt."

"I believed it was more difficult to interrupt such a system than a wired system. I never would have believed an attacker could simultaneously take down every single tower in the city."

"That's another splinter in my backside. How did such an attack take place with absolutely no one seeing a single attacker?"

"Like they're saying in the press, the attackers must be in invisible aircraft."

"Invisible aircraft? Preposterous. No one has an invisibility cloak— except possibly the GA. Was there any activity at the GA embassy?"

"None. It's as quiet as a cemetery. No invisible aircraft left the compound or landed."

"How would we know— if they're invisible?"

"I imagine the pilots would have to walk out to their ships. And the ships would have to be fueled, inspected, and armed. We'd see people moving around if such activity was happening there."

"Not if the aircraft were all stored below ground."

"Then we'd see the covers roll back to allow the invisible aircraft out to perform their attack. I tell you, there's absolutely nothing going on at the GA embassy. You're keeping your APCs there for nothing. Did any of *your* people see anything?"

"They say there was no activity at all at the embassy."

"So you're wasting resources that could better be used elsewhere."

"Where, for instance?"

"Guarding your home, for one."

Plelillo made an angry sound in his throat before asking "Why did the planned ground assault on the city never take place?"

"Unknown. Perhaps the confusion caused by the destruction of the com systems forced them to cancel that part of their operation as well. Perhaps one of the radio stations was supposed to keep them appraised of our movements by using live satellite information."

"Perhaps we should attempt to reconcile with the Rebels and agree to share power," Mewaffal said.

"Don't be a fool," Plelillo said. "They don't want to share power. They want to take all the power for themselves. They're not fooling me. They don't give a hang about the people. They're only using the idiot population to fight their war for them."

"Isn't that similar to what we do?"

"Of course. It's what every *professional* politician does. The idiot population is too dumb to govern themselves. Without us to run every minute aspect of their lives for them, the planet would fall into complete anarchy."

"Assuming the Rebel ground assault plan has only been delayed," Danttan said, "how are we going to prepare for it?"

"The first thing we have to do is increase the security around our residence compounds," Plelillo said. "I'm also going to station a couple of APCs in my side yard so I can be safely evacuated if such an attack occurs."

"Do you think a couple of APCs for each of our compounds is adequate?"

"Not completely. I wouldn't have believed the Rebels could mount an attack like the two we've seen, but the GA appears less and less likely. I'm going to pull my APCs away from the GA embassy compound. And if it's not the GA and not the Rebels, it has to be the Blenod."

"I'm not sure," Danttan said. "It might be the Kweedee Aggregate."

"Or the Aguspod," Mewaffal said.

"No, not the Aguspod," Plelillo said. "They're too busy fighting the Raiders. They might attack some of our border posts, but they don't have the available resources to attack us here. We're too deep inside Clidepp space. The Kweedee is a distinct possibility. They hate everybody equally."

CHAPTER TWENTY-TWO
~ April 27th, 2287 ~

"So you were, in fact, responsible for both attacks on the capital," Winston said as Sydnee finished relating the events of the first attack, which was the effort to recover him and the people taken at the time of his capture, and then the failed attempt to recover the people at the embassy.

"I'm afraid so. But SCI ordered me to recover you at all costs."

"I doubt they intended you to start a war with another nation. Not that I don't appreciate your unbridled enthusiasm in the effort."

"Perhaps I took them too literally, but to me 'at all costs' means nothing is off the table and that I throw everything I've got at the problem. SCI is a bit too far away for me to have requested clarification and received a timely response. And when I did later request help, I got the old 'you're on your own, kid' speech. So, yes, I used my own judgment regarding what they meant by 'at all costs.' I assumed they're worried that under torture you'd betray the GA. Congratulations, by the way, on your successful escape."

"Thank you. I was very glad to have the opportunity for a little payback against the two guards who beat me the worst. And I told them nothing, which is why they beat me senseless a couple of times."

"No truth drugs?"

"That probably would have come later. I think they wanted to release some of the hostility they felt for us, meaning the Aleoxlene Reqoppl, making them look like such fools for so long."

"You don't appear to be any the worse for wear."

"You should have seen me when I first escaped. I was one big bruise from my toenails to my scalp. So now you've told me about the attacks on the capital, recovering the former slaves, and finding a whole lot more. I calculate you have about a thousand mouths on board, and yet the corridors are lined with food crates. When did you get resupplied?"

"While we were waiting to recover the people from the embassy and you were healing from injuries sustained at the hands of the guards, we made a little trip to where several heavily trafficked space routes intersect. That pretty much guaranteed we'd encounter freighters on a regular basis. After skipping every freighter that appeared to be transporting mainly ore, we encountered one that appeared to be nearly maxed out with normal cargo. I managed to get them to heave to, although I had to threaten the use of deadly force. We examined their manifest, decided what we needed to procure from them, and had them assemble the food and send it over."

"Just like that. They just sent it over."

"Well, I did pay for it. Actually I paid about three times its value. But we were desperate, and price is pretty far down the list of imperatives to be considered when your stomach is grumbling about the lack of groceries being pushed down your throat."

Winston grinned before saying, "You're nothing if not resourceful, Captain."

"Unfortunately, the second attack on the capital didn't accomplish my goal."

"Which was to draw off the APCs so the shuttles could leave the embassy without being seen?"

"Yes. And we can't afford to remain here waiting for them to tire of sitting around because, in addition to eventually running out of food— again, the habitat container is getting more and more crowded every week."

"From newborns," Winston said, nodding.

"Yes. And we don't have a pediatrician on board. Our medic is doing the best he can, and we appreciate all his hard work, but if an emergency arises, we might need a full MD. If it wasn't for the help by the midwives, I don't know what we'd have done."

"I understand— and agree. Let's get these people to the GA, and then we can come back for the others and perhaps more."

"Winston, I want to come back for the others in the embassy— but I don't know about getting more. That is way above and beyond our mission. I don't even know if Space Command will approve *my* coming back into Clidepp space."

"You have me in your corner, Captain, but what you still haven't told me is what your original mission was."

"And you haven't told me what happened to the earpiece the Major gave you to wear but which mysteriously went silent just after you headed for the caves."

"Gee, I just don't know, Captain."

Sydnee smiled. "Com'on Winston. You know, and so do I."

"You do? And I do? Enlighten me."

"You told us there were only forty-nine more people waiting for a ride to the GA because you wanted to get me fully committed to saving slaves before you dropped the bombshell. You figured that once I had almost ninety on board, I'd be more receptive to taking the rest. But you couldn't risk having the earpiece pick up some loose talk about there being a lot more slaves than you had so far let on. So before entering the cave you removed the earpiece and smashed it with a large rock. It almost cost you dearly. We could have tracked the earpiece to wherever you were on the planet and we might have saved you the beating you got from the Qummuc. If you hadn't escaped, busting the earpiece could have been responsible for your death by beheading. How am I doing? Did I miss anything?"

Winston smiled. "I'm impressed. You're clever, Lieutenant. Ever consider transferring to SCI? I might be able to wangle a promotion for you. You're too smart to be a mere lieutenant(jg)."

"I'm not."

Winston looked at her with narrowed eyes. "You're not what?"

"That's not my true rank. I'm not a lieutenant(jg)."

"But you're only wearing one and a half bars."

"And you're not wearing any bars at all, *Lt. Commander.*"

Winston smiled again. "This is a head game, right? You're getting even because I pulled a fast one."

"It's not a lie. I'm really not wearing my true rank. But this is all you'll ever see while we're in Clidepp space."

"Then what is your true rank?"

Sydnee just smiled slightly.

"Not going to tell me? Is this a way of avoiding being charged with impersonating an officer of superior rank? You can't be higher than a Lieutenant because you don't look old enough."

"Admiral Carver looks even younger than I do. I know that for a fact. I've seen her— in person and very close."

Winston's smile disappeared. "You're not trying to tell me you're another victim of that Raider DNA manipulation system, are you?"

"As far as I know, the Admiral, Eliza, and Christa are the only Space Command officers who can make that claim."

"Then what is it? Your rank I mean."

"It's definitely not lieutenant(jg). And I'm not presently at liberty to reveal my true Space Command rank."

"You know, I've had this feeling all along that something was seriously wrong with this picture. I couldn't understand how a Lt.(jg) could be put in full command of a powerful warship, albeit a small one, with a crew of this size, composed mostly of SC officers, plus a Marine Special Ops team, *and* a Marine Wing commanded by a Lt. Colonel who reports to the j.g. and obeys her orders without question. It just didn't add up. The captain of this ship, at the very least, should be a Lieutenant commander. Am I close?"

Sydnee raised her eyebrows for an instant and smiled, but offered nothing else. She had been frustrated with Winston's reticence to reveal important facts since he'd come aboard, and she was now deriving a small pleasure from doing the same.

"Okay Captain, you win. Is that all?"

"Anxious to hurry down and pump Colonel Dennier to learn my true rank?"

Winston grinned before saying, "God, when did I become so transparent? I think I may have been on Yolongus too long. They can't read Terrans at all."

"Let me respond by saying I'm glad we were able to recover you from the planet. I truly apologize for the rough ride in the FA-SF4 weapons bay, but if I returned to the GA without you, Admiral— I mean Space Command, probably would have shipped me off to the former Tsgardi territory where I would spend the next decade on patrol, watching those apes to make sure they never escaped from their solar system."

"Admiral who?"

"What?"

"You started to name an admiral."

"Slip of the tongue. I meant to say Space Command."

"Sure you did. Was it Admiral Carver?"

Ignoring the question, Sydnee said, "Now that you're back aboard, we'll be immediately departing for GA Space. The people in the embassy have plenty of food and will just have to remain there until the Yolongi get tired of watching— nothing."

Sydnee grinned widely after Winston left. Saying 'admiral' hadn't been a slip of the tongue. It had been intentional, but she wanted it to appear as a slip of the tongue. She could imagine Winston racking his brain trying to figure out who she really was, what her secret mission was, what her true rank was, and why she was wearing just a bar and half. He had been right of course. She *was* playing a head game. Winston deserved it after the head games he had been playing since they met. Eventually, she would tell him the truth, if he didn't learn it first on his own. She knew that if he asked anyone other than Dennier, that person would swear up and down that her true rank was lieutenant(jg). Dennier would probably say that Marcola's rank was lieutenant but that she couldn't confirm that because Sydnee had told her that her true rank was the result of a special promotion by the Admiralty Board.

◆ ◆ ◆

"Sierra-Leader," Blade heard through his CT as he sat eating lunch in the underground bunker, "this is Bravo-One. The APCs are on the move." The report came from one of his Special Ops people acting as a spotter on the second floor of the embassy.

Dropping his sandwich and touching his Marine Corps ring, he said, "Bravo-One, this is Sierra-Leader. Are they positioning for an attack?"

"They appear to be leaving the area."

"All of them?"

"So far only twelve have actually changed position, but the others seem to be buttoning up."

"I'll be right up."

Blade pulled on his helmet and casually walked to the door of the large cafeteria. He would have run, but he didn't want to upset the women in the room who were having lunch.

Once outside the room, Blade walked swiftly to the elevator and ascended to the top floor of the embassy. The spotters never set up positions on the roof until well after dark.

"Sitrep," Blade said as he entered the room where Bravo-One was spotting.

"All APCs now seem to be on the move. Bravo-Two, Bravo-Three, and Bravo-Four all report that the APCs in their sight range are heading out. Now we can go up to the *Justice* once it's dark."

"Damn," Blade said angrily.

"Sir?" Bravo-One said, obviously confused by the exclamation."

"The *Justice* left for the GA two days ago. Now that we're stuck here for at least several more months, and possibly a lot longer, the APCs pull out."

"The *Justice* left us here, sir?"

"Yes. I didn't say anything because I knew it would depress everyone. The APCs hadn't moved since they arrived, and the *Justice* faced the problem of running out of food again if they didn't return to the GA and offload their passengers. The captain had no choice. She said she'll be back as soon as possible, but God only knows when that will be. The top brass may not want anyone coming here again until things have quieted down."

"Then we could be stuck here for years, sir?"

"I don't know, Staff Sergeant. I hope not. At least we don't have to worry about food or shelter. If you've got to be in a prison, I can't think of a better one, even if we can't go outside during daylight hours."

"Do we have to remain inside now that the APCs are gone, sir?"

"During daylight hours, yes, because we'd be visible to satellite reconnaissance. After dark, we can go outside as long as we're wearing our armor because the Dakinium will prevent us from being seen on thermal imagery equipment."

"I was hoping we might be able to strip down to shorts and tee shirts and run around the inside the perimeter wall. I'm getting tired of running around the shuttle bay."

"I understand. I'd love a good ten-kilometer run outdoors in the fresh air myself. I wish the Perimeter Defense System had been upgraded with the newer system."

"What does the newer APDS have that we don't?"

"I understand the first new system was installed at Admiral Carver's residential compound on Quesann when the governor's mansion was built. In addition to the automated protection it offers from any attempted outside penetration, it projects a three-dimensional hologram dome over the entire compound. The hologram can make the estate appear to be woodland, farmland, a regional recreation park, or anything else they wish to portray. It appears that way both from the ground or the air. If we had that, we could park the MATs on the lawn and the Yolongi would never know they were there. We could also run around the inside of the perimeter wall whenever we wanted without fear of being seen."

"That would be great. Sir, since we're not being watched by the APCs, and we're not really needed for protection detail here, perhaps we could get everyone interested in a good long run and go somewhere in one of the shuttles."

"That's a possibility, Staff Sergeant. We could head up into the mountains where the slaves were hiding out. It's pretty wild territory up there. We'll have to map out a trail first. And we still have to be careful regarding satellite reconnaissance."

"With the instrumentation in the shuttles, maybe we can plot the recon satellite paths so we know when an area is being observed and when it's clear."

"Yes, we might be able to do that. You've just given me another idea, Staff Sergeant. There might be another way we can get our exercise and help the GA at the same time."

"What way would that be, sir?"

"We'll get the team together at 1400 local and discuss it. Right now, I'm going to go finish my lunch, if someone hasn't cleared the table and thrown my food away."

◆

"By now you may have heard that the *Justice* has left for the GA," Blade said to his Special Ops team, the fire-teams from the *Denver*, and the shuttle pilots in the special meeting he had called in a cordoned off area of the shuttle bay. "They waited as long as they could, but they're busting at the seams with all of the former slaves we brought up. Another problem was food. The captain has already had to stop a freighter with threats of using deadly force on one occasion and then demand they give the *Justice* food. The food was paid for, naturally, including a sizable bonus, as I understand it, but we didn't want to have to do that again. There were other problems as well, such as not having a medical doctor on board while dealing with hundreds of women who haven't received the best of medical care over the years and who are now giving birth to artificially inseminated children. We face the same serious problems down here, being limited to midwives for handling the births. The midwives are great and working tirelessly, but they're not doctors. We just have to hope we don't have physical issues they can't handle.

"So the *Justice* has left and hopefully will return in a couple of months. But we can't establish any kind of date for their return. The main reason is that Space Command SHQ and the GA Senate Council are going to be damned upset that our efforts here have brought us to the brink of war with the Clidepp Empire. They might want to allow a cooling-off period before they allow the *Justice*, or another ship, to come here to pick us up. But come they will. Make no mistake about that. We never leave our people behind if there's any alternative. Here in the embassy bunker we're as safe as we would be in the GA. If necessary, we could survive for up to ten years before we'd even have to think of replenishing food supplies. I'm confident we won't be here anywhere near that long.

"Now, on to the real reason for this meeting. I'm sure you're as tired as I am of sitting around on our sixes. So I have a proposal. I want to rescue more slaves and bring them here. This will accomplish two key objectives. First, we'll free more Terrans from a life of slavery in this crazy, mixed-up nation. Second, we use the new attacks to shift attention away from the GA as being the primary suspect for the past attacks."

"How do we do that, sir?" Lt. MacDonald asked.

"We create a new, fictitious group that will be sort of like a cross between the Rebels and the Aleoxlene Reqoppl. The stated goal of our new freedom force will be the overthrow of any government who endorses slavery of sentient beings. We can call ourselves something like the Sentient Life Freedom Soldiers. Or perhaps the Terran Liberation Fighters since Terrans are the only sentient species being enslaved in this nation."

"How about the Terran Freedom Coalition, sir?" MacDonald asked.

Blade thought for a few moments and said, "I like it. The first two words clearly define our goal while not implying that we are strictly a violent group, and the 'coalition' suggests an organization that has developed from members of other groups, such as people from the Aleoxlene Reqoppl and people supporting the Rebels. Does anyone have another suggestion or think of a reason why we shouldn't use Terran Freedom Coalition? Feel free to speak up."

When no one spoke after thirty seconds, Blade said, "Okay, we're now the Terran Freedom Coalition or the TFC. When we conduct our raids, we'll spray-paint our coalition's initials on all of the buildings we assault."

"Who are we going to attack, sir?" one of Blade's Special Ops team asked.

"We don't have SF4s as cover, so our targets will have to be more remote than the previous targets. We want to make sure the response time of the secret police and the regular police will allow us to do what we intend to do and bug out before they arrive. We still have the DS shuttles, so we can get in quick, do what we have to do, and get away quick. As to our specific targets, we should break into groups and interview all of the slaves to get their suggestions. Then we'll study all available maps or perform flyovers to study the terrain and locate key enemy structures, such as military and police locations. The locations we'll assault will be guarded, and we'll take out the guards if we can't first stun them so they never see us. It's of paramount importance that there are *no* witnesses, but we don't want to take down any ordinary civilians if possible. We're all military people, so we know what to ask when we interview the former slaves. I want all officers and noncoms to remain, but everyone else is excused for now."

The enlisted who weren't noncoms rose from their chairs and left the bay as the others gathered around Blade.

"Lieutenant MacDonald," Blade said, "after we're done here I want you to arrange for work parties to move the food stored in the belly of the shuttles back to the embassy warehouse areas. We can't bring it to the *Justice* and it only adds extra weight to the shuttle."

"Aye, Captain."

"Okay, break into two-person teams for the interviews. I'll make a PA announcement that we want to interview everyone regarding their experiences under slavery because we hope to further advance our effort to free more slaves. I'll ask that everyone whose first name, or only name, begins with the letter A and who aren't in their final trimester please come to the dining hall. As we complete the interviews, we'll advance down the alphabet until we've talked to everyone. Once we complete the interviews and select a few places as prospective targets, we may need to get more information from the person or persons who provided the initial data. Any questions?"

No one spoke up, so Blade said, "I'll go to the communication room and make that announcement."

As Blade left the room, Jerry Weems asked Lt. MacDonald, "What do you think, Kel?"

"I wish Syd was here."

"Why?" Pete Caruthers asked. "We can handle this without her."

"Pete, Syd has an absolute genius for tactics. I'm not saying the Major isn't good, but Syd is the best I've ever met and as good as any military person I've ever heard about or read about."

"What about Admiral Carver?"

"I personally believe Syd's every bit as brilliant as Admiral Carver. No disrespect is intended towards Admiral Carver. We all know she's a tactical genius. I just happen to believe Syd is right up there on a par with her."

"We'll be fine, Kel," Weems said.

"I hope so, Jerry. I guess I just can't forget that the Major was ready to abandon us to those snake things during our first mission to Yolongus. Blade ordered Syd to pick him and his team up immediately and forget about us. He told her we were lost. Syd ignored him and saved our sixes. He's the senior officer so he's in charge, and I will follow every order he gives. But I still wish Syd was here."

◆

After hours spent interviewing former slaves, a long list of possible targets had been developed. Then the targets were put in order according to the remoteness of the location and likelihood of law enforcement arriving during the raid. Finally, the targets were prioritized by estimated size of the slave population at the target location.

"We have our first target and topographical images of the area from the embassy's database," Blade announced. "Now all we have to do is plan our approaches on the terrain maps to create the final plan for our first attack. We've gleaned every last bit of information we could from the women who have knowledge of this location. We know where the slaves are housed and how many guards are normally on duty at night. Naturally, there are a few things they're unable to tell us, such as where the guards reside when off-duty, how often the guards make their rounds, etc. But we're going to hit them fast, hit them hard, get the slaves, and bug out.

"We'll shove off at 2300 local time. That will put us over the first target at 2318. Literally. We'll land on the roof of the factory and follow the same highly successful plan established by Captain Marcola for the attack on the slave pens in the capital. Our goal is to get as many of the slaves out as possible. Remember that they'll be scared to death, so display your alternate Terran face on your helmet mask once we reach the factory. Remember to set your armor's translator to Yolongi. I've had some flyers printed up for us to drop at the site, and don't forget to spray-paint the TFC letters on the walls. Each team must do that at least five times. We want that to become the most feared thing a slave owner can imagine. Almost as important as freeing the slaves is our effort to convince the Triumvirate that the group behind all of the attacks, including those on the capital, is a new Yolongus insurgent movement. And remember to use the Yolongi translation and letters. One slipup with Amer could destroy the entire effort. We'll load up the shuttles with as many slaves as we can and return here. Based on the interviews, the number of slaves at each location will not exceed our ability to transport them in one trip.

"The individual assignments for each team are here in my viewpad. After we're done, you can download them to your viewpad. Okay, any ideas that will improve the plan I've laid out? Don't be afraid to speak up. I want to hear your ideas."

"Sir," Lt.(jg) Weems said, "is there sufficient room for all four shuttles on the factory roof and can it support the combined weight?"

"Good question, Lieutenant. I admit I don't know. How did you check that information when we attacked the Qummuc facilities in the capital?"

"The Qummuc facilities had symbols painted on the roof showing that oh-gee vehicles could land there and the weight restrictions. I see nothing on the images here."

"That might mean the roofs can't support the weight of even one shuttle," Caruthers said.

"I'm glad you noticed that, Lieutenant. Do you have a suggestion for how we can determine if it's safe to land there?"

"No, sir, but I suggest that instead of the plan calling for us to land, we simply hover a meter or so above the roof. You can then rappel down. It will make it a little more difficult for the slaves to climb in, but it will be far safer because the roof will already have the weight of over a hundred slaves. In fact, perhaps we should only allow the slaves out on the roof when the MATs are ready to load, and then only allow enough out on the roof as can be accommodated by one shuttle until most of them are aboard. I'm not suggesting that we only load one shuttle at a time but that we limit the number of people actually on the roof at one time to about forty. We can't know how safe that roof is. We're not talking about a government building with regular maintenance and inspections. Who knows how good their maintenance program is there."

"Then that's what we'll do. All pilots will hover slightly above the roof. Can we reduce the distance to say— twenty centimeters or so?"

"We'll do our best, sir," Weems said. "As the load changes with people climbing aboard, we'll have to stay right on top of it. But while I can't promise a precise distance, we should be able to keep almost all of the MAT's weight off the roof while holding the ship steady for loading."

"Good. Let's plan on that then. Any other questions, suggestions, or comments?"

"Sir," Lt. MacDonald said, "May I suggest that you share the code used to open the shuttle bay cover? If something were to happen to you, the rest of the team would be prevented from uncovering the bay so the shuttles could enter."

"As every military person knows, the CT implanted in every officer candidate when they enter one of the academies, and the ID chip implanted in every enlisted man and woman when they are inducted into the service, identifies them to the computer system aboard every ship and at every military installation and facility. When the system recognizes that identification, it allows them to access the areas they're authorized to enter. To use the special code I have for embassy access, I contact the embassy's computer system via my CT. Once both the code and my CT are recognized as valid by the embassy computer system, I can enter any part of the embassy not specifically forbidden to myself and other Marine officers who share the code. So you see, I can't simply share the code because it wouldn't work for anyone else unless that individual has already been granted access privileges by virtue of their status in the military.

"But I understand and appreciate your concerns. I believe I might be able to set up a temporary code that every officer and noncom can use to control the cover over the B1 level at this facility. I'll do that immediately after we finish here. Anything else? Anybody? No? Okay, then come download the plan for your team from my viewpad."

CHAPTER TWENTY-THREE
~ May 3rd, 2287 ~

At exactly 2300 the two-meter-thick cover over the shuttle bay at the embassy rolled back to allow egress from the underground area. All lights had been turned off so there was no illumination to betray the activity. Since oh-gee engines were whisper quiet, there was nothing louder than the sound made by a light breeze to betray the activity as four black MAT-14 shuttles climbed swiftly into the dark night sky.

◆

The four shuttles arrived over the factory building at 2318. Shuttles One and Two descended to just a meter above the roof, and the attack teams slid down short rope lines to the surface. All TFC insurgents were in the two shuttles to reduce assembly time on the roof. Shuttles Three and Four remained above and off to the side because their function on this evening was limited to the transportation of freed slaves. The MAT-14s were designed to accommodate up to forty Marines in full armor with their weapons, plus two pilots on the flight deck. But they had already proven that when the seats were folded against the walls, the main cabin could be used to accommodate up to sixty-six standing passengers, plus two in the head, and two in the rear airlock.

"The roof door is locked," Blade heard over Com 1, the general communications frequency. "Nothing fancy, just a simple lock. Blow it or burn it, sir?"

"Burn it," Blade said. "Let's keep the noise to a minimum until our presence is known."

Several Marines huddled around the door to hide the light flashes as much as possible. As far as they knew, no alarm had yet been sounded, and Blade naturally wanted to keep it that way for as long as possible. The act itself was almost noiseless as a laser rifle was pointed at the lock assembly and fired several times. When the lock fell apart, one of the Marines reached out and pulled the door open.

Within a minute, all of the Marines had poured through the doorway and begun descending the stairs to their designated floor assignment.

Once all Marine groups reported they were in place, Blade said "Go." The teams then opened the door on that floor and spread through the factory floor looking for guards or employees.

Most of the factory was empty, but there were a few guards sitting or standing around, plus a handful of maintenance people working on equipment. Blade wanted to avoid harming civilians while limiting violence to the overseers and the owners, but stealth was critical, so the Marines dispatched everyone they found in order to prevent there being any witnesses.

The operation moved at an incredible speed. The factory was not prepared for an invasion by trained troops. For that matter, it probably wouldn't have presented much of a problem for raw recruits. Within five minutes, the Marines were at the basement entrance to the slave quarters and had eliminated the two overseers there.

"Terran identity faces," Blade said and everyone changed the image on their faceplate to show the animated Terran face developed for each Marine. In some cases the image didn't look even remotely like the actual visage of the Marine, but it appeared real and moved just as a real face would when the helmet wearer spoke. The intent was to ensure identification of the Marine by witnesses was impossible once they removed their helmet.

The basement slave quarters were like a large barracks. There were no interior walls— just rows and rows of beds. When the door had been unlocked and opened, the Marines saw that most of the slaves were asleep. Since they had made every effort to be stealthy, that was understandable.

When the lights were turned on, the women began to stir. The Marines then moved through the dormitory shouting in Yolongi, "Terran Freedom Coalition. We're here to set you free and take you away from here. Get up and get dressed. Quickly."

The dormitory was suddenly a mass of confusion as some of the women began screaming while others began shouting and a few began weeping out of fear.

The Marines changed tactics at that point. Instead of trying to appear as saviors, as they had with the women who had reached Sanctuary and were waiting for someone to come get them, they started barking orders as they'd had to do at the slave pens. "Get up and get dressed. Now."

The women, used to following barked orders immediately to avoid the lash of an overseer, quieted down and began dressing quickly.

"Pick up anything you wish to take with you," the Marines barked. "You will not be returning here ever again. Take your blankets and other bedding."

The women began stuffing their pillowcases with their few personal items and wrapping up their blankets.

When the women were about ready, Blade said, "Follow the Marines out the door and up the stairs." He then turned off his external speaker and said on Com 1, "Don't forget to drop the leaflets and spray-paint TFC on the walls at every floor in the stairwell using Yolongi letters."

As the Marines leading the women emerged on the roof, the shuttles dropped down as close as possible without actually placing any significant weight on it. The number of slaves at this factory had been estimated at one hundred thirty-five, so the seats hadn't been folded.

When the first two shuttles had each taken forty women and two Marines on board, they pulled up so the other two shuttles could move in. Those shuttles were able to take the remainder of the women and the Marines. There weren't enough seats to accommodate everyone, so many of the Marines stood on the eighteen-minute trip back to the embassy. As the shuttles pulled away from the factory, Blade triggered explosive charges planted to destroy the video systems, computers, and all records. The Marines who had planted the explosives had downloaded the terabytes of information the computer contained before preparing the detonation trigger.

286

The information might help as the GA worked to build a database of slavery on Yolongus.

◆

Upon reaching the embassy, the four shuttles settled quietly into the bay. Once they were down on the B1 deck, the tennis court cover was closed so lighting could be restored in the bay.

After the pilots had carefully glided their ships to their proper parking locations in the large bay, they shut down the engines and turned off the systems. They then notified the Marines that the hatches could be opened. As soon as the rear cabin was open and the ramps extended, the Marines stepped out of the shuttles.

As the last of the Marines left the shuttles, Blade realized that the slaves were still seated inside. He climbed the ramp of one shuttle and peered inside, then entered the small ship. None of the newly freed slaves were moving or talking. They were just sitting upright, staring at Blade. He realized they had been so conditioned to slavery that they were waiting for someone to give them orders before moving.

Using Com 1, Blade notified the one fire team he had left with the slaves in the embassy that they could now allow the previously freed women to enter the shuttle bay. Within seconds, the former slaves were pouring into the bay and rushing to the shuttles. They stopped short when they saw the Terran wreckage and recognized it for what it was. Most of them had been there before being freed themselves.

"Ladies," Blade said to the women in the shuttle, using the translator and speaker in his armor to speak to them in Yolongi, "you are now on GA property. You are o*n* GA property, you are *not* GA property. You are *free*. I want to welcome you to the underground bunker at the Galactic Alliance embassy on Yolongus where you'll wait until we can transport you to Galactic Alliance space. I'd like you to leave this shuttle in an orderly fashion and join your sisters. They were freed not too long ago and can help you adjust in what I'm sure is a tremendously traumatic time."

When none moved, Blade left the shuttle and gestured to the women waiting at the bottom of the ramp. "See what you can do for them, ladies."

Blade then went to each of the other shuttles and said the same thing to the just-freed slaves, after which he invited the women from the embassy to help them.

As the newly freed slaves were led out of the shuttles, fear was written all over their faces, and many were physically shaking. Perhaps they hadn't fully grasped the true situation. Perhaps they believed it was a dream from which they would awaken. Blade hadn't noticed earlier, but all were marked with scars, bruises and welts. Slavery was the only life most had ever known, and changes were taking place too quickly. Blade could only silently curse the overseers who had physically beaten the women and beaten them down mentally as well. He suddenly felt anger towards himself because he had let the overseers die too quickly. He should have made them suffer as had their victims. Unfortunately, there hadn't been time. But he knew he would never feel any sadness at killing another overseer on this miserable planet or, for that matter, anyone involved in Terran slavery anywhere.

◆ ◆ ◆

"Where did you get this?" Gustallo Plelillo demanded of his Intelligence Minister.

"They were all over the factory," Danttan said. "They're asking the people of Yolongus to support them and their cause. The attackers also painted their initials on the walls."

"Their initials?" Mewaffal said. "Then we should be able to find them easily."

"Not the initials of their own names. The initials of the group name."

"Where are the slaves now?" Plelillo asked.

"We don't know."

"This could be a Rebel plot," Mewaffal said. "They might be trying to divide our forces so half are hunting for an imaginary group."

"This attack was not imaginary," Danttan said. "They took all of the slaves and severely damaged the factory with the fire they set to destroy the computers and video records."

"Were any video records salvageable?" Plelillo asked. "Do we have any usable images?"

"None."

Plelillo looked at the sheet of paper and read it again. "Who is this TFC?"

"I've never heard of them," Danttan said. "Nobody in my department has ever heard of the Terran Freedom Coalition."

"And yet they're claiming credit for this attack *and* the two in the capital, which they say was only done to raid the prisons and slave pens. They want the citizenry to forgive them for destroying the power systems and communications towers."

"Yes."

"But no slaves were freed in the second attack," Plelillo said.

"No, something must have gone wrong. Perhaps the com tower destruction messed up their own chain of command communications as well. That gives credence to the idea that the group doesn't have military training and are really just a bunch of amateurs."

"They seem remarkably disciplined and effective for amateurs. Could this be the work of the AR?" Plelillo asked.

"The Aleoxlene Reqoppl has never advocated violence," Danttan said. "Their goal is only to help escaping slaves reach freedom. That's why catching them has never been a top priority."

"Perhaps this is a group that has splintered off from the AR because the AR wasn't doing enough to eliminate slavery as quickly as this TFC desires. As for the AR, we make a lot of money when we recapture a slave because we then charge the slave owner a healthy recovery fee if he wants them back. That's the real reason why eliminating the AR hasn't been a high priority. If not for them, there'd be far fewer escaped slaves. They put money in our pockets."

"I don't know if the people behind these raids are former AR members or not. All I know is that the slave owners are getting riled up. In addition to the slaves they've lost, factories are now being burned down."

"And their overseers are being killed," Mewaffal said.

"The owners don't give a damn about their overseers," Danttan said. "They'll just hire new ones. It's the destruction of their factories and the loss of their slaves that's costing them money and making them angry."

"How many slaves were taken in this latest attack?" Plelillo asked.

"One hundred twenty-three."

"One hundred twenty-three," Plelillo repeated as he rubbed his hands together. "We'll make a nice fee when we find them."

"*If* we find them."

"Of course we'll find them. One hundred twenty-three slaves can't just disappear."

"This TFC must be well organized because we haven't been able to find a single lead."

"A lot of the people sympathize with the AR," Mewaffal said. "They probably wouldn't tell us anything even if they knew."

"They'll tell us with the right persuasion," Plelillo said.

"Money?" Mewaffal asked.

"That's one way. But we know a better way. Pain."

◆ ◆ ◆

By the next day, most of the women freed from slavery at the factory had recovered from the initial shock of finding themselves free. It would take a long time to recover from a lifetime of beatings and punishment, but if they hadn't been as strong as they were they wouldn't have lasted this long. A few would take much longer to accept that they were really free and acclimatize to a new lifestyle, but with the support of the stronger women, they, too, would make it. It would just take time to put all the misery and fears of their past lives completely behind them, if that was even possible.

Blade spent a lot of time the next day walking and thinking about the mindset of the most recently freed women. The women from Sanctuary had already seemed to be fairly well adjusted, although that may have just been a mask, while the women rescued from the auction market seemed strong and were making good progress towards a reasonable recovery. This made him wonder if there was anything he could do to help the newest women along. He knew that whenever he approached any of them, they cowered and pulled away, as if expecting he would harm them. Once the Marines had removed their black armor and changed into fatigues, the fear seemed to lessen. But when all was said and done, it would just take time for the women to learn to trust the Marines in the embassy and understand they were not like the overseers at the factory. Perhaps it might have been easier if there were more females among the Marines, but only two of Blade's Special Ops team were female, and only five members of the four fire teams from the *Denver* were female, not counting Lt. Kelly MacDonald.

Blade tried hard over the rest of the morning, but he just couldn't let go of his animosity towards the Yolongi slave owners over what he had seen at the factory and the fear he saw in the eyes of the women they'd brought back. He wanted to hit something, or maybe a lot of somethings, but knew he couldn't release his anger in the embassy bunker because it would further frighten many of the women who had lived a life of fear. So he decided another attack was definitely called for. He knew that freeing more slaves while destroying the property of people who engaged in slavery was the best catharsis for him and many of his Marines.

◆ ◆ ◆

The next attack went off as well as the first, but since priority had been given to the factories with the highest slave count, the number of freed slaves from the second raid was

291

lighter. Still, every slave rescued from the Yolongi slave owners was considered a victory, so freeing eighty-six women in the second raid was considered cause for celebration. But Blade announced that any celebration would have to wait until they had completed their tasks.

Unlike the first time when Blade had tried to allay the fears of the freed women after returning to the embassy, he just got out of the way and let the previously freed slaves take over.

◆　◆　◆

Over the next few days, the Marines conducted two more attacks and rescued a total of sixty-one more slaves. The rescued count since they had started the operation under the guise of being an organization called the TFC was two hundred seventy.

On the afternoon following the most recent raid, Blade called the entire Marine contingent together in the shuttle bay to address them.

"Everyone has done a tremendous job, and we've accomplished a great deal. While it's true we've only put a very small dent in the slavery business here on Yolongus, we've shown people what can be done, and I'm confident we've scared the bejesus out of factory owners who buy slaves for their companies. Every one of them on this part of the world is probably thinking their factory is next. And none of the four factories we visited will be producing anything for a long time, if ever. Maybe they'll try other methods in the future instead of relying on cheap slave labor, although I'm not counting on that. They'll probably need to learn a harsher lesson than the one we've delivered to turn them around.

"I think we can put this down as a great victory, but it's time to end our efforts now. I don't want to stop, but we have to be practical. We're going to be stuck here for perhaps as long as two years, and we can't afford to have the food shortage problems they had aboard the *Justice*. In addition to we in the military, we now have over five hundred former slaves to feed, a number of whom are pregnant. Our food stores are naturally finite. What we've got is all we'll have, unless we raid grocery markets or something, and I'd prefer not to do that.

So tonight we're going a eat a hearty meal, then perhaps drink some of the embassy's alcoholic beverages which were no doubt intended for honored guests. Tonight, all of you are the honored guests. I thank you for your efforts and I know you are all rightfully proud of the remarkable job you've done."

◆ ◆ ◆

"So, the count now is four factories in three different cities and two hundred seventy slaves?" Plelillo said.

"Yes, and not old slaves. The factory owners always trade in the old ones when they become less productive because they can't work as hard as the younger ones, they take up just as much space in the cells, and they eat almost as much. The older ones make better house servants, unless the owner there is still looking for sex."

"How can they have pulled this off without leaving a single clue to their identities?"

"They have identified themselves," Mewaffal said. "They're the TFC."

"I'm talking about personal identification. We can't find the ones responsible simply by knowing they're part of the TFC unless we learn who's behind the TFC. We need to get an informant inside and learn who's running the operation."

"But I can't get anybody into the inside until we find someone— anyone— who knows something about this phantom organization," Danttan said.

"How can they be operating without at least one of our operatives hearing something?" Plelillo said as he began pacing around the room. "It's neither logical nor reasonable."

"That's why I've said it involves the Rebels," Mewaffal said. "We haven't been able to infiltrate that organization or even learn who is masterminding the group. It's as if they've infiltrated *us* because they know our moves and countermoves before we even make them."

"I still believe the Blenod are somehow behind this," Danttan said. "It's taking more and more of our resources away from confronting them. They pull a few small raids and we devote our limited resources to tracking them down instead of going after the invasion fleet that has taken a huge part of our territory."

"It's not the Blenod," Plelillo said. "I don't know how I know, but I know. It's someone else. Someone powerful."

"Which is why you kept your APCs stationed outside the GA embassy for months," Mewaffal said. "And what did you learn? Nothing."

"I still think the GA is behind it."

"Why?"

"I suppose it's because I don't believe it could be anyone else. And no, I have no proof. It's just a gut feeling."

"The attacks on the factories are an annoyance," Danttan said, "but that's all. It's time to take down the enemies we know."

"Okay, we'll make one last major effort to learn who's behind these attacks, and then we'll take on our other enemies. I want every member of the Metawasa, Riwaxgo, and Qummuc on alert in all large cities tonight. When these TFCs attack again, we need to catch at least one of them. And when we do, we'll squeeze him like a Chileeka fruit until his eyes pop out of his head and we learn everything he knows."

CHAPTER TWENTY-FOUR
~ May 9th, 2287 ~

For the first time in months, Sydnee had been able to relax as the *Justice* headed for GA space at Light-9790, even though she knew she had to do whatever was necessary, and agree to whatever her superiors required, in order to return to Yolongus to recover the people she had left at the embassy. While leaving them behind certainly wasn't her fault, she still felt responsible for their situation because she was in command of the mission.

Looking for some activity to help her pass the time each day, Sydnee began spending time in the nursery, helping to feed and change the babies, or just hold and rock them while their mothers caught up on their sleep. It was the best experience she'd had since they'd arrived at Yolongus months earlier.

Can it really be just four months since we left GA space? Sydnee thought as she fed one of the babies. *It seems like a year.*

As she lay the sleeping infant down in one of the improvised cribs while intending to pick up another, she received a message via her CT.

"Captain, please report to the bridge," she heard Lt.(jg) Olivetti say.

Stepping outside the nursery area before touching her Space Command ring, she said, "I'm on my way."

◆

Less than two minutes later, Sydnee entered the bridge. Lt.(jg) Olivetti was the Watch Commander and started to rise when she saw Sydnee, but Sydnee waved her down.

"What is it? A problem?"

"You might say that, Captain. We just received a strange audio message from the embassy. In the clear."

295

Turning to the com chief, Sydnee said, "Play the message."

It was definitely Blade's voice, although a little garbled, that said, "Sierra-Leader to Juliet-Leader. We're all alone down here. Can we please come home now?"

"That's all of it?" Sydnee said to the com chief.

"That's all we received."

"And it wasn't encrypted?"

"No, ma'am. It was sent in the clear."

Sydnee frowned. "Blade knows we left the Yolongus solar system days ago," she said to Olivetti.

"Aye, Captain."

"I don't like this. Why would he be asking to come home, knowing we've already left?"

"I don't know, Captain."

"Better turn us around."

"Aye, Captain." Raising her voice slightly Olivetti said, "Helm, reverse course."

"Aye, Commander, disengaging the drive and turning one hundred eighty degrees. Now resuming course under full power. Estimated time to Yolongus twelve days six hours and fourteen minutes."

"Carry on," Sydnee said, then turned and walked to her office. The muscles in the back of her neck, which had finally begun to untwist as she began to relax following the departure from the Yolongus system, were retying themselves, and they seemed even tighter than before. The delicious feelings of relaxation that had begun to spread through her body had disappeared completely. As they headed back towards Yolongus, she knew that once again she would be unable to think about anything other than the mission.

The package was still aboard, although she could have had him dropped off using the same transport system used to retrieve Winston. But his sudden appearance following two attacks on the capital would certainly have resulted in the Triumvirate once again turning an eye towards the GA as the assailant. So they would have to take him all the way back to the *Denver* and return him to Yolongus in a few months. If the Triumvirate then tried later to publicly associate his sudden reappearance with the attacks on the capital months earlier, they would appear foolish.

◆ ◆ ◆

"Sierra- Leader," Sydnee said as she recorded a vid message that would be sent to Blade now that they had reached the Yolongus solar star system, "we've returned. We received your last message twelve days ago, but we were confused by what you said. Please acknowledge this message. Juliet-Leader."

After encrypting the message, Sydnee had the com chief send it, then she sat back to wait.

About ten minutes later she received a reply. It was a vid message and was properly encrypted.

"Welcome back, Captain. I'm sorry for the confusion of the last message. I'll explain when I see you.

"The APCs pulled out a couple of days after you did. I've had my people up on the roofs every evening and they swear no one is watching us. The power is back on in parts of the city near its center, but it's still dark here, and the locals go to sleep early. If any were watching us, we'd see their thermal heat signature moving around the house. If you approve, I'd like to bring the four shuttles, fully loaded to your location. We would depart this base five hours before dawn.

"Sierra-Leader out."

Sydnee released the breath she had been holding. She hadn't even realized she'd been holding her breath until the message ended. She had been expecting dire news, and it was nothing of the sort. She immediately sent another message in which she gave Blade permission to come to the ship after dark when he was sure they could leave the compound without being seen.

◆ ◆

Some eight hours later, four shuttles approached the *Justice* and began their docking procedures. Sydnee was waiting by the airlock hatch where Shuttle One had docked. When the hatch opened, there was exuberance both in the shuttle and in the *Justice*."

"Permission to come aboard?" Blade said with a smile.

"Granted, Major. Welcome home."

"Thank you, Captain. I'm glad to be home. We're going to need some help here. For this first trip, I've brought all the women who are in their second or third trimester. We couldn't bring them if they had to stand up, but we folded the seats and rigged the shuttle for ambulance mode for the women closest to delivery. We had midwives standing by, but fortunately none of the women went into labor during the trip up. The others all had a seat with room to stretch out. Shuttle One has the women closest to their delivery date, with Shuttle Two having the next closest group, and Shuttle Three having the third closest group. Shuttle Four contains all of the women who have delivered, and their babies."

Sydnee turned to the ship's medic and nodded. He stepped past Sydnee and Blade and entered Shuttle One.

"So you still have to return to make another trip?" Sydnee said matter-of-factly."

"Uh, actually we need to make two more trips."

"Two?"

"Yes, Captain. Uh, it's a long story."

"Summarize it."

"Well, uh, we were only able to bring sixty-six on this trip because of their physical condition. So, including the Marine personnel, we still have four hundred fifty-six in the embassy bunker."

"Four hundred fifty-six? How did two hundred five former slaves and their children become almost five hundred?"

"Well— as I said, it's a long story and I'd prefer to tell you over a cup of coffee once we've completed our trips."

Sydnee sighed and then said, "Very well, Major. Get those people up here and then we'll talk. I can't wait to hear this story."

"Thank you, Captain."

◆　◆　◆

By the time the last of the people from the embassy had been brought aboard, the *Justice* crew had run out of places to put them. Every spare space, including the mess hall, was being utilized. In the morning, the people sleeping on the floor of the mess hall would have to vacate the area so food could be prepared and meals served. Food for the people in the habitat container that had originally held satellites would be delivered there because there just wasn't enough space to feed everyone in the mess hall. The final group from the embassy would live, eat, and sleep aboard the shuttles.

Once Sydnee was assured that everyone from the embassy was aboard and the embassy bunker had been resealed to prevent access by anyone not authorized to be there, Sydnee gave the order to again head for GA space.

She was in her office when Blade knocked.

"Captain, I want to thank you for coming back for us. I thought I would go crazy in the bunker with all those women and with babies crying constantly. I need to apologize for the message I sent. After we learned you were leaving and we understood your reasons, we believed we would be there for possibly as long as two years. It was maddening. I knew you would want to come back for us, but I also knew that once Space Command learned what we had done they probably wouldn't want you to ever enter Clidepp space again. So we'd have to wait until the pickup was authorized and someone else could be found who would take on the mission."

"Tell me how two hundred five slaves became four hundred ninety-three."

"After you left, we pulled a few raids with the hope we could make the original attacks appear to have been the work of a new Yolongi insurgent group called the Terran Freedom Coalition. That's how we came to have more slaves than when you left."

"A little more detail, please. I need it for my report."

"Ah, yeah. Well, you see, we were going a little crazy in that bunker, so my Marines and I started to exercise and practice our combat skills. This was before the *Justice* left. Some of the younger slaves were watching and asked to be taught, so we started showing them some self-defense basics and teaching them exercises that build strength and stamina. One thing led to another and before we knew it we were talking about ending slavery on Yolongus.

"The discussions got more and more serious every day and finally I decided that rather than sit on our sixes for the next two years, I would try to make a difference. I also believed we might be able to make the Yolongi believe the earlier attacks were purely a domestic effort.

"We named ourselves the Terran Freedom Coalition. Most of the slaves had been slaves their entire lives and knew about slavery all over the planet. Pooling their information, we identified some of the worst slave owners and decided to do whatever we could to help the slaves at the factories owned by those bastards. Once the APCs left, we had free run of the planet.

"One night, the night of our first raid, we dropped flyers where the TFC took responsibility for the two attacks on the capital and asked the population to support us in our efforts. We used the shuttles to fly to the city where the slave owner with the worst reputation had his biggest factory. We landed on the roof, as we did in your plan for the capital, and stormed the factory. We had been told the slaves were kept in the basement. We took out the overseers, guards, and a few employees, then herded all the slaves into the shuttles. A few of the slaves were literally paralyzed with fear, and we had to carry them into the shuttles.

"And that's basically the story. In all, we burned down four factories and rescued about two hundred seventy more slaves. As with your plan for the capital attacks, we collected a ton of data from their computers before we burned down the factories."

"And you were never identified?"

"I don't believe so. We never lost a man on a mission, and the APCs never showed up at the embassy compound again. After the fourth factory, we stopped the raids. We just couldn't continue to grow the size of the groups in the bunker in case it took longer than two years to be rescued. As you know, survival often comes down to simply having enough food.

"Anyway, I threw a combination bon voyage party for the *Justice* and a celebration for the slaves we had freed and the factories we had destroyed.

"I'm afraid I drank a bit more than I should have. I'm told I went to the communication's center and sent a message to the *Justice*. I really don't remember it. And I would be forever grateful if you destroyed it."

"Without even knowing what you said?"

"It couldn't have been too coherent."

"I think it was priceless. Here, let me play it."

Sydnee tapped a few keys on her computer keyboard and the message played from the overhead speaker. Blade's jaw dropped as he listed to the very brief message.

"I'm sorry, Captain."

"Well, at least now we understand the reason for the garbled tone."

"And I sent it without encryption?"

"I don't think that fact is important. You didn't say anything that could identify us."

"I said it in Amer."

Tapping the delete button, Sydnee said, "I don't know what you're talking about. There's no such message in the computer."

"Thank you, Captain."

"You've performed bravely, above and beyond the call, and you've done a wonderful job for the GA and those poor women. My official log repeatedly states that. Since we're on a clandestine mission, the log can never be made public, but people with access at Space Command and the Space Marine Corps will know of your success, Major."

◆ ◆ ◆

"The TFC has stopped their raids on factories being operated with slave labor," Danttan said. "There hasn't been a single one since we activated our forces all over the planet."

"How many of the hundreds of missing slaves have we recovered?"

"None. Not a single one has turned up."

"A few months ago I would have said that was impossible. Where can they be hiding them? They must have other caverns like the one our informant uncovered."

"They may have gotten off-world somehow."

"And gone where? This is the Clidepp Empire. We control every square meter of space."

"Except the billions of cubic kilometers the Blenod have annexed," Mewaffal said.

"Shut up, you fool," Plelillo said. "I have to think."

"The fleet has received their orders to proceed to our border with the Blenod and engage them with the intent of driving them out of Clidepp space, Kurrost," Danttan said. "They'll be departing within a matter of days, leaving just two *Bernouust*-class destroyers in orbit here. As to the slavery issue, Gustallo, I know of no place in the empire where slaves could run free. We control the slave markets on all occupied worlds within our borders."

"Do you think the TFC somehow learned that every police officer on the force was waiting to pounce?"

"The activation should have been secret," Mewaffal speculated. "Perhaps we have a traitor in one of the forces."

"It's unlikely anyone talked about the activation," Danttan said. "It's more likely that someone in the AR noticed the increased presence and reported it to the TFC."

"So you believe they're in collusion?"

"Not necessarily. They have similar goals but vastly different approaches to achieving them. I can't see them working closely together, although they might share a little information."

"Perhaps it's time we cracked down on the AR," Plelillo mused.

"But you said they're responsible for a significant part of our wealth," Mewaffal said. "Wouldn't that be cutting off much of our income?"

"If the AR has become so adept at hiding slaves that we're unable to find them, they're not adding a thing to our bank accounts. We must do something. How are we as politicians supposed to survive if we can't collect the graft we so richly deserve for our ceaseless efforts of using our positions of power to guide and control the sheep? I work tirelessly for the people of this empire. Haven't I earned the right to live well?"

"I suggest we resume normal operations until the TFC strikes again," Danttan said. "When they do, we should take a more enlightened approach and attempt to infiltrate their ranks so we can crush them all at once."

"Very well," Plelillo said. "See to it."

◆　◆　◆

"Come," Sydnee said when the computer announced that Lieutenant Kelly MacDonald was outside her office. As the door opened, Sydnee stood up and came out from behind her desk to welcome her friend.

"It so great to see you, Kel. I've really missed you. You have no idea how much."

"I think I know because I've missed you just as much. There wasn't anyone I could really talk to in the embassy bunker. Blade's my superior officer and leader, but he's not much into normal conversation."

"I felt really lost without you, Jerry Weems, and Pete Caruthers. You're my closest friends, and you were all on the planet for so long."

"Tell me about it. It seemed like we were there forever. I did take my meals with Jerry and Pete, but I missed the girl talk we enjoy. If you have time, let's catch up on things. Tell me what you've been doing out in the vastness of space while I was buried below ground in the bunker."

"It's been one worry after another. I've got three times as many people aboard this ship than we had as crew on the *Perry*. And we're so squeezed for room they can't get a moment's privacy. We've crammed the former slaves into an area about one-twentieth the size they should have available to them. Those poor women are practically sleeping on top of one another on the floor in the habitats."

"At least in the embassy we had tons of space and a few dozen real bedrooms that we shared by rotating daily on three sleep shifts."

"Our main problem was food. We ran out while waiting for you guys to join us, and I had to highjack a freighter."

"You highjacked a freighter?"

"Yep, just call me Bluebeard Without the Beard."

"What did you do with it after you took all their food?"

"I didn't take *all* their food. In fact, I'm sure they hardly missed it. And I paid for it. Actually I overpaid for it. But I was trying to buy a little goodwill along with the food, and the captain of the ship seemed content with the arrangements once he got over being threatened to heave to or else."

"Good Lord, Syd, that's going to get back to Space Command. The story has probably spread all over Clidepp space by now. You know how freighters are when they meet in ports. They discuss their trips and pass on anything interesting or exciting that happened because their trips are usually so terribly dull."

"I had no choice. We were out of food. I requested help from the *Denver*, but Captain Lidden was denied permission to enter Clidepp space."

"So Space Command left us here to fend for ourselves and will probably disavow any knowledge of our being here if the Clidepp Empire files a formal complaint."

"Well, this was supposed to be a clandestine trip."

"Yeah, but they're the ones who kept changing the mission parameters. What do you think they'll do to you?"

"I have no idea. We started off with the simple task of dropping off the package. Then they ordered us to travel all over Clidepp space seeding spy satellites. Then they ordered us to do whatever we had to do to recover Winston. The last part proved to be so challenging that we couldn't accomplish either the original mission or the second mission. We still have all but eight of the satellites piled up in the bottom level of that habitat container. On top of that, I twice ordered air strikes on the capital city on Yolongus that wiped out their power generation and distribution, then destroyed their communication systems. I guess they'll bust me back to Lt.(jg), or maybe to Ensign."

"Bust you back? You mean you got a promotion while we've been out here?"

"Uh, yeah. Captain Lidden told me the Admiralty Board approved my early promotion and that I had been named to fill one of the vacant slots aboard the *Denver*."

"That's great, Syd. Congratulations. How come you're not wearing the proper rank insignia?"

"I felt it would be less embarrassing if people didn't see I had been promoted when I'm busted back to my prior rank. Don't tell anyone, okay?"

"Syd, after what you've done out here, they should advance you to lieutenant commander."

"Thanks, Kel, but we both know it doesn't work that way. Every time I think about the things I've ordered since we left the *Denver*, I hear the words Milty once said, playing in my head."

"Don't never do no wrong?"

"Yeah. He told you too?"

"No, *you* did— while we were still on the *Perry*. And a couple of times since then."

Sydnee grinned before saying, "Well— I guess I can't stop thinking about that— and he was right. We've seen it time and again. You can win a chest full of medals, but slip up just once where the number of negatives outweigh the number of positives and your career in the military is over. I think *my* career might be over. I didn't do just *one* thing wrong. My wrongs could fill an entire chapter in a book. I'm probably going to be thrown to the sharks when we get back. My next posting could be as a mess cook assistant on a dirt-side base."

"You've got way over a thousand positives down in the habitat container, plus you recovered Winston— twice. Maybe they won't take away your half stripe. Maybe for punishment they'll just send you back into Clidepp space for two years to complete the two assignments from this crazy mission. I think that would be worse punishment than being a mess assistant."

"I'd like to do that anyway. I hate not having finished the missions properly. It's only because we're busting at the seams and food would have become a problem again if we had remained in Clidepp space that I made the decision to head home."

CHAPTER TWENTY-FIVE
~ June 2nd, 2287 ~

"I've received a new message from Sydnee," Captain Lidden said to his XO when they met for their daily briefing.

"It's about time," Commander Bryant said. "She takes the order to limit messages to Space Command while in Clidepp space a bit too seriously."

"The latest message is proof of that. She says they're headed back."

"Back? They couldn't have seeded the satellites throughout the empire in a couple of months. Is it because of the slaves they picked up? What does she give as her reason for returning?"

"She doesn't."

"What does she say?"

"Only that they're returning to GA space."

"Uh oh."

"What?"

"This can't be good. Do you think she might have started a war?"

"I don't know. God, I hope not."

"So we don't know why she's returning or if she completed either of her two missions?"

"That's right. The last communication we had was when I had to tell her she was on her own."

"Wow. What will you tell SHQ?"

"All I know. She's on her way back."

◆　　◆　　◆

"We just received a message from our man on Yolongus, sir," Captain Salido said to Admiral Kincaid when he reported to the Admiral's office after requesting a meeting.

"Which one?"

"Lt. Commander Gravely, code name Cornwallis."

"He was the one we asked the First Fleet to recover because they already had a warship there on a mission for us?"

"Yes, sir."

"And after recovering him they lost him."

"Well, it wasn't their fault, sir. He makes that clear in his report. He told the captain of the *Justice* that he needed to return to the planet after they had recovered him, and she refused to let him go until he had sent us a full report. So he says she's not to blame. In fact, he praises her actions."

"Who's the ship's captain of this— *Justice*?"

"Marcola, sir. Sydnee Marie Marcola."

"Marcola— Marcola. Why does that name sound so familiar?"

"She was the Space Command officer who took command of the Marines on Diabolisto and beat back an attack by superior Yolongi Rebel forces that had been stranded on the planet. It was actually a rout. She then commandeered a defunct Clidepp destroyer stolen by Rebel forces, managed to get it partially functional, and took it into battle against another Rebel-controlled Clidepp destroyer and a freighter with hidden missiles, saving the crew of the *Perry* as a result."

"Yes, I remember it all now. She's reported to be brave and highly intelligent. Is that all Gravely reports?"

"He has a question, sir. He wants to know what official Space Command rank Marcola holds. He says she's only wearing lieutenant(jg) bars but told him it's not her true rank."

"Why is a warship's captain wearing j.g. bars? Isn't she a captain?"

"The ship was the one sent to seed the communication satellites, sir. It's not technically a warship, so it doesn't require the ship's captain to hold the official Space Command rank of captain. It's just a CPS-14."

"A CPS-14? Oh yes, the tiny, highly-reconfigurable mini Scout-Destroyer that can be altered to make it the ideal ship for special missions. I remember now. But don't regulations require that the captain of a Scout-Destroyer hold the rank of Lieutenant commander at the very least?"

"Space Command has never established a minimum senior officer rank for the CPS-14. I believe they envisioned the small ship merely as a space tug that can be deployed in unique situations where the firepower of a Scout-Destroyer isn't needed."

"A space tug?"

"The keel of the ship is designed to hold habitat containers that very closely resemble the containers hauled by freighters. If one of our forward bases needed food or support materials quickly, the CPS-14 could be used rather than forcing the base to wait for a Quartermaster ship to make its rounds.

"However, after the ship went into production, someone decided that it should have some basic form of self-protection. So they designed a container that housed weapons. They probably got the idea from that freighter used by the Milori to kidnap Admiral Vroman."

"Ah, yes. The freighter where the ends of a container flew off and they fired missiles at the ship ferrying him to Stewart SCB."

"Yes, sir. The Clidepp Rebels also used that disguised freighter container tactic. The weapons containers designed for the CPS-14 house both laser cannons and missiles. The *Justice* carries two of the containers so they can fire fore and aft within seconds of needing their weapons. It makes them a deadly addition to the undeclared warship category initiated with the development of the Scout-Destroyer. Then someone decided that the ship should be able to transport FA-SF4s inside containers. And not only that, they added the ability to launch the SF4s from the special container so they could function in a support role on special missions."

"The *Justice* has two weapons containers and an SF4?"

"Actually it has eight SF4s. It has its own Wing. They're also carrying a Marine Special Ops team and a full platoon of Marines from the *Denver*."

"Well, they're certainly armed to the teeth. That's a tremendous amount of firepower and Marine manpower to put into the hands of a lieutenant(jg). Why was she chosen to command a mission of this importance into Clidepp space?"

"It's an unusual situation, sir. This is the same ship sent to capture and bring back the government official suspected of being responsible for the Freight-One attack. Lieutenant(jg) Marcola commanded that very successful mission, despite having severe mechanical issues with an early production model of the CPS-14. The *Denver's* commanding officer, Captain Anthony Frederick Lidden, decided she was the best officer for the new mission. We agreed based on her past impressive successes."

"Lidden? Yes. Good man. Excellent leader. Too bad he got tied up by that awful freighter mess. If he selected Marcola, she has to be an excellent leader as well. So what's Marcola's true rank?"

"Officially, she's a full lieutenant."

"But she only wears lieutenant(jg) insignia?"

"That's what Gravely says."

"When was she promoted to lieutenant?"

"The Admiralty Board approved her early promotion to lieutenant just a few months ago."

"And when did she leave on this mission?"

"Four months ago."

"There it is then. She left on the mission before being notified of the promotion. She's probably been so busy she hasn't had time to have the insignia changed. She probably doesn't even have the right insignia available. That's a tiny CPS-14, not a destroyer."

"Yes, sir. Should I tell Gravely about Marcola's promotion and correct rank?"

"Of course. Why wouldn't you?"

"It's just such a strange situation that she wouldn't tell him. I didn't know if there was something else going on here. Something I might be unaware of."

"Such as?"

"I wondered if she was ordered to keep her true rank secret."

"I doubt that. It might be as simple as he's a man and she's a woman. If she's attracted to him, she might just be trying to seem more mysterious."

"Yes, sir. Gravely might be attracted to her as well. He says she's an amazing officer and leader. He recommends we try to recruit her for SCI."

"What do you think?"

"Her record is impressive. Top grades at NHSA and then seventh in her class at the Warship Command Institute. She was assigned to the *Perry*, but the record has been corrected to state a clerical error was responsible for the mix-up. She was originally selected for posting to a battleship in Admiral Carver's Region Two command. She reported to the *Perry* as ordered, and as a crew member of the *Perry*, her record is outstanding. The fact that she's one of just a handful of officers who have received early promotion this year shows the high regard Space Command SHQ has for her."

"Okay, run with it. If her captain approves, feel her out when she returns and see if she's interested in Intelligence work. What is she— about twenty-six? She's far too old to become an agent. We need to bring them aboard before they graduate from the Academy and develop the strong habits consistent with SC ship leadership, but we always need good people for other duty assignments."

◆ ◆ ◆

As the *Justice* crossed into GA space, Sydnee breathed a sigh of relief.

"Com, contact the *Denver,* give them our position and get theirs."

311

"Aye, Captain."

Some four minutes later the com chief said, "Captain, the *Denver* reports they are on their way here and instruct us to hold position. They anticipate arrival in sixty-three hours. They say you're to send a copy of the ship's log and all other information regarding our mission to Captain Lidden."

"Helm, all stop. Tac, check the Detect. Helm, cancel our envelope if we're clear," Sydnee ordered. "Navigation, send our revised location coordinates to the com. Chief, transmit our location to the *Denver*." Her next act was to address the ship. "Attention crew of the *Justice*. We have just crossed into GA space. We're home. The *Denver* is coming to meet us and will arrive in two and half days. To our passengers, welcome to the GA. You will now start to enjoy the freedoms extended to all sentient life in the Galactic Alliance. That's all."

The message was then repeated in Yolongi.

◆

Sydnee's announcement was met with jubilant shouting in every part of the ship. Many of the former slaves fell to their knees and wept tears of joy as they hugged the people nearest them. It was a day many had never expected to see in their lifetime. Anese hurried to her daughter and they hugged one another as they also cried tears of happiness.

As the former slaves regained their composure, Anese called for silence. When the habitat deck was as still as could be expected, she said, "My sisters, I want to suggest something. Today is the ninth of June on the GA calendar. I want to propose that from this day forward, every June 9th be celebrated as the day we officially gained our freedom. I don't want to diminish the efforts of the Aleoxlene Reqoppl or the entire crew of the *Justice*, but Captain Marcola was the driving force behind getting us here. We wouldn't be here if not for her. I know that I, my daughter, her children, and their children's children will observe a minute of silence on this date forever as we and they think of and remember the captain. Do you agree? June 9th is Captain Marcola day?"

312

A cheer went up and someone started yelling, "The 9th of June is Captain Marcola day— forever." A few others picked it up and soon the entire habitat container was rocking as they shouted in unison. The chant quickly spread throughout the rest of ship, finally reaching the people living in the shuttles, at which time they began chanting as well.

◆

"Com, what's that noise?" Sydnee asked from her command chair.

"I'll check, Captain."

A few second later the com chief said, "It's the former slaves, Captain. They're all chanting, 'The 9th of June is Captain Marcola day forever.'"

"Permission to put some vid images on the front monitor, Captain?" Lt.(jg) Templeton at the Tac station asked.

"Go ahead, Tac."

Images from the security cameras around the ship began to play on the large monitor at the front of the bridge. In every image women were hugging, kissing, weeping, and chanting.

Sydnee was shocked at first but then recognized it as the way the women had chosen to release the angst they'd still had that something might happen to prevent them from reaching the GA. They needed to remember and celebrate the day— the moment, when they learned they were definitely free.

◆   ◆

When the *Denver* arrived sixty-three hours and twenty-two minutes later, it was accompanied by a Quartermaster's ship. The *Justice* was ready to be disassembled into separate components and merged with the destroyer. All living areas had been organized and bedding stowed. All of the former slaves were gathered in the habitat container originally used just for satellite storage. The three twenty-meter by ten-meter deck areas were crowded to the maximum, but the women had grown used to it, and they knew things would be substantially better once they were aboard a larger ship. No one was going to complain that the journey to freedom was anything other than the best trip they'd ever taken.

The food stores had naturally been reduced since being acquired in Clidepp space, but there were still massive amounts of food piled up in the passageways. All corridors had to be cleared, so the food was being piled up in the Marine mess hall.

Sydnee examined every area before declaring the preparation work complete. The gravity decking would ensure that the deck was always the center of gravity regardless of its position relative to the ships, but Sydnee warned the former slaves to be prepared for some slight inertia issues as that habitat container was separated from the *Justice,* then moved into the quartermaster ship. The other habitat containers were likewise sealed and would remain that way until they docked with the *Denver* and the connection was declared complete and airtight.

When Sydnee was confident the *Justice* was ready, she gave permission for the four shuttles to detach and enter the *Denver's* shuttle bays and for the small, unmanned tugs to begin disassembling the habitat container section. When the *Justice* had been reduced to its main CPS-14 component, it would move into the special shuttle bay aboard the *Denver.*

"It's kind of sad, isn't it, Captain," Lt.(jg) Olivetti said as they watched the exterior work on the large monitor at the front of the bridge.

"Sad? I'm actually *glad* to be back, even though we didn't complete our main mission or our secondary mission," Sydnee said.

"No, I'm not talking about reaching the end of our mission; I meant seeing our home dismantled into individual segments. We still have the *Denver* of course, but I've kinda thought of the *Justice* as our home also."

"Oh. Yes, it's sad to see it pulled apart, but we have to remember that the next time it's needed, it'll be quickly reassembled again. Outside of the core, the *Justice* may not have the same configuration, but it'll seem like home again— a home that's merely undergone a bit of remodeling work that changed the appearance a bit to give us a better configuration."

"Yes, that's true."

"The *Denver* says it's ready for us to enter the large shuttle bay, Captain," the com chief said. "The hatch is being opened."

"Notify them we're ready and have been standing by to enter the ship. Helm, take us in."

"Aye, Captain," Caruthers said as he began applying power to the maneuvering thrusters.

As the *Justice* entered the large bay, Caruthers slowed the ship so much it hardly seemed to be moving at times. The fit was tight enough that it wouldn't take much for damage to occur from a slight scrape with the sides of *Denver's* hatchway. There was little chance that the *Justice's* Dakinium-sheathed hull would be damaged, but the hatch framework could be damaged enough so they couldn't establish an airtight seal. Sydnee knew that Caruthers, of all the pilots on the *Denver,* was the best helmsman with the CPS-14, whether tight maneuvering was required or simply general piloting of the small ship, so she never had to pay close attention when he was at the helm.

As the *Justice* settled to the deck after completing the temporary airlock procedure and then gliding to an available parking location once the temporary airlock walls were raised, Sydnee breathed a silent sigh. She dreaded what was to come. Until receiving the request for her log, she hadn't filed a full report since the first attack on the Yolongus capital, so no one aboard the *Denver* or in Space Command had known she was returning with one thousand three hundred ninety-six civilians.

"Captain, Captain Lidden wants you to report to the office in his quarters ASAP," the com chief said.

"Acknowledge that I'm on my way."

"Yes, ma'am."

CHAPTER TWENTY-SIX

~ June 23rd, 2287 ~

It was 0200 GST so naturally Lidden wouldn't be in his office just off the bridge at this hour. As she approached the door to his quarters, the Marine Corporal on duty there braced to attention. Sydnee moved to where the annunciator system could identify her and ascertain she wanted access to the captain's quarters. After it notified Lidden she was in the corridor and he approved her entrance, the door disappeared into the bulkhead pocket.

Sydnee was surprised to see Lidden in uniform at this hour. She'd expected informal wear. Even more surprising were the five other officers standing in the sitting room. All were in uniform except one— Winston. The *Denver's* XO, Commander Bryant was there, and Commander Knight, whom she had met during her mission briefing. She didn't know the others, but she understood their presence when she noticed that each had an SCI insignia on their collars. Sydnee stopped a meter away from the group of officers and braced to attention. "Lieutenant Sydnee Marie Marcola reporting to the captain as ordered."

"Lieutenant, you're out of uniform. You're wearing the wrong rank insignia."

"Yes, sir. Sorry, sir. I didn't have the correct insignia and there was no one else onboard the *Justice* from whom I could borrow one. Now that I've returned to the *Denver* I can procure the insignia during first watch."

"You're excused owing to unavailability of the insignia aboard the *Justice*."

"Thank you, sir."

"At ease."

Sydnee noticed that Winston was grinning. She wondered if he had previously learned her correct rank.

"You know Commander Bryant, of course," Captain Lidden said, "and the SCI lieutenant commander and agent who wishes to be referred to today as Winston Cornwallis. I'm also sure you remember Commander Knight from your pre-mission briefing. These two other officers are Captain Salido and Commander Brookstein."

"Sirs," Sydnee said as she nodded to the men and, "Ma'am," as she nodded to Commander Knight, although Space Command regulations and protocol permitted her to include all officers in a group with the male designation.

"You've had quite a voyage, Lieutenant," Salido said. "Winston tells us you somehow managed to avoid starting a war despite attacking the capital city of the Clidepp Empire not once but twice, crippling their power and communication systems."

"Uh, I hoped my actions wouldn't result in war, and I did everything possible to conceal our identity. If there had been any other way I would not have ordered the attacks, but my orders were to get Winston out at all costs, and I only took the actions I deemed necessary."

"The second attack took place after you knew Winston had escaped from the facility where he was being held."

"Yes, sir. Following the first attack, a large part of my crew had been forced to take refuge in the GA embassy. They couldn't leave because the Qummuc had arrived after they entered the bunker. With the APCs watching the embassy, they would have been observed if they tried to leave. That would have been sufficient proof to the Triumvirate that the GA was responsible. The second attack was an attempt to pull the Qummuc APCs away so my people could vacate the embassy."

"But your ruse didn't work?"

"No, sir. I don't know why it didn't."

"We're indeed fortunate that the Triumvirate didn't accuse us of being responsible. It would, no doubt, have gotten very

317

messy, and you might have lost those shiny new bars you haven't even acquired yet."

"Yes, sir. I expected my actions might mean the end of my career, but if I had it to do over again, I'd do the same things. And if you could have seen the faces on the slaves when they knew they were finally free after we crossed into GA space, I think you would have done it also."

"Where's the package, Lieutenant?"

"He's in Shuttle-One with two of my Marines as guards. He can be returned to his accommodations here on the *Denver* until another mission is sent to complete our work. The *Justice* was so packed with slaves it would have been impossible to perform the satellite placement, but we did get the eight satellites placed around Yolongus."

"I don't know what's going to happen when the news is released that almost one thousand four hundred slaves have reached freedom here in the GA. I'm sure we can't keep it a secret, but we intend to try to keep Space Command's responsibility for the escape a secret."

"Why, sir? The entire GA should know and be clamoring for action against the Clidepp Empire. The Aleoxlene Reqoppl estimate the number of Terran slaves in the Clidepp Empire to number in the millions. Only a quarter are Terrans who were captured and enslaved. The others are part of a breeding system to supply slaves to anyone who can meet the price. We have to end that, sir."

"I agree. But I don't make the rules, Lieutenant. Winston speaks just as passionately about correcting these wrongs, and in time things may change. People's eyes are being opened with every slave who is freed. Newsies looking for breaking news and authors looking for book subjects will probably learn of the slaves you freed before too long and start writing those stories and biographies, but we must conceal our participation in the Great Slave Escape of 2287 lest we be accused of perpetrating those very attacks you worked so hard to cover up."

"Yes, sir. In that regard Marine Captain Blade created an imaginary insurgent group he called the Terran Freedom Coalition. After we departed for GA space, he carried out four more raids where he rescued the slaves being forced to work in four factories. He also downloaded all data from their computers before setting fire to the factories. The Marines involved in the operation dropped leaflets and spray-painted the walls with the TFC initials to support the fabrication. With luck, it will further help to deflect attention away from Space Command and the GA. I might suggest you report that the slaves were freed through the efforts of that group and returned to GA space in a freighter. We've also interviewed all of the former slaves and collected a lot of information for SCI. And by the way sir, we were able to download all of the files in the government database when we raided the slave pens to recover the slaves Winston was trying to bring out."

"What?" Winston said. "You never told me you were able to access and copy their slave census files."

Salido looked over at Winston and frowned.

"Sorry for interrupting, sir."

"It was a busy time, Commander," Sydnee said.

"Lieutenant," Captain Salido said, "I've asked Captain Lidden if you're free to take another trip into the Clidepp Empire."

"If I'm allowed, sir, I'd like to go back and finish the mission we started."

"He thought you'd say that. But this would be a different mission. Winston believes he has discovered the true identity of Citizen X. We'd like you to take him with you and track down X, returning the Rebel leader for questioning as you did with the package. If he's responsible for the attack on Freight-One, he'll receive the maximum punishment for that crime. Would you be willing to go back into the Clidepp Empire and track him down for us?"

"No, sir."

"No? That's hardly the answer I expected from you, Lieutenant. Everything you've done in the past indicates this is a mission you'd relish."

"Sir, going back into Clidepp space to search for Citizen X would be a complete waste of everyone's time."

"You don't believe he's guilty of ordering the attack on Freight-One?"

"It's not that, sir. The trip is unnecessary because I've already captured Citizen X. He's sitting in Shuttle-Two with the Marines I assigned to guard him."

"What?" Winston practically shouted as he unconsciously took a step forward towards Sydnee.

Salido looked over at Winston again and once again frowned at the SCI agent, then returned his gaze to Sydnee after Winston stepped back to where he had been standing. Winston's face mirrored the embarrassment he was feeling for his outburst.

"I'm as surprised as Winston, Lieutenant. Who, exactly, do you have in Shuttle-Two?"

"I have Citizen X, sir. He's cuffed and under guard by four of my Marines, sir. You can begin interrogating him whenever you wish. So you see, there's no need for us to travel back into Clidepp space for that purpose."

"You couldn't possibly have X!" Winston yelled.

This time Salido glared at Winston for his outburst and continued to stare at the SCI agent.

"I'm sorry for my outburst, sir." Winston said. "I'm just— I'm just— I'm just…"

"Stop repeating yourself, Commander. And stop interrupting."

"Yes, sir. Sorry, sir."

Returning his gaze to Sydnee, Salido said, "Who do you have in custody? What's his proper legal name, not his Rebel code name?"

320

"His name is Plelillo. Aderses Plelillo. He's the son of the Clidepp Prime Minister. He's in Shuttle-Two, and his two top Rebel deputies are in Shuttle-Three. They're also cuffed and under guard by a fire team of Marines. I've kept the Rebels separated since their capture."

"Impossible!" Winston shouted.

"Commander, for the last time, control yourself!" Salido said. "If you don't, I'll have you removed from the room under guard."

"Uh, yes, sir. Sorry again, sir. It's been a very long time since I've had to follow proper military protocol. I apologize."

"I understand, which is why I've gone easy on you up until now. Agents are recruited before they graduate from the academies for the very reason that we don't want them so indoctrinated in military protocols that they can't properly assume the role of an undisciplined individual. Now just stand there and say nothing unless you're specifically addressed."

"Yes, sir."

"Now, Lieutenant, tell us how you managed to capture the individual we believe might be X and his two top deputies."

When Sydnee had explained about the strange communication stream that appeared to be coming from a stationary space yacht just outside DeTect distance from the planet, then destroying its temporal generator when it refused to heave to and tried to escape without calling for help from the Clidepp fleet, and subsequently learning who the yacht belonged to, all of the senior officers in Lidden's quarters, including Lidden, seemed to be in shock.

Winston finally found his tongue and asked, "Permission to ask a question, sir?"

"Granted." Salido said.

Looking at Sydnee, Winston asked, "And just how did you learn Aderses Plelillo was suspected of being Citizen X?"

"Why, you told me, Commander."

"I never said a word to you about Citizen X."

"No, not verbally. I read it in your report to SCI."

"She couldn't have read my report, sir," Winston said to Salido. "I never showed it to her, and it was triple encrypted."

"Yes, the encryption did present me with difficulty for a few minutes," Sydnee said, "but I knew I had to break it because I thought it might give me a clue to your whereabouts on Yolongus. I had an unfair advantage in that you used a computer system aboard my ship to write and then encrypt your report. Even though you tried to cover your tracks, I had access to computer files you either don't know about or were unable to delete. I used every trick they taught us at the Academy and managed to peel away the encryption levels one by one until I was able to read the message. I know the report was not for my eyes, but I believed it might provide me with a clue as to who had grabbed you. And it did because it mentioned Aderses Plelillo. I already knew his father controlled the Qummuc secret police, and my people were able to learn from an Aleoxlene Reqoppl coordinator on the planet where the Qummuc had taken you for questioning. I knew I had to get to you before the Yolongi crippled you for life or even killed you while trying to get you to talk. I didn't learn you had already escaped until after we raided and secured the Qummuc facility where you had been held. And, in your defense, only the captain of the ship has access to the files that allowed me to decrypt your message. It should also be stated that the appointed captain of a Space Command warship, even a warship as small as a CPS-14, routinely has access to data classified as Most Secret."

When Salido heard a chuckle, he looked around until he found the source. Then he said, "You find this amusing, Captain?"

"Yes, I do, Captain," Lidden said with a grin.

Salido smiled and said, "As do I." Returning his gaze to Sydnee, he said, "While we were busy strategizing on how we might locate X and capture him, you caught him and had him in custody. But why did you wait until now to inform us you had the suspected Citizen X under lock and key?"

"I didn't want to risk anyone else aboard ship learning about it before I had a face-to-face meeting with my captain, so I never told anyone aboard the *Justice* what I had learned from the encrypted message to SCI or what I suspected regarding Plelillo's secret identity. My Marines believe he's just a gunrunner. I felt that SCI should be the one to break the news and respond to questions when news of his capture is released— if it's to be released."

"*If* it's to be released?" Salido said with a questioning look.

"I've never heard anything in the news about the package being collected from Yolongus on my first mission into Clidepp space. I know it occurred only because I was there and in command of the mission."

"That was because we later learned he was innocent. We didn't want to publicly tarnish his name."

"It's not my position to praise or condemn the actions of the SCI, sir. I simply felt the decision would be better left to you."

"But you didn't even mention it to Winston after you recovered him the second time?"

"He had previously informed me he was a lieutenant commander in Space Command. Although I was the officially appointed captain of the ship, I didn't want to deny a senior officer from SCI access to a suspected terrorist. Especially not Citizen X. However, I believed he would have demanded access if he'd known about Plelillo being aboard. I felt that Plelillo's repeated interrogation would raise questions among my crew. You know how it is aboard small ships, sir. It's usually impossible to keep a secret. I believed this one was far too important to risk spreading while we were in Clidepp space. Now that we're back in the GA, you can interrogate the prisoner using all of the resources at your disposal. Other pressing problems aboard the *Justice* placed increased demands on my time and required my full attention, so I've had limited contact with Winston on the return voyage. I was the commanding officer of a ship designed around a crew of just twenty-five individuals, and yet I had almost one thousand five hundred persons under my care and protection. I was a bit busy."

Salido smiled and nodded. "One thousand five hundred. That's almost three times the crew size of this destroyer, and you were doing it with limited staff. I would guess you *were* a bit busy. Well, all I can say is you've done an incredible job, Lieutenant, and the people of the GA owe you more than just a pat on the back. Would you be interested in coming to work for me at SCI?"

"Me? An agent? No, sir. But thank you."

"You're too old and too well known to become an agent, but we have many other positions in SCI for highly intelligent people with the other skills you possess that don't involve field work. I've never been a field agent, and neither has Commander Knight nor Commander Brookstein."

Sydnee looked over at Captain Lidden.

"I would hate you lose you, Lieutenant," Lidden said, "but I have no right to interfere with your decision."

Looking back at Salido, she said, "Thank you for the job offer, sir, but I want to be in space. I think I'm going to remain aboard the *Denver* for now."

"Okay, Lieutenant. I understand. Would you be willing to go back into the Clidepp Empire and complete the original mission? We still have to return the package. And we still might need more ears over there. That may change if we can verify that Plelillo really is Citizen X and whether or not there's anyone ready to pick up the reins of the Rebellion now that he's our guest here. I'm sure you remember that the purpose of the project was to monitor all transmissions on all frequencies from every planet until we identified the Rebel leaders, then act to take down the leadership responsible for the attack on our space station. We should know if the satellite distribution part of the mission is still desired before you reach Yolongus and release the package."

"If Captain Lidden wishes me to return to Clidepp space and complete that mission, I will. I do hate not finishing jobs I've begun."

"You would be my first choice, Lieutenant," Lidden said. Sydnee looked over at him and smiled but said nothing.

~ finis ~

♦♦♦ *Sydnee's exciting adventures will continue* ♦♦♦

Watch for new books from this author on the websites of major book sellers, in bookstores around the world, and in announcements on the author's own website:

~ www.deprima.com ~

Or sign up for the free announcements newsletter at www.deprima.com to immediately receive news when future books are about to be released.

APPENDIX

This chart is offered to assist readers who may be unfamiliar with military rank and the reporting structure. Newly commissioned officers begin at either ensign or second lieutenant rank.

Space Command Officer Hierarchy:
Admiral of the Fleet (5 Star)
Admiral (4 Star)
Vice-Admiral (3 Star)
Rear Admiral – Upper (2 Star)
Rear Admiral – Lower (1 Star)

Captain
Commander
Lt. Commander
Lieutenant
Lieutenant(jg) "Junior Grade"
Ensign

Space Marine Officer Hierarchy:
General (4 Star)
Lt. General (3 Star)
Major General (2 Star)
Brigadier General (1 Star)

Colonel
Lt. Colonel
Major
Captain
First Lieutenant
Second Lieutenant

The commanding officer on a ship is always referred to as Captain, regardless of his or her official military rank. Even an Ensign could be a Captain of the Ship, although that would

a

only occur as the result of an unusual situation or emergency where no senior officers survive.

On Space Command ships and bases, time is measured according to a twenty-four clock, normally referred to as military time. For example, 8:42 PM would be referred to as 2042 hours. Chronometers are set to always agree with the date and time at Space Command Supreme Headquarters on Earth. This is known as GST, or Galactic System Time.

Admiralty Board:

Moore, Richard E - Admiral of the Fleet

Platt, Evelyn S. - Admiral – Commander of the First Fleet

Bradlee, Roger T. - Admiral - Director of Intelligence (SCI)

Ressler, Shana E. - Admiral - Director of Budget & Accounting

Hillaire, Arnold H. - Admiral - Director of Academies

Burke, Raymond A. - Vice-Admiral - Director of GSC Base Management

Ahmed, Raihana L. - Vice-Admiral - Dir. of Quartermaster Supply

Woo, Lon C. - Vice-Admiral - Dir. of Scientific & Expeditionary Forces

Plimley, Loretta J. - Rear-Admiral, (U) - Dir. of Weapons R&D, and SC Shipyard Management

Yuthkotl, Lesbolh - Rear Admiral (U) Admiral, Director of Nordakian Forces Integration Section

Ship Speed Terminology:

Plus-1 - 1 kps

Sub-Light-1 - 1,000 kps

Light-1 - 299,792.458 kps or (*c*) (speed of light in a vacuum)

Light-150 or **150 c** - 150 times the speed of light
Light-450 - 134,906,606.1 kps

Hyper-Space Factors:
IDS Communications Band - .0513 light years each minute (8.09 billion kps)
DeTect Range - 4 billion kilometers

Sample Distances:
Earth to Mars (Mean) - 78 million kilometers
Nearest star to our Sun - 4 light-years (Proxima Centauri)
Milky Way Galaxy diameter - 100,000 light-years
Thickness of M'Way at Sun - 2,000 light-years
Stars in Milky Way - 200 billion (est.)
Nearest galaxy (Andromeda) - 2 million light-years from M'Way
A light-year - 9,460,730,472,580.8 kilometers (in vacuum)
A light-second - 299,792.458 km (in vacuum)
Grid Unit - 1,000 Light Yrs^2 (1,000,000 Sq. LY)
Deca-Sector - 100 Light $Years^2$ (10,000 Sq. LY)
Sector - 10 Light $Years^2$ (100 Sq. LY)
Section - 94,607,304,725 km^2
Sub-section - 946,073,047 km^2

Mission Descriptions for Strategic Command Bases:

StratCom-One – Base - Location establishes it as a critical component of Space Command Operations - Serves as homeport to multiple warships that also serve in base's defense. All sections of Space Command maintain an active office at the base. Base Commander establishes all patrol routes and is authorized to override SHQ orders to ships within the sector(s) designated part of the base's operating territory.
Recommended rank of Commanding Officer: Rear Admiral (U)

StratCom-Two – Base - Location establishes it as a crucial component of Space Command Operations - Serves as homeport to multiple warships that also serve in base's defense. All sections of Space Command maintain an active office at the base. Patrol routes established by SHQ.
Recommended rank of Commanding Officer: Rear Admiral (L)

StratCom-Three – Base - Location establishes it as an important component of Space Command Operations - Serves as homeport to multiple warships that also serve in base's defense. Patrol routes established by SHQ.
Recommended rank of Commanding Officer: Captain

StratCom-Four – Station - Location establishes it as an important terminal for Space Command personnel engaged in travel to/from postings, and for re-supply of vessels and outposts.
Recommended rank of Commanding Officer: Commander

StratCom-Five – Outpost - Location makes it important for observation purposes and collection of information.
Recommended rank of Commanding Officer: Lt. Commander

The map on the following page shows Galactic Alliance space after maps were redrawn following the end of hostilities with the Milori, and the war with the Uthlaros, Tsgardi, Gondusans, and Hudeera. Unclaimed territories between the three regions were claimed to form one contiguous area. Regions Two and Three are so vast that exercising control and maintaining law and order has been largely impossible to this date.

The purpose of this two-dimensional representations is to provide the reader with a basic feel for the spatial distances involved, and readers must remember that GA territory extends through the entire depth of the Milky Way galaxy.

.jpg and .pdf versions of the maps created for this series are available for downloading at:

http://www.deprima.com/ancillary/agu.html

should the names be unreadable in your printed or electronic media, or if you simply wish to gain a better overall perspective.

---

e

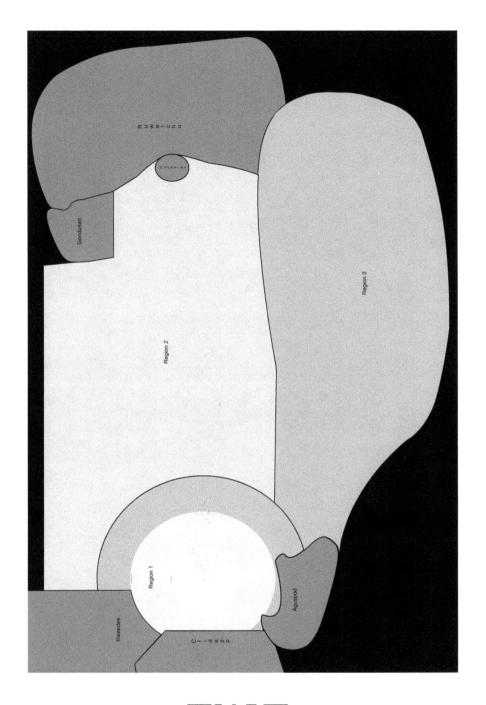

CPSIA information can be obtained
at www.ICGtesting.com
Printed in the USA
LVHW05s1928300818
588665LV00026B/703/P

9 781619 310315